CHANCE HARVEST

LUKE ADAMS

First published by Limelight Publishing 2025
@authorlukeadams.bsky.social | authorlukeadams@gmail.com

ISBN (p): 978-1-326-62540-5
ISBN (e): 978-1-326-62541-2

Tithe Note: Ten percent of all annual royalties I accrue from sales of this book will be evenly divided in donations to: *QueerWasAlwaysHere.org* [partner of the *Choose Love* fund]; *Intersectional Environmentalist*; and the *Elton John AIDS Foundation.*

Author cover photo by Jemima Marriott (https://www.jemimashoots.com/)
Layout and typesetting: Limelight Publishing

Limelight Publishing
PO Box 65, Narangba
Brisbane, Queensland Australia 4504

limelightpublishing.com

Contents

NOTE: This book, as with many books targeted to audiences that include younger readers, is accompanied by a suggested musical playlist that matches the reading, section by section. The Chance Harvest Playlist may be listened to on Apple Music, Amazon Music, or Spotify. Each song suggestion may be found either at the conclusion of the section or, in episodes, at the conclusion of the introductory quotes. The suggested overall book theme song is *Heaven*, performed by *Niall Horan*.

Praise for *Chance Harvest*

"Luke Adams has given us contemporary literature with structure and echoes of *The Jungle* by Upton Sinclair, yet set in the context of today's upheavals. Redolent with queer sensibilities and magick, the novel provides immersion in both the pressing events of the moment, and the enduring camaraderie of friendship and romance. This is a must-read."

—*Amy E. Warman, award-winning educator, feminist essayist, artist-activist, trauma and conflict resolution specialist, and international consultant advocating for marginalized communities*

"In the midst of social upheaval and climate crisis, Luke Adams has embraced the wizardry that can come from unexpected queer romance and chosen family. Chance Harvest offers a powerful narrative of self-discovery, inclusion, resilience, and love — and of making good trouble."
— Stephan Ferris ("Blue Bailey"), author of Blue Movie; activist attorney and legal scholar

"We're in dangerous times. With his first novel, Chance Harvest, Luke Adams has used the lens of young queer romance to highlight the importance of empathy, solidarity, and standing up for what is right."
— Cathy Coley, author of Felix the Comet; children's fiction writer, poet, and essayist.

"As we all navigate turbulent times and the existential threat of global climate change, Chance Harvest offers crucial queer joy and inspiration through the compelling love story that Luke Adams has told — a celebration of the strength of human connection and diversity."
— David Mixner, best-selling author of Stranger Among Friends, Brave Journeys, and At Home With Myself; peace and human rights activist

[Playlist reference, overall book theme:
Niall Horan — Heaven]

CONTENT ADVISORY
(WARNING: Spoilers)

This story has been written for an audience of mature readers, of ages ranging from young adults to elders, but has been especially centered on new adult main characters from the ages of 18-29. It was also written to appeal to all genders and sexualities, but specifically looks at the world through a queer and progressive lens. Politically right-wing readers may find elements of the book disturbing. The characters spend a lot of time in their heads, as sensitive new adults often do. Reading the glossary at the end may help readers with unfamiliar terms. In the story, there are generalized descriptions of a character being parentally neglected and bullied by peers, even violently, in early grade school. There are also suggestions of minor potentially violent confrontations, but it is made clear that they do not occur. There is mention of a violent crime committed against a restaurant worker in a labor struggle. There is a scene in which several common infractions of local beach ordinances and drinking age laws take place. There are also frank descriptions about incidences of overt homophobia. While there are no explicitly pornographic sexual scenes, the descriptions of sexuality and sexual behavior are frank, age-appropriate, and sex-positive. The use of mind-altering substances — alcohol, cannabis, or psilocybin in these cases — is discussed in the context of the aforementioned scene, of social situations and a dinner, and of one character's alcoholism, and another character's realization that he does not want to return to use of a psychedelic. Ultimately, in the context of strong emotions, this is a positive story of liberation, joy, deep friendship, and romance.

Foreword

THE PROLOGUE
TO CHANCE HARVEST

"Without you, without me, everything is different. …
It's huge if you think about it. … Infinity.
It's funny we have a word for that concept,
but there's no way we can understand it. …
Maybe... love? … When it goes on forever.
Maybe that feels like infinity."
— *13 Reasons Why, Season 2 Episode 7 Script,*
Mandy Teefey/Kristel Laiblin

"Along your path,
whether you end up choosing a person or a place —
may you choose a home that you deserve.
One that allows you to feel safe, to relax, to be yourself.
… A home that allows you the space
to grow and to challenge yourself …
yet whose roots support you
and will uphold you along the way,
even if you fall down."
— *Sasza Lohrey*

[Playlist reference: Baby Queen — We Can Be Anything]

Ekkheya: Welcome to me

If you're reading or hearing this memoir: cheers. My name is Ekkheya (which when spoken sounds like *eh-KAY-yuh*). The English translation is: "the way home." That makes me seem homey and cuddly, right?

Well, I'm not.

Believe me, I've been called a lot of names. Being gender non-binary has earned me a few more — not nice ones — ever since those judgy, genocidal missionaries came. They're not my favorite people.

Back then there were many bands of people, indigenous to the areas around the San Francisco Bay and the Monterey Bay, who comprised the Ohlone tribes. They actually somehow figured out I'm called Ekkheya. Although I was here long before they were, they were the only ones to get my name right.

Do I sound like a storyteller? Well, I *am* one. We get to know ourselves and each other over time by telling our stories, after all. I'm about to tell you one that will take you on an emotional rollercoaster through parables of friends and lovers, self-discovery, chosen family, romance, and making good trouble in your world — a world that now faces the threats of climate change and social upheaval.

We're in the midst of a time of collective grieving, so this is an ode to love in all its forms. I hope it will resonate with you deeply, whether you're searching for your own identity and place in a world in crisis, or you're seeking recommitment and purpose. While my perspective on it may be bathed in wizardry and a sort of queer joy, the story I am about to tell you is a story about the power of love and acceptance. It underscores the crucial need we all have for understanding, mutual support, and service.

I have had a lot of time to learn people's stories and I know I need to tell you this one. I'm good at telling them and at carrying their messages. If I'm nothing else, I'm tenacious. With what I've seen, I've had to be.

Part of my job is to know things. I figured *you* have to know about my role in all this, and to understand the impact of the surroundings on this story. The thing is, this part of the tale isn't like the rest of it at all. I think this introduction might be the less exciting part of the bigger picture.

Maybe it'll help if you start to think about it like this: Trying to make sense of today's news about people and the planet probably leaves you feeling lost. And that's before we even get into talking about relationships, because those are another messy ball of wax. The institutions and economy of the USA's democratic republic are crumbling because Republicans keep abandoning the Constitutional rule of law. In the midst of it all, I want to try to keep you from getting lost.

I mean, *even I* sometimes feel disoriented, and I'm what some folks consider "a supernatural being."

Yeah, that's a news-bite about me that probably caught you a little off guard. See, this is why I need to give you more backstory on me. For example, people used to believe I deserved to get daily offerings so that I'd watch over the people and places of their community. I could forgive you if you find that weird or absurd; I did.

Back in the classical Roman world, though, I had a nice little title. I'd be described as one of the *lares* — a guardian and a messenger — and folks actually worshipped beings like me. These days, I'd be happy if you people would just stop treating each other like disposable commodities, and treating the Earth as though it should be fuel for your growing dumpster fire.

I rate humans overall as a third-class honors, D+ kind of species — as conscious life forms go in the various dimensions of the cosmos. But you folks do have one saving grace. It's that at least you have the *capacity* not to be as stupid and evil as you usually are.

I'm sorry if I seem grumpy. I just know you humans can do better, and I've been desperately trying to help. Welcome to me.

As one of the *lares,* I am perhaps in the unenviable place of actually being able to read minds. That does have some advantages, though. As this story unfolds, I think you'll see some of the fun things I've been able to discover about people. Sure, I'm going to tell you parts of this memoir directly. But I am also going to give you a tour through this important story by way of my access to the minds of the three key people who saw it unfold in their lives.

The first was Matteo Poulsen, whose parents, born in the United States, are of Danish and Italian heritage. Matteo is pronounced: Mah - TĀY - oh. He was a nineteen-year-old surfer, and stood out from the crowd with his ginger hair, emerald eyes, and fiery political activism. He chose a major Political Science and Government at UCSC.

The second was Ferran Bosch, whose parents are Castilian and Spanish. Ferran is pronounced: FEH - rhaan (with a trilled "r"). He was an eighteen-year-old soccer star who was born in the California central valley and lived in a town called Santa Nella, near Los Banos. He chose a major in Classical Studies at UCSC.

The third was Maura Byrne, whose parents were both Irish-American. Maura is pronounced: MAW - ruh. She was nineteen years old, and chose a major in Physics at UCSC. A smart, lively, animated, voluptuous young woman, she also enjoyed being a kind of nosey project manager for her group of close friends. She started her second year at university with romantic designs on both Ferran and Matteo.

***

I've been guarding Santa Cruz, California, for as long as I can remember. Certainly, it's been since long before it had that name. In fact, the Ohlone tribes used to call this place by *my* name.

Ever since then, I've been trying to tell stories about differences and about making a difference. You know that Vulcan saying: that the cosmos seems to have "infinite diversity in infinite combinations." I'm definitely gratified that in Santa Cruz everything is — well — a little bit different. It's kind of like a witchy circle of earnest hippies sitting on a cluster of ley lines.

It has been a place where people can try to be themselves in new ways, and try to change the world — to be different. I think of Santa Cruz as a mindset as well as a character, a persona as well as a location. And like its quirky home town, the principal university there is also different.

The campus of the University of California at Santa Cruz — UCSC — is literally a city on a hill. A couple thousand years ago, one of your prophets, a rabbi, said that you shouldn't hide your light under a basket — that a city on a hill cannot be hid. I kid you not: the student newspaper at UCSC is even called, *City on a Hill Press.*

Santa Cruz is a thing, a power. The surprisingly cosmopolitan and intercultural university that got planted here amplifies that power. On one side of the Santa Cruz Mountains is the mundane Silicon Valley outpost of San Jose. On the other side, closer to the rumble of the San Andreas Fault and bathed in a Mediterranean climate, is this human-scale sanctuary for the wonderful and the weird.

Santa Cruz is also a haven for surfers, boasting two of the best surfing areas in the country: Steamers Lane and Pleasure Point. I feel it has also served as a living laboratory for new ways of loving people and the planet. The area sits poised on the Central Coast of California, with a backdrop of redwood forests, farmland, and a mountain range.

It certainly has the problems that any town in the United States might have. But progressive community members — affectionately called *Cruzistas* — go out of their way to find new solutions. I think it is a living proof that the personal is the political.

Let me tell you more about it's more recent history. That will set the scene.

The Backstory

It shouldn't come as a surprise that difference scares the powers-that-be. Over time, some powerful people had come to see the university and the town of Santa Cruz as a threat. The first targets of authoritarians are always a community's efforts at diversity, equity, and inclusion.

These powerful people tried to suppress the history and purpose of UCSC. After all, one result of the university campus being planted here was that the very sleepy, white, conservative seaside fishing and retirement village of Santa Cruz had become a mixing bowl of different races, ethnicities, and alternative lifestyles, and a hotbed of left-wing political activism.

UCSC had been founded to be different in a town that had become quite different. The '60s had hit the world and UCSC had hit California. People started to remember that the United States had been built on land that was stolen from indigenous tribes, and often by labor from people who were enslaved. Folks also began to open up their minds in other ways.

In the late 1970s and early 1980s, when the country was moving rightward and eventually elected Ronald Reagan as President, Santa Cruz was one of the communities that moved decisively to the left. Socialist majorities won elections in Santa Cruz on both the city and county levels. Voters enacted transformative ecological initiatives, starting with area greenbelts. An openly gay man became mayor. In her College Handbook, author Lisa Birnbach listed a concise commentary on UCSC. "Sex," she wrote, "is casual."

Predictably, the campus had been devised during the heyday of the movement to transform the goals of higher education. Most universities at the time, for academics and students alike, were intensely competitive pressure-cookers designed to create corporate tools. They followed the German educational model, with research faculty having little interaction with undergraduate students and everyone being siloed in rigid academic departments. UCSC instead, staffed with radical faculty reformers who developed the campus on the Oxford-Cambridge collegiate model, sought to encourage a lot of cross-fertilization between academic disciplines, alongside more diverse, cooperative, human-scale communities.

There would be no money-draining NCAA Division I sports program to distract from the pursuit of knowledge, and no Greek System of fraternities and sororities to displace the role of the colleges in encouraging diversity, equity, and inclusion in university life. Every faculty member and every undergraduate would belong to one of the small colleges that dotted the campus, threading through the edges of the redwood forest. Most of the graduate students would also work in one of the colleges, in addition to working in their labs and studios. Distinguished faculty would work directly with undergraduates.

UCSC became victimized by its own successes at creating change. Those powerful people who felt resentful about Santa Cruz seized on the economic uncertainty of the late 1970s, and the campus suffered under their pessimistic scrutiny. The University of California Regents decided to do the bidding of a cadre of rich, right-wing, bigoted, anti-tax crusaders who were gaining public support. The Regents sent a hatchet man to become the campus chancellor, a biologist named Robert Sinsheimer. He imposed a "reorganization" of the campus operational and power structure, bringing some very ugly results.

From my vantage point as an elder — okay, ancient — messenger and guardian, it seemed as though the campus and the town were having an experience of complex trauma. Santa Cruz is a character in its own right, and that character was being violated. Sneeringly, one student leader explicitly called-out Sinsheimer's agenda as an attempt to create "a general campus, having a general catalogue, with general students, for the general use of vulture capitalist corporations."

I remember when the early shifts were happening, back in the 1980s. Chancellor Sinsheimer made an early proposal to pave over a huge portion of the campus's on-site forest to build a profit-making industrial research and development park. We have only one Earth, only one home, and we have to cherish it. I was happy that Sinsheimer's idea was crushed by local and campus opposition within a year.

But among other things, the social atmosphere Sinsheimer was trying to foster meant the campus was facing the possible introduction of a "Greek System" of fraternities and sororities — which in some ways were an old-guard network to protect race and class privilege. The Student Union Assembly — UCSC's internal student government — considered issuing a policy against allowing the formation of such a system at UCSC. They had strongly believed that it would be counterproductive to the campus's college-based community structure, as well as fraught with problems that were counter to the ethos of UCSC and of Santa Cruz.

At one point, it had become very dramatic. I may have encouraged the Assembly to take a chance, and they had done so. They had decided to send a delegation of their members — two young men named Austin and Sabin — to the nearest University of California campus with an active Greek System, to conduct a sort of reconnaissance mission. If a Greek System was to be installed, the Assembly had wanted to shine a light on the reality of what might come to Santa Cruz.

***

Taking advantage of the free inter-campus library shuttle bus that ran between UCSC and UC Berkeley, Austin and Sabin got a ride to Berkeley on a Friday shuttle. They spent the day touring UC Berkeley and walking around "Fraternity Row," investigating which houses they might be able get into to chat with the "brothers."

Because there was a huge party raging there, they ended up settling on the Tau Kappa Fraternity House on the corner of Channing Way and Piedmont Avenue. They walked in and found a large number of drunk guys in t-shirts and backwards baseball caps, scattered everywhere. There were also many scantily clad women drinking from ubiquitous red plastic cups. Sabin remained upstairs chatting with some of the fraternity brothers — the *frat bros,* while Austin explored the party and ventured downstairs into a basement bar, where he chatted with some women about what they thought about the Greek System and why they were at this particular house party.

The women explained that they went to the parties because the drinks were free, the music was usually pretty good, and they could dance. As they did, a frat bro named Jason Praeger, President of the UC Berkeley College Republicans, overhead the conversation and butted-in. "Who are you and what frat are you with?" he demanded. Austin explained that he was a student at UCSC and was there to better understand the pros and cons of the Greek System.

Praeger told Austin that he was not welcome and pushed him back, which caused Austin to stumble and fall. That showed Praeger's true character. It was only the first of several gloomy shadows that Jason Praeger would project into the bigger story here.

After Austin got up and turned around to confront him, another fraternity brother came forward and threw a punch that hit Austin squarely in the face and caused an immediate bloody nose. Austin sought to escape the two charging fraternity brothers by running upstairs. When he got to the landing half-way up the stairs, he pushed an empty beer keg down toward the two frat brothers chasing him, buying himself time to get to the main floor.

When he reached the top of the stairs, another group of frat bros who'd been watching and waiting grabbed Austin. Fortunately, Sabin was there and swung his book bag in circles above his head. This helped him hit a number of the assailants with it, and allowed him to grab Austin's arm and lead them both out of the house and out into the street.

As they arrived in the street, they were fortunate that a campus security car rolled by and stopped. The campus officer saw that Austin's face was visibly bloody and that a group of frat bros were in pursuit. When they saw campus security, the frat bros stopped on the lawn of their house while the officers questioned Austin and Sabin. The officers asked Austin and Sabin to ride with them to the campus security station. There, they provided a detailed story of what had happened and were then released.

After they returned to UCSC, Austin and Sabin were summoned to the office of the Vice Chancellor for Student Affairs and Success. They were told that the Berkeley fraternity had filed formal charges against them for allegedly sneaking into the frat house party and threatening their female guests, and for supposedly pulling a knife on one of the brothers who had come to the defense of the women. Appalled at the fraternity brothers' lies, Austin and Sabin reiterated their own story which matched the facts determined by UC Berkeley Campus Security. One of the women Austin had chatted with at the party had given him her phone number, so he also called her and asked her to speak with the Vice Chancellor. She corroborated Austin's and Sabin's story.

The UC Berkeley fraternity was then cited for filing a false campus security report, and the specific Tau Kappa brothers and pledges were put on campus probation. Austin and Sabin then informed the California Department of Transportation about having witnessed many stolen California State Highway signs and City of Berkeley street signs on display in the fraternity house. *City on a Hill Press* ran a graphic security photo of Austin with his bloody nose, accompanied by an investigative report about the incident.

The Student Union Assembly issued a scathing condemnation of the prospect of beginning a Greek System at UCSC. Chancellor Sinsheimer, however, followed his pattern of flagrantly disregarding the shared governance structure — mandated by the California Constitution — of the state's research university system. He argued that any student organization could call itself a fraternity or sorority as long as it followed campus regulations, even though he would implement no formal Greek System. That fudging made the public relations shills in the Administration happy.

Shortly afterward, Sinsheimer even took his efforts so far as to try to formally get rid of the beloved tongue-in-cheek campus mascot: the banana slug. For people dedicated to the ideals of Santa Cruz and UCSC, that made the bigger political issues feel far more personal. At the time, it was the final straw for many students. Sinsheimer was stuck facing a major and multifaceted backlash of his own.

Still, the creeping divisions he'd set in motion didn't stop. In fact, they persisted — and have right to the present day. Setting a public tone that attracted more conservative and reactionary elements to the student body and to the town became the legacy of Sinsheimer's fellow-travelers — cog-in-the-wheel careerists who had been lurking among the faculty and administration, ready to pounce. They ushered in a larger presence of active classism, racism, misogyny, and homophobia to a campus that until that time had been a bastion of fighting against such oppression.

I can't be absolutely sure that the corporate lackeys had *intended* to create a safe space for narrow-minded, ruling-class dolts to make their way into Santa Cruz. They might claim it was an accident, but I feel strongly that they should be known by their results. For example, there are some students these days who feel they have permission to be overtly bigoted.

At the same time, a few of the marginalized students who've grown more reactive have taken to fearfully policing each other for doctrinal purity. Having student clubs on campus that call themselves "fraternities," and "sororities," many of whose members are also members of the College Republicans, has not exactly shouted "diversity, equity, and inclusion" to the world.

In some ways, though, geography has become destiny at Santa Cruz. Sinsheimer and his drones wound up with only marginal success in killing off the radical UCSC spirit. In comparison to most research universities in the US or Britain, UCSC remained a far more welcoming place for differences and change. The town, too, has maintained its circle of happy weirdness.

***

Locally and globally, personally and politically, things were cooking. They were about to get very different again. And that's the more interesting part of the story, which I'm about to help unfold for you in the book that follows.

A Dedication

FOR ALL THE LOVERS.

Short of the Vulcans
coming to save us from ourselves,
loving each other and our planet is all we've got.

BOOK ONE

1
ENCOUNTER

"… How on Earth can you explain in terms of chemistry and physics so important a biological phenomenon as first love?
… It seldom happens that you can plan your whole future just by looking at someone in the eyes, but think of how it feels when that does happen."
— *Albert Einstein*

[Playlist reference: Oilvia Rodrigo (Disney) — Start of Something New (Mini Version)]

Matteo

Ferran Bosch had just whizzed past his opponents. The crowd cheered wildly as he scored the winning goal, securing victory for the Division III university men's team. As they surrounded Ferran, his exhilarated teammates cheered, yelling the name of our campus's infamous mascot: "Slugs! Slugs! Banana Slugs!"

Me? I'm Matteo Poulsen.

I was a second-year student at the University of California, Santa Cruz. Ferran Bosch was a freshman, but the mostly older members of the soccer team seemed to consider him a star. His teammates were rushing-in and surrounding him, patting him on his back — his broad, muscular, magnificent back.

Oh, my.

We couldn't have asked for a more perfect day for a soccer game. It was a breezy mid-September. The wind was carrying the lingering scent of summer grass and just a slight hint of the approaching crispness of Autumn. Above the spectacular horizon where the Monterey Bay meets the Pacific Ocean, the sun was hovering and casting golden hues across the field. Further up in the hills, the forests were at last recovering from the terrifying Bonny Dune Wildfire — one of the resulting nightmares of global climate change.

The evening dusk was reliably on the way, and so was Maura Byrne. Curvy, vivacious, and effervescent, Maura was conducting our group of companions across the field as if she were our cruise director and kibitzer-in-charge. Even two cats engaged in a field war with a ground squirrel stopped their battle to get out of Maura's way.

Apparently, I was her newest friend, and she was grasping my hand as she relentlessly tugged me along with her.

During the game, Maura told me that in high school, Ferran had conclusively earned his record as a soccer prodigy. A team captain is often called a *skipper* in soccer, and he'd been the skipper of his high school team for the association football club in the central valley. He impressed his coaches and teammates at home in Los Banos. Clearly, he was also winning fans at Santa Cruz.

Maura turned to see me and commented breathlessly: "Look, Matt! I mean, *look at him!* Isn't Ferran incredible?"

Now, I'll tell you: I spent a lot of my life moving around and adjusting to new people and surroundings. I was used to trying to be alert and confident — to trying to keep my wits about me. In my freshman year at UCSC, I even managed to gain a reputation for being both aloof and a so-called "chick magnet." After all, a good mix of ennui and charm can have its benefits.

Not on *this* day, though. No, on this day I found myself feeling tense and anxious. I was nodding absentmindedly at Maura, but my attention was laser-focused on Ferran's every move. Maura didn't know I was bisexual, and I managed to shift my attention to her just long enough to sputter: "He's … amazing … on the, um … on the field."

O my gods, how embarrassing.

I have to say I felt puzzled looking at Ferran. It almost seemed to me that I was seeing a strange light revolve around him. But maybe it was just the evening's atmosphere working on my imagination. Or maybe I was just a horny 19-year-old? Couldn't say for sure.

When Ferran caught sight of Maura, he was still panting and covered in sweat. He also saw his roommate, Stu, and the rest of us in Maura's group of friends. We were all glowing with pride while we eagerly waited to greet him. Still out of breath, he looked at Maura and at our group, and then seemed to take-in a lingering eyeful of me.

The sheer intensity of Ferran's gaze caught me off guard. I tried to pull myself together to say something — anything.

I was *not prepared.*

Maura

A couple of weeks before this game, I'd decided I really liked Ferran Bosch. Of course, I also thought he was incredibly sexy. Besides being tall — six-foot-one, in fact — with a solid jawline and sporty features, the most obvious of Ferran's physical traits were his well-toned muscles. I imagined — often — that his thighs could probably crack walnuts.

Thanks to his parents being from Spain and having a distant Moorish touch in their lineage, his skin was another boon. It was the color of deep, golden-brown *dulce de leche,* His sparkling eyes were beautifully set off by it. Ferran definitely had the look of a well-built contender — gifted with athletic genes, and dedicated to practicing and working out for soccer.

In addition to being a soccer prodigy — moving up the pitch to be positioned as striker within the first few practices — I thought that his decision to major in Classical Studies was kind of hot. A super-smart jock. Swoon. I met him at a student sports fair at Cowell, my home college at the university. That was where his dark, chocolate-brown, doe eyes had done their magick and left me spellbound.

All right, fine. I was enraptured, okay?

Ferran

Maura Byrne was a striking young woman, and she was greeting me excitedly. Along with her was a young man I didn't know, and she was pulling him by the hand. "Ferran!" she called. "You were amazing out there!"

I thanked her and smiled a very happy smile.

I met Maura the first hour I was on campus. I learned that she was studying physics, and I was considering asking her out on a date. Her looks showed off her Irish heritage: jet black hair, porcelain skin, and deep blue eyes. And those eyes were fixed on me.

Beaming at me, she said, "I want you to meet someone!"

"Cool! Who is this?"

I focused more directly on the guy she had pulled by the hand. And then I couldn't look away. Standing in front of me was a young man about my age, whose chiseled features suggested he might be a fashion model.

I guess I could describe the rest of his looks as a cross between a ginger Santa Cruz surfer and a northern Italian hippie. He was wearing black trail shoes, well-fitted black jeans, and a very colorful knit Baja hoodie. I looked to his eyes, and saw them flash a sparkling emerald green.

So … Maura's friend was … strikingly handsome? Was I allowed to think that, even though I wasn't a player for Team Gay? I mean, I could appreciate a guy's remarkable looks, couldn't I?

Maura was still holding his hand, apparently fully in charge of her interaction with him. I wondered whether she might have devised this introduction to see if she could spark a competition between the two of us for her attention. She was giving him the kind of look that suggested she found him especially alluring. If I'm being totally honest, I couldn't argue with that finding.

"This is Matteo!" she exclaimed. "He's my newest friend, and I thought you two should meet."

The instant she said it, his cheeks turned a hot crimson red. I became even more acutely aware his features because of it. I had to admire that he seemed confident and sure of himself, in spite of his blush. Also, I could swear those green eyes were projecting a sensitive warmth that seemed both strong and gentle.

As if campaigning, he reached out his hand for me to shake. "Matteo Poulsen," he said firmly. "Call me Matt."

As I shook Matt's outstretched hand, an unfamiliar, inexplicable sensation flooded through my body. Suddenly I was flushed and hot, and my chest was pounding. I wondered if I was having a panic attack.

My mind also raced with an unusual cluster of thoughts.

What's with those eyes?

Can he really *be that pretty?*

Wait, what? Pretty?

Where the fuck did that come from?

I struggled to gather myself together, but my valiant attempt wasn't helping as much as I wanted it to. How dare some kind of insolent whirlwind thrash my usual sense of sportsmanlike calm!

Okay, all right. He's undeniably pretty.

I was relieved I hadn't said any of that out-loud.

Since I couldn't decide where to look, I focused on trying to pass judgment on Matt's decidedly "Santa Cruz hippie boy" outfit. But that didn't work either, because I couldn't help seeing his longish, dazzling ginger hair. He looked awesome, and I needed to know more about him.

I must have been projecting, because I thought maybe *he* seemed flustered. As I made an effort to hide my own nervousness, Matt offered me some praise. He called my plays in the game "brilliant." Something inside me was changing, because his words made my stomach do a happy dance.

I summoned all the *soccer jock* confidence I could present while I fumbled through my mind for something to say. I did my best to look Matt in the eye and smile broadly. With a lot of effort, I finally managed to put words together: "I'm glad you're interested in soccer."

Ugh. Was that the best I could do?

Matteo

My hand was still in the grasp of the soccer star's hand. I tried to speak more, but I couldn't. I was feeling the way I did in those times when I'd fallen from my surf board and I'd been towed under by the cold, crashing surf.

The thought crashing through my head was anything but cold, though. It was blazing-hot: *I just might be all too happy to drown in this man's sweat.*

I realized that I was also losing control of my own physical reaction to all this. And, wow, that was annoying. I was unnerved.

Staring down at my shoes, I tried to ground myself. Worrying thoughts slid their way into my mind.

Don't fall for a straight boy. Don't do it.

God only knows where this could go.

I looked back at Ferran, and he appeared to be every bit of the suave, calm, cool soccer phenom Maura had described to me.

He told me he was glad I was interested in soccer, and I tried to come back with a cheerful response. "Apparently, when you're winning the game for the Banana Slugs, I become a big soccer fan." I couldn't help that my long eyelashes were fluttering as I looked at him, could I?

I noticed Ferran shiver as his cheeks turned pink. Was he blushing, or just cold? In spite of his shiver, he gamely pressed ahead trying to make conversation with me.

Maybe sounding a little nervous, he asked: "So … uhm … how do you know Maura?"

Was the bright-shining Ferran Bosch worried that I might compete with him for Maura Byrne? I grinned at him and tried to relax. "We met last week at Stevenson College — at the Stevenson Coffeehouse — when they were playing an old Tom Lehrer vinyl album. She was sitting across the table from me and I just started singing along. Then we started talking about him and we couldn't stop because we're both such fans. And he actually used to teach here."

As if on cue, Ferran's roommate, Stu, began to sing: "I got it from Agnes, she got it from Jim…"

Another of their friends, Alicia, chimed-in with him: "We all agree it must have been Louise who gave it to him…"

Maura rolled her eyes. "Do you have to sing his one song about sexually transmitted infections?"

"Also, his funniest song," Stu offered, in their defense.

"Ew."

The banter provided me with just enough space to catch my breath. "And also," I spoke up again, "Maura is *always* talking about you."

Ferran seemed bemused by that, and he shot Maura a smile. "Wait, really?" he asked me. "What does she say about me?"

Maura grinned and quickly waved her hand dismissively. "Don't you worry about it, Ferran Bosch. They are all good things, I promise."

Ferran

I told Maura I was flattered, but I was more distracted. I was trying to scrutinize the surprising appeal I felt from this new guy, Matt.

I couldn't decipher whatever signal it might be that was rattling my inner core. I guess I could describe the feeling it gave me as a weird mix— fascination combined with a stringently contained psychic meltdown. Okay, maybe I was exaggerating. Maybe not?

But just at that moment, Matt's eyes dropped again, except this time not to his feet. When I followed the direction of his gaze, my own eyes widened. I wasn't sure how to feel about what I thought was happening, because I was almost certain that Matt was checking out my bicep.

I tried to interact more with him, but I think it just came out as anxious chatter. It must have looked to Maura as if Matt and I had some kind of instant camaraderie, because her smile went up to her eyes. If we had camaraderie, I wasn't feeling it over my inner turmoil, and Matt seemed — scattered maybe?

Maura looked back and forth at both of us, and she seemed a little surprised. I felt bad that she wasn't the center of my attention, but she didn't seem to be the center of Matt's either. Maybe she felt deflated? Maybe she didn't know what to make of either of us.

She raised her eyebrow while glancing between us and then slightly shook her head.

Maura

I met Matteo Poulsen at the coffeehouse about a week and a half after I met Ferran. I admit I felt an instant attraction to him. Our conversation was pithy and easy. And he was a Politics major who loved Tom Lehrer. What was not to like?

I also couldn't deny Matt's striking beauty — a combination of his mother's Italian heritage and his father's Danish background. The boy really was just so darned *pretty*. A barely five-foot-seven ginger with a lithe body, a gorgeous face, and what seemed to be a gymnast's build.

At the East Field after the game, Matt and Ferran and I continued to talk with each other. Alicia, Alex, Jake, Stu, and Emily — more of our new and deepening circle of friends — joined in with us. Matt and Ferran started to joke and laugh as if they'd known each other for years.

Now, I confess, I like to stay in the loop about social news I find important. I'd heard some talk about Ferran from a few friends in the Administration. They told me that the campus's Office of Physical Education, Recreation, and Sports — dubbed OPERS for short — had been very intentional in urging their Admissions Office colleagues to look extra closely at his already first-rate student application.

Whether you were talking about the vistas or the athletes, you could say that the main OPERS facility on the East Field had gorgeous views. The coaches intended to keep it that way on all fronts. With the handsome and talented Ferran Bosch boosting them to a winning season, they were sure he could help make the sports programs thrive.

I had at least as much determination as the coaches. So I decided I wasn't about to let go of the winning possibilities I might have with either of these hot guys. Or both of them, for that matter.

"Okay, people!" Coach Janaya Hasan loudly announced, with the vocal projection characteristic of soccer coaches. "We're going to be turning off the big lights soon!"

"Move your butts!" yelled her fellow-coach, Thuso Mokone. Coach Mokone generally seemed prickly and ill-tempered. In contrast, the very affable Coach Hasan — or

Janaya as she preferred to be called by the team — was striking up a friendship with Ferran and with our crew.

Ferran

I felt this weird pull towards Matt, and I was having a tough time resisting it. Jolted from my reverie by the coaches, I was saved from becoming even more thoroughly confused at the weird feelings I was having.

Suddenly, I noticed that the evening air was getting really chilly, and I remembered I was a sweaty mess. So, I made my announcement to the group: "I have to go hit the showers, folks."

Maura intervened to serve as social chair. "Come on, you two, she said to Matt and me, "Exchange numbers, and we can all keep in touch." She watched our ensuing awkward exchange with what appeared to be vague concern and puzzled amusement.

Then I was walking off to hit those showers.

Matteo

I watched Ferran walk toward the Field House and I couldn't stop staring.

Maura apparently enjoyed acting like a mother hen for the brood, and she took Ferran's departure as her cue to dutifully collect us. She flipped her obsidian-colored tresses in the breeze, and prompted the rest of the friend circle make their excuses and walk back to their dorms.

I wasn't living in the dorms for this school year. I had chosen to live off campus with other students in a house on Pleasure Point in Live Oak. So, I said my goodbyes and began to walk to the shuttle stop.

I was still in a daze.

2

BEFORE

"You're not supposed to be in a relationship
because it's comfortable, it's supposed to be
because they make you a better person."
— *Dominic Riccitello*

[Playlist reference:
Elton John, Dua Lipa — Cold Heart]

Ferran

Back in early June, the San Francisco fog was blanketing the entirety of the Velo Rouge Cafe.

That was often the case at that time of year in San Francisco. The marine layer would provide air conditioning for The City that would make the climate frigid until the sun burned it off mid-morning. Then it would return at dusk, flowing in from the Pacific. Residents had affectionally nicknamed the fog, "Karl."

Karl was everywhere in San Francisco on the day after April Challoner and I had graduated from our high school in the Central Valley.

I had just finished my senior high school year. As had my girlfriend April, a cheerleader who had sung in the school chorus and had the definite look of someone who might succeed as a model. We looked like a storybook couple — on the outside. The beautiful cheerleader dated the attractive, athletic soccer player, and we had been the class royalty of Los Banos High School. We had also pulled in the two highest scores on our university entrance exams. Stereotypical, I know.

Our parents were well aware that April and I had a sexual relationship. Since we had been together since junior high school, they had also taken to mentally planning what they believed would be our inevitable future wedding. For our graduation present our parents actually had been cool enough to buy us a weekend bed-and-breakfast vacation in San Francisco. If we were being honest, we couldn't wait to get out of the heat of the Santa Nella - Los Banos area to take our trip to The City.

We were having a light — and also solemn — breakfast at Velo Rouge on that foggy morning. April walked back to our table with her cappuccino. She did not seem happy, and neither did I.

Adopting her cogent, dry, matter-of-fact delivery style that she'd usually used for public speaking, April began making her case. "Look, Ferran. We've had a good run. Dating for six years. Everybody sure we were destined to be the king and queen of the prom. But you know as well as I do that this relationship as it is isn't going to survive long distance. I mean, we're going to be on opposite sides of the country."

I sighed. "I'm not disagreeing with you."

The truth was that I was feeling myself fall apart inside. In my mind, this was confirmation that the people I most wanted in my life — and needed to rely on — would abandon, or neglect, or betray me. After all, I'd come to the conclusion that my own parents had done that throughout my childhood, when the demands of their high-powered, major-money careers and of their own lives seemed to always take precedence over me.

In early grade school, the other children had quickly caught on to the fact that I was intellectual, and they labeled me a "nerd." They had relentlessly bullied me for it, and that had included physical violence. It felt as though my parents were oblivious to it all.

That was when I resolved I'd create an image that would overcome my reputation as a nerd. I think I succeeded, but I felt that the result ensured that my parents only knew me on the surface. They saw me as their athletic soccer star and high-performing student who had a gorgeous, smart, steady, long-term, cheerleader girlfriend. They had never seemed to take any real interest in my actual life.

April's story was nearly identical to mine, which had drawn the two of us together. We embarked on our relationship with both mutual affection and mutual calculation. Over time, I began to express to April some of my most covert feelings — to bounce them off of her. It was a kind of confidential trust we shared with each other

— a mainstay of our friendship. For the rest of the world, April hid her shrewdness and steely determination underneath her soft external beauty — but she let down her guard for me.

I worried that today was coming, and here we were. After we were together through junior high, we promised each other to be together in a monogamous relationship in high school. Still, I figured April would eventually find a far better catch and would want to be with him instead of me. I told myself that a breakup would come some time — probably because April would cheat on me. But neither of us had cheated, so I was surprised that she was breaking up with me.

Alex Garcia was my longest-running friend. He and I had been talking about my prediction of a breakup as if it were a looming inevitability. "I hate to break it to you," Alex argued, "but you two are basically a high school public relations campaign that's run its course. At least you can take comfort in this: when things go wrong, it's a sign that you're genuinely human."

Alex never minced words with me. He was the bookworm of his family, and April was an only child. Throughout junior high and high school, as popular as I had become, I considered Alex and April to be the only peers I could count on to keep me going. I hated that they seemed always to be competing and bickering with each other. But I didn't want to argue with either of them about it; I felt they were all I had.

At the table, I grumbled to April: "This is just sad."

I also reached over to take a swig from my now-tepid, pour-over house coffee. It was a French roasted, charcoal-tasting blend that I had long decided I detested. If most people knew "French roast" means a batch of all the garbage beans that hadn't made it through the roasting process, which are then thrown back into the roaster to burn and sell to customers with a poor palate, it might not be so popular. I'd only bought it because house coffee is just what I always drank.

Distraught, I had tried to come up with excuses to give to April for us to stay together. "We're good friends," I protested. "We've definitely had good sex."

"I cannot complain about the sex," April smirked.

"I understand there's no heart fire, April. But passion has never been our vibe. Alex says that we're like a PR corporation. It's always been about our friendship and curating our image."

"I am so tired of keeping up a damned image, you have no idea."

"Oh, no." I had to acknowledge. "I *definitely* have the same idea."

I think that too early in life we became cynical. We were young, but also worn-down. It was April who called it out: "How did we get so jaded at 18?"

Believe me, I'd already pondered that. I tried to offer April a series of ideas: "Maybe because our parents' and grandparents' generations fed us a steady stream of lies about what life is? And they wouldn't recognize social justice if it slapped them in the face? And they're burning the planet, and they've stolen our futures, and now they tell us we're lazy and we're on the hook to live with their disasters and pay for it all?"

"Well, there's that," she replied in a deadpan voice.

April had often told me she loved how deeply her favorite soccer jock could analyze the world, and that she didn't find me at all depressing. She claimed that she found me stimulating — in several ways. I was not feeling stimulated in any way at that moment.

Emphatically and *a propos* of nothing, I proclaimed: "As we say in Catalan, this coffee is *merda*."

She pressed on, unperturbed: "Let's be honest, Ferran. Your parents are not evil incarnate."

I tried to argue the point: "My father is a glorified computer peddler. Maybe he's not the devil himself, but he works for the guy. At least your parents run an organic farm."

With the first sign that morning of any animation in her voice, April laid it out for me: "Your mom has used her platform at the university to wrangle more investment for social housing out of the State of California than any other advocate. So, maybe you could give her a little credit?"

"Being depressed and whiny and easily-offended is part of my generational job description, isn't it?" I countered.

"Look, don't sell your parents short. They really do care about you."

"I'm going to have to trust your word on that," I answered in monotone. "And whatever their affections, they did split the cost of our bed-and breakfast with *your* parents. And, you know, 'You can't build up areas liberated *from* the system without using the existing material *of* the present system.'"

She smiled at my attempt at using an intellectual quote to parry. "Did Marx write that?"

"Rudolph Bahro, the Green fundie, but he was riffing off of Marx. So, are we now having the most San Francisco conversation *ever?*"

"I'll remind you that we have these kinds of conversations all the time — despite the fact that at the moment I know you're trying to avoid the subject at hand."

I grimaced.

"How many of our classmates would even know who Marx and Bahro were?" she asked.

"Alex."

"Exactly."

"Well, at least there's one righteous man," I quipped.

"You should become a Political Science and Government major at UCSC," April suggested, "not a Classical Studies major."

I'd thought about it before — I really had. But I shared my conclusion with April: "I can't do the kind of work involved in a Politics major and *also* do soccer. I've been team striker for three years and I'll be lucky to even be made a center forward at UCSC, so it's going to take a lot of work on the pitch. And I am not going to have you there to have these kinds of conversations with. So, if I don't have soccer, I will lose my fucking mind."

She paused for a moment to think. But then she made her emphatic announcement: "We definitely need to break up and get on with the next stage of our lives."

I couldn't help having my frown grow deeper. *"I know.* I just don't want us to disappear from each other's lives. I want us to stay friends and touch base when we're in the same city. Can we do that? Can we please not just dissolve a whole six years?"

"Ferran … *obviously,"* she sighed. "But we need to break up so we can *keep* our friendship. We were never going to be the happily married couple walking off into the sunset. We are going to stay true friends, I promise."

"Okay," I agreed, again feeling deflated. I felt as if the floor was pulled out from under me and that I was sinking fast.

"Both of us need to go out there and grab life," she said. "We need to find our passions and our people. And we need to get away from the rut of each other for a while to do it."

"Truth," I reluctantly admitted. "Just *hard* truth. You're not going to forget about me, are you?"

"I'm never going to forget about you, Ferran."

"Karl is being especially aggressive today."

"Yeah."

3

CONVERGENCE

"Once upon a midnight dreary,
while I pondered, weak and weary,
Over many a quaint and curious
volume of forgotten lore—
While I nodded, nearly napping,
suddenly there came a tapping,
As of someone gently rapping,
rapping at my chamber door."
– Edgar Allan Poe, The Raven

*[Playlist reference: Taylor Swift, Ed Sheehan
— Everything Has Changed]*

Ferran

The sun was bright a day after our winning soccer game, but a cool breeze flowed through the redwoods.

UCSC has a quirky "shopping for classes" exercise to start off each quarter. Students who were to live on-campus at UCSC had begun arriving for the Autumn Quarter on the first day of September, and the rest would roll in over the next several days. Some instructors would offer a kind of early power-point presentation on what to expect from a given course, prior to the start of classes. It was a ritual students could use to get acclimated and find their routines before instruction actually started.

I was lucky to be allowed into this History of Consciousness course as a first-year student, and to be able to fit it into my schedule. The "luck" was that the professor knew my mother and would give me a waiver. I was sitting in the back of Kresge College Lecture Hall 3201. As I scanned the room, my eyes locked onto a familiar face occasionally looking back at me — the confusingly breathtaking face of a young man sitting a few rows ahead of me. It was Matteo Poulsen. And that's how we had both discovered we were hoping to take the same course.

I was only ever attracted to women in the past, but I could always acknowledge when another guy was handsome or interesting. I thought that was perfectly normal. But why did my stomach swoop when I thought about Matteo? Fuck. After meeting him, I wasn't so sure I knew what normal was anymore.

Sitting in the lecture hall, we waited for the presentation about this course that was set to begin in two weeks. I couldn't help fidgeting. I was busily twirling my pen between my fingers, and I was not exactly displaying the most chill of looks.

I tried, but I couldn't stop looking at Matt. I couldn't help feeling drawn to him—wanting to bask in his energy. I certainly couldn't stay focused on what the professor was saying, especially since Matt would turn and look at me every few minutes. This was not me having butterflies in my stomach, was it?

Whatever it was, this unsettled feeling had become a distraction. Each time I looked closely, I'd wonder at Matt's engaging smile, his perfectly angular face, and those bewitching green eyes. They seemed to look right into me. I don't think I'd ever felt that way before.

It was weirding me out.

Along the way, I also noticed that the climate control in the lecture hall, still set on cold for summer, had left the room really chilly. I saw Matt seated in his chair with the desk up, apparently shivering. And then I had some unusual thoughts — thoughts that felt really strange to me.

I could let him wear my jacket.

I could take him to my room and make him some hot tea or something.

He looks as if he needs to be cuddled to get warm.

I surprised myself, okay? I shuddered at what I was thinking, so I tried to empty my mind of any thoughts at all.

Despite feeling unsettled, I wound up waiting after class. I'd told myself that I just needed to get a glimpse of Matt as he walked out. You know, to confirm that I wasn't going crazy or something.

I crouched down, pretending to tie my shoelaces. As Matt walked past me, I found I was unable to resist, and I called out to him: "Hey, remember me?"

Matt looked down at me and smiled. "Of course, yeah. Hi, you're Ferran from last night's soccer game? We talked."

Why was I so nervous? As I stood up, I said, "Yeah, that's me."

Matteo

I was motivated to take this class to have my eyes opened. Right now, though, I could only see Ferran Bosch. It was frustrating and it made me nervous.

The data points indicated that UCSC accepted only the top five percent of university-eligible students. I really wanted to believe that most of my fellow students were intellectually reflective and thoughtful. But, after living through a year's worth of my academic colleagues, and after being dragged last night by Maura across a sports field to be introduced to a perilously charming straight boy, I was starting to consider an alternative. If we were the top five percent, I thought, that might explain why the republic was in such dire straits.

Maybe I was obsessing about Ferran. I'd only just met him, but my intuition was telling me that there was something important and exceptional about him. Besides the fact that he was especially handsome and likable, of course. I was feeling torn between having faith in my hunch about him, versus trusting my fear of getting hurt by falling for a straight boy.

It was confusing, because this was the same inner knowing that always told me something was watching over me. That same intuition kept telling me I needed to somehow amplify what a place like Santa Cruz could be and do, even though I wasn't sure how. But now I couldn't tell whether it was telling me to run away, or to let Ferran get closer to me. I had a lot of challenging thoughts running through my head.

I was drawn to this class because I wanted to see the big picture of how consciousness gets raised. I knew that there always has been a kind of knowledge that doesn't make it into the standard history about a community, or into coursework at schools. Powerful people try to suppress it. I had come to Santa Cruz to study Politics — officially

"Political Science and Government" — and to continue my political organizing work.

I was starting to feel some burnout, but I worked hard to keep my hand in several activist projects. The History of Consciousness course that Ferran and I both seemed to want to take was going to provide a fascinating overview of the evolution of political thought. I hadn't suspected that a soccer jock like Ferran would have any interest in it.

I'd also come to Santa Cruz because I wanted to surf. I wanted to meet new people. I especially wanted to be near my wonderfully flamboyant grandmother, who'd always amused me to no end.

Mostly, I came to forget. Forget that I'd never been good at making friends while my parents had moved around for work during most of the time I was growing up. That the first girlfriend I ever had broke my heart by dumping me for a much taller boy. I admit that I'd thrown myself into the concretely sexual aspects of my bisexuality, carefully avoiding any mindfulness about it or any real intimacy. That was one way I tried to deal with it all.

Somehow after meeting Ferran, though, my boiling urge to do that evaporated.

That change I was feeling was already making me anxious. Then after class, there was Ferran, crouched down at the entrance and tying his shoelace. Well, I think he was pretending to tie it. From the way he'd been looking at me during class, I thought I might be picking up some vibes from him. Maybe he wanted to be friends? Maybe.

Ferran blurted out a sort of greeting: "Hey, remember me?"

I answered that I did, of course. But, O my gods, even the sound of Ferran's voice was becoming beguiling to me. I was trying my best to appear calm and removed but I didn't think it was working. I kept repeating in my mind: *Don't fall for a straight boy.*

But I was worried that it might be too late.

"I didn't know that we'd both be interested in this lecture," I said. "But I didn't know they let freshmen take it. I was able to option it because I got approval last Spring."

"They don't usually let freshman take it," Ferran said as he stood up. "But I really wanted this course and my mother is friends with the professor."

"Aha! A little extra maneuvering!"

No question: Ferran made quite an impression on me last night. Standing across from him, I was having a hard time — literally — with a persistent image of kissing him. I hoped it would just leave my mind, but that was wishful thinking.

I continued to walk slowly by Ferran's side out of the lecture hall. I laughed nervously as he chatted with me. I was making a major effort at appearing to be measured and calm, but it wasn't working. Then I tried to make a case for a quick exit: "I need to rush to my next preview or I'll be late."

Ferran suggested that maybe we should meet at a dining hall for dinner some time, and I panicked. "I live off campus, so I don't have a meal plan," I offered, feeling stupid. "But maybe we can do coffee with Maura or something. Take care. Gotta go!"

Mind racing, I sought to escape by hurriedly walking away.

Ferran

I guess I was hoping for some kind of green light, some "yes" that would make this weirdness easier for me. Matt seemed to have effortless confidence, and I asked myself why that was making me sweat. As my nerves got more frazzled, I kept scrambling for things to say.

Matt told me he didn't think freshmen could get into the lecture course we were both looking into. I joked with him about my mother getting me an inside track. But as soon as I'd thought we were going to get a chance to talk more, Matt said he was going to be late for his next preview and needed to go. "Oh," I said, feeling like my bubble had been burst.

I don't know why I was feeling so dejected, but I kept babbling at Matt. "Okay. Well, I'm a newbie at UCSC and I just thought I'd take the opportunity to get to know you better. We exchanged numbers last night," I said, hopefully, "so… shoot me a text sometime. Maybe we can grab some dinner at the dining hall."

I was ruffled. It looked to me as if he wanted to run away. I couldn't deny the fluttering in my chest or the sudden unusual feelings I was having about him. I never felt this way before — not toward anyone. I tried to brush it off, but the weird feelings wouldn't go away.

4

TANGLED

I have to face life with a newly found passion.
I must rediscover the irresistible will
to learn, to live, and to love.
— *Andrea Bocelli*

"Anything is possible when you have
the right people there to support you."
— *Misty Copeland*

*[Playlist reference: Charley Puth
— One Call Away (Acoustic Version)]*

Ferran

A few foggy days later, I ran into Jake and grabbed some tea with him. With a few strategic — okay, prying — questions, I got him to open up about his secret crush on Maura and I'd asked him if he was going to try to date her. I told Jake that I would never compete with him over a woman, and said he should tell Maura about his crush.

"She's such a goddess," Jake said. "She intimidates me. I don't know how to tell her what I feel."

I was there at the ready to offer Jake some relationship advice. I guess I was missing the irony. "You don't need precision," I told him. "You just need to speak up and tell her you like her and you want to spend time with her."

"And what about you?" Jake asked, with his eyebrow raised. "Who's on your dating radar?"

He caught me in the midst of my confusion, so the best I could come up with was to speculate about my emotional state. "I think I'm not ready yet after my breakup. I feel like it might take more time."

Honestly, I had been telling myself that. But I think the deeper truth was that I was still preoccupied with my thoughts about Matt. I found myself checking my phone more often than usual, hoping for a text message from him. I'd even found myself actually *daydreaming* about what it would be like if I could just hang out with him and get to know him.

I guess I couldn't shake the feeling that there was something strangely special about the man. But thinking that way left me uneasy, so I tried to distract myself with soccer and schoolwork. It was always there, though — this nagging feeling that wouldn't go away. Whether I could understand it or not, I was wanting — maybe needing? — to see Matt.

I finally gave in and texted him.

hi! it's ferran bosch
and i hope you still remember me
don't want to bother you if you're busy
but I had an idea
and I want to chat with you about it
could I call you on an actual voice call?

It took several minutes for Matt to respond and I was worried that I'd made him nervous. But his reply

Ferran! Of course I remember you –
(I believe in capital letters, btw)
Press those numbers
I'm only one call away

It wasn't easy, but I mustered the courage to actually make a real-time phone call to Matt instead of continuing to text. I clicked on the call icon, and in less than one ring he answered the phone.

"Hey Ferran. What's up?"

I tried hard to sound chill. "Hi, Matt. Or, should I call you Mr. Grammar?"

Matt scoffed. "Hello to you, too, mister. Did you call me just to gripe at me about my texting style?"

"No, no, no. … The reason I called is that I just got the new EA Sports FC 26 game. My roommate isn't here to play 'cause he's staying with his girlfriend at Kresge College. So, I need for somebody to challenge me. Do you wanna come hang out at my dorm room tonight for some gaming?"

Matteo

I can't deny it; I got excited. I cleared my throat, trying my best to hide that I was *thrilled* with Ferran's invitation. "Oh! Yeah, sure!" I answered him. "That sounds like fun. Just let me know when and where."

"Great! How about around seven o'clock? My dorm room is at *Casa Sexta* at Stevenson. Just text me when you get to the lower quad."

There were my unhelpful thoughts again: *Oh sure, Casa* Sex-*ta. Let me try not to think about that.*

I took a deep breath, trying to settle my nerves. "Sounds good! I'll see you then. I think Emily and Stu are really cool, by the way."

"I like them a lot. But sometimes it's also nice to have the room to myself, obviously."

"Obviously."

O my gods. Did that mean anything? And then Ferran mentioned something that, despite sounding a bit foreign, was really thoughtful. "Oh, hey," he said in a honeyed voice that made me hungry, "it's really damp and chilly out. You might have to wear a *jersei.*"

A what now? I was confused at that word. "What's a *juhr-SAY?*"

"Ah! *Jersei* is the Catalan word for a sweater, a jumper, whatever you like to call it. It's like the British word 'jersey.' My mama is from Madrid, but she lived a long time in Barcelona with my papa. So that's the word we always used around my house for a sweater."

Oh. His *mama* was from Madrid and his *papa* was from Barcelona, and my cheeks were growing hotter by the second. Aside from having felt a jolt of lust just then, I'd wondered about his sweet advice.

He's trying to look out for me. What's that mean?

I don't know, but I like it.

"Wearing a sweater will never be the same for me," I'd tried to say flatly, to tease him.

Ferran laughed. "Matt Poulsen, are you acting like a smartass before we've even played a video game?"

"Of course I am. Before we play a virtual soccer game, I have to take the soccer star down a peg, don't I?"

Ferran

I liked Matt's sense of humor, and I chuckled at our give-and-take. "Okay, smartass," I said. "Just come over so I can beat you at FC 26."

"On my way."

Matt made his way to Stevenson College and came up to my room. When he arrived, I thought he looked effortlessly adorable, and I tried not to stare at him. We wasted no time in breaking-in my new game. The games were exciting and amusing overall, but unsurprising.

Except for the fact that I kept losing.

We were having such a good time together, though. I was loving the banter and the teasing, but I was also noticing a peculiar feeling in my gut. As we passed our second hour of gaming, I just wanted Matt to stay. Probably more than I should have, because I had a quiet freak-out when I thought about what it might look like if he did stay.

Despite a part of me not wanting him to leave, I knew that eventually we had to part ways a third time. I was becoming more and more aware that our evening was drawing to a close. As I was ruminating about it, I had a very odd experience. I honestly thought I heard someone say something in my ear that sounded like "okay, yeah."

Obviously, nobody else was there but Matt and me. So that was weird. Maybe I was just searching for any message at all because I felt so bewildered by my initial encounters with Matt. I needed to refocus, so I jokingly grumbled at him.

"You're killing me!" I said, "You gotta be cheating, man. I just don't know how."

"There's no way I cheated," Matt protested, as he bested me at yet another game of FC 26. "You are just clearly outmatched." I threw a pencil at him playfully, and we both snickered as he ducked to avoid it.

"Outmatched!? At least I have the ability *in real life* to actually score goals while running in the right direction. It's a useful skill, you know?"

Matt dropped his jaw in mock surprise. He taunted me: "You're such a soccer star that you can't even beat a surfer at a video game version of it?"

Ouch! I couldn't help laughing at that, and I responded in kind: "Ohhhhh … this from a student of Politics? Studying so you can become an expert in the art of making promises you won't keep, and blaming the other guy for the failure?"

Matt smiled but looked sheepish, and lowered his eyes. *"Rompicoglioni!"* he growled.

That sounded Italian, but it was close enough to the Catalan phrase that I thought I understood the playful insult. I feigned disbelief: "Did you just call me a ball-buster in Italian?"

"You're not the only one who has parents who sometimes speak foreign languages."

"It's almost the same in Catalan," I said, feeling oddly energized by what felt like a buzz starting in my own balls. *"Tu torracollons,"* I dubbed him. Matt's eyes widened as he grinned from ear to ear.

"Okay, fine! I see how it is," he declared. "So *you* just want to act like you're a Republican so when you can't win fair and square, you project your inadequacies onto your opponents."

He definitely clipped my wings with that one, so I chortled. I didn't know which was worse: Matt saying I wanted to act like a Republican, or his implication that I might be inadequate.

"Wow … *Inadequacies?*" I challenged, with as much sarcasm in it as I could pour. "I'll have you know that my boys on the field think I'm a lot *more* than adequate!"

Matteo

I had a string of erotic thoughts run through my mind as I visualized Ferran being *more than adequate,* on or off the field.

I was getting nervous despite our playful words, and I think I was sensing Ferran's inner discomfort, too. I tried to put him at ease with some small talk. As we played more rounds and during our breaks, we talked about our families, our interests, and our goals for the future. Before long, it felt like we were back to behaving the way we did the night we'd met — as if we'd always known each other.

Was it the game bringing me so much joy, or was it the company? Why was I still dwelling on these questions? I knew it was time for me to head home.

"Seriously, though: thank you," Ferran told me. "You were here to save the day."

I raised my eyebrow. "Were you gonna die if you couldn't play with your toy as soon as you got it?"

Ferran was laughing. "Something like that," he said.

I was thinking that both of us had become almost giddy. When we exchanged numbers and parted ways back on that first night on the sports field, I felt as if the world had shifted between us. On this night, by the time I had to take my leave to go home and get some sleep, I was feeling it had happened again.

I spent the trek home by bus berating myself — for every word, every gesture, every look, every thing I was convinced had been something that would scare Ferran away from me and put an end to this budding friendship.

But that wasn't what had happened at all. Before I even reached home, my phone chimed with a text from Ferran:

Meet me at my soccer practice tomorrow?
(I'm using caps, ok?)
If you want
we could be workout buddies at the gym after

At home, upstairs in my room, I eagerly texted him back, taking a chance at adding a vague but suggestive emoji at the end:

I'll bring my gym bag
Tomorrow I was planning on back and arms Thanks for
letting me kick your ass at FC 26
[purple heart emoji]

Ferran

By the time the clock on my smartphone was nearing midnight, I had already spent at least ninety minutes consumed by my thoughts of Matt — my very mixed-up thoughts.

I don't understand. Why do I feel this way?

I couldn't deny that I wanted to see him again. I was feeling conflicted, but something moved me to text Matt and ask if he wanted to hit the gym together the next day. He texted me back right away, and when I read it I felt warmth all the way up to my ears.

Then I kept re-reading his text — especially the purple heart emoji he'd ended it with. That's supposed to stand for admiration, support, loving-care, close bonds. For all my confusion, I wasn't able to stop smiling.

Maura

As the days went by, I noticed that Ferran and Matt were hanging out together a lot. To me, it seemed that an undeniable friendship was growing between the two sexy young men. Believe me, I was fantasizing about the possibility of getting both of them to be a lot more involved with me. Why shouldn't I have both of the hottest and smartest guys on campus?

I was starting to think of them as a unit, and to refer to them as "the boys." I also noticed that Matt had been going to Ferran's soccer practices. Stu told me they were gaming in the dorm a lot and that they'd also started hiking together around town and around campus.

One night, I saw them lying down on the lawn between Stevenson and Cowell colleges, having a conversation and staring up at the sky. It was so cozy looking; I wanted to join them. But since their talk looked serious, I decided I didn't want to interrupt.

On a Monday morning, Ferran and I ran into each other on our way to a class at Cowell College. As we chatted in the breezeway, we also had the opportunity to revel in the sound of the provost's children noisily playing and running around the fountain. I made a decision to take more initiative in pursuing Ferran, so I asked him directly: "Are you dating anyone?" He seemed a bit startled.

"What? Um, no. I think I'm still trying to recover from my breakup with my high school girlfriend. April and I were together for six years. I'm not sure I'm ready to date anybody yet."

I was surprised when he then immediately asked me: "Who is Matt dating?"

It seemed strange that his follow-up question to me was about Matt, instead of asking me about my own dating life. "You guys hang out so much," I answered him, "I figured you'd know more about that than I would." His answer was that Matt had never talked about it with him.

"Hmmm," I pondered. "I guess I should admit that I asked around a little. I know that last year he got a reputation as 'a player,' but that seems to have died down. I also heard that there was this Persian woman who was always after him. I mean, I don't know if she and Matt ever got together. Her name is Laleh — pretty sure she's a Merrill student. I think she's friends with one of your soccer coaches, Janaya. What I was told is that Laleh was always drunk at parties and that she used to always hit on Matt."

Ferran

Maura's news about Matt being 'a player' in his freshman year made me feel queasy, and I wasn't sure why. But I did try to quickly change the subject: "Have you seen Jake lately? I think he had a message he wanted to give you."

"Really? I haven't seen him in a couple of days, but I'll text him and ask him what's up and if he wants to grab dinner tonight at my dining hall."

I was already feeling awkward, but I think I managed to dodge more of it. I was wishing I could guard Matt from people like Laleh, but I kept telling myself it was none of my business. What I couldn't bring myself to do, though, was to tell Maura that I was having feelings of dread and annoyance over what she'd told me about Matt. I was relieved that she had to go to class.

One Thursday afternoon, Matt took a video of me playing at soccer practice. He later posted it to his videos on two social media platforms, tagging me, and using the #ucscmenssoccer and #boschtalent hashtags on the post. I saw the posts, and within seconds I pressed "like" on both of them.

The remarkable thing about it was the number of likes from random people that showed up on Matt's posts. He told me he didn't even know most of them. Within a few hours, Matt had almost eight hundred new followers on his accounts. Even the official account for the San Jose Earthquakes — the professional soccer team just over the hill from Santa Cruz — had liked both posts. They commented on one of them: "We've seen him play. Genius."

Matt claimed he was impressed by that, but I was astonished. I couldn't bring myself to believe that someone from the Earthquakes had even taken notice of me. "Of course they did," Matt said, shrugging. "When it comes to soccer, you're gonna give Ronaldo a run for the money, man. And you're the best as a person, anyway."

I'll admit I actually felt a tug at my heart when he said that. But I kept telling myself: *It's not like I'm in falling in love with the guy or anything. It's just that I get along with him. Right? And it's not like when I started to get hard it had anything to do with him comparing me to Cristiano Ronaldo. Right? University life is for making new friends.*

Okay, I admit I was also still thinking of my jumbled feelings as a looming threat — one that would steal this blossoming friendship from me.

Days after that, I noticed Maura and Jake sitting at a table in the Stevenson Coffeehouse. They were having a very animated conversation. I was curious if Jake was finally making his move, so I caught his eye and raised up my open hands as if to ask a question. Jake slowly shook his head "no," and I rolled my eyes at him.

I decided it was better to skip getting coffee. I hadn't stopped thinking constantly about Matt, and that was frustrating enough without adding watching Jake's seeming inability to tell Maura how he felt about her. Maybe that meant I was being a hypocrite, but my situation was different.

Or was it? I kept replaying in my head the conversations I'd had with Matt. I kept noticing that I missed Matt when we weren't hanging out together. I kept wondering if there was a way to make our friendship closer. When I considered all that, it made me feel like I was melting inside, but I was doing my best not to think about what that meant.

I suppose I should have been noticing instead that other troubles were building up inside me. Ever since April and I broke up, I had been repressing my intensifying stress. I tried to lock it away, but it was triggering the fears I'd held since I was a kid. I felt the pressure building — the compounding of all my sadness, anxiety, confusion, and frustration — exacerbated by a layer of disturbing curiosity.

I didn't see it coming, but I was reaching a crisis point. One day during a particularly grueling soccer practice, I totally lost my temper. A bunch of my teammates had to hold me back from swinging at another teammate who had inadvertently tripped me.

That was very uncharacteristic for me. The guys told me in strong terms that I needed to chill and to hit the showers. So, I went to the locker room, sat on a bench near my locker, and found myself alone and feeling raw.

I was lost in thought when the locker room door suddenly creaked open. I turned around to see Matt standing there, his ginger hair shining and his emerald eyes looking worried.

"Hey," Matt said, clearing his throat. "I just wanted to see if you were okay."

That look of worry in Matt's eyes was more than I could bear. Inside me, a mental dam burst that had been holding off my emotional flood. In a flash, it was all starting to pour out of me. Tears flooded my eyes, and I shook and slumped over, burying my head in my hands. I really didn't want Matt to see me like this.

He calmly walked over and sat on the bench beside me. I could feel his warmth like a fire. He reached out his hand and placed it on my back, beginning to massage me in small, gentle circles. "Whatever is upsetting you," Matt said to me quietly, "I'm here. You don't have to tell me what's going on. But if you want to, I'm always ready to listen."

I wanted to pull myself together and answer, but my tears gained intensity and I needed something to hold onto. I managed to sit up far enough to grab Matt with my arms and then cry on his shoulder. I felt vulnerable and embarrassed, but Matt held on, trying to comfort me.

Finally, I was able to breathe through my weeping enough to sputter: "I'm just overwhelmed." He nodded, but he didn't say anything right then. The respite in Matt's arms helped my sobs ebb away.

I struggled with the reality that I was resting my head on the seemingly absorbent shoulder of another man — such a truly caring man, a man who was disturbingly pretty. I got frightened all over again about what all these feelings might mean. But even as that was happening, I could still feel peace slowly descending on me. I could see it was just the two of us, but I swear it felt like a circle of people were filling the room with a comforting presence.

"I've had some pressures and confusion weighing on me ever since my breakup," I confided to Matt. "I guess they finally hit home. Tonight was the last straw, that's all. I hate to lose my temper, but when I tripped and I fell down hard I totally lost it."

Matteo

I definitely recognized *that* pattern of dealing with pressure. It was also my own. I tried to call it out to Ferran, for my sake as well as his: "You've been trying to stuff-down your feelings."

"Yeah," Ferran admitted. "I'm not even sure what all of them are. So, I've been trying to keep them in a lockbox."

"Please don't do that," I pleaded. "You know you can talk to people. You've got Alex. You can see a counselor on campus. And don't forget I'm your friend and I'm here. I care, too."

"Yeah? I'll try, Matt." He paused and seemed to be trying to fix a more controlled look onto his face. He cleared his throat and suggested, "I should get cleaned up and go home."

"You sure you're okay?"

"I'll be okay," he answered. I think he was trying to come across convincingly — to himself as much as to me. "Thank you, Matt,"

"Okay, then, I'll leave you to it. Text me when you get back to your room so I know you're home safe."

"I will."

I turned and walked to leave, but Ferran called out after me: "Matt?"

"Yeah?"

"Could we take another one of our walks tomorrow?"

I felt a rush of warmth run through me and I smiled. "Of course! I can be by your room in the evening, a little after six-thirty. Will that work?"

"Yes," Ferran said with a sigh. "Thanks Matt. … I'm sorry."

"You have nothing to be sorry about," I replied, walking out the door. "I'll see you tomorrow, six-thirty"

Okay, my feelings were definitely in uncharted territory. I guess I had become adept at second-guessing myself, because I went right back to thinking that my stupid feelings could ruin this blossoming friendship. I kept repeating that well-worn mantra I'd been using since I first met Ferran at the soccer game:

Don't fall for a straight boy.

But I didn't know if I could hold myself to that anymore.

5

UPFIELD

"Everywhere is walking distance if you have the time."
– Steven Wright

[Playlist reference: Christina Perri
(featuring Jason Mraz) — Distance]

Ekkheya

I had a vested interest in this small group of friends, as you well know by now. You also know I was paying close attention to the developments between them — particularly to what was going in the minds of Ferran and Matteo.

The two young men were making important discoveries about themselves and each other. And even if Ferran felt that the people he most needed to trust couldn't see him for himself, I was trying to let him know that I was with him. I think I almost got him to hear my name.

Was I prying? Maybe, but you try turning off hearing people's thoughts and feelings when you're a nosy supernatural being. In any case, it was going to take some work for me to break through to offer guidance.

I was looking in on an unusually balmy early evening in Santa Cruz. Ferran's roommate Stu and his girlfriend Emily were leaving Stu's and Ferran's dorm. They were late on their way to the dining hall.

Matt was just arriving to pick up Ferran for what had become their almost nightly walks or hangouts of some sort. Emily yelled to Matt as she saw him walk toward the entry of *Casa Sexta:* "Hey! Pretty boy!"

"Look at you" Matt yelled back, grinning. "Shamelessly flirting with me right in front of your boyfriend!"

"I have to be understanding, Hot Stuff," he yelled back to Matt, laughing and holding tight to Emily's hand, "'cause if I weren't straight, *I* would be shamelessly flirting with you!" Stu was about as confident in his sexuality as any progressive straight guy might be in an uncommon place like Santa Cruz, but he didn't mind having Emily reassure him that his inclusivity wasn't a bad thing.

Just then, the elderly Stevenson night proctor ambled down the walkway and called out to Matt in a slightly quieter tone: "Hey, Gorgeous George! Keep the bellowing to a lower volume!"

"Okay, Mario," Matt said, smiling.

Matt went up to Ferran's room and knocked on the door. As he answered the door and saw Matt, a wide smile lit up Ferran's face.

"Hey there!"

"Hey," Matt said, smiling back. "What's up?"

"Just finishing up this paper." Ferran gathered up and stored his laptop and some paper notes. Matt snapped a photo of him poring over his desk.

"What's that for?"

"Gotta show your fans you have an academic side," Matt answered, grinning.

Ferran grumbled: "I did just finish writing an analysis of the Aeneid, and now I need some walkies."

"Walkies, eh?"

"Don't give me grief about my Barbara Woodhouse reference."

Matt teased him: "You're damned smart for a soccer jock, funny man. If only *I* could spend my days thinking about dog training shows and reading ancient literature in a dead language. The lure of all that nostalgic charm. How exciting!"

"Did you just disrespect my thoroughly respectable liberal arts major?" Ferran laughed. "And by the way, I also know French in addition to the Latin and Greek. And I doubt you've got the stamina to surf the mighty waves of Aeneas's epic journey, hippie boy."

Matt's smile made the corners of his eyes crinkle. "Hippie boy?!" Matt croaked. "Just because I'm a leftist studying Politics makes me a hippie?"

"No, I think it has more to do with the long hair and the billowy sweatpants, and the fact that you always smell like sandalwood."

Matt could feel his face turning red. and wished he didn't blush so easily with Ferran. "At least it's not patchouli," he joked.

"Thank the gods for small mercies."

"How did you guess it was sandalwood?"

"I like sandalwood, I suppose. I noticed it on the field when we met. And I've noticed it every time we've hung out. I guess I've become sort of like a well-trained dog. Now, I smell sandalwood and I think: *Matt.*"

"Dogs don't speak classical Greek."

"And surfers don't usually get a whole bakery's staff to go on strike and win themselves a labor union work contract."

Matt's heart rate accelerated at the idea that Ferran remembered any of the political work he'd talked about having done. The fact that Ferran also seemed to like the way he smelled was making him … flustered. Trying to school his emotions, he felt he should try moving the conversation along.

"So, where do you want to walk tonight? Stay on campus and walk to Elfland?"

Elfland — let me tell you about that. It is a sector of the campus forest that had once been a burial ground of the Amah Mutsun band, an indigenous Ohlone tribe. Students over the years had reverently placed totems, talismans, and other artifacts there to honor the land and the spirits. It was a sacred place where many a UCSC student had gone on psychedelic trips.

Matt offered another option: "Or should we go downtown and grab fried 'chokes at Foster's Freeze and maybe walk to the beach? What's your pleasure?"

Ferran looked at Matt, wondering if he'd ever be able to come right out and say that the pleasure was just being with him. But instead of that, he answered, "I think it's a Foster's Freeze night."

After taking the bus down the hill to the transit center, the boys noticed that there was some "queer night" event happening at the Blue Lagoon bar, with a gaggle of fabulous drag queens and their admirers vaping something or other to the left of the entrance.

It wasn't surprising to me that neither of them mentioned it, since they were both trying so hard to avoid any consciousness or mention of sexuality, or of queer *anything.*

Side by side, they headed west to Laurel Street. Matt opened his smartphone and posted the photo of Ferran writing his Aeneid paper. He added the caption: "Soccer forward crushes the classics x," along with the #boschtalent hashtag. Ferran's smartphone pinged and he looked at the post.

"What have you gone and done?" he asked.

"The Sharks hafta see that you have a mind, too," Matt said. "I'm being your publicist."

"What's that at the end?"

"Maybe a hug?" Matt fudged. It was actually the symbol for a kiss, but he was afraid to say so.

Ferran was feeling an uncanny fondness for Matt wash over him, but he had no idea what to say.

Matt's cheeks were heating, so he felt he should change the subject. Looking around as they walked, he posed a theoretical question to Ferran: "Have you ever wondered what it would be like to have a superpower? Like the ability to fly, or control the elements, or something like that?"

Ferran laughed softly under his breath as he stole a look at Matt's compact, sinewy frame. "Sure! I mean, I think we all fantasized about it when we were kids. It would be pretty amazing to have that kind of control over nature. Especially these days."

Matt nodded. He always seemed to find himself soothed by Ferran's somewhat mysterious charm. And by his chiseled cheekbones.

"Well, it crosses my mind sometimes, especially when we're walking around, and it feels like we're surrounded by this … I dunno … mystical energy."

"Sometimes that's fog, Matt," Ferran said, giving Matt some side-eye. "Although, I can't help but wonder what it would be like to tap into a power like that."

Now, since I am one of the nosiest *lares* I know, Ferran was really piquing my interest. Over the past year, I'd been able to feel Matt's openness to the energies around him, and maybe even to me. But the feelings and conversations between Ferran and Matt were showing me new options to get an important message through.

Matt raised an eyebrow. "Wait, so are you telling me that you would want to tap into that kind of spiritual stuff? Like, energy from the mementos in Elfland, or using tools from Moonkissed or one of the other metaphysical supply stores here?"

"Well, I think it's just physics, not metaphysics. Butterfly effect on a whole series of quantum levels. The Dalai Lama says we live in a contingent reality and I think he's right."

"I agree with him on that. When you have the Higgs boson *deciding* whether or not to help things to *exist* in a given situation, it really begs the question. Isn't metaphysics really just the physics that our science hasn't found a way yet to measure?"

"Yeah. I think that's valid," Ferran said, pondering. "See, this is why I love walking with you. I never have conversations like this with my other friends."

"Let's just say I'm open to new ideas," Matt replied, grinning mischievously. "I mean, there's so much that our science doesn't yet understand about the world. Most theoretical physicists today say that there's something more to it all."

Perhaps it was wishful thinking on my part — and as a magickal creature I suppose I'm entitled to do that — but I was starting to notice that Matt could vaguely sense my presence. I was hoping that this connection between Matt and Ferran might open up a channel to help them work on some necessary transformations. Certainly, I was growing acutely aware of *their* energy.

Ferran responded to Matt: "You always have a way of making things intriguing, don't you?"

"I aim to please," Matt replied. "*Soooo* … Are you okay after last night?"

"Well, I'm fairly certain that I'm still not dead. And that I still have a lot of things to work through. But I have this friend who came along and saved the day."

Out loud, Matt told Ferran: "Me? I was just doing what a good friend is supposed to do." But Matt was wishing he could tell Ferran how he really felt inside:

I'd reach for you until the last sunrise.

He told himself he was becoming overly dramatic. As he tried hard to regain his bearings, Matt decided to deflect. "Okay," he said. "Now we can get back to what might be your ideal superpower."

"All right. Let's say I entertain this game for a minute. What kind of power would you want to have if you could choose?"

Matt paused to consider the question. "Part of me wants to say the ability to control water, like Aquaman or something, just so I could have a splashy entrance in any situation."

Ferran laughed quietly, but Matt noticed.

"Hey," Matt smiled. "Just imagine the possibilities."

"Okay. Well, in that case, I would have to go with teleportation. Think of all the places we could explore without needing to drive or take a jet."

"Oh, the places you'll go!"

"That's a Dr. Seuss book!"

Matt answered: "Yes!" triumphantly, amused that Ferran was so excited about the reference. Ferran told him it had been one of his favorite books when he was little. Immediately, Matt envisioned Ferran as a small child, being read bedtime stories. Then he thought he might die of a cuteness overload.

"I'll bet when you were little you were adorable," he said, before he caught himself. "I mean, your parents reading that book to you and all," he added, in an attempt to make a save.

"Are you trying to tell me I'm not adorable now?"

"No comment, Teleportation Man."

"But teleportation would be great! Think about it: No more struggling up Cardiac Hill to get to Crown College! We could just blink and be wherever we wanted."

Matt was taking notice of Ferran's repeated references to "we." He playfully nudged Ferran as they arrived at the Foster's Freeze. "All right, maybe you're onto something. You wanna get the fried 'chokes, or something else?"

Ferran reached for his wallet "Could we share a big bag of fried 'chokes? I also want to get an Oreo Twister. I'm buying."

"Sure, we can share," Matt agreed, looking up at Ferran's height and surveying his pectoral muscles as he unzipped his light jacket. "With this kind of food, it's a good thing we've been working out and taking so many walks."

Ferran suggested that maybe their evening walks were just training sessions for when they'd finally unlock their hidden superpowers. I was cautiously optimistic that it wouldn't turn out to be just humor. I could feel that Matt was getting ready to let Ferran see him more deeply.

Matt smiled and his eyes sparkled. "Now wouldn't that be a story to tell? Two ordinary, everyday university students turned superheroes, all because we have a backstory of fried food, ice cream, and walkies."

They laughed together, and the vibration of warmth between them felt to me like being in a soothing hot tub. Ferran turned to Matt and they both stopped walking for a moment. He raised his eyebrow and softly said, "I'm glad we're friends, Matty."

Matt took a deep breath and answered: "Me, too!"

Having decided to hold the Foster's Freeze bag so that Ferran would be able to eat his Oreo Twister ice cream, Matt nervously looked down at it. He reached into it to grab a fried artichoke heart, pulled it out, and munched it. Then he looked up at Ferran and asked, "Am I *Matty* now?"

"Is that okay?"

"Yeah," Matt answered, blushing. 'It's good."

After an awkward, silent moment, they began to walk again, but quietly. Matt broke the silence: "So, I think this friendship of ours means I should probably tell you that my interest in metaphysics isn't exactly mundane."

Ferran was distracted by droplets of ice cream running down his hand. "I am clearly not eating this ice cream fast enough. It's starting to melt on me. You wanna lick some?"

Matt swallowed hard. "You have no idea."

"Then here," Ferran fussed. "I'll switch with you."

Trying to give himself plausible deniability, Matt dramatically licked all around the Twister making an *"Mmmmmm"* sound as he did.

Ferran meanwhile, wolfing down the fried artichoke hearts, tried in vain not to stare at what Matt was doing with his tongue. His thoughts raced again.

Am I turning gay for him or something?

No, that's crazy.

I mean, if I was gonna go gay for somebody…

Trying hard not to pursue those thoughts, he again tried diversion. "So," he asked, "what did you mean about the metaphysics?"

"Well … some of my friends are very spiritual. Here, take back this Twister and hand me the last couple of 'chokes."

Ferran followed the directions.

"So, you mean spiritual like A.A. or maybe they're really religious or something?"

"No, none of that. I mean spiritual like … I dunno. Like gray Jedi, except my friends actually cast spells and stuff."

"Oh!" Ferran said, absorbing the information. "So, like, neopagans, or spiritualists, or witches, right? My parents were raised as Spanish Catholics, but we still have *saludadores* in the extended family. So, I guess I've been consorting with witches my whole life."

"Well, you're also consorting with one now."

Ferran's eyes widened. "Oh! Wow! Cool. So …
you, like … get naked under the full moon and stuff?"

I'm a largely unseen spirit guardian and maybe
those two couldn't hear me, but I cheered.

Matt was throwing the bag from the artichokes into
a recycling bin on the side of the road and then took a
bandana from his back pocket and wiped his fingers.
Folding and returning the bandana — a vibrant shade of
robin's egg blue — to his right rear pocket, Matt replied:
"Only if you ask nicely."

For several reasons he was considering
simultaneously, Ferran blushed. "Oh, I didn't…. I didn't
mean to make light of your spiritual practice. I'm so sorry."

"No offense taken. You and I are hanging out a lot.
I just wanted to let you know that I cast circles and all. I
didn't want to shock you if you see me with some friends
doing a spiral dance and singing on the East Field some
night."

"I'll join you!" Ferran said, images of Matt dancing
naked awakening a hunger he didn't know he had.

"Well, *you're* full of surprises, aren't you," Matt
answered.

As your old intrepid angel (as it were), I should tell
you that this was a *moment.* It was when I became even
more sure that these two young men were going to need
more of my protection and guidance. Obviously, I'd
contemplated the possibility that they were embarking on a
special kind of relationship. But this was a turning point; it
could mean they'd become a team that could change all the
lives around them for the better.

"I guess every spiritual practice sees some variation
on the idea that the unified field got fractured in the birth
process of the cosmos," Ferran ventured, "and the cosmos is

groaning to find it's fullness again. So, all of them have some kind of magick to breathe wholeness back into the world, right?"

Matt looked at Ferran in awe. "Yes," he answered, "and that's a very wise and succinct way to say it."

"I *told* you we have *saludadores* in my extended family, Matty" Ferran reminded him. "I paid attention to what they and the other *brujos y brujas* were doing when I was growing up, even though my parents didn't want me to. I've never believed in any of the dogma that passes for organized religion; I'm a science guy. But I know that Infinite Intelligence is real. And I study the classics, right? So, I know what Pausanias documented — the Delphic maxim inscribed in the *pronaos* of the Temple of Apollo at Delphi."

"Of course. Mr. Classical Studies major."

"*Gnōthi seauton*; know thyself." As he said this, Ferran opened a wet wipe he'd taken from the Foster's Freeze and wiped his hands with it.

Matt marveled. "I didn't think it was possible for you to be even more cool, but you just proved me wrong."

"And who knows what other surprises await, sir?"

Matt looked over at him. "Well, I can't be sure."

"I think one thing is sure, Matty. You're a pretty extraordinary person."

Matt's face lit up. "Ferr, I think *you* are. And I think we are good at exploring. And that you're fun to do things with."

Ferran nodded while his thoughts rushed. "Imagine the possibilities."

"I will."

Ferran looked up and out. "We've been walking so far, we're at the clock tower. Do you want to head back to the transit center?"

"Yeah. We should."

So, they began to walk back.

"So, I'm *Ferr* now?"

"If that's okay."

"I like it. '*Ferr play.*'"

"Exactly."

Another moment of silence passed between them.

Ferran broke it with a question: "What's your favorite non-campus Santa Cruz built thing?"

"Definitely the Walton lighthouse."

"Iconic."

"What's yours?"

"Probably the roller coaster at the Boardwalk."

"I *love* riding that roller coaster, Ferr."

"You do?" Ferran got excited. "We should go do that some time!"

"I'm definitely down for that," Matt said.

Matt stopped walking for a moment and looked around. Ferran paused with him. "It's surprisingly peaceful out here tonight."

They were standing next to the Moonkissed storefront. Ferran insisted they needed to take a selfie in front of it, and they posed for it getting the store logo in the background. He posted it with a #magick hashtag and a smiley face emoji. Matt saw him make the post and couldn't figure out whether Ferran was trying to flirt with him or was just being super concrete about their chat. He felt both confusion and a bit of pining.

Then Matt began to walk again, as did Ferran with him, side by side.

"It's peaceful, but not as peaceful as strolling through the redwoods on campus. That's like our own little sanctuary."

"Exactly! It makes me feel … maybe knit together with something greater, you know? There's just something magickal about being surrounded by nature."

"I *do* know. I like that feeling. I really like the redwoods. I feel connected to them." Ferran took a deep breath, and looked over at Matt. "That's why I like it when we hang out, 'cause I also feel connected to you. We've only known each other for a few weeks, but you have *best friend energy,* Matty."

Matt felt his heart beat faster. "That is an honor."

"Can I tell you something?"

"Sure."

It took all the courage Ferran could muster at that moment to say what he felt in his gut: "It really makes me feel good when you come to watch me play soccer. I like it; it totally pumps-up my game. It's like you're on my wavelength when I'm out on the field, and I know exactly which way I'm supposed to move the ball."

Matt was trying to fight his urge to grab Ferran into a hug and kiss him. He choked back a whimper of desire, and commented affectionately: "I don't know how that works, but I definitely like watching you play. You are *masterful* on that field. And you really love the game. That's why you're such a star."

That gave Ferran a feeling of encouragement — and also that maybe the butterflies in his stomach were taking up permanent residence. "I just enjoy what I do. But,

Matty, it would really mean the world to me if you could make it to *all* my home games. I know you probably can't fit them all in your schedule. But, any time you can, I'd love to have you there, rooting for me."

At that point, Matt wasn't sure whether he was feeling fear or awe. He answered quietly. "You're an incredible athlete, Ferr, and I will *definitely* come to every one of your games that I possibly can."

"That's *so* cool."

At that moment, they arrived at the transit center. Matt's Live Oak bus was already there, ready to board. Ferran was going to have to stay to wait for the University bus. They looked at each other as if they needed to say something more. But, instead, they just stared into each other's eyes, searching.

"Okay. I gotta get onto this bus," Matt groaned.

"Text me when you get home so I'm sure you got in safely?"

"I will, Ferr. Check in with me, too, okay?"

"You got it."

The bus door closed. The driver began to pull away from the curb, and the somewhat shaken soccer star looked at the departing bus with longing, but also with a sense of happiness that felt entirely new. He was nervous about the risks, but he was also sad that he wasn't more courageous in telling Matt how he felt. To no one in particular, Ferran asked, "Why am I like this?"

6

MAJOR

***

"Each friend represents a world in us,
a world possibly not born until they arrive,
and it is only by this meeting
that a new world is born."

— *Anais Nin*

[Playlist reference: Steven Dawes: It Could Be Me]

Ekkheya

On this October day, the sun had been surprisingly hot.

Ferran was pondering how life had been going in New Haven with April, so don't think I wasn't checking in on her. I was getting information from other *lares* about her, and I wouldn't let you miss out. April had too much importance to the unfolding of Ferran's approach to the world and to what I've been telling you about for me to leave you in the dark.

April's path, in fact, was becoming as strange to the previous life that she and Ferran had shared as Ferran's path was becoming to him. April was discovering — as I had a while ago — the confusingly entertaining phenomenon of having Episcopalians pop-up in one's life as a transformative *non sequitur.* I guess that witches and neopagans and gnostic types were more my cup of mead, but I had to admit that progressive Anglicans had blown open their minds since the 1960s.

Maybe it was because I'd tried to be one of the spirits who comforted some radical bishops — bishops who pushed things ahead and got flack for it. But they opened up an interfaith discourse that has challenged rigid hatreds about the ancient ways. They allowed gnostic scholars to help with research, dispel some of the smears and falsehoods about alleged gnostic hatred of the material world, and unearthed information about that rabbi Jesus that shocked the sensibilities of people who prefer their Jesus to be a neutered, right-wing Republican.

From the realm of spirit, I encouraged James Pike, the fifth Bishop of California, to take stands against racial segregation and for women's ordination. When his son committed suicide, I tried to bathe him in the warmth of sympathy and prod him to get sober.

When that obnoxious fogey James Stanton attempted to get Walter Righter tried for heresy for ordaining an openly gay man to the diaconate, I surrounded Righter with encouragement. When Otis Charles came out late in life and moved to San Francisco, I helped guide him to Felipe, who became the love of his life. I whispered in the ears of the committees that it was time they finally ordained an openly gay bishop in Gene Robinson. Late in life, when Bishop Jim Montgomery was finally living openly with his male partner, I led him not only to acceptance but also to joy in having women serve in the priesthood.

When the question of where the consecration of Megan Rohrer as the first (present-day) openly transgender bishop would take place, I hope my influence is what brought it to Grace Cathedral in San Francisco (and I was disappointed, but not surprised, when transphobic Lutheran leaders forced him to resign under false pretenses).

I could pretend that I'm unsure about how Episcopalians went from being generally "rich people at prayer" to being sacramental socialists, but the truth is I had a hand in persuading them. It has been a slow but refreshing change. It certainly was for April, who was never big on religion but loved a good show.

Over the long weeks she'd been in New Haven, April had become fond of attending high mass at Christ Church, an Episcopal parish in the heart of Yale. An ever-practical explorer, she considered it to be pretty good theatre for the price of a tenner in the collection plate on a Sunday. She was also a fan of frankincense, and the place was always redolent with clouds of that.

It shouldn't be lost that she was also fond of Father Ethan, the young curate who'd arrived at the parish when she arrived at Yale. It was his first call to work in a parish, and both the rector and the vestry had been impressed with his ability to connect with all kinds of people and get them involved. I especially liked Ethan because he was a member of the Churches' Fellowship for Psychical and Spiritual

Studies — something that endeared him to the many fans in the greater New Haven area of the regionally close medium, John Edward. Ethan's singing voice had also been a selling point, considering the tone-deaf chanting from Mother Jessica, the assistant pastor.

April was not the only woman in the parish who had her eye on Ethan. He was handsome and popular, and garnered a lot of attention. He'd easily smooth-talked April into helping with the parish food kitchen for people in the area who were poor or unhoused.

There were plenty of men in the parish who were smitten with Ethan as well, since one of the good Father's tasks was to serve as chaplain for the parish chapter of Integrity, the group for Episcopalian queerlings. One of those men with a crush was the parish sexton, Sebastian "Bash" Corbin. At coffee hour between masses on one of April's Sunday visits, Bash was — unabashedly — flirting with Ethan.

April heard Ethan gently rebuff Bash's advances. "Sorry, Bash," Ethan told him, "you flatter me, but I'm terminally heterosexual." He looked over at April as he said it and flashed her a bright smile. When Bash went to the other side of the parish hall in defeat, April walked over to Ethan and suggested, "I think you made his world a little grayer today, Father."

Ethan chuckled and asked, "Hasn't Bash told you his story? He tells everybody."

"Not yet, but I'm still fairly new."

"Let me give you the synopsis, then," he smiled. "I couldn't have made Bash's world as gray as his teen years in a low-church evangelical parish. Not many of those places in Connecticut, you know, but his parents sure found one. They'd grown up in high-and-dry parishes filled with liberal Republicans."

"Ah … those long-lost liberal Republicans," April commented, rolling her eyes.

"I know. Obviously liberal Republicans pretty much became extinct, and both of those parishes eventually had to shut their doors. So, Bash's parents lurched to another end of the scales. Imagine how he must have felt as a gay boy. Obviously, he couldn't wait to break out. He discovered a love for weed and Anglican chant, and now he's probably the most consistently high Episcopalian here."

That gave April a good laugh, and a chance to notice that Ethan's cassock was very nicely tailored around his impressive pecs. She was also aware that he was giving her more eye contact than any of the other women in the room, and she found that unusually enticing. She hadn't ever considered that she might swoon for an Episcopal priest, but Ethan was quickly becoming her favorite compassionate cutie in a clerical collar.

"I'm actually off this afternoon for a change," Ethan told her. "I'm out of here in about an hour. Would you like to join me for an early dinner at Pepe's? I've been craving a clam and bacon pizza."

"Wow, clam and bacon, Father. A *traife* pie," she teased him.

"Don't tell my Jewish friends," he joked. "And please, call me Ethan."

Okay, so he was handsome and funny, a social justice nerd, and he could sing. Now he also showed that he could assertively ask for a date, and that he knew from good pizza. April felt her fondness level kick up a notch.

"I'm afraid I'm going to have to accept your invitation, Ethan."

"Afraid?" he laughed. "Am I in trouble?"

"We'll see if your luck holds up."

Ferran

April and I hadn't touched base since we'd each moved into the dorms at our respective universities. She'd told me that we should wait to talk again until the winter break. I had no idea what was unfolding in her life, and she had no idea what was unfolding in mine. I wondered, and I was feeling really sad about it.

But then, I was shaken from my brooding by Matt calling out to me as he opened the door to my dorm room: "Yo, Ferr! It's another beautiful day in paradise. Want to go for a walk on the beach?"

O my gods, yes. Yes, I did. I looked up at his beaming smile and answered, "That sounds so good, I could use a study break." I gathered a jacket and my wallet and I was ready to go. "Are we taking the bus or did you drive?"

"Bus, mister man," Matt answered cheerily. "Mass transit or person-powered is always preferable to cars, even if the car sustainably runs on electric or hydrogen."

"Totally agree," I said. Gazing at him, I was struck by how at ease and confident he looked. I got a sudden urge to scoop him up into my arms in a bear hug. Before I knew what I was doing, I just stepped forward and hugged him tightly. I guess I caught him by surprise, because he stiffened for a few seconds. I was afraid I'd overstepped the line, and I wasn't sure I even knew what I was doing. But Matt didn't seem to want to interrupt it, and he relaxed into the enclosure of my hug.

When we moved apart, Matt asked me, "What was that for?"

I didn't know what to say because I was still caught up in the moment. I was pondering how Matt could look adorable. So, I punted: "You're just such a great friend and I'm really happy you're here."

"I like to hang out with you, Ferr. You know that."

"Yeah. Just … Thanks for being my friend, Matty."

"I'm glad we're friends. Really. Thanks for being such a great friend to me."

Was that actually what it was? I truly didn't know. The thought of the spark between us being more than a friendship seemed to me to be completely out of reach. I was meant to be straight, right? At least I'd thought so. But I was experiencing pangs that made me question everything about my feelings. In all my confusion and fear, I didn't feel like it would be a smart move to confide in Matt about it.

I reached for my courier bag and we left my room and my dorm. We caught our bus downtown and walked the few blocks to the main beach, discussing our upcoming schedules and what our roommates were doing. We also bantered about our prognostications over whether Jake and Maura would start to date.

I was kind of hoping I'd begin to feel normal again after a while. But instead of things going back the way they were, they kept taking unexpected turns. I didn't know if it was curiosity or something else. But whatever it was, starting to question my sexuality was really freaking me out.

I was finding myself thinking a lot about what it might be like to touch Matt more — maybe even to hold him. I supposed that straight friends — good bros— maybe did that. But I asked myself how I could be thinking any of this stuff about a guy — about holding him tight — and not even feel slightly disgusted or grossed out. A *guy!*

I guess all of it had deeply shaken me. So much so, that I'd recently taken to ruminating about my breakup with April, which was making me feel lonely. So there I was, wallowing in my increasingly bizarre emotions. With the way things were going, I was even struggling with how to continue my friendship with Matt. The potential outcome of "all my crazy" scared me.

One night when Stu went to Emily's room to sleep over, I spent hours alone in our dorm room, crying. The fact that Matt and I saw each other almost every day wasn't helping. Every time we were near each other, the idea of a kiss with Matt would force its way into my mind. It rattled me, but it just wasn't something I could turn off anymore.

Having my head racing about it all was disturbing enough, but I also couldn't get it to leave my heart — or even my gut. The thoughts and feelings insisted I pay attention. Why couldn't I just dial it down? I wanted to think of Matt as I would any other close friend, but my mind had other plans.

Matteo

I was clearly having trouble with my "don't fall for a straight boy" mantra. He *was* straight, right? I felt there was this spark between us, though. I was sure it couldn't be more than friendship, and that was frustrating me to no end. It felt as though my pining for Ferran was as heavy as the end of the world. I was beginning to fear that I might never be happy with anybody else.

When I reflected back on it, I felt as though Ferran and I had been clicking from the beginning. In a matter of several weeks, we'd developed an extremely close friendship. It was confusing. What, if anything, should be my next steps? Should I acknowledge the tension and the desire that I was feeling about Ferran — tension and desire that just kept growing? Should I throw caution to the wind and try to kiss him, and let the chips fall where they may?

If I'm being honest, I was consumed with thoughts of kissing him. At the same time, he was becoming my best friend and I was terrified of losing him. The thought that we could ever be more was something I felt I would just have to shove far outside my mind.

I considered distracting myself by hooking up with someone — anyone but Ferran — but I was feeling no interest in a mindless hookup, and that surprised me. I got queasy even thinking about doing that now. That strategy wasn't working the way it always had before Ferran.

When Ferran would hug me or tell me how important he thought I was, it would drive me crazy. The stress of trying to figure it out made me wish I could just stop thinking altogether. It wasn't making sense to me, and my head too often felt like it would explode with conflicting needs.

I repeatedly told myself that friendship was all it could ever be. I was attracted to a straight guy, and I was becoming deathly afraid of ruining a friendship I'd come to treasure. Even though I was now feeling that my attraction to Ferran was undeniable, actually acting on my feelings with this straight guy seemed impossible.

Ferran

I couldn't bring myself to stay away from Matt, but I was feeling like this whole situation was impossible. On top of that, I couldn't believe I was thinking about kissing a guy — *any* guy. The problem was that, more than anyone ever before, it was Matt who I wanted to kiss. When we were both in the same space together, I had to use all my willpower to keep from trying it.

One night, Stu was over at Emily's room and I was stuck in my weird thoughts and feelings about Matt. I decided it was time to try to shock myself back to my senses with a marathon of straight porn and beer. It didn't change a damned thing.

I mean, that's not to say I didn't enjoy the porn. I reacted to it the way I usually did, and I didn't hold back on pouring the beer or the lube. But I had to wonder if it was just the women in the scenes who were turning me on, or if it was the men, too. The drunker I got, the more I thought about my actual feelings for Matt. I was starting to wonder if maybe I was bi and just hadn't realized it before.

I woke up the next morning from a dream about Matt with a sense of dread, both for my throbbing hangover and for another part of me that was throbbing. I grabbed my towel and shower caddy, and I walked toward the bathroom feeling like someone had planted cotton in my mouth and swords in my brain. For the first time in my life, I took an ice-cold shower.

Over the weeks that followed, I came to feel as though a thick tension was growing between Matt and me — a tension so thick that I ached any time I wasn't near him. And when I *was* near him, I was boneheaded and giddy. I was spending even more nights feeling stuck — lonely and sad about my life and crying myself to sleep.

As Matt and I walked toward the beach, my face must have given away that I was brooding. He commented on it: "You seem preoccupied."

"I've just got a lot on my plate."

"Maybe you're just too tense, but walks are good for relieving stress," Matt said with a grin. I knew he was going to try to gently rib me, and I appreciated his effort to lighten the mood. "You know what they say about Classics majors, right? They say you guys are as rigid as temple statues."

"I've never had any complaints about getting rigid before," I quipped, laughing. But then, I caught myself and got embarrassed. Matt blushed a bright red that matched his hair.

On the way to the beach, we ran into a picket line and a small crowd of people chanting in solidarity with them, outside a fast-food restaurant. A young blond woman, about Matt's height, ran up to him. He later told me he knew her from his numerous activist involvements and that she knew his reputation for stirring up a crowd. Speaking rapidly, she told him the store's workers were trying to unionize and asked him to "please, just say a few words." Matt looked over at me, and I nodded in favor.

Taking the bullhorn handed to him by the young woman, Matt introduced himself to the small crowd and told them he recognized a lot of faces. "I didn't even know you folks were going to be picketing tonight," he said. Then he dove into a rousing extemporaneous speech praising the efforts of the workers to organize and to get paid a living wage. "I'm going to get the Student Union Assembly to give you some solidarity and mutual aid," he told them. "I wanna make sure UCSC students stand with you."

The small crowd cheered Matt as I got busy taking video and stills of the whole thing. Matt looked over at me briefly, and then told the young woman he was in the middle of an important talk with a friend and he had to go. She thanked him profusely for his pep talk. Then she ran her hand over his chest. She leaned-in to kiss his cheek, and he returned the kiss to her cheek.

My body temperature rose and I could feel anger churning inside me. I felt my chest go tight and my fists clench. How dare she kiss Matt when I was right there? She didn't seem to notice that I was glaring at her. Matt shot me a look and his brow knitted, as if he was trying to decipher why my eyes suddenly looked so furious.

What the hell was wrong with me? He wasn't mine, and I had no right to feel so possessive. I needed to push these feelings out of my mind and put them in a lockbox. He was just a really good friend, and a guy, and I was being an idiot.

Looking concerned, Matt walked back towards me. "Is something wrong?" he asked, understandably. "Are you okay?"

That look of concern in his eyes — I couldn't stand it. Just like the first time, all my emotions were threatening to flood out of me. I summoned every bit of energy I could to school my expression so I could look chill and unperturbed. "False alarm. I saw a group of cops riding by, and I was afraid they were going to break up the picketing," I lied.

"Thanks for watching so closely. I'm glad nothing like that happened."

Just his presence near me helped me calm down. If I leave out the cheek-kissing incident that set me off, Matt showed great finesse at inspiring a crowd. Watching the whole interaction he had with them, I think I was becoming even more of a Matteo Poulsen fan.

While he was still giving his impromptu speech, I posted the video and stills I'd taken to my social media. Underneath it, I wrote a synopsis of the picketing and the demands, along with hashtags: #livingwage #unionstrong and #poulsentalent. I let Matt know that I did it, and told him: "It was my turn to be your publicist."

Matt gazed at me with his emerald eyes looking soft. He opened his mouth and then closed it again a couple of times, seeming to be at a loss for words. Eventually, he told me that he felt grateful about my post in a lot of ways.

When we got to the edge of the sand, we took off our shoes and wandered down, close to the water's edge. I didn't know what I was going to say, but I felt I had to say something about my confusion. But then my throat went dry. I thought maybe I should just try to see where our conversation would lead. Finally, I managed to croak out a sound: "Matty."

"Yeah?"

"I think I might need some *'talk about anything with Matty'* time, if that's all right. I don't get to talk with many people where any subject or question can take a new and different road. And I think I need the mental exercise."

Matt peered at me with his sparkling eyes, as if he were making mental note. "Yeah?" he said. "I think you summed-up that feature pretty well. So, talk to me."

"Hmmmm. Let me think."

Damn, I was struggling. I wanted to tell Matt about the feelings I was having about him that were scaring me, but I didn't want it to scare *him*. I fought the urge to just reach out and grab Matt's hand to hold it. The thought terrified me — especially out in public. After some frustrated rearranging in my head, I decided to take a mental detour.

"Okay. Here you go. What's your most treasured childhood memory? And how does it shape the person you are today?"

"Wow," Matt said, his eyes widening. "Just had that big intimate essay question ready to go. Did you just whip that one up right now? Seems like that was waiting right there on the tip of your tongue."

"I've been curious," I told him. Did I really say *that?* Maybe I was hoping that Matt would wonder if we could both be curious about some other intimate things.

Matt hummed thoughtfully. "Well, I have an answer," he said. "My most treasured childhood memory would have to be the time my grandfather and I spent hours stargazing in his backyard. That really ignited my love for cosmology and the cycles of the Earth. It taught me to always be in awe of the mysteries that are in and beyond the cosmos. He helped open my mind to infinite possibilities."

I was struck with awe: "Dude."

"What?"

"That answer was perfection."

Matt tilted his head and gave me a wink. "It also taught me to dream big, and to set my intention and walk forward into it."

"Matty, that is amazing."

"Thank you."

"Thank *you* for sharing that with me. Really. It sounds like your grandfather had a profound impact on your life."

"He did, Ferr. You know, I don't usually open up to people as much as I open up to you. It's easy to share stuff like that with you."

My stomach swooped, and I wondered if he was aware he was having that effect on me. But I pressed onward: "Okay, but now I have another question."

"I guess I'm the contestant in the hot seat tonight."

"Bear with me," I pleaded. "So, we both have majors that aren't exactly typical choices. Like, I'm studying Classical Studies, and you're doing Politics."

"True," Matt replied, eyeing me cautiously.

I flashed on a brief memory and laughed at myself.

"What?" he asked.

"There's this woman, Nancy, who lives in the upper quad at Stevenson. And back at the start of September at the parties when freshmen were getting to know each other, she would begin almost every first conversation with another freshman using the same phrase: 'Hi, I'm Nancy. What's your major?' So, some of the women who live in my dorm started calling her *"Nancy Whatsyourmajor."*

"That's awful," Matt said, pretending to clutch his pearls. "And funny," he added with a giggle. And, sure, his giggle was cute. There was no denying it.

"Now, I don't want to sound like Nancy, but I do feel her curiosity. What motivated you to choose Politics?"

"Ha! Are you ready?" Matt exclaimed. "It might sound deep. I chose a Politics major because I've always been fascinated by the complexities of power dynamics and how they shape both the self and society. I've always been passionate about making a positive difference, and advocating for social justice and ecological sanity. It's a field that gives me spaces to fight for what I believe in."

This guy just kept impressing me. "I like that answer."

"Now it's my turn," Matt ventured. "What about you and Classical Studies? What drew you to that?"

"I think the classics have always fascinated me. I love learning about the classical period civilizations, and their languages, their cultures, and what led to their demise. I would ponder all of that a lot and I wouldn't have to think about harder things I was facing. I guess it also kept my mind busy when I was taking care of the vegetable garden in my parents' yard."

"You had a vegetable garden?"

"We still have it, and I love growing stuff. Tomatoes are my specialty."

"What do you think of the Agro-ecology Farm and Gardens here?"

"I love it. For real, I hope that's the planet's future. That's one of the things that drew me to UCSC."

"Cool! I love it too. I want to figure out how to get involved."

"Me too. But I'm not sure how much time I could give it, because I have to think about maybe getting a work-study gig. Plus, I'm knee-deep in learning more advanced Ancient Greek at the moment. I think languages are a way for me to connect with the past and understand our present better. And I'll admit I have a soft spot for ancient Greek and Roman mythology."

"You do a lot of living in your head for a sportsball player, mister."

"If I'm being honest, I guess I'm making a confession to you about that?"

"What do you mean?"

"I mean that while most people might use sports as a recreational diversion from academics, I used academics as my recreational diversion from sports — at least from all the scrutiny of my soccer playing."

"Did it work?"

"In a way it did, but here's the thing about that. The more deeply I delved into the classics, the more interested in them I got. I realized how rich and nuanced studying the classics can be. The ancient civilizations, their myths, and the art they left behind — it all spoke to me in ways that keep giving me new eyes on the world."

Matt smiled at me, and I felt like his eyes lit up everything around us. "That's kind of great, you know," he commented. "It's amazing how sometimes we find our true passions in the most unexpected places."

And his mention of passions sent my mind racing again:

"Find our true passions in the most unexpected places?"

Am I just imagining it, or has he been dropping double-entendres on me all afternoon? Am I supposed to follow them to the witch's door like proverbial breadcrumbs? The witch in that story had evil plans, so maybe that's not a great idea. But my witch doesn't have evil plans.

There it is again. *When did Matt become* my *witch? Now my pulse is rapid. Am I panicking?*

Matt's voice broke me out of my racing thoughts as he offered a turn of subject. "Speaking of unexpected things…"

I took a deep breath to try to calm my heartbeat. "Should I fear what's coming next?" I asked him, with a little trepidation.

Matt's ears turned red, and he looked away. "I do feel a little vulnerable talking about what I'm about to say."

He felt vulnerable. About *me*. Go figure.

"Give it to me, Matty; I'm your friend," I said, bracing myself. "I care about you. You can say whatever you need to say."

"You care about me?" he asked me quietly, almost timidly.

Wasn't this old news by now? "Well, yeah," I told him. "Matty, wasn't that obvious? We hang out *all the time*. You *get* me."

Matteo

He told me he was curious, and my mind went spinning so fast I could barely keep track of what he was saying. I tried to stop fantasizing about the many intimate things Ferran could be curious about. Then he told me I *got* him. Man, how I'd love to get him.

O my gods, I was being so pathetic!

But then I tipped him off that I had something weighty to talk with him about, and he seemed to get a little anxious about that. I wanted to calm any fears he might have, but he told me to give him my thoughts because I was his friend and he cared about me. I hoped I didn't look like a heart-eyed puppy when I responded to him.

"Listen, Ferr. First, I love how you love the classical world. And, when I consider what you said — that I understand you — I do actually feel like we've done some growing together …"

Were his dreamy eyes looking at my lips? Whether he was looking at them or not, I forced myself to press on: "Because … we've been sharing a lot of personal stuff and exploring each other's lives." I couldn't help feeling a wave of passion, even though I was trying to suppress it. "I like it a lot when it's just you and me, away from everybody else and just being ourselves."

Ferran nodded, but his face seemed set on blank. Then he said, "So do I. Honestly, I'd rather spend time with you than anybody."

That was what prompted me to finally voice my fear. "I'm sort of worried about it, though. I feel like I've probably been monopolizing your free time and screwing up your chances with all the girls who are after you. I can't help but think it may have got in the way of either one of us dating Maura. Or anyone, really."

Ferran breathed out, shaking his head right and left. "Matty, I was in a relationship with a remarkable, sexy girl for six years. And we weren't even in love. I don't think I'm in a hurry to find the next girl to play house with to make my parents happy."

If this was how he thought about his relationship with April, this was the first time he had let me know those details. Sure, he'd told me they broke up because they didn't think long distance would work. But he also said they were best friends, and she seemed pretty absent from his life right now.

He also said some words that got me sad: *the next girl.* I suppose I should remember that guys don't do it for him. I guess I really wasn't even on his radar for being more than friends. I hated the thought of him meeting someone and being intimate with her. I wanted him for myself, which was stupid because he was straight.

"I mean, I'm at university," Ferran continued to muse. "I know I'm supposed to be finding someone to make my mother anxious, but I'm just enjoying taking some time off."

My fears rushed out of my mouth before I could edit them. "I don't want you to resent me for being an obstacle, Ferr. I mean, I'm honestly not interested in any hookups right now." My throat was feeling thick and I had to clear it. "I feel like I've been hoarding your attention, and I hope that isn't going to ruin our friendship. I don't want to give you claustrophobia and have it change things between us for the worse. Last summer was rough for me, and … my attention … is elsewhere."

He snapped at me in a low voice: "Matteo Poulsen, I am here because I enjoy being here." I'd learned that when Ferran used my full name, he usually was intending to chide me about something. "Sometimes it's a little mystifying or confusing to me, but I feel like there's some center of gravity that's pulled us together as friends. And I'm pretty sure I got an amazing friend out of the deal, so I consider that a win."

Okay, this man was making me melt all over again. Gods, how I wanted to kiss his soft, beautiful lips. But thinking better of that, I instead tried moving to ideas that could help preserve our friendship. If I couldn't have everything, at least I'd have something.

I tried to think of things he had told me made him happy. "You know, I have such a good time hanging out with you," I ventured. "I've been wishing we could bring your dog to campus sometime and run around and play with her. Wouldn't that be cool?"

Ferran's eyes glistened as he gave me a wide smile. Then his lower lip quivered and his hand went to his stomach as if he were protecting it from something.

"Adelina? That would be really cool. And she'd love it. I know Zipcar has some cars that are especially dog-friendly, and I can ask my parents if they'll let me bring her. But I can't keep her in the dorms; I'd have to drive her back to Santa Nella."

"She could stay with me!" I offered. "Then you wouldn't have to drive her here and back in one day."

"Would your housemates be okay with that?"

I made a firm declaration: "Without a doubt."

"See Matty," he said, his shoulders obviously relaxing. Ferran's voice turned gravelly. "This is what I meant when I said that you *get* me. You know Adelina's my buddy. And you're right there, reading *her* wavelength, too. That's some kind of special thing that happens between you and me."

Suddenly, I felt as though my stomach were taking flight. And…oh! Was *that* why Ferran's hand had gone to protect his stomach? No, it couldn't be that, could it?

He went quiet for a moment. "I will definitely check with my parents. Who knows what they'll say? But Adelina would love the adventure."

"So would I."

"She's uncanny, you know. Since she was a puppy, she's known everything about my emotions. It's like she's the one non-human who knows me inside and out."

"I like her even more now," I confessed.

The silence hung in the air between us for a moment. My mind wandered with possibilities. When I could get up the nerve, I asked: "So, are there any intimate questions you've been dying to ask *me?*"

Ferran

As if my flipping stomach weren't distracting enough, when Matt asked if had any intimate questions to ask him, a jolt of fear shot through me. I wasn't sure I was ready to ask Matt the questions I really wanted to ask, and I definitely didn't know how he'd handle them. So, I decided to take another conversational detour.

"What makes Santa Cruz really special for you?" I queried. "What it is that you love about this place?"

Matt's face seemed to display some sort of disappointment, but he gamely offered an answer: "That's easy. Hands down, it's the sense of freedom that comes with living by the ocean. The vast expanse of it, and the crashing waves — it reminds me that the Earth is alive — that we all come from her and we'll all return to her. That's grounding, and it makes Santa Cruz a place where I can become more truly myself."

I swear, this guy knew how to earn my wonderment and admiration. "Your mind is an awesome thing," I replied, the butterflies soaring in my stomach again.

"What about you?"

Time to get honest about that part, at least. "Well … I feel like I can say this to you when I can't say it to many other people. I feel like there's a magick here, and that it ties into the Deep Magick running through the world. There's some ultimate law of cause and effect at work in the world and, I dunno, Santa Cruz seems to be some sort of circuit for it …. And I also agree with you, Matty. There's something about the ocean that makes everything feel alive and full of potential. Like every wave brings new possibilities."

Matt was silent, and he looked over at me with wide eyes and a slackened jaw before looking forward again. I was feeling as though someone was hovering near us, but when I looked around there was nobody close. It felt like a warm hug, so maybe I was just feeling the vibe between Matt and me. We both fell silent again for a bit as we continued to walk along the beach.

After that little while, I broke the silence: "Do you ever feel like anything's possible, Matty?"

He stayed quiet for a moment, seeming to contemplate my question. Then he answered: "I sure do hope so."

7
NICKNAMES

"You cannot say something about something
without revealing something about yourself."
— *Mokokoma Mokhoana*

"I love nicknames.
It makes me feel loved.
It makes me feel less alone in this world."
— *Elliott Page*

[Playlist reference:
Dusty Springfield — The Look of Love]

Maura

It was a humid autumn day, but the lower lobby of McHenry library always seemed to be cooler than the rest of the building. The Global Village Cafe was located off the lower lobby and it provided a convenient place to for us to grab lunch with our friends — especially if we were likely to have to split off into different areas of the campus for our next classes.

Matt and Ferran were sitting at a table in a far corner, engrossed in each other while they were chatting and eating lunch. Alex, Alicia, Jake, and I were at a table closer to the center of the lobby. I felt like we were being sneaky, but we were watching them as we picked at our food.

Alicia whispered a question in a low, conspiratorial tone: "Have you guys noticed how close Matt and Ferran have been getting lately?"

In fact, one afternoon I had seen them heading down to Ferran's soccer practice, and I told Stu: "Those two are like the closest best friends I think I've ever seen. What does Matt even do down on that field while Ferran is practicing?"

"Matt sits with all the other guys' girlfriends," Stu reported. "He watches the team practice and does reading and homework, like the girlfriends do." He paused and looked at me whimsically. "I dunno. Maybe he fits that role better than either he or Ferran thinks he does?"

Thinking on that, I answered Alicia: "How could I not notice? You saw me introduce them to each other. They were like fast friends right from the start. I've definitely noticed."

Emily, Stu's girlfriend, interjected: "They look an awful lot like a couple."

"I don't know if they've figured that out, though," Stu noted.

Alex suddenly seemed agitated. Apparently, he needed to add his expert commentary as Ferran's BFF: "People, maybe that's a leap. I mean, true: I've known Ferran since junior high school and I've never seen him be like this with anyone before. I'll admit they seem really connected. I'm not denying that they're close and that the whole process has been interesting to watch — sort of like watching a bromance on some reality TV show. But I feel like there's something not right about the way you're looking at it."

I asked Alex what he meant, and he made a suggestion: "Didn't they both seem into you, Maura? Maybe we're actually watching some kind of tension or rivalry between them unfold."

I'll admit that I was pondering the idea of friction and tension between them, but it wasn't the bad kind. Then, as if Jake knew my lascivious thinking, he jumped into the conversation with an observation: "Maybe that's it, but I'm confused about what kind of tension it is. They're more like magnets or something — like they're always drawn to each other. Have you seen their social media posts? You gotta admit, it's all sorta cute."

It was definitely cute. I turned to Jake and looked at him appreciatively. "It's like they have their own little world."

Alicia provided us with some news: "I've seen those social media posts, and apparently so have the San Jose Earthquakes. So, what is it, almost a thousand likes and comments by now? Plus, a lot of talk about Ferran's soccer prospects. And plenty of posts about Matt's fiery speeches."

Alicia being ever the voyeur (and I loved that about her), she noted that watching Matt and Ferran was like endlessly scrolling through all the sexy guys on social media. "And there are plenty of dreamy-eyed fan posts about both of them. I mean, I think it's all sort of hot, actually."

Jake wondered aloud if they were even aware of the way they looked. "Like … did you notice that oversized lavender printed t-shit Matt's wearing. I think that's Ferran's *Quarter Life Crisis* t-shirt from Baby Queen. So … they're wearing each other's clothes? That's about as sweet as a Wonka Bar, but it also makes you wonder, doesn't it?"

With her eyes narrowing, Alicia asked Jake if he was jealous of them.

"Envious," he admitted, quickly correcting her. "How is anybody else supposed to get noticed when you have two guys who look like *that* hanging out together."

I had to agree. "It's kind of a beautiful thing to see."

Alex gruffly called us out: "Is this a spectator sport?"

I quickly shushed him: "Quiet down! They'll hear you! But listen, it really does seem like their friendship has become something … *different.* No?"

"What exactly do you mean by 'different?'" Alex asked. "Are you really trying to suggest that they're getting it on?"

For sure, I was now mulling over the idea. "I don't want to jump to any conclusions," I hedged, "but their connection looks pretty deep. It's like … they seem kind of inseparable now."

"Definitely looks like a bromance to me," Jake's assessed. "I mean, they're glued at the hip."

"It's like they have some *secret friend* bond," Alicia added. "They're always laughing together and sharing inside jokes,"

Alex seemed bothered again, quickly telling Alicia he wanted to examine what "*secret friend* bond" meant to her.

Alicia bit out a sharp whisper: "You know, you seem to always become a little testy about Ferran getting close to any of the rest of his friends. What's up with that?"

Alex's shoulders sank, and he acknowledged she had a point: "Right to the heart, Alicia. Wow. But, okay, I guess I always get a little worried that he might forget me. He was the most popular guy in our high school, but he trusted me to be his main anchor during the hardest parts of our teenage years. I keep wondering if we still have that."

Alicia gave him some firm reassurance: "Alex, you're like his brother. He's always saying he would be lost if you hadn't decided to come to UCSC."

I briefly saw Alex nodding at her when I noticed Jake locking eyes with me. In a quiet voice, he asked me: "Could you be thinking what I'm thinking?" Yeah, I could. But I thought it better to demur, so I said I couldn't be sure.

"I do have one tidbit of information that might be relevant, and I'm sure some of you already know it," I told the group. "A while after the game where I introduced you, Matt and I shared some big getting-to-know-you facts with each other. He told me that over the summer he was reeling, because he kept getting harassed at his touristy gig at San Francisco's Pier 39. In order to explain to his parents why he left the job, he had to come out to them that he's bisexual."

Jake blinked his eyes in genuine surprise. "Is he really bi? I've heard stuff here and there, but I guess up 'til now I've had trouble believing it."

"Why would it be hard to believe?" I asked, giving Jake a quizzical look.

Jake answered with a sly grin: "He doesn't really have any — you know — *swish* with his swagger."

"I cannot believe you just said that," I groaned.

Alicia shot him a look and huffed: "Stereotype much?"

"Well, come on," he huffed defensively. "Matt doesn't mince around or anything."

"Aw jeez, really?" I grumbled, rolling my eyes at Jake. "Quit while you're only a little behind, bucko, or I'm going to find a way to electrocute you." He held up his hands defensively.

"And for the record," I snapped, "a lot of women find a little swish with the swagger to be really hot. Why do you think Elvis was such a hit?"

"Okay, okay!" he backtracked. "I take it back. You don't have to swish to be a queer dude. But you gotta admit, neither of them swish, do they."

Alicia looked at him in disbelief. "What the hell is up with you today?" she growled. "And, so what if they do swish or if they don't?"

Alex's eyes flashed and his chest puffed out. He tried to directly counter the whole narrative: "I have known Ferran for longer than anybody here, and he's straight," he emphatically declared.

I wasn't convinced, and I was keen on digging for more data. "But didn't Ferran break up with his cheerleader girlfriend before starting here this year?"

Alex made a sound of exasperation. He offered us more detail, reaching again for his inferred expertise on the matter. "I think they had just become comfortable with the sex, and with their image of being a soccer star with a cheerleader. Ferran told me it was an amicable breakup, because neither of them felt it would survive long-distance. Personally, I don't think it would have survived, either."

Alex hesitated a moment. Then he added: "Honestly, she and I used to bicker a lot." Maybe his insecurity was showing.

Jake also seemed to take notice of that insecurity, and chided Alex: "Now this is getting intriguing. Are we having a little friend group telenovela?"

I made an attempt to be decisive about our whole discussion, but I probably sounded as worried as I really was about potential problems between Matt and Ferran. "Matt seems so nice to me, but maybe Ferran needs to be told about his sexuality. I mean, come on; the poor man needs to know. I think I should tell him," I announced.

Alicia grumbled, not even bothering to refrain from rolling her eyes at me. "Never mind all those inconvenient bigotries underneath all that."

"What do you mean?" I retorted, glaring back at her as I began to arrange cookies that I had bought from Pacific Cookie Company on a paper plate in front of me.

"That isn't yours to tell," Alicia insisted.

"But what if one of them breaks the other one's heart?" I pleaded. "We just can't stand by and let Ferran be blindsided. I feel some responsibility for the boy."

"You only met him a little while ago," Jake argued.

"I'm the one who's known him forever," Alex reminded everyone.

"I just don't understand why it would be an issue anymore if we just got it out in the open," I insisted.

Alex glared at me in disbelief. "After all the anti-queer and anti-trans backlash and everything lately? You can't figure out why Matt might not want to shout his sexual orientation from the rooftops right now?"

Alicia agreed. "If something really is happening with those two, we don't need to out them. We could just ask them about it. And I don't think being bisexual and hanging out with Ferran is just his plot to flout tradition or something."

"Nothing traditional about that bromance," Jake chirped, watching Matt's and Ferran's interaction several tables over from us.

"Maura, I really like you," Alicia continued, "but sometimes I wonder if you actually believe some of the stuff that pops out of your mouth. Or if you're just a master at being oblivious. As well as at procuring the best of all things chocolate, that is, because these cookies from Pacific Cookie Company are *delicious.*"

I slapped Alicia's hand as she reached for a cookie: "Not yet. And that was an okay save you just did. But we might be able to use these cookies as a way to have that special conversation with the boys."

Alicia heaved a long-suffering sigh. "Maura, somebody's heart *might* get broken. Of course. That's what can happen anytime somebody puts it on the line."

"That's not what I meant!" I groused, pursing my lips. "Listen, what if we try to set up a date for them somehow?"

Alex and Alicia looked at me, and for a moment I thought they might both explode. "That is *way* out of bounds," Alex nearly barked.

Leaning in, Alicia nearly growled at me. "And … what? What then? Even though I'm pretty sure I know exactly what."

I tried to press my case: "Maybe they'll end up kissing and figure things out."

"Okay, that's just way too much," Alex said, rolling his eyes. "Too many assumptions. Too much interfering. And what about that girl, Laleh, from last year? Wasn't she all over Matt at parties?"

"She *tried* to be all over Matt," Alicia said, "but I heard that Matt wasn't all over *her*. She always seemed to be pretty drunk at those parties. And Matt wasn't exactly hurting for other women to hook up with."

"All that's beside the point," Jake interjected. "I agree with Alex. Trying to set them up with each other is way too manipulative."

Why were they all being so blasé about this? "Then I don't want to hear 'oh, poor Ferran' from any of you if this friendship of theirs goes sour," I complained.

Alex grimaced at me. "Aren't you the least bit shocked at yourself for trying to play puppet-master?"

Out of the corner of my eye, I saw Alicia snatch a cookie and stuff it in her backpack while I was trying to defend my idea. "I just wouldn't want to see either of them heartbroken."

"Sure, sure," Alicia quipped. "What kind of nosey-ass matchmaker would that make you?"

Sigh. "Okay, Okay," I conceded, starting to laugh at myself. "So here, all of you can eat the damned cookies."

Looking back and forth between Jake and me, Alicia asked the question directly: "So, let's make sure we all have this right, just for the record. You two are definitely putting out there that you think they might already be dating?"

"I think it's a strong possibility," I suggested. "Maybe they're exploring? Matt told me he's never seriously dated anyone before. But he also told me he *has* had hookups with at least four genders that I know of."

Jake actually giggled at that: "This whole story is getting better and better."

That was when Alicia said she was curious as to which four genders Matt had been with. "From what he told me: cisgender female, cisgender male, a trans woman, and a trans man," I reported.

Alex looked quite surprised. "I am duly impressed," he announced.

Alicia winked at Alex and called him a horn dog. He huffed out a laugh and said, "Look who's talking. You're the Sexual Psychology major." She dismissed him with side-eye.

"All right. If we can expand the category on this gossip fest, I did get some tea from Stu and Emily," Alicia told us, apparently deciding it was time to add enticing morsels to the notes we were all comparing. "Did you know that Matt's housemate Ayesha is trans? And that a guy on Ferran's soccer team has a crush on her?"

"Bakari?" I guessed.

"No. I mean, I think he has a crush on her, too, but I think she and Cameron are actually dating."

"I couldn't tell she was trans," Alex responded, tilting his head. "Not that what I could or couldn't tell matters. And it doesn't affect how I look at her; trans women are women. And she's a fascinating woman."

"That she is," Jake concurred. "And also, she's very quiet. Sort of an introvert, I think. But whichever team member it is, I hope they get to be happy together. And that's pretty much how I feel about Matt and Ferran, if they're getting together. I think maybe I'm just a hopeless romantic."

I nodded. "I like them all. And I think if you add them, and Stu and Emily, and Janaya, and all of us, our whole group are some of my favorite people in Santa Cruz. I don't think we'd all be hanging out with each other so much if it wasn't for Ferran and Matt, though."

"I think you're right," Jake agreed. "Maybe, whatever glue there is between Ferran and Matt, it holds us all together, too — even if it's just for gossip at the moment."

"I think I'm okay with us being pulled together," Alicia commented.

Alex still seemed reluctant to relinquish his image of Ferran. "Listen, though. Ferran's never been sexual with a guy before. At least, not that I know of. And I *am* his bestie."

That sparked my intrigue again; I couldn't help it. This could be my opening for more detective work. "I think it's worth sleuthing over," I mused. "Not that I want to invade their privacy…"

Alicia threw some sarcasm at me for that: "Oh, heavens forbid."

"But," I pressed forward, "if they really are in a romantic relationship, I feel like they could use our support."

"I'll agree with that," Alicia said. "So again: maybe we should — you know — *talk t*o them?"

Jake confessed that he was concerned by that idea, and he asked us how our group would even proceed to do that. Alex suggested that maybe each one of us should separately approach Matt and Ferran, one at a time, to gauge whether they'd open up about it. "We don't want to put them on the spot or make them super-uncomfortable," he advised. "And, unless we find very clear evidence of anything nefarious, we definitely don't want to make accusations that either of them would be trying to take advantage of the other one."

I groaned. "I guess it all does seem like prying," I relented. "I suppose if they want to confide in us, they will."

"I understand the concerns," Jake commented, "and I definitely hope neither of them is playing games with the other, but whatever's happening we have to trust they'll work it out. Remember, even if they can't figure things out together, there's no reason any of us need to abandon them as friends. We can help them through whatever might happen. I think they'd tell us if and when they were ready. And if they didn't tell us, we would have to respect their privacy anyway."

While Jake was making his point, Alicia peered over at Matt and Ferran. "Geez, look at them," she commented, ruminating about her hesitancy. "Maybe I'm wrong and our plan lacks boldness after all. It's like those two have their own magnetic field."

"I'm the physics major here," I joked. "I'm the only one qualified to determine if they have their own magnetic field." But then I looked over at them some more. "Yeah, okay, sure," I conceded. "I suppose they do."

"I still say it's important to approach the topic delicately," Jake reminded us. "We need to avoid pushing them away or making them feel like we're being judgy." He suggested that each member of our group should keep an eye out for any signs or hints that Matt and Ferran might give us.

"Yes, but whether we're satellites in their orbit or not, we still have to wait for Ferran and Matt to come to us," Alex insisted. "If it's even a thing." He also warned us that we should refrain from broadcasting Matt's sexual orientation to the world.

I agreed with both of them. "All right; fair enough," I said. "Look: Whatever Ferran and Matt are to each other, they both deserve happiness. They don't deserve a toxic situation or a crazy reaction. I'm sure we can be there for them regardless of whatever they're doing or going through. They're our friends, right? That's what friends do."

"I guess, yeah, I actually agree with that." Alicia said. "This has been one very weird discussion, but I'm glad we've landed on the same page with this. We all have to have each other's backs, right? And theirs, too."

"And we get to be snooping busybodies while we're at it!" Jake chuckled.

"Yeah, let's not forget that part," Alex joked.

Of course, I asked them all if that was not why we were even having the conversation in the first place.

"That's true," Alex asserted. "We've already been doing that, right? So, whatever happens, we've gotta be there for them. I really don't know how it would go if it turned out to be true. You never know how people will react if their stereotypes get challenged," he said, with an arched eyebrow. He told us he was sure we all could navigate through it together and be the best friends Matt and Ferran could ever ask for.

"Aren't we already?" Jake asked.

I was thinking over what I'd already observed from the boys. "Did you notice they've created little nicknames for each other? Ferran calls Matteo, 'Matty,' and Matteo calls Ferran, Ferr.' So, it's like it has already become 'the Ferr and Matty Show.'"

"That's true," Alicia noted. "I heard some of Ferran's soccer buddies call them that. And if the soccer guys are commenting on it, there must be something about it to notice, right? Maybe it's a little too cozy?" Alex also voiced concern about the soccer buddies speculating. "Not surprising, though," Alicia observed. "Emily said that Matt sits with the soccer girlfriends and watches them practice all the time."

"Interesting," I whispered, peering over to the other table. I couldn't help tilting my head a little and smiling when I looked at them. "They're freakin' adorable."

Jake abruptly demanded to have a cute nickname, too. "Matt and Ferran's nicknames for each other have me feeling left out," he pouted.

"You don't just get one assigned," I told him. "They have to come naturally."

Alex huffed sophomorically: "Come naturally, Jake," and both of them laughed rudely.

"So mature," Alicia mocked.

Pretending to ignore her, Alex went back to teasing Jake: "Maybe you could start with finding a love interest, man. Then, if you do that, the nickname will come rolling in after."

Jake's eyes went wide and he laughed nervously. "Shut up," he huffed. "All I said was that it would be nice to have someone who calls me some kind of term of endearment."

"Better start working on your flirting skills, then, Romeo."

Whatever the subtext of their banter might be, it confused me. "Just remember," I offered, playfully nudging Jake, "I'm always here for you if you need some love advice."

Jake seemed flustered as his cheeks went bright red. He fidgeted nervously, and then he mumbled, "I think you *could* give me some advice." Whatever that might mean, I was ready to turn back to the subject at hand.

"Should we give them a couple name?" I asked.

Alicia groaned. "Ugh! Noooooo! Already there are people spreading rumors that they've gotta be boyfriends. And then I also overheard some women from Merrill College saying they thought Ferran was queer-baiting Matt. To like, you know, try to set him up to knock him down."

I felt some annoyance that people I thought of as outsiders would be speculating about the things I felt entitled to speculate about. "Like Ferran is some grimy, barbaric, manipulative heterosexist dross?" I groused. "I guess when it comes right down to it, I honestly don't think Ferran is just trying to use a willing Matt for a little secret side action. If we're totally serious, do any of you think that?"

"Maybe?" Jake responded. "It wouldn't be the first time a queer boy got totally used by a straight jock. And how is that any worse than thinking Matt might try to seduce Ferran against his will?"

"I implied that, didn't I," I admitted, feeling deeply embarrassed. "Wow, I am such a jerk. I don't think I really believe that deep down."

Alex got very defensive. "Ferran would *never* do something like that! He's always been an upstanding guy. He would never act like such crap to someone, just because they're some flavor of queer." He shook his head. "I don't know what people are even talking about. Come on, he used to date the hottest girl in our junior high and high school. They were together for six years! I really don't think Ferran's gay. But, so what if he was?"

Alicia peered over at Matt and Ferran, but spoke to Alex. "Bisexuality exists, mister. Look, you know how I am about '60s music, right? Do any of you know that ancient Burt Bacharach song, *The Look of Love?*"

"I do," I chimed in. "I love that song. And Sandra Bernhard used to say that sometimes you just need a little Burt."

"Look at their eyes," Alicia said softly. "I think it's pretty obvious. That's some kind of love affair, even if it isn't a sexual one."

We all turned our attention back to the boys. Just then, Matt and Ferran stood up and left their table. We watched as Ferran walked over to Matt and grabbed him into a big hug, leaving Matt looking surprised. He seemed to just go with it, though. They separated again and grabbed their bags. Then they headed off outside the library, turning back to wave goodbye to our crew of friends.

All right, I could see it. "They do look like they're totally gobsmacked, don't they."

"Maybe we should give them a couple name after all," Alicia comically suggested.

Jake seriously asked: "Why can't we just call them Matt and Ferran? Come on, they're iconic. Everybody's always just gonna refer to them as a unit anyway."

"And at this point, that would be the problem," Alicia reminded us. "Maybe we should just leave it be. The other gossips are already in full flower."

"Are we really gossiping?" I asked.

"We're their friends. We're just … Ugh, I don't know," Alex grumbled.

"Admiring them?" Alicia suggested.

"Honestly," Jake confessed, "it's intimidating to have friends who look like that and who seem to have a language they speak that doesn't require talking."

"That just sounds to me like they really are a couple," I suggested.

"They'd tell us if they were, wouldn't they?" Alex asked. "Wouldn't Ferran tell *me?*"

Jake seemed to take a moment to consider. "Ferran has this image of the soccer jock, right? The one who had the hot cheerleader girlfriend? That's the total stereotype of 'straight,' isn't it?"

"Kinda," Alicia remarked.

"If Ferran dated a guy, all that straight privilege might vanish overnight," Jake pointed out.

Exasperated, I fussed: "We're their friends! If they're boyfriends they should just tell us."

Jake looked at me pitifully and whispered: "It isn't always so easy to tell someone about your feelings, Maura." That was when I noticed that Jake's gaze was full of what might be described as longing. What the actual…?

Suddenly, I was feeling oddly nervous myself. "Okay," I hedged, standing up from my seat. "Ehhmmm … I need to get to class. Who's going towards Oakes College?"

"Me!" Alicia called.

"Me, too." Alex announced. "I have a class at Rachel Carson College."

"Great!" I said, quickly gathering my things. "Let's go! So, Jake, you wanna come with, just for the stroll?"

"No," Jake answered, flatly. "I have to go up to Crown. But I'll chat y'all up later." He grabbed his backpack and waved to us as he walked off toward Crown College.

As Alicia, Alex, and I walked down a path toward the east side of campus, we were all strangely silent.

Eventually, I had to ask them: "Does Jake like me?"

They both looked at me with bulging eyes. "*Jesus, girl!*" Alicia exclaimed. "What was your first clue?"

Alex asked me if I'd really been that oblivious, and I had to consider it for a moment.

"I haven't been paying attention," I said. "But maybe I should."

Then we continued our walk through the redwoods in silence.

8

PANIC

"There is no greater agony
than bearing an untold story inside you."
— *Maya Angelou*

"In any moment of decision,
the best thing you can do is the right thing,
the next best thing is the wrong thing,
and the worst thing you can do is nothing."
— *Theodore Roosevelt*

*[Playlist reference: Peyton McMahon
—Fear of the Unknown]*

Ekkheya

It was dark and cold outside, and Ferran was having a nightmare.

He'd been having horrible nightmares on and off for years. They still came even though things were going well at school, and even though Alex was with him at UCSC. They still came despite the fact that he'd met Matt, who had become an amazing new friend.

It was hard for me to be the spirit guarding him and checking-in on him when he was having such distress. He and Matt could find so much happiness on their paths if they worked together. In fact, though, the worst of Ferran's nightmares these days were when he'd dream that he told Matt about his feelings, and Matt decided to break off all contact with him.

Ferran kept asking himself how he'd arrived at such a strong feeling that he didn't just *like* having Matt in his life, he also *wanted* him. When I heard Ferran's voice inside his mind, it saddened me, because he kept asking himself: *Why am I being such a coward?*

He was torn between the desire to tell Matt that their friendship made his life better and that he really did love him for it, and the fear that it would somehow bring an end to their connection.

The nightmares would shake Ferran awake in a cold sweat. He decided he had to tell his roommate, Stu. about them. He reasoned that Stu should at least know what was happening when he heard Ferran gasping in the middle of the night.

So, before Stu could get stuck some night trying to sleep through Ferran's tossing and turning across the room, Ferran apologetically told him about the kinds of dreams he was having. And Stu did hear Ferran that night. He went to Ferran's bedside, and tried his best to comfort him.

"Look, man," he said, trying to give Ferran reassurance, "I don't think you have to worry about losing your friends, especially if you tell people how much they mean to you. What happened to you that you're so afraid of that? Everybody really likes you."

"The truth? My parents were always too busy doing their own thing when I was a kid. They never cared about how the other kids treated me at school, or what I was interested in, or anything except how it all looked to other people. I never really felt like anybody cared about me until Alex and April came into my life. And then, you know … April broke up with me."

"But Alex is here, man. And so are the rest of us. Especially Matt."

"Yeah? But maybe that's what I'm so afraid of losing."

"Ferran, friendships are like a garden. If you tend to them, they keep yielding the good stuff."

"I don't know why it is that the closer people get, the more afraid I am that I'll get hurt. But sometimes that's how I feel."

"I think you need to talk with a counselor about that."

"Maybe."

The only thing that actually seemed to calm Ferran after one of his bad nights was spending time with Matt. On that following day, though, Matt's obligations meant they wouldn't see each other.

Ferran

As the day wore on, I rushed through the light drizzle, headed toward the Stevenson Coffeehouse.

When I got inside, I saw my favorite of Matt's housemates, our friend Alicia. She was sitting in a corner and I called out to her. "Alicia! You have a class here?"

"Yeah, sexual psychology. We just finished. How's it going?"

"It's going," I said flatly as I approached her table. I felt so nervous. I needed to be able to talk about this stuff with someone. "But I need to talk to you about something," I said in a near whisper, "if you have a minute."

"Okay."

I sat down at the opposite side of her corner table. I was trying to maintain hushed tones "Okay … So maybe this will seem weird to you, but I've sort of been feeling strange about Matt. And I need to be able to talk with someone who knows him well and who can also keep it confidential. Could I do that with you?"

"I'll confess I'm a little concerned about that intro," she said quietly. "But I'll do my best. What's on your mind?"

"Well … Matt and I have been hanging out a lot."

"I know."

"And that hasn't left much time — any time, really — for either of us to go on dates with the women who've been sort of in-pursuit. Wait, that same out all wrong. I'm not saying the women are chasing me down 'cause I'm *all that.*"

Alicia smiled at me and gently shook her head. "What did they used to say? Both of you are 'all that and a bag of chips,' darlin'".

I huffed out a smile. "Thank you, flatterer. Of course, it isn't like you don't have a lot of guys chasing *you.*"

She rolled her eyes. "Sometimes that's annoying, Ferran."

"Yeah, I imagine it must be."

Alicia tapped her pen on the table. "That's not what you wanted to talk about, is it."

"No" I admitted. "Okay, so, here it is. I'm feeling confused about Matt."

Alicia arched her eyebrow. "Confused?"

"Yeah … I'm probably spending too much time thinking about my friendship with him. But, I dunno. It sure feels … this will sound strange maybe? It feels like a long day when the day is without him."

Alicia hummed quietly before she spoke. "It's true you guys have become like the 'dynamic duo' since the quarter started. You're always together. Not that it's a bad thing. I mean, the rest of us get to indulge in leering at you from afar. It's all eye candy."

An uncomfortable laugh escaped from inside me. "The rest of us?"

"Ferran, *please*. When two guys look like the two of you look, and they're best buds who hang out together all the time, it's damned hard not to notice."

I was feeling more anxious all of a sudden. "Look like what?"

She peered into my eyes with all seriousness. "Look like you just walked out on the runway together for a Loewe campaign at Paris Fashion Week, that's what."

Really? She thought I was model hot? I knew Matt was, but me? "Alicia," I complained, "it really makes me nervous that people are paying that much attention."

"Honey, I think that comes with the territory."

"But it gets worse," I groaned. "People apparently feel the need to tell me stuff I don't think I wanted to know." I wanted to highlight for her some of the peculiar ways other people were acting about Matt's and my friendship. "I guess there are people who know that me and Matt are like two peas in a pod."

"Yes," she observed. "I'd say so."

"Like yesterday, for example. I was up at Merrill College and the girlfriend of one of my teammates was sitting by the Merrill Wall, so I went over to chat with her. She and her friends gave me an earful of gossip. Like, they said, 'Your friend Matt is a total player.' They told me they used to see him hanging out at Merrill a lot last year and he'd have a different girl hanging on his arm every day. I know Matt and other people have told me he didn't seriously date anybody, but I started to wonder if he was just having a lot of random hookups with all these women."

"Why is that important, Ferran? Would that matter to you?"

Fuck. Talking about this with her was going to be harder than I thought. "Alicia, I … This has to stay between us. Please? Promise me? The last thing I need is people starting to talk about me with … well, just stuff I don't need. Obviously, people can be judgmental creeps. And please don't say anything to Matt. I need this to just be between you and me."

Alicia's features softened and she looked at me with gentle eyes. "You can confide in me, Ferran. I'll give you the sanctity of the confessional."

"I think …" I could barely get the words out. "I think I might be jealous."

Then both of Alicia's eyebrows raised high. "Jealous as in envious that he got all those casual hookups with the ladies, or jealous as in you don't want your bromance buddy to be hooking up with anyone?"

Wow, she cut right to the chase, didn't she.

But I did have to sort out my thoughts, and maybe saying them out loud to Alicia would help. "Both? Maybe? I don't know for sure. Look, lately I've been feeling … *gahhhh!* … like he's my friend, but I want to have him all to myself."

"I see."

I know it's bizarre. It's like some crap Reality TV show," I sputtered. "I feel like I want to protect him, though. Like: from the world, from numbing-out his feelings with lots of casual sex, maybe from the lineup of women trying to get with him for a night. And I know it's really none of my business, but it twists me up inside. When I think about how he was last year, I get angry thinking about those women having him. I start to wonder if I even fit into his life."

Ekkheya

Alicia was now well aware that Ferran's distress was not really about Matt's hookups. She wasn't sure, however, how much of Ferran's disclosures she should tackle at once. She settled on a strategy of just trying to reflect empathy.

"I hear you," she said, "and I understand why you might feel that way. But bear in mind that what you're worried about happened last year. There hasn't been any of that since he got here this year. Matt's past hookups, good or bad, don't define who he is today. I've noticed a change in him, and maybe your friendship has something to do with that."

"You think?" Ferran asked, seeming especially vulnerable. "I guess you're right. But it's really confusing for me. I don't know why I feel this way. Why am I like this?"

"I can't answer that for you. There are always trade-offs in life. I think you need to figure out how much of a priority Matt is to you. Or, maybe you have to look inside yourself and find out why Matt *is* such a priority for you, and why you feel so possessive."

"Do you think I'm being possessive?"

Alicia tried to summon every tool she had in her undergraduate psychology arsenal. She asked Ferran what it felt like for him to be around Matt.

"All of a sudden," he described, "I lose focus and things fade into the background. I think of everything he and I have done together from the time Maura introduced us, and then everything makes me think of him. It's like he has a halo around him and I just wanna be around it all the time — like I yearn for it. I don't want any of the time I get with him to end, but I'm also afraid of that."

Alicia was now fairly convinced that the straight boy wasn't so straight, but she had no idea when Ferran would catch up to that reality.

Weighing everything he'd told her, Alicia replied carefully: "I think that you want your friendship to be the way it has been since you met, perfectly and without changes. And that you're worried Matt's libido is going to leave you behind in the dust. And that you also know you're not in a position to control any changes that might happen with you guys. So, I think you might be afraid of that."

Ferran felt like she'd stripped his mind naked. "Maybe you're right," he pondered. "I really wish I could talk with him about that. But I'm afraid if I tell him how I've been feeling, that'll be the end of our friendship."

Alicia reached for his hand on the table, and gently placed her hand on top. "When people are as close as you two are, it's completely normal to feel confused. Sometimes, the emotions can be overwhelming. I get the impression that you haven't felt this way about anyone before."

"I haven't."

"Give yourself a minute," she advised him. "It's definitely important to figure out your own feelings before you even think about bringing it up with Matt. You definitely don't want that conversation to sound judgmental. When you think you can be gentle and clear and honest, with yourself and with him, then maybe you two ought to talk about things."

"Okay. You're right," Ferran sighed. "Thank you for talking with me. I'm sorry I'm such a mess."

"At least you're a handsome mess, Ferran."

"You are too kind," he answered, trying to smile. "But I'm supposed to go meet Alex at Ivéta for dinner, and now I haven't even given myself enough time to grab a coffee for the walk."

"You'll live."

"Thanks again," Ferran said as he waved goodbye and walked out of the coffeehouse.

Then he made his walk as brisk as he could, so he wouldn't be late to meet with Alex. He was already going to confide in his oldest friend, because he needed Alex to help center him. But at this point, after talking with Alicia, he felt like he was falling over a cliff.

Ferran

When I arrived at Ivéta, Alex was already sitting at a table.

He watched me closely as I walked over to him. At the table, I sat down across from Alex. He looked me up and down, and observed: "You don't look so good."

"Maybe a burger will fix it."

A server came up to the table and asked us if we wanted to order drinks. Alex tried to be subtle and not to appear too creepy while he gazed at her intently, clearly impressed with her looks. If I'm being honest, I couldn't even focus on her.

He managed to choke out an order of boba tea, and I asked for a cappuccino. We agreed that we were ready to order, and we both ordered burgers. This dinner and catching-up time were long overdue.

I think Alex and I were still learning how to adapt from our high school lives to our university lives. I knew I was struggling with the fears I'd been carrying for a long time, but hadn't been able to fully put into words. For the past six years, Alex had been the only person besides April whom I could think of as a reliable, go-to friend.

Alex always showed up for me and I could be real with him, so I was feeling I could trust him with this. Still, I felt scattered and nervous. I leaned back in my chair and stared off into the distance, unsettled. After almost a minute of quiet between us, I tried to tell Alex my big news.

"Alex … I can't stop thinking about him."

My longest-running friend gave me a look somewhere between confusion and intrigue. He leaned forward across the table toward me. "All right. Him *who,* Ferran? Who are you talking about?"

"Him ... I'm …," I cleared my throat. "I'm talking about Matt."

I knew I'd be unsuccessful at suppressing it, but I still felt ridiculous giving-in to the stupid smile that was taking over my face.

Alex tilted his head slightly toward his right shoulder and cupped his right ear with his hand. "I wanna be sure I heard that correctly," Alex remarked slowly, in a gentle voice. He repeated the name and asked for clarification. "Matt …," he said. "Your attached-at-the-hip new-best-buddy Matt. Right? The Matt who looks like a model, and you can find him at every big activist thing. The guy who always gets me to fumble in hackey sack?"

"I didn't know he had mad hackey sack skills, but yeah, that's the one."

"Okay, man. Well, I don't suppose he's easy to miss."

"Yeah," I said, as Alex regarded me with a wary look. "So that's the him I can't stop thinking about."

My friends were apparently getting really good at arching their eyebrows, and Alex raised both of his high. "Okay. Well, it *does* seem that you guys have been hanging out a whole bunch."

I agreed, sheepishly: "I kinda want to see him all the time."

"That's interesting."

"Interesting, sure. It's … weird. He's like a work of art, you know?"

Alex seemed to consider the statement, and then quietly asked me: "Are you, like, having a major bromance, Ferran?"

"Man, I …" I hoped I had it in me to dismiss the idea, but my throat was clutching. I took a breath and tried again: "Alex, man, you're my oldest friend. We went to junior high and high school together, and we grew up together. *You know me, buddy.* I think if I was gonna be in a 'bromance' with anybody, it would be you."

Alex chuckled, but shook his head. "Aw, shucks," he commented with a smile, oozing sarcasm. "But I don't feel convinced."

"Man, you *know* I dated April the whole time back then. You know we were doing the deed. We just got bored."

"Dude," Alex grumbled, "how do you get bored with *that?*"

"We just did," I protested. "The best part with her was just being able to talk with her about the most random stuff. It was an intense friendship, Alex, but it was never a romance. And at the start of the summer, she said she just felt we needed to really make a break so we could grow — that we could reclaim our friendship later. And I agreed with her, even though it hurt. There was never any — you know — *passion* between us."

"Well, you know I figured that would happen. But now we're having this conversation and, I have to tell you, it's a little peculiar. I also feel weird, 'cause I'm beginning to wonder how much you've ever really opened-up to me about the stuff going on in your life. How did you not tell me this before? If you had let me know, I wouldn't have made jokes about you two being a public relations campaign."

I knew how Alex and I first bonded. It was from talking about our mutual love of all things intellectual — something out-of-the-ordinary for two brown boys in the Central Valley. Alex's mother had died in a farming accident when he was eleven years old. I appeared in his life just at the time when he seemed to need a purpose, and a sense that he wasn't going to be abandoned. I needed that, too.

We became best friends. I feel like Alex became very possessive of our friendship over the years. I had decided that was okay, because I had no intention of ever abandoning one of the only two people I felt I could trust.

Alex was starting to look perturbed, so I pathetically apologized: "I'm sorry."

He spoked with his lips drawn tightly. "Before you go on, I have to tell you about something that was bugging me before, and is bugging me even more now. Could we talk about that for a minute?"

I felt my chest get tight. I worriedly asked Alex what was going on.

"I wish both of us would talk about our feelings more, not less," he told me. "I'm sorry to bring up old stuff, but this has been eating at me."

"Please, Alex. What is it?"

"You didn't tell me about how close you were with April as friends, Ferran. You left that part out, even from *me.* It actually hurts that you kept the truth away from me — the truth about the kind of level that your relationship with April was on. I mean, why would you hide that? It feels like I didn't matter to you."

"Oh, no. Alex, you always mattered to me sooooo much," I insisted. "That's why it hurt so bad when you and April would fight with each other. You two bickered constantly. I think you both felt like it was a competition, and I didn't want to say or do anything to make it worse."

"I guess. But I think we might have been okay if you had let me know. Without knowing what was up, it just looked to me as if she wanted to be in the middle of every minute that you and I ever hung out. It was annoying."

"When I started asking you if you were considering UCSC for school," I tried to explain, "my goal was to reconnect with you. You're like my brother, and I'd be lost without you. I didn't keep quiet about the BFFs-with-benefits thing with April because I was trying to use you somehow. I was trying to keep peace between the only two people I felt like I could trust."

Alex looked up. "I did *not* know that. I couldn't understand why you let the tension keep building, when you could have been really transparent with both of us about what was going on with you."

"I felt sometimes like you hated her."

"I never hated her."

"Well, you two sure had a strange way of showing it," I shot back. "I should have figured out sooner that it was some kind of fear."

"Look, are you really the one to be talking about *my* fear right now? You seem to be paralyzed by your own. Without giving me the details about what was going on with you, you left me lost between you and April a lot of times."

"I'm sorry for that," I confessed.

"Just don't leave me out like that again, please."

"Not going anywhere," I assured him. "I was there for you for both of your high school girlfriends and all the heartache you had when they stupidly dumped you because they wanted to try to go after more popular guys. You're my anchor, and I hope I'm yours, too."

"I know, and you are," Alex confirmed.

"Could we try to assume we're gonna be there for each other," I asked, with some hope, "and actually have some real talk about it before we jump to conclusions?"

"Yeah, I think that's reasonable," Alex said with a smile. But how was I supposed to know how to explain to you about the strife between April and me, when I was supposed to be your best friend but you didn't let me in so I could understand? You gotta let me in, man."

"Alex, please," I pleaded. "That's what I'm trying to do now. I've been going through a lot of confusion. This hasn't been easy. Besides, it's hard to admit out-loud that April and I were just best-friends-with-benefits and that we were consciously curating our image."

"You were definitely doing that. It was a cliché. The trope of the soccer star and the cheerleader."

"Okay, yeah. But we sure looked good together."

"Sure," Alex teased me. "It was like a bad Candace Cameron Bure *Family TV* movie."

I had to grimace. "Yuck. Aren't all of them bad?"

"Abysmal. And yeah, it was especially chafing that we all knew you were getting some, when half of us weren't."

We were quiet again for a minute or so, and I started losing focus. I was staring out the restaurant window and beginning to muse, so I tried to get back on track. "Alex, I'm trying to say something else important here. To let you in this time."

"Okay. Go ahead."

"Matt's just …"

Alex paused. I think he was waiting a beat or two for me to finish the sentence, but I couldn't.

So, he jumped in: "You can tell me anything, and you know that, Ferran. What's going on with all this?"

My constipated mind relented: "I don't even know how to describe it, Alex. When Matt and I are not hanging out, I think about him all the time — and they're thoughts that are super-strange for me. I've thought about holding him, man — even kissing him. It's making me nuts."

I gave Alex a moment to try to digest the information I just revealed to him — and he took it.

"Wow," he finally replied. "Okay, I have to be uncomfortably honest about something to you, too. The other day at the library, a group of our friends were having lunch together. Remember?"

"Yeah…"

"We saw you guys in whatever conversation you were having over at your corner table, and you two were looking really deeply involved with each other. I have to admit that a few theories about you two got advanced. What you just told me was one of them."

Our friends had been talking about this? I was surprised, and maybe even a little annoyed. "You guys were gossiping about us?"

"I have to confess, man. We were. You two looked so fascinated with each other. We were starting to wonder if it was more than just friendship, although we didn't know what to make of the sexuality aspect of it. We got around to hoping that neither of you were just trying to use the other one, because we didn't want someone to end up getting hurt."

"I would never do that," I snapped.

"I know, and I told them that. All of us agreed we were overstepping our bounds and that we should wait to see if either of you told us more."

"And here I am, telling you more. Are you going to tell any of them what's happening with me?"

"Ferran, no, man. That's not mine to tell. You can trust me. But I do feel protective of you, you know? And, knowing what you've been thinking about, I feel like I should ask if things are gonna be okay in your living situation. I mean, there's Stu. Have *you* talked about any of this with your roommate?"

I'd thought about it, but the idea frightened me. "No!" I quickly replied. "Alex, I can't do that! He and his girlfriend are already tossing jokes at me about Matt. They referred to him as my 'bromance' before you did. And they call him my 'little boyfriend'. What if I told them about this and then they decided I might be leering at everybody — that I might try to come on to Stu?"

"I don't know. And I don't think that would happen. But Ferran, you live with Stu. Somehow, if you keep having a crush on Matt, I don't think it's gonna stay hidden from somebody you live in close quarters with in a dorm room."

All I could do in that moment was groan in frustration. "What do I do?" I asked him. "I don't know if I could tell him anything about this, Alex. You're calling what I have a 'crush,' but I don't know what it is. I wouldn't even know *what* I would tell Stu. And whatever I'd say, then he'd tell Emily."

"Yeah," Alex replied, in a measured and reassuring tone. "But hey, listen: Maybe I should tell you some information I've been told *about Matt*. Obviously it's gossip, but I think it's from reputable sources."

"Tell me."

"Well, they said he's bisexual."

"What?"

"Bi, Ferran. They said he likes more than one gender."

"Some other gossips told me he was always with a different woman last year."

"Well, from what I was told, cisgender women were only part of his buffet."

"Oh," I choked, feeling my heart sink and my jealous anger flare.

Alex continued: "So … like … if he's such a 'player,' what if he tried to hit on *you* or something?"

I grumbled in frustration. "See? You're already jumping to the conclusion that he might hit on me, and wondering if I'd be concerned. That's why I'm worried about what Stu and Emily would think of *me* if I said anything to them."

"Ferran, don't forget that they're your friends. And, like I said, your roommate is eventually going to notice what's up with you — it would be too hard now to hide your social life or lack of it. But I don't think you understood what I was getting at with my question."

"No?"

"What I meant was more like … if Matt hit on you, then you'd know he'd been thinking about stuff with you, too."

"Matt hasn't come out as bi to me, so this is all new information for me. But if he did, and if he hit on me, I'm not really sure what I'd do. I've never felt this way before. *Ever.* I'm freakin' *obsessed* with him, man. I mean, I've only been with girls in the past, but then Matt... "

"… What? …"

"I don't know, Alex. He's different. He's gentle, and confident. And I have to admit, I think he's really beautiful."

"Well, yeah, he is really, really pretty. Even I can see that."

"Alex … He's breathtaking."

Alex broke out in a wide smile.

"O. my. gods. Ferran, you have it *bad.* What is this, man? Did you catch a case of 'love at first sight?' I think you *have* gone gay on me."

I could feel the heat rising into my face. My heart was pounding. I knew I must have been blushing hot.

I sputtered what I thought was an explanation. "I really don't know what it is. I haven't stopped being attracted to girls. I walk around campus, and I see so many women who are total eye candy. And they're *here,* you know? So, I know they're smart. But I can't help it: Matt is always on my mind."

I paused. I wasn't sure if I should tell Alex the rest, but I took the risk: "I saw him eating an ice cream cone the other day, and what he was doing with his tongue made me crazy. And then I got scared. Alex, I am so confused. Every time I see him my heart skips a beat."

"That's … well, *that's* something."

"I even tried to search through porn to see if it would turn me on at all, and then I looked up on the internet to see if I could take a test to figure out if I'm gay."

Alex tilted his head and seemed to think that over for a moment. "Are you kidding?"

"No."

"Okay," he said, stretching out the syllables of the word. "So, what did you find out?"

"I found a bunch of stuff, but it just kind of weirded me out. I went to a porn site but I couldn't make myself watch anything. They had this link to a gay leather site. And that one discussed this 'hanky code' thing where people wear bandanas to signal sexual stuff they like. Then I remembered that Matt has worn this cool blue bandana around his neck or in his pocket sometimes, so I figured I'd research what that was supposed to mean. Then I found a Wikipedia entry about the 'hanky code,' and I started to read it. Alex, I swear: I got a few descriptions in, and I felt like my brain was gonna explode. It was like an input overload. I had to stop reading."

"Kinda sounds like you were jumping in the deep end of the pool, man."

"I know. So, then I found this web site for a quiz at an Alphabet Soup health center. They had a quiz about identity and the dimensions of sexual orientation — and I took it."

"Alphabet Soup?"

"You know: LGBTIA2Q+. And maybe l, m, n, o, p. They've got a letter for everything."

Alex chuckled. "Ah. So, what did your test tell you?"

"The results said that my answers fell within the clinical definitions of bisexuality, because I seem to like more than one gender. It all looked really political and clinical to me."

"Ferran, not gonna lie," Alex confided, his eyes gone soft with his concern for me. "This will be a bigger thing for you than you might think. You tell me it's scary, and it might be. But it could also be the best experience you've ever had. One thing is for sure, though: you're gonna have to figure out if you're willing to put the rest of your life on the line … to try getting with Matt."

"… On the line? …"

"You two are already too close for people not to notice it if you guys actually do hook up. You laser-focus on each other as it is. Even if you try to keep it on the down low, there's no way people won't figure it out. I can't see you dialing back the romance in order to hide the rest."

"Why would that put the rest of my life on the line?"

"That straight jock persona you cultivated for years?" Alex reminded me. "If you guys become more than platonic friends, nobody is gonna buy that image anymore. And that probably means that all the privilege you get for being the dashing, manly soccer star would evaporate. You have to figure out if going for it with Matt is important enough to take that risk."

Oh, damn, damn, damn, damn, damn.

I whinged at my longest-running friend, feeling as though my stomach was doing backflips. "I've been worrying about that and about a million other parts of this."

As I pondered that question, our server arrived and set down our food and asked if we needed anything else.

Both of us looked up at her and answered together, "No, thank you," so she went on with her work. Alex leaned back in his chair, looking deep in thought.

He clasped his hands into the shape of a steeple, which he held to his lips. After a bit, he said: "My dude, who knows? Maybe you've really been bi all along and the right man just hadn't come into your life until now."

My throat felt constricted, and it wasn't an allergic reaction.

"So … I'm wondering. Are the feelings you're having mostly … *emotional?"* he asked. "You know, you could just work out all the sexual mechanics later."

I was already slightly queasy, and I was really hoping not to have to think about the sex part. I dropped my face into my hands, feeling defeated. I replied in what seemed like a choked voice: "Oh, my gods, … *sex."*

"Well yeah, man. What did you think?"

I felt lost at sea. "I think I'll need to go online and study this more. I don't know if this is a test I can pass! I'm gonna have to, like, watch the porn and read some journal articles. Jesus, Alex! I need to learn how to play with my …"

"Stop right there, buddy," Alex said, cutting off my hectic rambling. "That's already more information than I need to know."

"I'm going to make a disaster out of all of this, I just know it."

Alex tried to lift up my spirits: "It will work out if it's meant to work out, buddy. But you have to answer that big question about whether he's worth all that. And if you feel like he is, then you'll have to take the risk to find out."

I shook my head back and forth in my hands. "O, gods."

"Have you even talked to him about any of this? Maybe he feels the same way about you," Alex pointed out.

I nervously looked up and shook my head no. "I haven't had the courage, Alex. "

"You need to talk to him, man."

"What if he doesn't feel the same way? What if I can't do the sex part? What if I'm a coward about losing my privilege and status? Alex, I could totally ruin my friendship with him. You really are like my brother, man, but he's become another best friend."

I think I was traveling down an anxiety rabbit hole. I started shivering, and I looked into Alex's eyes as if that would help me grab onto a life raft. "I *can't* risk losing him as a friend," I told him, pleading. "April is, like, *gone.* You and Matt are my grounding cords."

Alex tried his best to comfort me: "Look, Ferran, you aren't gonna know unless you try."

I huffed.

"I've got your back, buddy," Alex promised. "I'm still your friend, whatever happens with this."

My voice quavered as I told him how thankful I was that he was part of my life.

"Look," Alex reassured me, "from what you've told me, it seems like there's something special that's happening between you two. Listen to me, Ferran. Even if you try to put all this on a back shelf, or if you go for it and it doesn't work out romantically, I want to believe your friendship with Matt can weather the storm."

"Up close, he smells like sandalwood," I said dreamily. "Did you know that?"

"Man. You know what he smells like up close?"

"Oh, yeah."

"Ferran…"

I took a deep breath. "Okay. Maybe you're right. Maybe I need to take a chance. Life's too short to hold back on love."

Alex laughed a quiet, breathy laugh. "Listen to yourself, man. 'Love.' You *do* have it bad."

That exasperated me, and I begged Alex: "Tell me what's happening to me."

"Maybe what you need is to find out who you are with Matt, and not just who you are living under a manufactured image. I think we gotta get you into the spirit, my dude."

"It's not like a soccer game," I grumbled.

"You know I'll be here to support you no matter what happens. And who knows, maybe Matt is just waiting for you to make the first move?"

"Maybe. But I need more time. I need to figure out how I can regroup if it all goes south when I tell him. And please, *please* keep this just between us."

Alex sighed with a smile. "All right, Ferran. But don't take forever, man. Nobody will win from that."

Alex was handling this news better than I'd ever imagined. I got choked up about it, but I tried to tell him without breaking into tears. "Thanks, Alex. I don't know what I'd do without you. I really appreciate that you're being supportive instead of giving me any crap about it."

"No judgments," Alex assured me.

"I'm going to try to talk to Matt soon. I just have to pump up my courage."

Alex raised his boba tea glass. "Good luck, Ferran. Really. I am manifesting even as we speak. Right now, in front of these cruelty-free, lab-grown burgers, I am solemnly affirming that everything is going to work out just fine. You need to get your 'happily ever after,' buddy."

"I will do my best, Alex. But I'm really scared."

9

BORDWALK

"When I walk down the boardwalk,
people stop me and say,
'Oh, your house is the one that glows.'"
— *Mary Matalón*

*[Playlist reference: Ed Sheeran (featuring Taylor Swift)
— The Joker and The Queen]*

Ekkheya

Rain was pouring relentlessly all day. Matt took a night away from his usual walks with Ferran to go to an emergency meeting in Santa Cruz that was called by some labor groups, fishing advocates, residents worried about recent crimes, and the Monterey Bay Aquarium's sustainable fishing project.

An angry union organizer, Yohei Tanaka, was speaking.

"This is how we live and survive, through our seafood," said Tanaka, President of the California Seafood Workers Union. "If we allow this to happen and they start to get more aquaculture than catching wild, it shoves us out of the way and pollutes the ocean for all of us."

Tanaka knew that poorly regulated fin fish farms posed a significant and ongoing ecological and public health threat. They were also a threat to wild fish stocks, whether by the spread of disease or by escaped farmed fish competing for food. Those sorts of aquaculture operations at full scale also produce an enormous amount of waste, which can result in higher nitrogen and phosphorus concentrations in the water. Those nutrients can cause toxic algae blooms, which choke off oxygen in aquatic environments and can lead to higher fish mortality and ecosystem disruption and death.

In the midst of the global climate crisis, some large corporations were seeking to compete with China for the fish consumption market by building fish farms all along the coast of the Monterey Bay. The profit motive for them was important enough that they were willing to sabotage small fishers and fisheries, from the Monterey Bay to Tomales Bay. There had been increasing acts of vandalism, violence, legal wrangling, and worse to advance their goals.

The death of a 40-year-old fisheries observer from Santa Cruz aboard an Aquaculture Cod purse seiner was under investigation by the Santa Cruz County Community

Safety Office. Matt was working with a group asking for help from the EPA and the Coast Guard, but they were getting nowhere. All of this was causing a renewed focus on the recent dark history associated with the job.

Along with all the environmental risks, the Monterey Bay's fishers worried that bringing more aquaculture to the Central Coast could push independent fishers out of business. Families and hangers-on who had been in the fishing business for generations were facing relentless upheavals disturbing their lives. Family secrets and corporate sellouts were beginning to cause major community rifts.

Cooper Collins, president of the Central Coast Fishers Association, said that fishers in her area were required to catch wild fish only according to a careful seasonal schedule of species. She believed that if aquaculture took hold in the region and one of those wild species that commercial fishers depended on was being farmed year-round, it would kill their business. In a decade or so, it could also choke off wildlife — including the important Northern California shellfish and fin fish industries — in the surrounding ocean.

Several of the local restauranteurs in Santa Cruz were on record refusing to buy farmed cod for their venues. After they did, there were a number of vandalism attacks on those restaurants. Audrey Mekonnen, another organizer with the union, dug around and discovered that the great grandson of a Central Coast fishing clan stood to make a fortune off of selling his fish prep factory to the Aquaculture conglomerate.

Then, one of the bussers at Jamey's Harbor Grill was beaten into a coma. People at the meeting were buzzing about that, wondering what she might have seen. The meeting's tone was understandably grim.

While Matteo Poulsen was ready to lend support to the organizing activity, the intense intrigue of the meeting convinced him even more that he wanted to be involved in projects for sustainable food sources. Working at UCSC's Agro-ecology Farm and Garden Project with Ferran was going to be the kind of effort that could bear fruit, literally and figuratively. They could help to feed the way forward with less ecological and social insanity. Matt decided he would start right after the meeting to do some digging about how to get a paid internship at the farm.

***

Matteo

It was a bright and clear day — a day I was eagerly anticipating. Riding rickety old wooden roller-coasters was one of my favorite things to do, and I knew the Santa Cruz Beach Boardwalk would not disappoint. I was also going to get to experience it with Ferran, which I was sure would make it even better.

I could accept that I was fascinated with Ferran; the problem remained that he was straight.

The summer before this quarter, I was bullied a lot at my job at a San Francisco tourist trap. I got hired for a gig at a restaurant on Pier 39. One morning when I noticed a hot silver fox taking his time in the store and stealing furtive glances at me, I made the mistake of confiding to a co-worker that I was bisexual. She told all of our co-workers and managers; I hadn't realized she was a bigot with a big mouth.

Despite San Francisco having a progressive reputation, in certain quarters there was still a persistent infection of lingering chauvinism and negative discrimination. My co-workers made my life miserable, day-in and day-out. They even recruited some of the tourists who were our customers to badger me. "Go work in the Castro, fag," became almost a daily taunt from them.

Then, the manager fired me on a completely bogus accusation. He claimed I was "being inappropriate" with male customers — which never actually happened. But I was staying with my parents, so getting fired meant I had to explain it to them. That was why I decided to come out as bisexual to my family and to some friends over the summer.

I could have taken legal action, but I had enough on my plate organizing for other people's labor concerns. I should have taken a stand for the sake of the next person to face it, and I was feeling guilty that I didn't. But I just didn't have the energy to carry all of it, and my parents told me I shouldn't feel ashamed of taking care of myself first for a change.

I probably could have taken better care of myself than by throwing myself into an explosion of sexual hookups. Although I had never seriously dated, I did have some furtive hookups during high school and a more constant parade of them during my first year at UCSC. I treated it like a smorgasbord, trying to sample all the plates.

Let's say I taste-tested a lot. I had been with cisgender folks who were assigned female at birth. I'd been with both cis and trans folks assigned male at birth. I stumbled on a trans man whom I found extremely hot, and got to sample him, too. And, while I liked it all, I didn't feel any serious romantic connection with any of them.

Obviously, there's nothing wrong with being an ethical slut. I was very honest and respectful with partners when sex and consent were involved. I did all my regular testing and took all my proper meds and had all my shots, like a good puppy.

I wondered if I might be aromantic. But I was also starting to feel that maybe I was having all these random hookups because, if I never took it beyond sex, I wouldn't be forced to feel my feelings about being different. When I would take a good look at my parents' relationship, I'd yearn to have something like it someday.

When I met Maura, she was wonderfully flirtatious with me. I decided that, in case we might hook up, I had to confide in her that I was bi. When Maura introduced me to

Ferran, though, I guess my gut feelings decided I couldn't get away with hiding-out in random hookups anymore. Alicia was the only one of my friends with whom I could bring myself to discuss my obsession with Ferran. I trusted her; I knew she could keep things confidential. And after all, she was majoring in Sexual Psychology.

When I talked with her about it, she asked me what it felt like for me when I was around him. At least that forced me to put it into words: "It's like I'm desperate to make time stop so I can make every moment I have with him last longer. Like everything else is in the background, and he's front and center with a glow around him. I think about him at the strangest moments — which are getting to be, like, all the time."

Alicia told me she was fairly certain I'd already fallen hard for the straight boy. I had to admit that whenever the man was near me, I got butterflies in my stomach. I was feeling very conflicted, but I resolved that I didn't want to add the weight of more secrets to the problem.

I was having contradictory feelings for a person who was now one of my closest friends. I couldn't stop focusing on him. On top of that, I was now confronted with that person nearly every day. Ferran had taken up residence in my brain, and it was wearing me down. My stress was threatening to cast a pall over the plan he and I had made for a fun day at the Boardwalk.

As wrong as it all felt to me at some moments, at other times just being with him felt absolutely right. I wanted to find peace again, and my feelings for him weren't going away. I decided that my mind and body were tired of fighting — fighting to keep at least the truth of my bisexuality away from Ferran.

I felt strongly that this was the day I was going to have to come out to him. I might be making a fruitless attempt to get closer to Ferran, but I knew I had to tell him the truth. At least if I told him, I would find out whether he would reject me or still want to be friends.

When we met-up the Boardwalk, hanging out with him felt as cozy and right as it always did. We rode the teacup, drove into each other in the bumper cars, got lightheaded from centrifugal force on the Cyclone, got splashed in the Logger's Revenge, and I stole longing glances at him while we rode the historic Looff Carousel. I don't know if I was just imagining it, but he also seemed to be looking at me more intently than usual.

We'd already been on the Giant Dipper roller-coaster twice and were heading back for a third when Ferran suggested we get funnel cakes. He said he wanted to sit and watch the ocean for a while, just to take a break. I sent him to find some seats, insisting on going to buy the tasty junk food for us. In the meantime, I was hoping I could manifest some bravery to tell him about me being bi.

When I arrived with the funnel cakes, Ferran had a panicked look on his face. "What's wrong?"

"Oh, nothing. I was just getting in my head about whether the team is as prepared as we should be for our next game."

"You're a passionate kind of guy."

Ferran looked at the funnel cakes and changed the subject: "Man, my mouth is watering. "Those look decadent."

"Yes! And they are! Also probably deadly, and I will enjoy every last second of indulging."

Ferran agreed: "That's the spirit."

As we began to pull at our funnel cakes, I screwed-up the courage to announce that I wanted to talk to him about something important.

Ferran

When he told me he wanted to talk to me about something important, I immediately wondered if this would be Matt's coming out conversation with me. Instead of being happy at that prospect, my anxiety started churning. Thoughts flooded my mind — of the numerous reasons Matt would reject me if I said anything about my feelings; of the fact that thoughts of him were always flooding my mind.

I remembered stories I had heard about straight jocks on the down-low, just using queer guys as an extra port in a storm to get themselves off. What if Matt thought I only wanted to use him as my sexual backup plan? That idea terrified me; I was sure he'd leave me behind if he imagined that I wanted him as just some kind of side-piece.

Or maybe he'd end our friendship because he really didn't like me like that, and I'd made it uncomfortable. Or maybe he'd end our friendship because I don't know how to actually *do* sex between two male-bodied persons. Or maybe he would leave because…

He broke into my panic spiral: "I've been wanting to tell you something for a while now."

I tried to force myself to stabilize. "Oh? What's that? 'Cause you know you can tell me anything."

"I hope so, because this is rough for me to do, Ferr. We've spent so much time getting to know each other and I haven't found a way to tell you this before. I was wondering if you'd just find out from the grapevine, but that doesn't seem to have happened. And with everything I have to do, I haven't exactly been super-social outside of you and our friend group."

For as long as I could remember, I identified as a straight guy. Why was I feeling such panic now? Probably because my self-perception and my efforts at image-making were churned out by society's expectations. I knew I was trying to create an impenetrable fortress around who I really was, because of all the taunting when I was a kid, and because my parents were so oblivious.

Meeting Matt changed everything, and the fortress was crumbling. With him, it never felt to me like the blossoming of an ordinary friendship. I was increasingly aware that I had an undeniable attraction to him, and it defied the boundaries I thought were set in stone. And here I was, panicky that it would all vanish.

Matt soldiered on: "It's just that … our friendship has been super important to me. … And I've been afraid that what I have to tell you will change things for the worse. So, it was tough to do, but I made a decision to take the reins and stop just playing along."

For me, that sentence struck a chord of distress, and sent me into silent rumination.

Has been.

He said, "has been," past tense.

He's gonna come out to me as bi. Then he'll tell me he's tired of doing all the extra work of having to deal with a clueless straight jock, and that he just wants to go back to his old life of easy hook-ups with whomever, and no strings.

I tried to insulate myself — to make my words a shield: "Just … whatever you tell me, Matty, don't make any assumptions about me or how I'll treat you. … Don't forget that being friends means I care about you."

Matteo

On the surface, I thought Ferran's words sounded kind, but I was left asking myself why such kind words could also sound like a warning. Maybe this was Ferran's way of saying he wasn't interested, and wanted to keep me at arm's length.

I pulled myself out of the mental speculation, and decided to take the risk.

"Ferr, I'm bi. … I know I should have told you right away so you could walk away if you wanted to, but I wanted your friendship so bad."

"You don't want it now?"

"What do you mean? *Yes,* I want your friendship now. I just didn't want you to think I was coming on to you sexually, or that I was trying to lie to you about anything. I definitely think our friendship is more important than my sexual orientation. Obviously, I've been more interested in hanging out with you than in getting laid with anybody — of *any* gender."

Ferran looked stung. Did I just wreck everything? All he responded with was, "Oh."

"So, are you all right with me being bisexual? Are we okay?'

Ferran looked dazed, and that scared me. He took a few seconds, and then he spoke.

"We are okay, Matty. Your bisexuality is just a part of who you are. It isn't a thing you decide to do to make a point or something. It just is. So, I hope it won't make anything weird between us. Let's just keep being "Ferr and Matty,' okay?"

I wondered what he meant about not making anything weird between us. But it seemed like it was traveling a dangerous road to ask questions about it. I settled on thanking him for being so open. "I'm relieved and really glad that you're being accepting. I didn't know how you'd react."

"I'm sorry if I seem out-of-it," Ferran answered, running his hand down his face. "Probably that second roller-coaster ride."

"Thank you for riding it a second time with me. I really love that roller coaster. And I'm really glad my queerness didn't make you run away from our friendship."

"I'm far more worried about climate change and our prospects for work in the future than I am about your bisexuality, Matty."

I didn't buy that. Ferran was staring at me as if he was a trapped animal. I could see that he didn't know which way to turn. He attempted a verbal parry. Maybe he was embarrassed to tell me how he really felt about it, and putting up a smokescreen was his first step towards distancing himself.

I started to feel desperate, so I scrambled to make a suggestion that might hold Ferran's attention. "I had an idea," I announced.

"What's that?"

"I think it would be cool if we both applied for student internships at the campus farm. We would each need to get a faculty member from Environmental Studies to sponsor us, and then apply at the internship office. It pays a stipend. They need more interns for the rest of this quarter and for next."

Ferran

Maybe Matt's emphasis on *friendship* shouldn't have stung me, but it did. I was facing the possibility that it meant I had no chance to be intimate with him, even if I told him I hoped to try. I was just getting used to the idea of wanting him, so I was sure I didn't like the possibility that it would be totally off the table.

But then he jumped right into the idea of us working together at the farm, and my spiraling thoughts and feelings began to calm. How did that happen? This man could lead me to stir up my anxiety in one moment, and in the next to find peace with him that I'd never felt before.

My head was making an analysis that gave me some reassurance:

This means he still wants to hang out with me for real. He even wants to do the nitty-gritty dirty work on the farm with me! He doesn't think I'm some stalker, some straight jock asshole.

And the farm! That's so us.

I felt relief surround me like a warm bath. It reanimated me, and I had an answer for him: "That is a freaking amazing idea! I was considering trying to pick up some work-study for about ten hours a week, but working on the farm would be so much better. It's a lot to learn, but I like what we'd be doing. TI hope for a green future, and that's actually something we can do to build it."

"Right? I am so glad you're down with this idea. It'll be great; you'll see. We'll be making a difference, Ferr. We do need to build it."

"I am definitely down for it."

"I was thinking. People lionize Greta Thunberg for her climate activism. But they do that, and then forget about her. If our so-called leaders had actually paid attention to her at the 2019 Climate Action Conference, we'd be well on our way to making a full agro-ecology transition. Instead, we're well on our way to baking the planet."

I loved it when Matt was lit up like this. To be honest, though, I also couldn't remember Thunberg's speech. So, I decided to de-stress in one of the ways I loved to: by giving Matt some room to expound.

"Remind me what she said at the summit?"

10
HARVEST

"I feel like I enjoy being able to tell
important stories that people can relate to
or that the world needs to know.
I think there's something really beautiful
about the art that we create as a society,
and it's great to be a part of that."
— *Joe Locke*

"Those who contemplate the beauty of the Earth
find reserves of strength
that will endure as long as life lasts.
There is something infinitely healing
in the repeated refrains of nature—
the assurance that dawn comes after night,
and spring after winter."
— *Rachel Carson*

[Playlist reference: Sufjan Stevens — A Running Start]

Ferran

The sun began its descent on a radiant autumn evening, and Matt and I were working at the UCSC organic farm. We had arranged to be working side-by-side in a field that day. The air was crisp as sunset was approaching, and the soil under our hands felt alive with possibility.

It was only ten days since our experience together at the Boardwalk. After Matt came out to me, my very strong — and maybe romantic — feelings toward him kept blooming, but his talk about friendship meant those feelings were also gnawing at me. I kept ruminating over my litany of worries, which led me to wonder if I'd ever muster the courage to talk with Matt about how I felt.

Sometimes I was angry at myself for wanting him so much. It wasn't just that he was so pretty — so *very* pretty. He also trusted me enough to reveal parts of himself that he shared with me but didn't seem to share with other people. I understood who he was much better now, and it felt like our connection was intimate. I wanted it to get even more intimate.

I worried that if I told Matt I was into him, he might think I was just a straight jock who wanted to use him. I was still afraid to say anything that might make me lose his friendship. Of course, I was assiduous in avoiding the topic of sexuality any time we were together, and Matt didn't bring it up either. Despite that, our friendship seemed to be growing stronger with every passing day.

When I arrived at UCSC at the end of summer, I was a guy who had never allowed himself to think about romance or sex with anybody but a smart, sexy woman. Then I met this smart, sexy man who rocked my world and had me in a tailspin. Now here I was at the farm, digging in the dirt with one of my closest friends — and pining over him.

Matt took a deep breath and wiped his brow. "Whew!" he sighed. "It's been a busy day, but I love being out here working. There really is something special about being this close to nature. It makes me feel alive."

I nodded yes and answered: "Completely agree. I know I'm gonna sound like such a hippie, but this Earth is full of wonders, and I feel like this farm connects us to them"

"Oh! He waxes poetic!" Matt teased.

His snark made me laugh. "Maybe," I said. "Or maybe doing this, I'm finally feeling some hope for the Earth. Like, maybe She's trusting that we can make a difference and keep us all from full-on climate catastrophe."

"Growing our own food and promoting sustainability?" Matt asked.

"Yeah, and fighting for social justice — the way *you* do."

Matt's face went bright pink as he looked down and dug deeper into the soil to add more mulch. "Hey now," he said, "you are being truly eloquent, my friend. But you're giving me very high praise."

How did this beautiful ginger wunderkind not understand how amazing he was? I told him: "You deserve it, Matty."

"It does make me think," Matt answered, giving me the impression he was trying to change the subject. "I became a Politics major because I was always passionate about political activism and organizing. But out here, actually getting our hands dirty on the land while we learn and work? Knowing we'll see the literal fruits of our labor? That's on a whole different level."

All right, what he said was *intense,* and I was pondering it. All of a sudden, the thought that he was *my* beautiful ginger wunderkind rushed through my mind. But there wasn't a chance he'd ever be mine if I kept being a coward about telling him how I felt. I hoped what I said next would help to find an opening.

"It's funny how life brings people together," I told him, as I amended the soil with more mulch. "I thought I'd come to UCSC to play soccer and study the classics. I didn't ever think I'd find myself working on an organic university farm — let alone enjoying it. I guess I'm not surprised that my parents were oblivious to how much I've always loved working in my grandfather's garden. They asked me why I would want to work on this farm — like this with my hands — when I could be focusing everything to get on a pro soccer team."

"If that's their dream for you, I guess it's an understandable question."

"Yeah, but what if my dream isn't all about that?"

"Then show them how you can be different from their image and thrive?"

"I want to do that, Matty." I was thinking I was going to have to do exactly that, in a bunch of different ways. "Look at this farm and look at us: *this* is life. If you think about it in political science terms, life is the first right listed in our Constitution, even before liberty or the pursuit of happiness."

Matt's face turned serious, even as he dug in the ground. "That's true, but maybe your parents don't understand what yours means," he answered me. "And people fight over what it means in the Constitution all the time."

"I don't think anybody back then thought it meant protecting zygotes instead of actual breathing humans. But with that fight going on, and with all the threats from climate change, soccer isn't going to matter when millions might be starving. That's one of the things that really moves me."

Matt's eyes grew wide. He took a deep breath and said, "You never cease to fascinate me."

"And my parents don't seem to care about what moves me at all."

"When you say that, I feel sad for you. So, what else really moves you?

"Well … it's thanks to you that we're having this experience together. That matters."

I could hear Matt swallow, and I hoped my talk about my parents wasn't getting him upset. He didn't answer me for maybe thirty seconds, but as anxious as I was feeling it might as well have been an hour. At last, he spoke: "I feel like the most important thing about doing this kind of work is that it helps increase our capacity to give loving-care — for everything."

My heart pounded like a timpani drum. My breath caught, and in my mind, I begged him.

Please.

Please give me your loving care when I tell you how I feel about you.

I came up with an answer: "I totally get that. Like maybe if we open up our minds, being loving to each other also grows more ecological sanity,"

Matt cleared his throat, and his cheeks turned pink. "Yeah, that," he said. "Maybe …maybe when we learn how permaculture works, and when we're digging in the dirt to grow sustainable food, the connection gives us more empathy. These days, the world is full of fractured communication and performative cruelty. It seems like the whole idea of caring for each other is fading away. We need to grow more empathy and love."

That idea might apply to my own life, too. "I think I understand that equation," I answered, grabbing more digging tools. "First, we treat ourselves and the other forms of life with empathy, and then we learn enough about them to provide that care and attention when and where it's needed, and then we understand that we have to do the same for the environment we all live in. Right?"

"Right. I also think that doing the whole process for the sake of love is what helps open our minds in the first place," Matt ventured, "and then the love has a chance to be exponential, so it helps us work for each other's well-being."

"I think that's what I'm finding out. ..."

"Ferr ... I feel like that's more and more true for me every day."

"Me, too, Matty. ... And ... I feel like being around you teaches me a lot."

"Yeah?"

"Yeah. It just makes everything better, really. I'd honestly rather hang out with you than with anybody else. I'm glad we became friends."

Matt looked up into my eyes and I felt like I could fall into his. "Friends," he said. "Right ... We're ... good friends." Then he turned away from me, looking down at the ground.

Matt's crestfallen description flipped some kind of switch inside me. I felt a rush, and I could swear I heard something like a whisper, telling me to strike the iron while it was hot. It felt like some power I'd been missing was with me now, pushing me to finally tell Matt that I wanted him as much more than just a friend.

"And here we are," I pressed. "And maybe it sounds all earnest and sentimental and stuff, but we get to learn about all this together. You and me — we're doing what makes the difference that we can make, and where we can make it."

Matt replied, still focused on the dirt. "It feels really personal when you put it that way, Ferr. I like it."

"I think it *is* personal, Matty. You're the person who got me here. I feel like it's our way to send good vibes out to the world."

I noticed Matt shiver, and he seemed to choke on something for a few seconds. I was worried and about to get up, but right then he said, "I think you're exactly right about that."

I relaxed some. "Not much makes me have faith, but this does."

Matt looked up again and he was smiling, but he didn't look at me directly because he caught sight of the beginning of a magnificent sunset.

He stood up facing the direction of the ocean, and looked out toward it. "That's so good," he said, quietly. My gaze lingered on him, and my heart slammed against my chest with nervous excitement. He was quiet for a moment looking at the glorious sunset, but then he commented: "All this farm work we're doing started because we were taking our walks and talking about our majors and what we believed in, Ferr. And then we started to talk about this farm. You're the one who gave me the inspiration, so I'm glad we're here working alongside each other like this. It was a leap of faith."

My heart fluttered. The idea of taking a leap of faith resonated with me to my inner core. I sensed a kind of gravitational pull in the air between us. The sun was dipping lower on the horizon, casting a warm glow of burnished orange across the farm. Whatever ideas you may have about astrology or astrophysics, I felt as if the stars were aligning. I got to my feet and softly said: "It's the best."

Matt seemed in awe of the sunset, and pointed to a stroke of color against the sky: "Look over there."

I looked out with wonder: "Truly awesome." I was riding a heady mix of fear and joy. I realized that it was a combined emotional package I'd only ever felt with Matt. If the whole galaxy had been linking itself together for my next move, it still might not have delivered me a more flawless opportunity, so I walked over to stand much closer to him. I saw the glow surrounding his body as he watched the sunset, and I gazed out over his shoulder at the vibrant colors.

Matt took a deep breath and sighed. "I don't want to take my eyes off of it. I wouldn't want to be anywhere else right now."

"There is definitely a lot here that's beautiful," I purred.

A long moment of silence hung between us. I stepped slightly forward, into Matt's personal space. I could feel the powerful, undeniable connection to him that was coursing through me. I noticed the heat coming off of his body, and I could smell the delicious scent of sandalwood mixed with his sweat from our efforts. He gently turned and looked up at me, and our eyes locked.

I leaned in very slowly, tentatively. Then Matt followed. Our eyes closed just before our lips touched. I joined my mouth to his and parted my lips just enough to swipe a lick of his. He returned my exploration with his own tongue and then we gently explored each other's mouths. He tasted of the herbal spearmint we'd been chewing while we worked the soil. A wave of warmth surged through my body from head to toe, and it sent my insides fluttering.

Matteo

He kissed me! That man I've been longing for since I first laid eyes on him *actually kissed me*. It shook me and flooded me with warmth all at the same time. Yeah, it's a cliché, but that was the *effing best* kiss I've ever had — as glorious as the sunset that was glowing around us.

I didn't want to stop devouring his delicious mouth and teasing tongue, but I had to catch my breath. I drew away from his lips just slightly and looked up at his beautiful face, where I noticed that his chocolate brown eyes had darkened with passion. That sent a jolt of energy right to my bulge. I wasn't sure I could even remember my own name.

Ferran slowly pulled away, but we remained standing very close to each other. Our faces were still just inches apart. He smelled of cedar and soil and clean sweat and mint. He looked down at my lips and said: "Wow."

Words? Was I supposed to be able to use words after my world just shifted on its axis? The best I could do for the moment was to say it back: "Wow."

"Yeah," he answered.

The realization of what just happened washed over me. It seemed my straight boy wasn't so straight, and he wanted to kiss *me!* I leaned in again and looked up at him. Putting my hand on the back of his neck, I pulled him to me and kissed him again — a kiss he returned with fervor. This time, he ended the kiss to catch his breath. We looked into each other's eyes, and I moved my hand back to my side.

Then suddenly, he scrunched his eyes closed tightly, and slowly shook his head back and forth. I got frightened. I looked up into that handsome face, and cautiously asked him, "Are you sorry we kissed?"

Ferran opened his eyes and then clasped his arms around my body and reassured me. "No, I'm not, Matty," he rasped before clearing his throat. "Not at all. But I never expected this before I met you."

Had he only had these feelings with me? He must have been so scared. I smiled at him and nodded.

"I've been really struggling with my feelings," Ferran told me quietly. "I think for years I told myself that any time I looked at a guy and felt a pang of attraction or an urge to be near him, it was just some kind of aesthetic appreciation. I think I hid any of those thought or feelings I ever had under the great chemistry of sex and friendship that I had with April. I never thought I'd find myself falling for another man. I didn't really know what to do with it, but it was like some weird synchronicity. This feels absolutely right with you."

Falling for me? I thought I must be dreaming. And if I was, I didn't want to ever wake up. I managed a roughly whispered reply: "I feel absolutely right with you, too."

He looked at me with lidded bedroom eyes that made my bulge vibrate again. "I have to admit I'm scared," he confessed. "I don't know if I want other people to know yet, but I'm grateful for kissing you. I'm grateful for you."

By this point, I was actually quivering. I was definitely glad that he took the initiative, and that my soccer jock was not some down-low user, trying to get an easy outlet. I had to tell him how much I wanted him. "I can't explain it, Ferr, but when I'm around you, everything feels different. I was afraid of losing our friendship if I said anything. We don't need to make a big deal to other people about this. But you make *me* feel alive in ways I've never experienced before."

"I feel that way, too."

The air crackled with tension and our eyes locked again. Slowly, we moved closer to each other and our lips met in another tender, gentle, magnetic kiss. I had my hand on his chest and I could feel his heart literally beating in sync with mine. It felt as though time stood still, but eventually we broke the kiss, staying close to each other.

I tried to speak, but I wound up stammering. "Um … uhm … uhhhh … would you … Ugh!" I was frustrated at my total lack of cool. Not cute.

"It's okay, Matty. Whatever it is, just ask me slowly."

I wanted this so much, so I made an effort to get it all out: "Could you maybe come to mine?"

I don't think I'd ever seen Ferran smile such a wide, joyous smile.

"I'm not trying to put the moves on you, I promise," I insisted. "You could stay tonight out at the house with me and sleep on the futon. I've just wanted you so much for all this time. I … I want you to be near me … so I can have more of your kisses."

Ferran laughed lightly and looked hungrily at my lips.

"Well, yeah," he answered. "I'm fairly certain we'll need a lot more practice."

11

CANOODLE

"Soul meets soul on lovers' lips."
— *Percy Bysshe Shelley*

"The kiss is a lovely trick
designed by nature to stop speech
when words have become superfluous."
— *Ingrid Bergman*

*[Playlist reference: Calvin Harris, Dua Lipa
(Oliver Heldens Mix)— One Kiss]*

Ferran

As the dusk and chill settled in over the farm, Matt and I packed up the equipment we had been using to amend the soil. After the kisses we'd just shared together, I was at a loss for words. It seemed that Matt was, as well.

After about twenty minutes with us only talking about work, everything was properly stored away. The whole time, I was thinking about why I had waited so long to kiss my beautiful ginger man. I had finally gotten past my fears enough to take the chance, and tasting his mouth was one of the most ecstatic experiences I've ever had. I felt like our energies were dancing together.

I caught myself thinking of him as *my* man, but I was hardly sending him the message that it was what I wanted. One of the first things that slipped out of my mouth after we kissed was wrapped in my stupid, lingering fear. I told him I wasn't sure I wanted anyone to know about us. Even though he told me he understood, maybe he felt that I was ashamed of my feelings for him.

I didn't want to do that to either of us, and it didn't take long for me to know in my bones that I wasn't going to. My mind wouldn't stop sending me a message, loud and clear: *One kiss was all it took, and now you know this feeing with him is right. You wasted too much time already. Don't let fear keep you from being together.*

I spent so much of my life building an image to meet other people's notions of who I should be. Now I was at a decisive moment: be who I wanted to be and embrace the life in front of me, or keep living an illusion to make others accept me. I had taken a leap of faith, and Matt didn't push me away. As sure as the sunset, I decided I was going to try not to push him away, either. I wanted our friends to know, and I wanted my parents to see me for me. If people couldn't handle me being with a guy — especially a guy as wonderful as Matt — I was ready to fight to stand my ground.

As we closed up the tool shed, I put my hand on Matt's shoulder and looked down into his happy face — maybe the most beautiful face I'd ever seen. I smiled back at him and shared my feelings. "Matty, you remember before, when I said I didn't want other people to know?"

"Yeah, Ferr, I remember."

"Please *don't* remember it. Please forget I said it. I was being a stupid coward."

"Ferr, you really don't have to tell the world right now."

"I think I could tell *our* world. I wanted you so much, and I wasted too much time being afraid. I just need to get past the habit of worrying about how people will react. And I already gave Alex a heads-up. You gotta know I had to sort out my feelings about you with him, right?"

Matt nodded a yes at me and asked, "What did he do?"

"He basically tried to give me a pep talk to tell you."

Matt huffed a laugh and raised his eyebrow. "Well, a big thank you to Alex, then," he quipped.

"I also may have talked to Alicia and told her I was getting super anxious about my feelings for you."

Matt laughed quietly. "You *may* have, eh?"

"Okay, I did. And I swore her to secrecy."

"Oh, I see."

"And Stu and Emily already think we're having a bromance."

"I think it's a *little* more than a bromance, Ferr."

I seized his lips with mine and kissed him until we were both breathless again. "It is."

"Ferran Bosch," he said with a sigh. "Do you know you're making my heart jump?"

His emerald eyes were glowing in the bright moonlight, and I smiled at him, overjoyed. "Good," I answered. "Then it matches mine."

Our plan when we started our work shift was that Matt would drive me back to my dorm. After we gathered our things, we hopped into Matt's Niro EV and drove up to Stevenson. But we'd made a new plan: I was going to put together an overnight bag from my room so I could go out to Live Oak and stay overnight with Matt.

I raced up the stairs and went in to my dorm room. I was quickly putting together an overnight bag while I told Stu I was going to be staying at Matt's house on Pleasure Point for the night. When I said that, Stu looked back at me and raised his eyebrow. Then with a sly grin, he said, "Say hi to your little boyfriend for me, buddy."

I would have told him more, but I didn't want to keep Matt waiting. So, I rolled my eyes and hopped down the stairs to head to the parking circle. When I got back to Matt's car, I opened the door, flipped back the seat, and threw my bag in the back. Returning the seat to upright, I sat down on the passenger side and pulled the door closed. I looked over at Matt, and saw the gleaming smile on his face.

I was about to take yet another leap of faith with him. I spoke excitedly: "I didn't spew out the news to Stu, but when I told him I was staying over at yours tonight, he told me to say hi for him to my 'little boyfriend'.

"Stu is … Wait, what? … 'Boyfriend'?"

"Yeah," I answered, feeling a little nervous.

"Well, that's……"

I interrupted: "Matty? So … um … Do you *wanna* be boyfriends?"

Matt's jaw dropped slightly. He looked at me with what I thought was disbelief. After a few beats, he asked, "You're kidding, right?"

I looked back at him trying to be as serious as possible. "No, I'm not kidding. Not after what we just did today. Please hear me out, Matty. For weeks and weeks, I've wanted you so much — just to be close to you all the time. Even before we went to the Boardwalk, I kept thinking about how much I wanted to kiss you. So, believe me, I am absolutely *not* kidding."

"Oh," Matt answered, looking ahead for a moment. I stayed quiet despite being anxious about what he'd say, to give him a chance to register what I'd just told him. He turned and looked at me with his eyes wide. "There were many times since we met that I wished you would ask me that question. And there were so many times I wanted to ask you that question, but I was too afraid you'd be grossed out and stop being my friend. So, I can barely believe I'm hearing this question from you now."

"Believe it," I answered.

Then his shining smile lit up his face. "Well, then *yes!*" he said, nearly shouting. *"*Yes, you big goof! I want us to be boyfriends."

I was so happy I thought my heart would explode. But I also had to tease him: "Oh, good. So … so, now you really *are* my 'little boyfriend.'"

Matt gave me some side-eye while he smilingly answered: "I don't know about that 'little' part."

"Come on," I said incredulously. "You're six inches shorter than me and you have at least 30 pounds less muscle than I do."

"We'll see." Matt chuckled.

"And also," I started to say, but the next words I had to tell him had so much emotion behind them, I choked up. When I could, I rasped them out: "... *You're beautiful. ... I think you're probably the most beautiful person I've ever seen.*" Matt blushed bright red and his eyes began to glisten with tears. And I confessed: "I have wanted to say that to you for *so* long."

A tear rolled down Matt's adorably freckled cheek. He seemed to be trying to speak, but the words kept getting caught. "I think you win most beautiful, Ferr. And now I'm sure I gonna have to tell Stu my 'thank you' in-person."

I reached out my fingers to wipe the wetness from his cheek. For a moment, all I could do was look at him in amazement. "This probably sounds weird, Matty, but when we were packing up after we kissed, I didn't like not touching you even for a few minutes."

My ginger *boyfriend* quietly huffed a happy laugh and told me: "You are a ginormous goof. And, may I ask you for something?"

"What would that be?"

"We're just starting out on this *boyfriend* journey, so could we make this exclusive between us — at least until we're sure that we're on solid ground? I would feel safer doing it that way."

I was beyond happy. "That is absolutely a 'yes' for me," I responded. I leaned back in my seat and looked over at Matt's hands on the steering wheel. I made a tentative request: "Would it be okay if I hold your hand?"

Matt's pinkish blush became a heated crimson. I was secretly amused by the stoplight combination of his green eyes, the amber in his ginger hair, and his red cheeks. "Oh, man, he sighed. "Yes, it would be okay if you hold my hand. Please do." I took Matt's right hand into my left hand and wondered if I looked as thoroughly contented as I felt.

"You are too good to be real," Matt said, shaking his head.

"This is long overdue. You make my spirit happy."

Apparently, Matt couldn't keep his jaw from dropping at that. He cleared his throat and said, "I have had a lot of fantasies and daydreams about this. I don't know how something this wonderful is actually happening."

I felt my heart swell in my chest again, as I gazed at him with a kind of reverent affection. "Come on, Matty. Let's get to your house. I need kisses."

Matt started the car, pulled out of the traffic circle, and began the drive. As we moved through town, as much as I wanted him to speed down Soquel Avenue toward Live Oak, I also wanted to get there in one piece. We had time to make up for.

Matteo

When we arrived at my house on Pleasure Point, we grabbed our stuff from the car and got inside as quickly as we could. I had permission to kiss Ferran now — to kiss my *boyfriend* — and I didn't want to waste another minute. I took Ferran's hand, and we ran up the stairs to my bedroom.

I reached for him, and he put his arms on my shoulders and pulled me close, looking down into my eyes. Our faces came closer still until our noses touched. I closed the distance between us and reached my lips up to his mouth to plant a soft kiss. It was such a perfect kiss, soft but eager. Ferran kissed me back with zeal, bringing a jolt of energy to me that had me gasping.

When we both parted to gulp some air, Ferran said, "We need to figure out how to breathe when we do that."

"Air?" I teased. "Who needs air? It's overrated anyway."

In the large room I leased in the house, I had both a queen-sized bed and a double futon. Ferran leaned into the crook of my neck and deeply inhaled. I pulled him down onto the futon with me, growling: "I know you said you like my sandalwood."

"I do. Truth is, it makes me feel sexy and cuddly all at once."

"And here I thought it was the allure of me being a beach bum."

"Maybe I can't resist that you ride the wild waves."

"You're a master of double-entendres, aren't you."

"It's from studying the classics."

"Okay, then," I grinned. "Now that I can say this, Mr. Classical Studies major, I just wanna tell you that you always manage to smell *classic.*"

"Classic, eh? Is that your way of saying I reek of old books?"

I nudged him. "Not at all. It's more like … like a heady man-mix of woodsy sweetness and your own musk. Smells like sophistication and mystery. I think it might be your secret weapon 'cause it drives me crazy. Makes me want to unravel you, layer by layer."

Ferran purred in my ear: "That's … kind of a turn on, the way you described it." He ran his fingers through my long ginger hair, and I felt as if I was in free fall.

"Ferr," I said, murmuring his name. "That feels so good. You have no idea what you're doing to me."

"I know what you do to me, so I think I'm getting a clue."

"A clue that you can't resist *me?*"

"Matty," he said with a short, breathy laugh, "I've definitely been having that idea."

"Good boy," I growled.

Ferran

I repeated that phrase silently in my mind.

Good boy.

Matt's words sent a vibration through my mind and body that I couldn't explain. In all my experience up until that moment, no one had ever told me I was a good boy — especially in a romantic or sexual context. I felt my heart welling up like a fresh spring.

To my delight, Matt kissed me again. At first, we brushed our lips against each other's gently, delicately. But soon a passion overtook me that surprised me. I pressed my mouth to Matt's and intently pried his lips apart with my probing tongue. I realized it then: this beautiful surfer boy was *mine*. I held him tightly, wanting to claim every part of him, starting with his delicious mouth.

"You taste like home," I whispered. That felt electric, and we devoured each other, wrestling tongue to tongue, teasingly biting lips, exploring each other's mouths.

"You taste like a feast," Matt said, as he grazed my neck with his teeth and lips.

I was so turned on, I thought I might burst my button-fly jeans. I stared into Matt's eyes with all the longing for him I'd been suppressing. As if we actually needed any more heat, we were grinding our bodies together. We kissed, and cuddled, and nuzzled, and kissed some more.

For hours.

Conveniently, Matt had a jug of water and a glass on his nightstand. It was keeping us hydrated through both our marathon make out session and the occasional trip to the restroom to send all that water back.

The night seemed to speed by. At about eleven o'clock, Matt was resting his head on my chest when he looked up at me. "Are you hungry?" he asked me.

"Super hungry."

"I can make us some quick *Penne alla Puttanesca.* You good with that?"

"Sounds delicious," I hummed. My *boyfriend* was going to cook for me and I loved how that felt. It also made me eager to find a way I could show him how much I loved to cook. "You're going to just whip that up?"

"Thank my mom. She's the Italian-American who taught me how to cook. Cooking is not my dad's thing. But there's a lot of good stuff I've got from his Danish heritage."

My make-out charged mind sent me images of Matt's bulge. "I'll bet," I said, grinning and lowering my eyes to his pelvis. His breath hitched and he wagged his finger at me. Smiling, he got up and summoned me to follow him downstairs.

He worked in the kitchen with quick mastery, producing a savory delight as I watched him. I was definitely falling for him. "What if we could do this all the time?" I asked him, "You and me, hanging in the kitchen together and making dinner."

"We could, Ferr," he answered, as he grabbed a bottle of crushed red pepper flakes from the cupboard. "I mean, why not? You do have a dining hall contract, but whenever we both have the time and space, and you want to do it, we could make it happen." He paused. "It would be like a date."

There had been times when the idea of a date with Matt made me panic. Now I was yearning to date him and romance him, and hold him in my arms. "It wouldn't just be *like* a date, it would be a real date. I want to have dates with you, Matty. I wish I had a kitchen so you could come to mine sometimes."

"Do you like to cook?"

"I love to cook."

"Then you can cook for me here! I'd love it."

"So would I. But our walks, and soccer practice time, and maybe getting to watch you surf, and movie nights, and just hanging out together — I like the idea of all of those being our dates, too. Dates don't have to be elaborate, right?"

"No, they don't," he said, looking at me with dreamy eyes. "I mean, it can be nice sometimes if they are. But since that first night playing video games in your dorm room, what I've loved most is when we just spend time together — whatever it is. I like being with you and talking with you."

That made me smile. "I like laughing with you."

"I like that, too. And now that I know that kissing can be on the menu, I'm gonna be hungry for a *lot* of that."

"I'm hungry for that, too. I'm also hungry for this pasta!"

"Me too. I'm ravenous."

We practically inhaled the *penne.* Having such great food filling my stomach helped sate some of my appetite. But, definitely not all of it. I helped Matt clean up, and then we went back upstairs.

Back in the bedroom, Matt wrapped his arms around me and looked up into my eyes. "I wasn't sure if we could ever get to this place together," he said, with a shaky voice.

I had been keeping my longing for him a secret from Matt since we met, but this day was clearly the day to show my hand. I admitted the truth to him: "I wasn't sure I knew what was happening, but I couldn't stay away from you. I worried that if I said or did something to give that away, I could lose your friendship. Then a little while back I was talking with Alicia about my confusion, and it hit me that I wanted *all* of you. I mean, *all of you,* Matty. That made me realize I could also lose you if I didn't take the risk and let you know how I felt."

"Ferr …"

"And then I got terrified that if I told you and you didn't feel the same, I might lose you anyway."

Matt's eyes had grown limpid and he tilted his head to the side, looking at me. "Why are we like this?"

"I don't know," I answered, "But I'm *so* happy we kissed today. You've relieved all of that worry for me. And I am very happy we'll be sleeping here together in the same room."

Matteo

"Sleeping is the operative term, mister," I reminded him.

"Bossy," he said, smiling.

"Maybe kinda."

"I think I might like that."

My chest fluttered. "This is brand new for you," I explained. "I'm not gonna take any chances of spooking you about sex before you're ready. I was scared too, and I don't want to have won you just to lose you."

His lips parted and his eyes turned fiery, as he assured me: "I can't see that happening, Matty." He knew the right things to say. My heart pounded and I immediately went rock hard.

But I was resolved: "I want you to feel sure. We can take it slow. I don't want to rush things and have you feeling like you don't know what you're doing, or like you're not meeting some laundry list of what guys do with each other."

He rolled his eyes and smiled at me. "All right, surfer boy, touché. It does feel a little out of my league. But even so, I still know this thing with you and me is right. And since you don't want tonight to be just a hookup, I'm thinking maybe now you're drawn to something out of your league, too?"

He knew. Somehow, he found out my reputation as a player, and he knew that was not what I wanted to do with him at all. He met my eyes, and a moment of understanding passed between us. "You're not a way for me to avoid my feelings, Ferr. You let me feel them all."

He placed a tender kiss on my forehead, and moved a lock of my hair behind my ear. Then Ferran smiled and his eyes smoldered. "Also, I have to say I'm not completely sexually lost," he confessed. "There are just … well … drives I can follow."

He was making me so hard it hurt. Then his lower lip quivered a little. "And I've been … kind of … doing research," he said. "Reading and watching stuff online, not in person, I mean!"

He was either going to be the death of me or give me a hands-free orgasm. "But Ferr," I pleaded, "let's go slow and easy, okay? Not low and sleazy?"

He laughed. "Okay, okay, handsome."

I took a deep breath and tried to will the blood to move to other places in my body. "Research is good, though," I told him with a grin. "We can talk about a lot of the options. The stuff you might think about from a 'straight bro' perspective probably doesn't cover all the bases of what we can do."

"Oh, really? Okay, then, I'm all ears!"

"Let's save that 'til later. Come on, we still have to get ready for bed. Busy day tomorrow," I said, briskly. I got Ferran a towel and a bathrobe since none of my pajamas were going to fit his tall, handsome frame. He'd brought a toothbrush in his bag, but I pointed Ferran to where all the soaps and toiletries were in the bathroom. Then each of us separately went through our nightly showering and other rituals. It felt so comfortable to be together getting ready for bed. Of course I ended my shower with a minute of cold spray. I was determined I wasn't going let things move along too fast sexually.

Ferran went back to my bedroom. After taking a detour to the hall closet, I gathered an extra blanket and extra pillows and pillow cases to use on what would be his bed for the night. Carrying them in, I asked Ferran to help me put the pillow cases on the pillows and to put the blanket over the futon.

He looked at me with those molten chocolate-brown eyes, and I wanted to melt into him. But I made it clear to him again that I was resolute that we shouldn't rush into sex. "Sleeping in separate beds for the night is probably the best idea," I told him, wishing desperately that it wasn't so.

"All right," Ferran agreed, surrendering. He chuckled quietly and said: "It'll be like we're having a slumber party — just the two of us."

We did agree that we would unequivocally need more cuddling time on the futon before calling it a night. We both crawled onto the futon to get cozy. Ferran had just comfortably laid back when I sat up and looked down into his eyes.

I spoke what I hoped would be a word of power: "I will never stop needing more of your kisses."

12

HEAT

"Sex is nice and pleasure is good for you."
— *Dossie Easton*

[Playlist reference: Ariana Grande — Into You]

Ekkheya

For seven weeks since the fateful soccer game, the advance of autumn had been rolling along at UCSC.

It was seven weeks since Maura had introduced Ferran to Matt, upending the world for both of them.

Seven weeks since Ferran's roommate Stu, and Stu's girlfriend Emily, had met Matt — asking Ferran to tell them more about who "the pretty boy" was, and later teasing Matt and Ferran that the two young men should ditch school for a modeling career.

It was six weeks since Matt started meeting up with Ferran nearly every day to work out at the OPERS main facility and grab lunch, and nearly every evening to study or take a walk or play some video game or watch a movie or cheer-on Ferran at a soccer game or hang out with their friends together.

It was five and a half weeks since they dubbed each other "Ferr and Matty" and a couple days later that they had their talk about what motivated them to choose their majors.

It was four weeks since Matt and Ferran went to the Boardwalk together and bonded over funnel cakes and rickety roller coasters. The same four weeks since Matt came out as bisexual to Ferran.

It was ten days since a sunset at the campus organic farm had led Matt and Ferran to their first kiss and an outpouring of feelings. Which also led to a marathon make-out session back at Matt's house that left them struggling to get to sleep in their separate beds. They'd suffered a mutual frustration of arousal, of course, mixed with the fear of moving further and faster.

It was four days since Matt had to bury himself in two major papers for his classes, which kept him from spending any time with Ferran.

It was three days with no "Ferr and Matty" hang-outs or lunches or working out together at the gym, leaving them in a wake of aching need after that first fateful kiss and a night of canoodling.

It wasn't that they'd refrained from burning up each other's phones with texts. They were becoming experts at finding synonyms for the word "amazing" to describe each other and what they were feeling. They also frequently used that word to describe the quality of their kisses. They'd also discussed how intensely they both wanted to do more than kiss.

For the first time, Ferran shared his worries about having sex with another man, wondering whether he'd be good — or even okay — at it. Matt shared about his worries that Ferran might not like it, or might feel too rushed or too scared. They texted about their sexual health and whether they both had all their shots, or any chronic problems. They discussed using condoms or PrEP or both. Matt let Ferran know he was on PrEP and had been for two years. Ferran was not yet on it, and asked Matt how to find out more information about it. They also texted to each other to hash out how they would talk about and process all this stuff.

They even discussed the fact that although they'd showered at the same time at the gym before, they carefully avoided looking at each other's bodies for fear of vividly displaying their attraction to each other to any other guys in the gym.

It was the night of the following day. Eight o'clock, to be precise. Matt and Ferran had finally been able to arrange to meet at the gym for a workout. Changing in the locker room to go out on the floor without becoming erector sets had been especially difficult.

During their workout, they determined that not kissing each other on the gym floor must be some kind of fresh Hell. At one point, Ferran had to go to the water fountain and splash his face with cold water — not because he was overheated, but because he hoped it would help him mentally shut down the growing bulge in his compression shorts. When he returned to Matt, he said: "I don't think I have any questions left. I'm definitely bisexual."

Matt finished his last set first and excused himself to go to the men's locker room to down a protein shake, and brush his teeth before hitting the showers.

The gym was going to close at 10:00 pm that night and the locker room was empty except for Matt. The gym floor was empty as well except for Ferran, Matt, and the two women who were working the front desk. The really gorgeous woman at the desk was Sakura, a Japanese-American trans woman whom Matt had met the previous year, and whom he had helped elect to the Student Union Assembly. And to be clear, with whom he'd had a hot spontaneous one-off hookup on an art workbench at Porter College.

Matt went into the shower area just as Ferran entered the locker room. As Ferran was brushing his teeth, Matt tried to adjust the temperature in the shower stream. Since the only other person there was Ferran, Matt didn't feel he would need to distract himself when Ferran came into the showers.

As he stood there naked in the empty shower room, the hot spray easing his overworked shoulders, Matt began to feel himself lengthen. Frankly, his endowment was difficult to hide during even the most innocent downtime. For someone who was built like a "short king" gymnast, Matt made up for a lack of height with considerable length and girth.

Ferran sauntered into the shower room naked, with his towel slung over his shoulder and his shower kit in his hand. He hung up the towel, put down the kit, and adjusted his shower spray. That was when he turned around to fully take in the view — for the first time without avoidance — of a naked Matt.

Ferran

Matt was standing under the spray of warm water with his longish ginger hair wet and slicked back from his chiseled face. He looked like a living marble statue of the classical *beautiful boy*. The kind of artwork you might find in the center of a glorious fountain.

I couldn't help it. I gasped, and it echoed off the shower walls. Then my jaw quite literally gaped, and I could feel my eyes growing wide.

Matt stared at me, asking: "What?"

"You really are a work of art."

"You are sort of embarrassing me," Matt scoffed, though grinning broadly.

"You're beautiful. And I am *definitely* into you."

Matt looked me over, scanning my own nude, wet body. "Ferr," he rasped, "you look *so* good and … you *are* so good. And so handsome. And tall. And hot. And *ripped.*" Then he focused his gaze on my basket. It was his first chance to ogle it while it was uncovered. "And … *all that!*"

"Are you kidding me?"

"Just … wow!"

"'Wow' for *me?*" I asked, pointing at him. Have you seen that *pendulum* you own?" I mean, I could tell the other night when we were making out that there was a lot. But, Matty… *Jesus.*"

He giggled and I could tell he was blushing, even in the shower. "Someone once called it a longsword."

"It *is* a longsword!" I responded with wonder. "And you're like … *completely hairless* from the neck down … like a Roman statue!"

Matt nodded a yes. "There's not a lot of hair there to start with. But I used to be on the swim team in high school and I always got waxed, so I've just done it ever since. Makes getting into a wet suit to surf a lot easier."

Surprising myself in my lust, I blurted out: "Damn! *Yes*, please," I gulped as my face grew hot.

Apparently, Matt was finding it difficult to keep himself from getting rock-hard. I wasn't having much more success at that effort myself. I turned to the wall to shut off my shower, and made an announcement: "I'm coming over there."

"What if someone comes in?"

"There's nobody here except the fine ladies at the front."

Approaching Matt, I placed my hands on his muscled shoulders. I moved him forward to be farther out of the warm shower spray. "We should probably turn this off for a bit," I suggested, turning the knob on the wall. Then I pulled him close and leaned down, and I kissed him deeply.

He sank into my kiss passionately and let me explore his mouth. Standing there naked and pressed up against each other, I felt ravenous. Matt moaned softly as his hardness intensified and his wet nipples rose and strained.

I let my hands wander down his back, and farther. I grabbed his body and kissed him more intensely. Matt looked deeply into my eyes when our kiss broke. He ran his fingers along the trail of dark hair on my torso that led downward.

"I'm glad none of our parents decided that cutting us would be a good idea," Matt observed.

"Me, too!"

Matt continued to wrap his fingers in the curls of hair between the cuts of my Apollo's Belt. He looked at my equipment and growled: "*So* hot"

"Please touch it," I begged him with a breathy urgency.

He looked up at me and asked, "Are you sure?"

"O gods, yes. *Please.*"

Matt did as he was told, and I moaned a deep, "*Ohhhhhhhhh.*"

I wanted him so much. I was so thirsty for him, and I needed to taste him. I kissed Matt tenderly again and then just dropped to my knees to satisfy my hunger.

Matteo

To say I felt glorious fireworks between us is an understatement. He'd obviously learned some mad skills from his research, and I marveled at Ferran's eagerness. He swallowed every gushing drop I fed him, and my legs went weak. When he stood again, his lips swollen and slightly creamy, I pulled him against me and reached up for his mouth with mine. We kissed deeply and I could taste myself on him, which started me growing all over again.

I began to reach down for Ferran's hardness, but he held onto my hand and said, "Just let me hold you; that's what I need right now." Trying to bask in the afterglow in the gym shower room was a bit difficult, though. So, when we caught our breath, we took our showers and began to dry off with our towels.

"I swear I have never done that before," Ferran offered.

"You're a natural," I told him honestly. "And thank you; no question I'll be returning the favor."

Ferran pretended a gentlemanly reply: "It was my unanticipated and wonderful pleasure, my good man."

I breathed a quiet laugh. "Now you have new and impressive sporting talents."

"Tomorrow," Ferran announced, "I think I'm going to go over to the clinic and meet with the PrEP navigator."

"Oh!" I exclaimed in surprise. "Well, you decided *that* question fast."

"Your point?"

"Ha! You know, if you want me so soon, the clinic will tell you how to use the pills at a 2-1-1 dosage before you start it daily. But if you're *eager* even before your blood tests come back, we can go get some condoms."

I was standing in front of Ferran, and he gazed at me with lust-filled eyes. "I'm eager! Okay?" he announced. "I have to do some — what should I call it? How about, '*Cave digging.*' ... I mean, I *need* to. Like, as soon as humanly possible."

"Oh, really?"

"Really." Ferran confirmed, giving me a huge smile.

"You're just going to assume I'll play catcher for you," I teased.

His pupils were blown and his grin looked fiery. "I really, really hope so."

I couldn't keep from blushing. "I want that so much it's driving me to distraction."

Ferran peered into my eyes. "I want *you* so much."

13

SAMHAIN
(SAU'—IN)

"As I have said, I am aware that,
whatever the circumstances,
there will always be speculation about me."
— *Cristiano Ronaldo, 31 October 2008*

"Back for a minute. I'm bi.

Congrats for forcing an 18-year-old to out himself.

I think some of you missed the point of the show. Bye."

— Kit Connor, 31 October 2022,
on a now-decimated social media site
of which he was formerly a member

"You owe nothing to anyone.

I am so proud of you, my friend. *[double heart emoji]*"

— Joe Locke, 31 October 2022,
on the same now-decimated social media site
of which he was formerly a member

"I truly don't understand

how people can watch 'Heartstopper'

and then gleefully spend their time

speculating about sexualities

and judging based on stereotypes.

I hope all those people are embarrassed as FUCK.

Kit, you are amazing."

— Alice Oseman, 31 October 2022, giving the last fuck,
on the same now-decimated social media site

"If you are not personally free to be yourself
in that most important of all human activities
— the expression of love —
then life itself loses its meaning."
— *Harvey Milk, 31 October, 1977*

[Songlist reference: Billy Idol — Eyes Without A Face]

Ekkheya

The vigil of the day reserved to honor those who have passed into the spirit world was set to arrive in two weeks, but the campus was already swept by a brisk wind.

Among witchy folks in the Northern Hemisphere, that festival was usually called by its ancient, pre-Christian Celtic name: Samhain (in Irish and Scots Gaelic, or in Manx Gaelic, *Sauin*). The Church had dubbed the day "All Hallows Eve," or Hallowe'en. Legend stated that it was a day when unruly, troublesome spirits would try to play tricks and create difficulties for those still in the mortal world. Sometimes — especially in the rare moments he doom-scrolled the news — Ferran thought every day felt like Samhain.

I don't consider myself troublesome, as *lares* go. But I definitely know some troublesome human spirits. And Matt, as a Politics major, was acutely aware that history is replete with troublesome spirits. Now, here is an important piece of history that you need to know.

Much earlier, I told you that Jason Praeger would cast more of his shadows into this story. He was the UC Berkeley frat bro who had punched the student delegate from UCSC and filed the false police report those many years before. Praeger eventually moved to the Central Valley and became the father of Kyle Praeger.

Three years older than Ferran, Kyle had gone out of his way in early grade school in Los Banos to bully and torment Ferran for being what he called a "nerd." Teachers at school ignored it. Ferran's parents had remained oblivious to the bullying, since they were preoccupied with their jobs.

Struggling in this crucible from an early age, Ferran had decided he needed to create an external image that would keep the bullies away. He worked hard to become a muscled soccer jock, buried himself in studying the classics as an escape, and found a gorgeous girlfriend who had endured the same traumas and had settled on a similar strategy. It allowed both of them to push away any thoughts about interests or appearances — or even attractions — that might prompt others to see them as anything other than a pinnacle of sporty, conformist, heteronormative popularity.

When he got to UCSC, Ferran was disheartened to discover that not only was Kyle Praeger a student at Stevenson College and a member of the College Republicans, but also that he lived in the same dorm. Although older than Ferran, Kyle had never seemed to mature emotionally — he hadn't amounted to much on the social hygiene scale. Also, while Ferran had grown more athletic, muscular, and popular, Kyle could still easily double as a five-foot-ten desiccated green bean acting in a grammar school play.

Lately, some of Ferran's classmates were telling him that Kyle was making a lot of insinuations about Matt and Ferran being secret lovers. They told him Kyle was saying that the supposed star of the soccer team was "just a pathetic faggot." Given his prior experience with Kyle, Ferran felt it was time to nip that in the bud.

***

Ferran

In the early afternoon of Samhain, Kyle was walking quickly down the dorm hallway and swiped by me. He didn't even hesitate to keep on walking. So, I called out to the human green bean: "Hey, Kyle, I'd like to talk to you for a sec."

Kyle turned and flashed a smug grin. "Oh, look who wants to have a chat," he said, taking a few tentative steps back down the hall. "What's on your mind, Ferran Bosch?"

I wasn't sure what motivated Kyle, but it was easy enough to see that he was still a bully. As he had in grammar school, he was again trying to stir up hatred toward me. But he was doing it here, and now I was no longer afraid. I felt as though this was my turf, and I was determined to draw a line against Kyle's troublemaking.

"Look Kyle, I've been hearing the rumors that are going around about me and Matteo Poulsen. It didn't take much to find people who let me know they'd heard the stuff from you. I just wanted to clear the air."

Kyle laughed. "Clear the air? So, are the rumors true? Finally, gonna admit you're queer and you have a needy little boyfriend? Is that what you wanted to say?"

"No, Kyle, that's not what I wanted to say," I answered in a measured tone. "Matt is not 'needy." And there's nothing wrong with how close I am with him, even if he happens to be a guy."

"Yeah sure," Kyle mocked. "Keep telling yourself that."

I was trying to keep calm, but I raised my voice a bit as I snapped back. "What are you trying to do Kyle? Are you a walking wannabe Rupert Murdoch tabloid? I'm not going to just stand-by while you and other people spread gossip about us. I care about Matt, and I'm not hiding that he's more than just my friend."

"Oh, what a surprise! The 'straight' soccer star all of a sudden has some 'deep emotional connection' with his pretty little boyfriend."

"At least you admit he's pretty," I countered.

"That's not what I meant!" Kyle grumbled, his hands balling up into fists.

"What is your problem, man?"

"It's *your* problem," Kyle barked. "You two flaunt your lifestyle in people's faces. You're like prancing GQ commie fags."

Wrong thing to say, Kyle. I took a deep breath and responded with contained intensity: "You do not get to ever use that word and still keep all that expensive orthodontic work, Kyle."

Kyle's eyebrows raised, but he tried to paste a smile on his pallid face. "Yeah? Threats?"

I replied to him in a steely voice. "Listen to me carefully, Kyle. A *threat* is something that someone might not actually carry out. This is not a threat. And for the record, you need all the cosmetic help you can get. It's just that your envy is not a beauty product."

Kyle's jaw went slack for a few seconds, but then he sneered and said: "You're Spanish, right *maricón?*"

Maybe Kyle was trying to see how many derogatory names he could remember for queer folk. But I decided to calmly *correct* this bigot: "Catalan," I answered. "Besides, I think you've got your list of insults all twisted. *I'm* the one who's a socialist who wishes I could walk the red carpet, wearing Valentino. My boyfriend is the one who's the tree-hugger who'd rather be surfing on a nude beach than hanging out at Fashion Week."

Kyle grimaced. "Prissy-ass homos," he spit out.

The anger gripped me at that point. I changed my entire demeanor to an aggressive stance. I glowered at him.

"You know what, Kyle? You can piss right off. No matter how much you want to mock me, I'm not going to hide who I am or how I feel about somebody. I'm bi. Matt means a lot to me, and I am proud of being with him. I've probably got 100 pounds on you, and it's all muscle. So, if you need me to use force to get the message across, I will."

"Oh, *wow,* Ferran!" Kyle said sarcastically, sneering at me again. "You're making such a big, bold statement there. I'm sure everyone will be thrilled to know that you're dating that little longhaired fuckboy, Matteo."

"And maybe they will be, when I tell *everyone* that Matt is more than just my friend! Your blowhard ass will get shut down, and any of their nonsense will get shut down. Jesus, dude! This is supposed to be 'Santa Cruz: home of hippies and open-mindedness.' You're an embarrassment to our reputation. You're just a bigot and a bully. Your constant judgmentalism and speculation aren't going to define me anymore, you pathetic excuse for a scarecrow."

Kyle scoffed. "Good luck with that, man. I know you used to date that chick who was a hot cheerleader at Los Banos High School. Now you've sunk so far down that you're chasing after some pretty little boy. I don't think anyone is gonna be surprised when I make sure they know the rumors are true."

"First of all, Kyle, Matteo Poulsen is not a 'little boy.' He's a year older than me. And you just *wish* you were that pretty and sported a bulge like his — because it *isn't* little."

Kyle recoiled. "Dude! *TMI!!!*"

"It doesn't matter if you and your douchey senior buddies like us or not, Kyle. What matters is that I'm being true to myself and standing up for the person who means everything to me. I'm not gonna let your ignorance bring me down."

Kyle paused, his eyes flaring. But then he caught a glimpse of the Resident Assistant down the hall. "Fine, Ferran," he huffed. "Do whatever the fuck you want. It's your life."

I made a sharp declaration: "Yeah, it is *my* life. And from now on you can keep yourself out of it, or you will definitely suffer the consequences."

Then I turned on my heel and stormed out of the main door of the dorm. I walked up to the Stevenson Coffeehouse, trying to calm down. When I walked into the coffeehouse and made my way to the counter, I was still feeling anxious.

I took a cleansing breath and greeted the barista. "Hi, Adah. May I get my usual house coffee, please? Not the French Roast; the Columbia Dark. Thanks." She nodded without speaking and went to get my coffee.

Adah was the Program and Advocacy Intern at the Lionel Cantú Queer Center on campus. She and Matt had met there and worked together on several activist causes. Matt was always happy about her knack for being a human billboard. She often dressed as a walking bumper sticker, and on this day, she was wearing a progress pride pin on a "Consent is Sexy" t-shirt.

I met Adah through her work at the coffee shop, but I knew we also shared the same French language tutor. While she was getting my coffee, she seemed to be getting very angry. "Here you go, soccer star," she said, her voice dripping with sarcasm.

I thought her behavior was odd, but I passed some cash across the counter. She squinted her eyes and seemed to become even more annoyed. "Look… you…," she spit out. Then she surprised me even more by spewing a venomous tirade at me: "You've obviously gone and got yourself what you *think* is some kind of side-piece, and I hope he hasn't fallen for it. How dare you just make use of all the benefits queer people have won, while you screw around from your closet like a typical jock and wind up hurting people?! And if you thought you were succeeding at hiding anything from anybody, you're not!"

I was stunned, but I tried to remain calm. I furrowed my brow and asked her directly, "What the hell are you talking about, Adah?"

She continued her accusations: "Don't play dumb, Ferran. You might be some straight, popular soccer stud, but people can tell what you and other jock asshats like you do to thirsty queer boys. You keep playing googly eyes with Matteo — and you're queer-baiting him, and it's gross. But, at least now I hear some people are calling you gay, so I hope that stings."

This day was shaping up to be crap. I felt as if I was having another one of my nightmares. Another trap like this, and that one more bad dream could bring a fall. I was getting even angrier at Adah than I'd been at Kyle, because I felt that her very public verbal attack was a betrayal from one of my own.

"If that's what *people* think," I snapped at her with a sharp edge, "then maybe it's time for me to set the record straight."

"Oh, *please.* If you're not being another DL game player and it's real, then why haven't you already admitted that you're gay with all the time you two spend glued to each other? I didn't expect Matt to be some clingy twink who'd be a straight guy's free use hole, but I think it's obvious that you're using him. And maybe you aren't even conscious of it, but that's even more pathetic."

As much as I wanted to knock her teeth down her throat, I was not going to be *that* guy. I leaned in and spoke loudly and sharply, so everyone around us could hear: "*Bisexual,* Adah! I'm bisexual. And you know what, you mouthy jerk? Matteo Poulsen *is* my boyfriend — my *real-life boyfriend.* I'm not hiding anything, even though it's all pretty new to me. And I don't care what you or anyone else thinks about where and how fast I'm supposed to meet your doctrinaire Red Guard grading scale."

Adah got a look of shock that transformed her face from surliness to surprise. My rebuttal left several of the people within earshot slack-jawed as well. The usual din of the coffee shop was replaced with silence.

In what seemed to be disbelief, Adah timidly asked: "Wait, seriously? You guys really are actually boyfriends?!"

I answered angrily: "Yeah."

"Woah…," she said, as her whole body seemed to slouch. She took a breath and tried to backpedal: "That's not what I heard at all. My bad; I fucked up. I'm sorry, I didn't mean to offend you, Ferran. I just thought…"

"You thought *what,* Adah?" I hissed. "That I was a straight piece of garbage who was intentionally queer-baiting a sweet bimbo of a guy, just to set him up to hurt him and laugh at him? That's seriously how you think? You learned nothing from our last French class, apparently, because look how *gross* your mind is. *Les yeux sans visage!"*

The blood rushed out of Adah's face. She got my reference because she saw the film in class when I did. Besides, her French was good enough to translate regardless. But I didn't stop my upbraiding. "I know I didn't meet your or other people's stereotypical expectations for a jock, but I don't owe you or the rest of the gossips a damned thing."

Adah appeared still to be reeling, and she softened her stance even more. "I didn't realize, Ferran. And I'm really sorry, I got this one wrong. It's just that it really *is* surprising. I actually did think you were setting him up to make him and other queer guys look foolish. I'm sorry … I'm sorry for being an ass."

"Great; glad to hear it," I snapped at her. "*I'll* be okay, but I wish I didn't have to deal with this toxic garbage from people who are *supposed* to have my back. Or from the bigots here, even at what's supposed to be such a freakin' progressive school. You all are buying into all that 'conservatives versus liberals' bullshit when the reality is that it's the ruling class against the rest of us!"

Adah tried to make an excuse: "We never know what the bigots are gonna try next, so we have to be vigilant."

"That's *hyper*vigilance, Adah. You're taking a trauma reaction and pretending it's activism. You and your gossiping friends act like Tankies," I told her bitterly. "Why can't you just accept that I could fall for Matt even though some people never expected I'd fall for a guy? What makes you think you're allowed to appoint yourselves as my judges? Do you *want* people to run out of hope?"

Adah finally seemed contrite. "I'm sorry, man. I really am. Sometimes, I guess I can get politically correct at the expense of human decency."

I wasn't in the mood to be patient. "That's for sure," I snarled as I started walking out of the coffeehouse. "You'd just better not be giving Matt any of this crap!" As the conversations in the coffeehouse began again, I exited the door and it slowly closed behind me.

Standing outside on the patio, I took a deep breath. Then, I reached for my phone and texted Matt.

Matty are you home?
Is it all right if I come over?
I just really need to see you right now
See I used caps
If I can get a quick Zipcar and drive out there
it'll only take me maybe 20 minutes

Ferr of course you can come over
Are you okay?

Yeah I am I think
I just need to be with you right now
[red heart emoji]

Okay I'll be right here waiting for you
[three double heart emojis]

14

TRUVEL

"Home is not just a physical address,
it's an emotion, a state of mind, a feeling, a person."
— *Henry Susanti*

*[Playlist reference: Noah Cyrus and Vance Joy
—Everybody Needs Someone]*

Ferran

As the wind picked up and the daylight faded, I was able to easily procure a Zipcar near the bookstore. After exiting the campus, I made my way across town headed to Live Oak. To try to help clear my head, I turned on the radio to listen to the campus public station on the way. "This is *Pack Rat's Rat Trap* on KZSC at UCSC: 88.1 FM, the far left on your radio dial," the announcer intoned.

"Oh sure," I muttered. "How comforting."

When I arrived at Matt's place on Pleasure Point, I found some rare parking on East Cliff Drive. Walking up to Matt's house, I knocked on the door — and for the first time I noticed it was painted an odd shade of pink. Matt opened the door and looked at me adoringly. He sucked in some air and then softly said, "Hi."

"Hi."

"Your texts looked like you were upset. Come on in and tell me what's going on."

"Yeah," I answered, taking a deep breath. "Could we go upstairs to your room?"

"Of course. Sure," Matt said, ushering me in. We climbed up the stairs to Matt's room, which had a big picture window overlooking the Monterey Bay. The room was suffused with an extra bright light due to the afternoon sun coming through the windows.

I was really nervous as we both sat down on Matt's bed.

I needed to ground myself, so I turned and looked in Matt's eyes. They seemed to have transformed into translucent pools of aching want. Those sparkling green eyes had me feeling aroused and calmed at the same time.

"Could you hold my hand?" I asked him, shaking a little. Matt reached out and clasped my hand. Then, gently and passionately, he kissed me. I felt the sparks fly between us all over again. We breathed each other's air and I felt home. After a while, we broke our kiss.

"Ferr," Matt pleaded, "please tell me what happened."

"Okay. So, ummmm … today I did something pretty bold — or maybe crazy. But I had to do it."

"What did you have to do?"

"I'm sure you've heard about the gossip going around about us."

"Sure," Matt noted, rolling his eyes.

"I found out it was that asshat Kyle Praeger who was one of the worst ones talking shit about us. He literally ran into me in the dorm hallway today and I stopped him. I just wanted to try to get him to mind his own business."

"Kyle Praeger? The really tall senior in your dorm? The one with his pack of senior buddies who act like slimy frat rodents?"

"That would be the one, yeah. He used to bully me when I was a little kid in grade school."

"O gods, Ferr. I had no idea."

"How would you know?" I admitted, "I haven't told you about all that stuff yet.

"And Kyle still seems like he's *the worst*. This is just crap — it's totally gross. Are you okay?"

"I'm gonna be okay, but I needed to shut him down."

"Ferr … he's a pathetic person. Gossiping about who is and isn't queer is just one of the things pathetic people do. I try to have pity on people like him."

"There's more, Matty."

"Okay."

"I went over to the coffeehouse to get some coffee, and Adah started accusing me of queer-baiting you."

"*What?!*" Matt said incredulously. "My Adah? The Adah I've done activist stuff with? The black Jewish lesbian in my Community Studies class?"

"Your Adah, huh? Well, I didn't know she was in your Community Studies class, but yeah. That's the one."

"What the hell? I don't get that at all. That's freakin' weird."

"Weird as fuck, Matty. … So, what I did was … I finally came out to both of them. I said I was sick of their bullying and I told them that you're my boyfriend. And I told them I'm proud of that."

Matteo

Ferran's news had me feeling both surprised and concerned. At that moment, I was also very curious about the decision Ferran made about how to deal with it. "Ferr," I asked him, "what made you do something like that?"

"I had to do it, Matty. I don't want to live like I'm hiding anymore."

I grabbed Ferran into a hug and then kissed him. "You're a strong and wonderful man," I told him.

"I really want to like who I am. And I told Praeger the absolute truth: I'm proud that you're my boyfriend. All that gossip was tormenting me, and I figured this was the best way to shut them all down."

"Ferr, listen: I understand your frustration. Are you sure you were ready to make that move, though? It's going to get around."

"No, Matty. The truth is that I'm fairly sure I *wasn't* ready yet for the whole world to know. I'm still 18, and I made it to adulthood playing a character that April

and I invented for other people: 'Ferran Bosch, the brainy
soccer star with the hot cheerleader girlfriend.' But I'm sick
and tired of worrying about what people will think. I've got
to embrace who I really am — and who I am wants to be
with you. I want to be able to embrace you out in the open,
and I can't do that if I hide."

There was no question I was going to learn a lot
from this man. Ferran leaned-in and gently kissed me,
sending tingles all the way down to my toes. He was my
guy, and he was fantastic.

"You know I've got your back," I assured him.
"And no matter what, I care about you. That doesn't mean
I'm not worrying about the repercussions this might have
with your parents, though."

"I know, and that's actually one of the main reasons
I'm here."

"What do you mean?"

"I mean I have to ask you about this. Would you be
okay with it — with me — if I drove out to my parents'
house this Friday night so I can come out to them at our
Saturday brunch?"

Okay, I was not expecting that, but I was starting to
think that expecting the unexpected might be our new
normal. Pardon the pun, but I wanted to approach this
gingerly. "Are you sure you're not rushing this?"

"I don't know. … I want them to know about who I
really am, and about us. … I want them to know you're
really important in my life."

Those words hit me deep. Man, was I ever happy to
feel *that* impact. "I'm important in your life?"

"Of course you are."

And there he was, making my heart sing again. And
I felt every bit the same about him. "You're important in
mine, too."

"Am I?'

"Oh … Ferr … Yes, you are. You are very important in my life."

I was trying to be protective of Ferran with what I said to him next. "I think it's amazing that you have the courage to come out to your parents right now. But you're not running down any kind of coming out clock, Ferr. I was forced to tell my parents that I was bi. I was getting harassed and bullied, and they needed to know why I quit my Pier 39 job. But when I did that, a few of my friends here had already known for a year that I was bi. Right now, this is all brand new for you."

"I hear you; I do. But, let me just put this out there for you to know. Sure, it's new, but I've never been more convinced of the way I feel about someone, romantic or otherwise. If I'm being honest, I was totally captivated by you from the first moment I laid eyes on you."

"That must have felt weird for you?"

"I mean, yeah. You know, I thought I was *straight?* Hetero? Normal, whatever the hell that means? But, I kinda knew I was in trouble with that whole idea when we started talking and I kept looking at your eyes. Every time I did, Matty, all I wanted was for you to be *mine.* "

I felt a shiver run up my spine — a good shiver.

Ferran explained: "It scared the hell out of me. I didn't even know what *your own* sexual orientation was." He laughed quietly. "Although… I did catch you checking out my arms."

O my gods. I covered my eyes with both of my hands, feeling caught. "Man, you saw that? I'm so embarrassing."

"There's nothing embarrassing about it. And I was smitten. I guess that's why I totally pursued you — so I could be closer to you. So, I could become friends with you."

Hearing how Ferran felt when we met, I got a shock of recognition about my own feelings. Which made me grunt in exasperation.

"What's wrong?" Ferran asked.

"I just feel stupid."

"Why?"

"Okay, let me tell you something. When I was watching that game with Maura, I was looking at you and thinking I had never seen anybody or anything so remarkable in all my life. The way you were moving showed so much grace and skill, it was like fine art in motion. Also, I have to admit: I was stunned by how incredibly handsome you were. Then Maura grabbed my hand and started walking toward you after the last goal, and I could barely keep it together. I didn't know how I was even gonna be able to speak to you. That's why I stuck out my hand like I was some third-rate city council candidate."

Ferran laughed at that, and I joined him. "I was a mess, and trying everything I could think of to look chill for you," I confessed. "I thought I was a fool because I was getting obsessed with a straight jock."

"I suppose I'm not so straight," Ferran said, cupping my chin with his hand, "because I want you so, so much. That's why I *need* to tell my parents, Matty. I have to let them know the full reality of who their son is."

"I understand, but you've got nothing you have to prove to me, You've already got me."

"Honestly, I want to get to the point that I can show you off to them."

My face heated in his hand, and I'm sure I was blushing again. He was good at getting me to do that. "I don't think I'm all that," I told him. "*You're* the one who is a serious athlete and just also just happens to excel at speaking ancient languages and modern Catalan and French. You're a fucking studly genius."

So, then it was Ferran's turn to blush, taking his hand from my chin and running it through his lush brown hair. "Matty, stop," he laughed, as a cherry hue mixed into his delicious caramel-colored skin. Being this close to him also bathed me in his scent, which was my kryptonite. Strong, seductive notes of cedar and hazelnuts, creamy tonka bean, mint and a sweet musk that made me want to bury my face under his massive arms and then move down to treat the spicy fragrance of his intact member as though it were aromatherapy.

A quote ran through my mind.

The spice must flow.

Maybe not exactly what Frank Herbert meant in *Dune,* but I felt it was apt.

Being close to him was like being hypnotized — by his virile build and aromatic aura as much as by his enthralling intellect. I ran my hand through the soft fur of his chest, and breathed him in. More of Frank Herbert's words reverberated in my mind:

He who controls the spice controls the universe.

But even as I was caught up in my reveling, Ferran was lavishing me with praise: "You're awesome. And in every way, you are the most exquisitely talented person — and the prettiest — that I have ever seen in my life."

Cloying? Treacly? Maybe. But it was heartfelt, even if we were drowning in sentimentality about each other. But I knew I'd have to tease Ferran about it anyway: "Listen to you. My boyfriend sounds like a Valentine's Day card."

"My handsome cynic."

I rubbed noses with him and kissed him. "Okay, if you say you're ready then I support you. Just please, keep in mind that it could be a lot for your parents to process."

"I know it won't be easy, Matty. But I want to come out to them — I want to be honest with my parents about this. They have to see me for me"

"No matter how it goes, I promise you I'll be right here by your side."

Ferran released a heavy breath. "Thank you," he choked out. "I'm glad to hear you say that — you have no idea."

"I believe in you."

"There's no doubt I'm excited and nervous. But I really believe this is the right step for me now. And I want to ask you something else now, Matty, but I don't want to seem too needy."

"Please," I encouraged him, "don't ever be afraid of asking me for reassurance. I'm sure I'm going to need to ask you."

"I can give you that. Now, ummm … could I stay here with you tonight?"

"Uhhh … *of course!* I would love to have you next to me tonight."

This man — what I was feeling for him wasn't mere infatuation. He was being everything I needed him to be. I just hoped I could hold on to him. We went downstairs and made some dinner and ate. Then we went back to my room and got into bed — the same bed this time — and cuddled, watching *Avengers Endgame* until I drifted off to sleep.

Ferran

Seeing Matt adorably curled up next to me, I was feeling as though my heart might burst out of my chest. I'd never felt this way about anybody before, I was sure of that. As I watched him fall asleep, I hoped against hope I'd never lose him. I grabbed the remote and turned off the video. Then I spooned next to him, holding him close to me until I drifted off to sleep as well.

The next morning, as the sun began to rise over Santa Cruz, Matt's surfing urge motivated him to leave our warm bed — and my arms — to join the Dawn Patrol on the heavy waves. The Monterey Bay's picturesque coastline constituted Matt's back yard at Pleasure Point.

Half-awake, I told him in a hoarse morning voice: "I want to watch you."

"If you want, Ferr," he told me as he leaned down and nibbled my earlobe, "you can watch me from the window here. Or you can pull together a few blankets to wrap yourself in, and grab a cup of tea from the kitchen, and then come watch me from the rocks. But, look: if you just want to stay in bed and keep warm, it's okay," Matt said, rubbing noses with me and kissing me on the forehead.

I didn't want to compare them, but it struck me that April never nuzzled and caressed me the way Matt did. He and I seemed to be naturally drawn to do that for each other. I opened my eyes more, though they were stuck with morning graininess. "I want to see you do your thing, Matty. Believe me, watching you ride the waves is gonna wake me up."

Matt looked out at the Bay's waves and seemed motivated, rocking back and forth on his heels and toes. "I've been waiting for these cherry waves all week. It was my prediction that this morning would give me the perfect conditions to fly on them."

He hummed with building excitement and left to leap down the stairs. "On my way out," he called, winking back at me. I stood and looked out from the narrow side window, where I could see that Matt had made his way to the outdoor shower stall and was retrieving his trusted gear.

Matteo

I opened the door to the outdoor shower, and a sense of familiarity washed over me. My three wetsuits were neatly organized, hanging in a row. I chose my black and green favorite, because the colors helped me feel adventurous.

I carefully slipped into the snug embrace of my wetsuit as I mused about how wonderful it felt to spend all night in Ferran's arms. I pulled the zipper tight and adjusted the neoprene around my shoulders, and that exhilarating mix of anticipation and adrenaline started to flow through me. This was my dance with nature, and I was all too ready to get out there and do it.

Equipped with my surfboard — I affectionately named it, "Maverick" — I trotted down the stairs from the house. Echoes of the sound of my feel on the steps helped to pump up my excitement. The air was crisp and salty, and the sound of crashing waves filled the atmosphere as I was approaching the rocks below.

I looked up and saw that Ferran had emerged from the house wrapped in several quilts and holding a tumbler of hot tea. How was he looking so hot while swaddled in blankets? He made his way down the stairs and perched on a rock not far from where I was going to hop into the water.

I hoisted my surfboard onto my shoulder with a precision I'd practiced countless times at surf spots in southern and northern California since I was a kid. I might have been showing off for Ferran — just a little. It was a familiar and joyful task, and I was getting a rush as I felt the weight challenge my muscles.

The Monterey Bay stretched out ahead, offering me a seemingly endless expanse of majestic waves waiting for me to join them. I tried to keep my footsteps sturdy against the jagged edges as I navigated the rest of the wet rocks. Maybe I was a seasoned adventurer, but the sight in front of me was still humbling and awe-inspiring.

I scanned the horizon, analyzing the patterns and intricacies of the waves. These waves were prime; every roaring swell carried the promise of a thrilling ride — an opportunity to connect with the raw power of the ocean. Ferran was with me to see it and I was overjoyed about that, because I could share with him the kind of surfing moment I treasured. I feel that they're thrilling flights with nature that hold few rivals.

Launching myself into the water, the cool ocean hugged my body and greeted me with an invigorating rush. The connection was instant — I deeply cherished my symbiotic relationship with the sea. I was marveling at the beauty that surrounded me as I paddled through the breakers — the vastness of the ocean, the mystical allure of the Monterey Bay, and my cozily cocooned boyfriend.

Another surge of adrenaline coursed through my veins as I felt the perfect wave building behind me. I positioned myself on my surfboard, precariously balanced on the edge of adventure while my hearts pounding in my chest. I felt the wave grab hold of me and propel me forward with a force that just might have matched my passion for it.

Time always seems to lose meaning when I surrender to the power of the wave. The glide along its crest felt effortless as my body moved in unison with the ebb and flow of the water. The sound of crashing waves was a rhythm that guided my every movement. It was a symphony in my ears.

That fleeting but powerful union with the sea always left an indelible mark on my soul.

Ferran

I stood on the rocks as the salty spray enveloping me was awakening my senses. I felt the sheer greatness that was present in front of me. The entire experience was sharpening my sense of awe for Matt's beauty and power. He'd acquired years' worth of experience chasing the waves, and each deft movement he made was a testament to it.

Was this the kind of fervor Matt saw from me when he came to watch me play soccer? I knew I felt rapturous inside when I was playing my best, but I wondered if Matt was seeing that in me the way I was seeing it in him. Was that what he was telling me last night about how he felt when he first saw me?

He was riding a wave that was reaching its crescendo. Just at the perfect moment, he executed a graceful turn. His surfboard carved through the water with a finesse that only experience and talent could bring. Watching this beautiful man superbly dance on the waves, my heart soared along with the salty breeze. I knew I was experiencing an unforgettable moment — one I never before believed I could have in my life.

I savored a fleeting but powerful union with the sea that I was sure was leaving an indelible mark on my soul. I sensed I was feeling what Matt was feeling. I could see the look of pure exhilaration on his face as he rode the wave to its ultimate conclusion and let out a triumphant cry. I felt as though Matt and I were experiencing a climax together from the most intense lovemaking. In that moment, I was feeling it in every cell — I wanted my future to be with Matt.

A profound sense of peace that had always been elusive in my life washed over me. This was pure magick. And I felt ready to draw my parents into the honest depths of my life — whether they really wanted to be there or not.

15

PARENTS

"I just followed my parents' example
and advice on living,
which was to leave the world
a better place than you found it.
They were professional do-gooders."
—*Sir Ian McKellan*

[Playlist reference:
Troye Sivan (featuring Betty Who) — Heaven]

Ferran

As was often the case, the heat in Central Valley was a lot to take.

After I watched Matt surf, I called and surprised my parents, Isabel and Ignasi, by telling them I wanted to drive back home to join them for brunch on Saturday. Their house in Santa Nella — the house I grew up in — was about an hour and a half drive from UCSC.

I was grumbling to myself about the shortsightedness of the people who had worked so hard to throw roadblocks in the way of high-speed rail statewide and in the area. Same people who'd thwarted construction of solar-powered desalination plants and projects to mine lithium, salt, and other key minerals from the brine. Same people who were fighting using nuclear power as a bridge to a fully sustainable energy system. Same people who fought against building and maintaining high-density, income-indexed social housing. Stupid, selfish, myopic people — but I didn't want to get sidetracked in my anger at them. I drove to Santa Nella with a purpose.

I was there at my parents' kitchen table, sitting down for a Saturday brunch with them. When they told me they were happy to have such an attentive son, I think the irony was lost on them. As usual, they were less-than-attentive to me — too busy focused on themselves. Sure, they were happy that I was there in their house with them, but they couldn't be bothered to ask what was really happening to me — or about who I really was.

This was no different from when I was being bullied in grade school — that's when I'd first realized that they had checked-out on me. It was as if they were contented merely with their image of me — an image I'd largely crafted — and didn't want to chance finding out that there was anything more than their own perceptions of me. Same as it ever was.

My papa looked up from his smartphone news app in order to lean a bit in my mama's direction. "Isabel, they want me to be on-site for a big meeting in Morgan Hill on Monday so I won't be able to walk the dog that day."

"Oh … I have to teach on campus on Monday," my mama said, never looking up from the research journal she was reading, "so I guess we need to call a walker for my baby Adelina." My mama doted over the dog.

Hearing her name, Adelina scuffled to the kitchen and rested her head in my lap. "Mama, she's twelve years old," I chuckled. She was a good dog, and she definitely played favorites. I scratched her on her head and behind her ears and she looked up at me worshipfully. "Hey Adelina," I said, "how's my girl?" Then she settled down, and comfortably curled up at my feet.

Mama declared that Adelina would always be her baby, and papa confirmed that he would call their dog walker, Howard, after we finished eating.

I fidgeted in my nervousness. I was going to have to interrupt their self-focus if I was going to get any message through to them. I took the leap of faith and broached the subject I came to discuss: "Mama, Papa, I'd like to talk with you about something."

"Of course, Ferran," Papa muttered, not looking up from his smartphone. "Is everything all right?"

"I just need to tell you both about something important."

I was hesitating, and Adelina let out a small, prescient whine. "I…," I was trying to get the words out, but they were catching in my throat… I don't know how to say this exactly, but I've sort of had a wake-up call about some things, and I really want you to know."

Mama was still reading her research journal. Finally, papa put down his smartphone, with a confused look. "What is it, son? Tell us, whatever it is."

I took a deep breath and launched into my revelation.

"You know when you guys came to my soccer game last week? You two already met my roommate, Stu, when I moved to campus. And obviously you've known Alex since we were both in seventh grade — and he still loves you, by the way."

"Oh, that's nice," Mama answered, looking up from her research journal with a polite smile that seemed pasted-on.

"And then you got to meet Cam and Bakari from my team, and Maura and Jake and Alicia and Matteo?"

"Yes," Mama noted. "And all of them are so lovely. Your friend group at school is so respectful and they seem so kind."

"They *are* kind. And there are more of them, in fact. But the ones you met were really excited to meet you."

"But, oh," Mama interrupted, "that Matteo. He must be a lady killer, that boy! *Déu n'hi do!* He's a heartbreaker."

She didn't, did she? "Mama," I said, feeling slightly embarrassed. "He's 19 years old and he's maybe my best friend. You're acting like a cougar."

Mama grinned and winked at my smiling papa. "Your mother has a thing for sexy gingers," Papa informed me.

"O my gods," I muttered, rubbing my face.

"So that really enthusiastic girl — Maura? I think she has a crush on you," Papa interjected. I suppose I had to agree.

"I think you're right. And that's sort of what I wanted to talk to you about."

Papa was suddenly more interested. "Are you getting serious with her, son?"

"Were you wanting to bring her home to 'meet the parents'?" Mama asked excitedly.

"Ummmm, no," I mumbled, growing more anxious. "That's not exactly it. This is a difficult conversation for me, but I wanted to be honest with you."

Papa tried to reassure me: "You know we're always here for you."

"I didn't feel that way when I was younger," I answered sharply.

"We were trying our best to make sure you had everything materially and that you were comfortable," Mama snapped.

"Are you sure it wasn't so that *you* could have everything materially and be comfortable?"

Papa broke in: "Ferran, please stop. Now is not the time to have this argument again. We want to hear what you need to tell us."

I hoped that knowing what was happening to me and who I really was might be worth a little discomfort. But it didn't seem that way. Tears began to well up in my eyes.

"Okay, here goes...I've come to realize that I'm bisexual."

Both Mama and Papa sat silently, unreadable.

I pressed on. "I liked girls. You know I dated April all through junior high and high school. And I still like girls. But... I also figured out I like a boy, and he's really special to me. I wanted you to know about it."

Papa silently opened his hands and moved them as if to ask me to tell them more.

"We were friends," I explained. "And then … well … I really liked him. But I didn't know if he would like me back. I was afraid and I didn't want to ruin our friendship. I didn't know how I would find the courage to tell him. But then he took a chance, and he told me that he was bi. Actually, I was surprised and it took me a little while to process the news. But when I took a chance and let him know about my feelings, I found out he *did* like me back — as much as I liked him. And that made me really happy. And so, now we're actually boyfriends."

I stopped for a moment, trying to get my bearings. Then I told them: "It's Matteo Poulsen."

Papa took a deep breath and paused, processing the information.

Mama's brow furrowed. "Ferran, are you sure about this? This could be just some passing infatuation? I mean, back when I was a little girl I was infatuated with my best friend Catalina in Madrid."

"Mama, please! You know I was in a relationship for six years with April. She's an amazing young woman. And I'm sure you didn't miss that she was obviously a sexy cheerleader. You got us a room with a king-sized bed in San Francisco for gods' sakes. I'm not naïve, okay?"

"Okay…"

"Mama, listen, please. I'm feeling a fierce kind of happiness. And I know it's Matteo who makes me feel so happy. I'm not just having some temporary boy phase."

"Okay, okay," she said in a placating tone. I think she was trying to absorb what I told them.

"Matteo is an amazing person. And it was Maura who actually introduced us. Which is kind of ironic, since she was nursing crushes on both of us."

"Does she know?" Papa wondered.

"She guessed it on Thursday, and we confirmed it for her."

"Was she upset?" he asked.

"Ha! No, she told us she kinda knew already, even before *we* figured it out. Looks like our other friends did, too. She said it was a good thing they weren't taking bets. She told us that she was waiting for *us* to tell *her*. So, she seemed to roll with it. I mean, by the time we left she wanted us to be her wing men to find her a guy so we could double-date."

Mama's face was still sullen as she was digesting the news. "That's … interesting," she offered.

"Mama, I've never felt about anyone the way I feel about Matteo. He's smart, and brave, and kind. And he makes me happy."

She answered me in a monotone: "Ferran, I have to admit that this is unexpected news for us." I could tell that Mama was trying to measure her words carefully. "We grew up with certain beliefs and traditions. That doesn't mean we can't learn and understand."

"I know, Mama, I was worried about how you both would react, especially considering your Spanish Catholic upbringing. But I'm definitely not gonna lose a piece of my soul to try get into *their* Heaven — that's for sure. You and Papa once told me that the truth has to run wild. So, I had to tell you about this."

Right away, Mama adopted the demeanor of a lecturing professor, and sought to disabuse me of any religious storm clouds. "The Church is not the issue, *el meu fill*. They're not exactly a bastion of integrity. I was just thinking more about family life."

"We *have* grown and evolved since we were raised," Papa added. "Just as you have, *fill*. We understand that a sexual orientation is not something you chose or just make up out of the blue."

"Thank you, Papa."

"As much as we can we'll support you, Ferran," he offered tentatively.

"That's part of our duty as your parents," Mama added.

"Duty," I grumbled, rolling my eyes.

"Ferran, please," Mama asked plaintively. She stopped and breathed. Then she said, "Okay, tell us more about this Matteo."

"What can I tell you? He's amazing, as I said. We developed the best friendship, and I liked him *so* much. But I started to get so afraid of my feelings for him, I couldn't bring myself to tell him. We kept talking and finding out more about each other. And we were working at the campus farm one afternoon and the sun was setting. It was beautiful and so was he, and I took a leap of faith and kissed him. It was the first time we kissed, and it was incredible."

Mama and Papa glanced at each other.

"*You* kissed *him?*" Papa asked.

"Yes, I did. … And, I was really scared. But, when he kissed me back just as eagerly as I was kissing him, it made me feel so right. Then we finally got honest about our feelings, and we figured out we were both feeling the same way. I'll tell you I was overjoyed. And I still am."

Mama's jaw seemed to slacken at how openly I was describing this romantic scene. But she couldn't resist some motherly probing. "Tell me, what is he studying?"

"His major is Political Science and Government. We're actually in the same History of Consciousness lecture — the one you helped get me into. He surfs, and he loves soccer — well, maybe he loves watching *me* play soccer. But we share music, and we both enjoy walks, and we both love working on the campus organic farm. We really have a lot in common, and he makes me feel…."

Tears came back to my eyes. "He makes me feel … I dunno … like I'm walking on air?"

Papa laughed quietly. "Oh my, *jove canalla!* You have it *bad!*" he teased. *"He must be pretty impressive to catch your eye."*

I know I was blushing. "Yeah, Papa, he is really special. And, Mama, like you said, he's also *really* handsome. I never noticed that in a guy before. You know? But Matt is just … he's *beautiful."*

Mama actually nodded in agreement. "I can't argue with you there."

"And I'm not exaggerating, Mama; I've never felt like this before. I'm just really thankful he's in my life."

"We want you to be happy," she said unconvincingly, in her most diplomatic academic tone.

"I *am* happy. And I'm finally feeling like I'm being true to myself. I don't know what kind of family I'll make, but I do know it will be full of love."

I could tell that Mama was trying to remain composed, but she seemed a little startled at my declaration about family.

"Well … thank you for trusting us with this," she said dryly. "It is just something we need to wrap our heads around. Give us a little time, okay?"

Disappointing, but not unexpected. "Okay Mama," I replied, "sure."

Adelina whined softly again, and I petted her head and blew her a kiss.

That was about as much of them as I could take at that point. I decided the time had arrived for me to get out on the road and drive back to UCSC. I was craving a hard run around the soccer field, and I needed to be close to Matt.

"I … I probably should start driving back to campus," I said to both of them. "We have practice later today. There's a big home soccer game for us on Friday night."

16
CHRYSALIS

"I've never been interested
in being invisible and erased."
—Laverne Cox

[Playlist reference: Roxy Music — More Than This]

Ekkheya

A thunderbolt sounded, as lighting cracked across the sky by the beach. It was rare to see that kind of melodramatic weather in Santa Cruz, especially when there was no sign of rain. As far as I was concerned it was a portent. In the bewildering and tumultuous world of self-discovery, after all, there are moments that forever alter the core of someone's being.

See, if the sky can be melodramatic, so can I. But seriously, as a guardian and messenger for Santa Cruz, noticing how magick is working is kind of my thing. Ferran was wondering — I could hear his thoughts loud and clear — if the magnetism in the skies might be tuned to the magnetism he was feeling from Matt. That gave me joy.

In the electric atmosphere, Ferran was standing nervously on the grass under the Wave sculpture in front of Porter College. Recently, he was told by a professor that the student nickname for the Wave sculpture was, "The flying IUD." It took him a good half minute to stop laughing when he heard that for the first time. He was wishing he could laugh as easily right at this moment

He checked the time on his phone for what felt like the hundredth time, then adjusted the collar of his jacket. He was trying to look cool and composed, but his heart was racing. Matt would be there at any moment and would probably want a kiss — right there in full view of traffic and of other students.

For Ferran, the coming out process still felt daunting. When he told Matt that he hadn't been ready but felt forced to come out to quell the bullies, he didn't realize that his fears of people seeing him differently would keep nagging at him. But nag at him they did.

Sure, he had grappled with a vulnerability he'd never anticipated. He had come to terms with questioning his previous assumption that he must be straight. He was now convinced that he wanted a romantic relationship with

Matt. But, the idea of telling people was still rattling him, even though he'd managed to get a little bit of practice at doing it. Confusion, doubt, and fear still waged a relentless battle inside him.

Since grammar school, Ferran had felt that he was slogging through a foggy world looking for answers about his life, but also that his honest answers usually would be met with rejection. His experience of neglect from his parents, and his observation of so much judgmental scrutiny from his peers, instilled in Ferran a deep fear of what other people would think of him. It instilled in him an anxious hyper-vigilance, and lurked in the shadows of his every interaction.

It wasn't easy — not by a long shot — for Ferran to come to terms with the reality that he was attracted to more than one gender. The expected social norms that he had long allowed to govern his image had come to feel like chains weighing him down and making him suffocate. That realization hit him like a tidal wave, crashing against the carefully constructed avoidance that was his standard operating procedure for so long.

Ferran had barely begun the process of overcoming his fears and learning to use better coping strategies. He hated his uncertainty and self-doubt, but coming out to everybody felt like it would be a monumental task. Still, he prided himself on being strong — both on and off the soccer field. He knew that his worries were stifling his ability to live fully and freely.

As he was walking this treacherous path of self-acceptance, Ferran leaned heavily on Matt's unwavering support. In the midst of his internal emotional chaos, at least that support was offering him some solace and a glimmer of hope. He and Matt were navigating the uncharted territory of their new kind of relationship together. He felt, when Matt was holding him, that he really could find the courage to confront his fears head-on and peel away the layers of other people's expectations.

Ferran

Matt was walking towards me across the field. His smile seemed as bright as the flashes of lightning I saw earlier. Just looking at him made me feel like my heart skipped a beat — an effect Matt always seemed to have on me. He was stretching out his hand with his palm turned upward, as if he was hoping for me to hold it right there in public.

I shivered. "I've been finding this so tough," I confessed, as I just stared at Matt's hand until he put it down to his side. "I feel like an idiot; I thought I knew better than to internalize the homophobia. But obviously it's in there, buried deep."

We were standing there together under the Wave sculpture, and we were both silent. I flashed on the idea that the sculpture might serve as a symbol of the fluidity and movement of my own identity. I was still so nervous. But I was determined I was going to have an honest conversation with Matt about what it might take for me to be completely open about the deep feelings I had for him.

I wanted to come out to more people, but it felt as if my insides were at war. It seemed to be a daunting task, and it filled me with uncertainty. The passion he and I shared ignited me like a fire, and I'd been brave enough to shut down gossips on both sides of me. I had been brave enough to kiss Matt. I had been brave enough to come out to my parents. Why couldn't I find the rest of the bravery I needed?

"Matty, I want to be able to hold your hand in front of everybody," I admitted, "but sometimes when I try, my body goes into, like, fight-or-flight mode."

"I want to protect you from it all," he said earnestly, "and I wish I could save you from all that turmoil. But I know I don't have the power to do that."

He tried to keep reminding me that nothing needed to happen overnight, but I was berating myself. "I'm failing to be the decent human being I thought I was," I told him.

"I really don't see it as a failure, Ferr. I look at it as an unfolding process. After all, I went through my own process and it took a *lot* of work on myself. And I'm nowhere near done."

I was also worried about potential rejection and judgment from my soccer teammates. And what about the cluster of my relatives who were conservative? Matt tried to reassure me that we could face any challenges if we faced them together.

"It can be really confusing for me sometimes," I told him. "I know we're good and valid, but I guess it's about how other people see it. And somehow, I went from being a regular guy who was having a good, long-term relationship with a smart, sexy girlfriend; to breaking up and feeling all alone; to realizing I'm a bi guy who is now lucky enough to be in an amazing, passionate relationship with a beautiful boyfriend. And it's all happened in just a few months' time. Sometimes, I guess I feel like I can't wrap my head around it all."

"Ferr, I can understand that. I was really afraid until you kissed me, you know. I was scared that the feelings I had for you wouldn't turn out to be real, or that you wouldn't feel the same."

"But you know I do feel the same," I confirmed, "even though it feels unbelievable sometimes."

"I'm very glad you do."

"I just get these moments when the idea of acknowledging my feelings for you in public gets me completely terrified. But then there are other moments where it makes me feel the happiest I've ever felt in my life."

"You have to make your way out when you feel ready, Ferr, whether you do it slowly in stages or all at once."

"I know I did the right thing in really trying to figure all of this out with you, Matty. It was right for me to kiss you. It was right to start a romantic relationship with you. It was right to face reality instead of running away."

"I'm going to be right here with you. Just, please Ferr, don't be ashamed of who you are or who you love. You're an amazing person. Too many people try to erase us. Don't let them."

I was anxious, but Matt was so right. Then all of a sudden, I could swear I heard someone say, "By your side; I see you for you." It wasn't Matt's voice, and there was nobody around but the two of us, but I felt a presence that enveloped me in affection and care. Then it was like a packet of information instantly downloaded into my brain, and I knew what I needed to do. I felt relief start to tangle with my feelings of fear. Even though I was torn about being ready for the world to know about our relationship, that part of me that didn't want to hide anymore was winning.

"I just had a bizarre experience," I told Matt, and related what I'd just felt.

"Ah. See what you get when you dabble in witchcraft with your boyfriend?"

"It's funny how I'm a lot less afraid of that than I've been about what other people think of me."

"I really do understand your fears. Coming out is never easy, especially when we live in a society where we're seeing so much backlash against us. But remember that we have a relatively supportive community here at

UCSC, and we have our friends, and we have each other. We don't have to face any of this alone."

"What if people get resentful at me for being 'the queer soccer player'? What if they treat me differently — like, in a bad way? I'm trying to figure out how to handle that. I guess I just don't want all the moralistic crap from the bullies, you know? I'm supposed to be this soccer star, and people don't expect me to be … *bisexual.*"

"There are queer soccer stars, Ferr. Yeah, it's hard to come out as one, but it isn't unique. And it's just a university team. Besides, people might surprise you. The ones who really care about us will embrace us for who we are. There might be some who react badly, but their opinions shouldn't ever make us disappear."

"Am I that brave?"

"I feel like you've already shown a lot of courage. Take your time. Coming out is a personal journey, and you get to decide when and how to navigate it."

"I realize that it's the storm in my head that makes it worse, Matty. But I also know that falling for you made me realize that this is part of who I am. I get stuck sometimes is all. I'm so thankful you're with me on this road, though. I think I got so used to the practice of 'looking the part' with April back in high school that I don't really know how to be this more real version of myself."

"I'm not grading you on your queer public displays of affection, Ferr. Please don't use that as a measure on yourself, either. You don't have to hold my hand, or kiss me, or anything out here — until you want to."

I groaned. I *did* want to; I was yearning to. That's why the conflict inside me felt so bad. "As messy as I am about all this, I can't keep hiding who I am. I deserve to be out, and you deserve not to have to hide anything for me. It's gonna take more courage, but I don't want to be a disappointment to you."

"You are anything but a disappointment to me, Ferran Bosch. You make me shine. If you need time to get used to this and we need to keep it more quiet, I respect that. I really do."

I looked over and saw a group of my teammates walking over the pedestrian bridge several yards away toward the family student housing units. They caught sight of Matt and me standing by the sculpture and began to wave at us as they walked. I couldn't help it; my anxiety level spiked.

I shouted to myself inside my mind.

It is time for my anxiety to back-the-fuck-off.
I have support. Fear is not going to own me;
I won't let it.

I reached out for Matt's hand and took it into my own. Then I leaned over and kissed him deeply. My sweet boyfriend seemed surprised and dumbfounded, but he hungrily kissed me back. Apparently, my four teammates who were walking across the pedestrian bridge weren't people who might want to bully or insult us. Instead, they made what sounded like wolf calls, and one of them yelled, "Get a room, boys!"

Matt looked at me and gently intertwined his fingers with mine. "You are crazy, mister. Why did you do that?"

"Hopefully because I'm still capable of learning? I've got to get over my cheap self. I can't live in fear of being who I am, and I'm not going to undermine how I feel about you by treating you like some dirty little secret that I have to hide."

"I don't feel like your dirty little secret, Ferr."

"And I would hate it if you ever did. I can't do that to you, and I can't do that to me."

"Sure you really can handle it right now?"

"You know I'm not sure about anything — except that I want you. Besides, those guys from my team didn't seem to have any problem with us."

"What if there are other guys on the team who are homophobic?"

"Then I'm gonna face my fear, I guess. Because being with you — that is totally worth putting everything on the line."

"Ferr…"

"I need to do this."

"Ferr…"

I took both of Matt's hands into mine. "Matty," I said, "the life you make, the life I make, the life *we* make …" I held both sets of hands up to my heart and went on, "There's nothing more than this. If any of the other guys on the team — or anybody else — gives me grief about it, I'm just going to have to follow through by giving them a lesson they won't forget."

"Ferr…"

"That's exactly what I told Kyle I'd do to him, and I meant it. If I have to do that to anybody else, I'll fight to live my life, and I'll fight for yours."

Matt shrugged and sighed, giving up trying to debate it with me. He just smiled and looked up into what I hoped were now my resolute and fiery eyes. He huffed a laugh at me. "You're going to be a champion for both of us, eh?"

"I will, Matty, and that's only possible because of you. I want my outsides to match my insides. And I want *you* to be able to be proud of your boyfriend — the boyfriend you can tell everyone about if you want to."

"Oh. really?" he asked, and I nodded yes. "Okay, but shouldn't we tell our friends first?"

A laugh bubbled up out of me, and I allowed myself to relax a little. I kissed Matt again, adoringly. "Yeah, I think so. Let's start there. And thank you for being so patient with me."

A jogger ran past us just then, and for a split second some residual fear had me to considering dropping Matt's hand. But right at that moment, I remembered my commitment. I took a deep breath and mentally thrashed my fears as I gripped Matt's hand even tighter.

"We're right here at Porter, Matty. How about we see if we can find Alex?"

Matteo

I reminded Ferran that he said he'd already made Alex aware of his feelings for me. I knew he was eager, but I didn't want him to have regrets about too much too fast in coming out to people. But Ferran insisted: "Alex doesn't know you and I are boyfriends, so let's tell him. I want to make it official."

In for a penny, in for a pound, I figured. Hand-in-hand, we strolled into the Porter College courtyard. Alex was leaving a classroom area door, and spotted us just as we walked in. He also looked at our joined hands and his eyebrows lifted in surprise and he broke into a huge smile. "Ferran, my dude!" he called out. "You finally told him! Seems like that went well." Both of us nodded and grinned.

Ferran put his hand on Alex's shoulder. "I wanted you to be the first of my friends that I told, Alex. But Maura guessed about us first, and then I had to tell my parents. And I had a couple of bullies I had to get rid of. As for any of our friends that we've been able to choose to tell officially, you are the first."

"Awwww, then I feel honored, guys. But exactly what is it that I officially know? That you two are not straight? That you're holding hands?"

I gave him my answer: "That we're both definitely bi, for starters."

"And … that we're officially boyfriends," Ferran added, dropping his hand from Alex's shoulder.

"Well, it's about time…. O my gods, you guys! I am *really* happy for you." Alex threw open his arms and told us we needed to all have a group hug. We agreed with that, and brought him in for one.

Then Alex gave us the full details about all the speculation our crew of friends had been engaging in about us. He wrapped it up saying: "Everybody was wondering if you guys would figure it out. And Jake! I think the one thing Jake has wanted is for you two to finally get together. I mean, almost as much as he's wanted Maura to notice him. That boy is a hardcore romantic."

"Ah, yeah. Maura and Jake," Ferran commented, "And you think *we* had a hard time figuring it out."

I agreed with that. "Right? I'm no one to talk, but how does she not see?"

"Oh, she sees *now*," Alex informed us. "They had a little breakthrough when we were comparing notes about you two."

I beamed at Ferran, and then looked back at Alex. "Were we an inspiration?"

"If I'm being completely honest, the two of you are kind of an inspiration to the whole group about a lot of things."

Choking up, Ferran told him: "I don't know if you're just saying that, Alex, but you don't know how good it feels to hear you say something like that."

"It's the absolute truth, man."

"Buddy … thank you for being so amazing."

"You're welcome. It's my job as the sort of elder BFF, right?" Alex joked. "But guys, I'm starving. I'm gonna go over to the dining hall, okay?"

I answered him: "Go eat, man. Thank you for being so cool. I think we have a few other stops to make and chats to send."

"Good! You guys, everybody's gonna be so happy. But, hey, text me later and let me know how it went."

We both replied in unison, as if we'd practiced it: "We will, Alex."

He laughed and began walking away from us towards the dining hall. About half way there, he turned back to us for a moment and called out: "Hey, I love you guys!"

Then he jogged briskly in the door.

17

SCORE

"Only those who risk going too far
can possibly find out how far they can go."
— *T.S. Eliot*

[Playlist reference: Peyton McMahon — Someone]

Ekkheya

The bright moon was shining a path of light across the Monterey Bay. Ferran and Matt stood in front of the large picture window in Matt's room, looking out at the magnificent sight. Ferran held Matt in his arms, his chest flush against Matt's shoulder blades as they slowly rocked in an intimate rhythm.

Maybe Matt had fallen first, but Ferran was falling even harder.

Neither Ferran nor Matt were lacking in classically handsome good looks. There were people of all genders who wanted one or both of them, practically falling over themselves trying to get a date. But since that fortunate evening in mid-September, Matt and Ferran had barely noticed any of their suitors — unless you're counting their attraction towards each other.

Neither of them could be described as sexually naïve, either. Both Matt and Ferran had their first sexual experiences back in high school, when they'd also both become more focused on training for their athletic endeavors. They spent years developing their muscles and their minds, as well as growing in genuine sweetness. Ferran dated a few times before settling-in with April, and Matt definitely had his flings — facts that by this time they had made sure to tell each other. Still, neither of them had developed a serious, passionate romance until they encountered each other.

Both guys were thinking about the way their high school classes had spun sex education. Basically, the message they were taught was: "sex could always mean death." Most of the students had considered that melodramatic, but it made them curious enough to ask questions about how to protect themselves and each other from a wide variety of risks. And obviously, those inquiries became especially important in the wake of the rescinding of abortion rights — and all the other nightmarish attacks on personal bodily integrity that the Republicans and their corrupt US Supreme Court had foisted on the country.

Ferran felt more incentive than usual to arm himself with facts. After their first sexual encounter in the gym showers, Ferran quickly obtained his blood test results and started PrEP-on-demand — on his way to taking it daily. He was making no secret that his urges for Matt were intensifying, and that he was longing to move forward sexually. Matt hesitated only because of how new Ferran was in experiencing his own queerness.

Ferran

I held Matt, and we swayed as we looked out at the moon. In a quiet, lilting voice, I sang a short quote for him from one of my favorite songs:

> And I know
> you could fall for a thousand kings,
> and hearts
> that could give you a diamond ring …

Matt quietly giggled, then purred, "Thank you, Ed Sheeran."

"I'm telling you the truth, Matty, and you know it," I replied. "My life has been a lot better since I've had you in it. You could have anybody you want, and I don't know why you chose me but I'm glad you did."

"I'm not so sure I chose you as much as we were chosen for each other. And we both said, 'yes'," And, Ferr, come on: you have to admit that my 'yes' was especially vigorous."

I whispered near his ear: "Yeah? I think you're making me feel especially vigorous right now."

I lowered head and nuzzled my lips into the crook of his neck. With a moan, he reached back and guided his fingers up under my shirt. He stroked my treasure trail, and then brought my arm tighter around his waist. He drove me crazy wiggling against me to snuggle-in more deeply. I let out a low, eager growl, and Matt said: "Shhhhh ... Just let yourself feel everything."

How could I not? My desire for him was already incendiary and it only intensified as I drank-in his intoxicating scent while he rubbed against me. His skin was supple and milky white with an adorable dusting of freckles that was typical of gingers. The lines of his face were clean and angular, his compact body a lithe, smooth, muscular masterpiece. His eyes, framed in a sexy fringe of strawberry blond lashes, glowed like well-lit emeralds on display. I was in awe of his looks, but his appearance caught the attention of most people who saw him.

Usually, when Matt walked into a room, he exuded a presence that commanded attention. He moved as if he owned the place and you were glad he did. It wasn't merely his striking appearance; it was also the kind of self-possession that others find inspirational. I felt grateful that he chose to be with me as if he were my treasure to hold. I closed my eyes and breathed a sigh into the luxurious hair of the beautiful man I was coming to cherish.

I was very studious about the ways men could have sex with each other. Matt was still saving one kind of sex because he wanted me to be absolutely sure about it before we did it. That frustrated me to no end. But in the moonlit glow of the moment, my hardness throbbing against his back, I think I heard an unintentional whimper escape from him.

"Okay, fine, mister," Matt sighed. "I haven't ever craved anyone as ardently as I'm craving you and you're making me acutely aware of it. Are you happy? You're weakening my resolve not to move along too fast with the sexual stuff. I just don't want you to feel like I took advantage of you."

"I don't feel taken advantage of, but thank you for saying that. I'm not that fragile. Come on: we've already been best friends, and we've already done some other sexual things."

"Yes, we have," Matt said, as the erotic charge in the air grew stronger and his body grew warmer against mine.

I nibbled on his earlobe. "I want you so much. If there's anyone I really need right now, it's you."

"Gods! You are hard to resist."

"Please," I begged, pulling him even closer to me. "Don't resist, Matty. Please?"

Matt put on his best frat boy voice, trying to lighten the mood. "You turning queer on me, bro?" he joked. "You tryna come on to me?"

I was determined that he wasn't going to deter me. "You know," I answered teasingly, "it might just be a little too soon for that, pretty boy."

"My game plan has failed."

"Yes, sir, it has."

"I'd better think up another one."

I groaned. "Matty, please! I know you care about me, and you know I care about you. I know we can just touch and play around if we want to. But I want *more*. I need you — I need to be *inside* you." I let out a deep breath, and so did he.

"Fuck. You know, in a way, you are already inside me. I feel like I've experienced the joy of getting to know your soul. And that just leaves me defenseless."

"What are you defending against? I'm not a danger to you. I'll be your protector if you want me to be."

"Ferr, do you feel that? You're making me tremble."

"Is that a good thing?"

"Gods! It's one thing to get turned on, but you light me up so much more than that."

"Oh? Do I, now?"

"You do," Matt said, leaning back and rolling his head against my neck. "Every curve and corner of your frame, every aperture, every nook, every tuft of your body hair."

"Yeah?"

Matt shivered. "And your scent, Ferr. … It gets me so riled up … I love it."

"Matty, you're making me so hard it hurts."

"And your hands, your lips, your eyes — all of you, Ferr. Everything about you floods me with excitement."

I grunted. "Flooding you is *exactly* what I had in mind."

Matteo

Ferran's innuendo was as ironic as it was enticing, because salacious thoughts about him flooded my mind all the time. My boyfriend's desire to take me seemed to have him climbing the walls — metaphorically, of course. For his sake, I was trying to avoid quenching my raging thirst for him. But I was out of ideas for that, and my longing to feel him deep inside me was growing much more insistent.

He kept telling me he was lusting after me, and I knew I was lusting after him at least as much. I also knew that Ferran and I would be spending the night together. I had prepared myself in the shower before he got to my house. I wasn't going to take any chances, just in case.

Ferran was no longer impressed by my protests that we should keep moving slowly. If I'm being brutally honest, I was no longer impressed by them, either. My depths were yearning for Ferran's attention, and it seemed nothing else would sate him except taking our lovemaking to the next level.

I knew we couldn't possibly get too close. I knew his hunger. I knew the right time was right there and then.

I gave Ferran my answer: "I don't want you to feel like there's any pressure. No stress, no performance anxiety. I want it to be just you and me joining together, exploring and making each other feel good. I want to be like home for you."

Ferran moved my hair aside and licked in a line from my collarbone to the back of my ear. I moaned. He spoke to me in a deep, soft voice. "What you want is my dream, Matteo Poulsen. You are so good in so many ways, and I want you *so* bad."

I turned around to face Ferran, and I kissed him as he ran his hands down my back. His large, strong hands settled on the round globes of my ass. As he grabbed onto and kneaded the muscles, I looked up into Ferran's eyes and then lowered my own eyes and rested my head against his chest. I asked in a whisper: "Is that what you want?"

"What I *need.*"

He stepped back and pulled his shirt off over his head. Then he took off his shoes and socks, and finally pulled down and stepped out of his jeans and his jockstrap.

I drank-in the vision of his beauty and prowess as Ferran stood nude in front of me. I felt like my whole body was crying out for him. My heart pounded as I heard my voice inside my mind.

This is definitely the night.
Look at all that! I'm in trouble.

"Matty, please," he said, closing the distance between us. "I'm so ready." Then he took hold of me and kissed me with passion and tenderness.

I returned his kiss — fervently, devotedly — our tongues meeting in a battle for dominance. But it was not only combat for control; it was also an excited duel to discover which of us could explore the other's mouth more extravagantly. I could tell that the vibrations coursing through his body were as electric as mine.

"I want this," he panted, breaking the kiss, "and I know you want this, too." Ferran was tracing down my body lightly with my fingers, and I could feel the goosebumps rise on my skin. In a low, gravelly voice he asked me, "Are you thinking about what I could do to you?"

Oh, *yes* I was.

He was hunting me, and I moaned his name: *"Ferran."* He growled and held me closer. And my deepest longings were being stirred by the very idea that Ferran would be inside me — and that my boyfriend would be leaving a part of himself in my depths to claim me.

"Do you want me to make it a reality?"

I begged him: "Yes, please, let me be *your* good boy."

Ferran swallowed hard. "Matty, you *are* my good boy."

I reached down and gently brought Ferran's hand to my lips. I slowly encircled and bathed his index finger with my mouth. I encased it with my lips and gently sucked on it while I caressed Ferran's hand.

"You're driving me crazy."

"I'm going to let you take me."

I moved Ferran's trembling hand to my chest, and he grasped my pectoral muscle. My nipple swelled and firmed in arousal. He kissed me more passionately and my pulse quickened even more. I was unbuttoning the shirt I was wearing as we smashed our hungry mouths together. I pulled it off of me and tossed it aside. Then I took Ferran's hand again and placed it on my chest, and moved it slowly down my torso.

He moaned and drew back from my lips. "Matty," he rasped, "you're making me ravenous. You have such soft, soft skin but such hard muscle. And you're so smooth."

I moved his hand lower until it was resting at the buttons of my jeans. "Just pull them open," I begged, and Ferran happily complied. I was going commando, so he reached in and softly caressed the family jewels that were tightening under my rigid staff. He leaned down and pressed butterfly kisses to my neck, making me mewl in pleasure.

From the excitement of our connection, I felt myself starting to relax and bloom. I broke from him only long enough to remove the rest of my clothes. Then he took hold of me and kissed me again. With a hint of power, he pushed me down onto my bed.

I looked up at him hungrily. Breathing heavily, I nearly sobbed the words: "I want you."

He lowered himself down onto me, his taller frame and rock-solid build covering me and making me feel wrapped in bliss. Then things began to move quickly. Lips tasted lips, and naked body covered naked body. Ferran began to run his tongue down my torso. "Don't stop," I pleaded. "I want your tongue on me, in me, everywhere."

"I want to feast on you," Ferran growled. And so he did.

After what seemed to me to be an achingly long time — his mouth all over me and probing into me, arousing me, lubricating me, opening me — I couldn't wait anymore. I grabbed onto Ferran's shoulders and begged: "Please. … I need you inside me."

"Where can I find lube?"

"I'm ready, Ferr. I'm still slick and open from your tongue. Please, just put yourself inside me now!"

Ferran's eyes met mine, and he must have seen my desperate, eager thirst for him. I could certainly see the potent desire in him. He placed himself, ready to enter me for the first time. Ferran gently breeched the ring and slowly advanced into me by only his tip. I sucked in air through my teeth and my muscles went tight. "Ferr…," I whimpered.

Even in getting used to the physicality of the muscle resistance, all of my hesitancy and fear melted away. Soon, I was relaxing and I needed more. I nodded to him to keep going, and as I keened for him, he slid into me, centimeter by centimeter.

Never before in my life — with anyone — had I ever known such intense connection during sex.

Ferran

The sensations were almost overwhelming as I slowly rocked into him. Being inside him felt hotter, smoother, and tighter than anything I imagined. I never wanted to leave, but it felt so amazing that I didn't know if I could last.

The first time I pushed into that pleasure lever inside him, he let out a joyous yelp and his eyes rolled back in his head. He begged me to move faster, harder. I took my time increasing the velocity; I was feeling like Matt and I were made for this moment.

The athletic ebb and flow of our rhythm went on for long enough that I wondered if we'd get dehydrated. As we pannted and groaned, the intense bonding lifted us both into ecstasy.

"I'm so close, Ferr," Matt cried in desperation.

I growled. "I want to see you come undone with me inside you!"

I gently took hold of his throbbing shaft and shoved myself deeper into him. He erupted in a moaning crescendo, spending himself in fountains everywhere. I exploded inside him and felt as if my soul was emptying into the deepest caverns of his being.

"I felt it. I felt you flooding me. O my gods," Matt whispered in a throaty voice, his eyes wide and pupils blown.

We collapsed onto each other, feeling glued together as we panted and held on to each other tightly.

After a while we caught our breath. I looked into Matt's glowing face and asked him if we should clean up. "Not now," he sighed. "I like this mess. I want to feel us bathe together in the gene pools." I chuckled and kissed his reddened lips.

Gently shifting him to his side, I reached down to the sheets and blankets that were folded at the foot of the bed. I pulled them up around us and then settled in behind Matt to spoon him. I nibbled on his earlobe and Matt purred with pleasure.

"Matty," I gently whispered into his ear.

"Mmm-hmm?"

"Now I've really claimed you. From inside you, with my own DNA."

Matt moaned, and pulled my arms around him more tightly. "Fuck yes, you have," he answered in a sleepy voice. "I love that so much. Now we're always going to be part of each other's bodies." And I marveled at the beautiful gift I was holding in my arms.

"I've never felt so safe and so truly at home," he purred.

Before we drifted off to sleep, I had one more thing to say.

"You're mine," I quietly declared to him.

"Yes, I am. And you're mine," Matt quietly answered.

18

SAGRADA

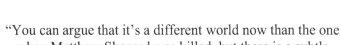

"You can argue that it's a different world now than the one when Matthew Shepard was killed, but there is a subtle difference between tolerance and acceptance. It's the distance between moving into the cul-de-sac and having your next-door neighbor trust you to keep an eye on her preschool daughter for a few minutes while she runs out to the post office. It's the chasm between being invited to a colleague's wedding with your same-sex partner and being able to slow-dance without the other guests whispering."

— Jodi Picoult, Sing You Home

[Playlist reference: Zzoilo & Aitana — Mon Amour]

Ekkheya

It was a cool night and an exciting sports event, yet Isabel, Ferran's mother, seemed lost in thought as she sat in the Ivíta Cafe after attending her son's Friday soccer game. Ignasi, his father, observed his wife's furrowed brow and silently began to sing a children's song to himself.

One of these things just doesn't belong here...

He returned to their table holding a cup of coffee in his hand. *"Vita meva,"* he asked, "what's bothering you?"

Isabel heaved a sigh and admitted to her husband that over the past week she had been obsessing about Ferran. "The situation with him and Matteo Poulsen," as she called it. "It's weighing heavily on my mind."

Ignasi placed his hand on Isabel's, and looked at her with kindness and understanding. *"Amor meu,"* he said lovingly, "it's a big adjustment. But we have to remember that Ferran is still our son and nothing can change that."

Teary-eyed, Isabel tried to make excuses: "I know, *rei meu,* I know. But our dreams for him... the expectations we had... they're all slipping away. I don't know how to handle it."

Ignasi took a deep breath. He tried to reassure his wife that it was okay if life doesn't always go as they planned it — especially if it wasn't actually *their* life. He told Isabel that sometimes, change is a good thing. She was hesitant, but she reluctantly agreed.

"Maybe we really weren't there for him as much as we should have been," he offered. "He surely seems to feel that way."

"Maybe," she acknowledged, "but that can't be why this is happening."

"Of course not, but maybe that's why he always tried to be *our* idea of perfect before."

She shook her head: "I don't understand it."

"Isabel, we raised Ferran to be a strong, kind-hearted man who stands up for the truth," Ignasi reminded her. "And that's exactly who he is. He hasn't changed for the worse because of his relationship with Matteo. … *Vita meva,* we *succeeded."*

"But it's not what we imagined for him," she lamented. "We thought he'd have a nice girlfriend, settle down, have a traditional family. This... it's so different!"

Ignasi looked at her softly. *"Bebe,* I understand,*"* he told her. "But we can't let our preconceived notions about what Ferran's life should be get in the way of his deepest happiness. Let's be honest: we allowed our careers do that for most of his childhood. I think that took a toll, Isabel. He deserves our love and support, no matter with whom he may be in love."

Isabel insisted that she was trying, but that it was hard to let go of what they had always thought was best for their child. She was shedding gentle tears and began to sniffle. Ignasi handed his handkerchief to her and she put it to use.

"I know it is hard," he said, caressing his wife's hand. "It's a challenge we never thought we'd face. But we have to trust that Ferran knows what it is that he needs to make him happy, and that he knows who he loves. In the end, *bebe,* isn't that what matters? That, and the love he gives in the world?"

"You're right. Of course, you're right," she answered.

"It is hard, I know."

"I think I am starting to believe that putting our agenda first when he was a child negatively impacted him. I felt that we were being so focused to give him more security, you know that. But maybe it did the opposite. Am

I adding to his stresses now by letting my fears and expectations cloud the love we have for him?"

"I know we're both coming to terms with this, but I am feeling like we can't let that happen."

"So, you are telling me that I have to find a way to accept him for who he is."

Ignasi relaxed then and grinned broadly. He shrugged as he looked at Isabel. "He could have done a lot worse than Matteo Polsen, my love."

Isabel also felt herself relaxing, and laughed very lightly. "At least our son has good taste, she said, smiling. "That boy is *so* pretty, isn't he?"

Ignasi gave a full-throated laugh at Isabel's fangirl observations about Matt. "Yes, indeed," he remarked. "First our boy was with an impressively hot cheerleader and then… Well, *bebe.* Matt's a *looker,* for sure. I'm jealous of that boy's hair!" They laughed together as their tension broke.

"Don't forget, though." Ignasi reminded her, "Matteo is also a really decent human being. Let me tell you something Ferran shared with me tonight when I was over near the locker room, *amor meu.* Do you remember when the books got banned in that Sierra school district, and the fight to get them restored?"

"Yes, I do. Those people got organized and fought, and they got the policies of that manipulative group of Nazi Trump-lodyte book-burners overturned."

"Matt Poulsen was the one who led the organizing, Isabel. That young man has soul."

"Oh, my. That's impressive."

"And I *know* you saw the way he looks at Ferran."

Isabel's breath caught, and she looked at her husband with all seriousness. "Ignasi," she confided, her hand over her heart. "He looks at our boy as if Ferran is the most precious and magnificent person in the whole wide world. *Rei meu,* he looks at him the way I look at you."

"Do you, my love? Even now that I'm a glorified, computer peddler who has gotten old and soft?"

"Ha!" she blurted. "I do. Always, *amor.* Always."

Ignasi looked lovingly into his wife's eyes. "We are going to face this uncertainty together, just as we have with every challenge that has ever come our way."

She sighed. "Okay."

"You know," Ignasi told her, his eyebrows raised, "it isn't just Matteo who looks at our boy like he's all the treasure there ever was. Ferran looks at him the same way."

"I saw," Isabel admitted. She took a deep, cleansing breath. "They really do care deeply for each other, don't they?"

"I am pretty sure they are ridiculously in love."

"So were we," she reminded him.

"So *are* we, Dr. Bosch. So *are* we," he emphasized. "I still go from zero to one hundred when I see you, Mama. Like a Formula One racer."

She laughed. They clasped each other's hands, and held them together tightly.

Isabel became resolved. "Alright, Ignasi. Ferran is standing up for the truth, and I am going to learn to embrace it. We will support him every step of the way."

Her husband gently kissed Isabel's hand.

"That's what our son needs, Isabel. Our backing, our love, and our acceptance. Everything else will fall into place."

Together, they sat quietly in a moment of silent solidarity, ready to face the unknown with their son. Feeling a sense of relief, she nodded a yes.

"Let's see if we can go talk with him at his dorm and tell him," Isabel proposed.

Ignasi sent a text to Ferran. He asked if he was alone and if they could come by his room to talk with him. He replied that Stu was out with his girlfriend, April, and that they were welcome to come up and chat.

But their request made Ferran nervous. He anxiously sat on his bed, and waited for them to arrive.

***

Finally, there was a knock on the dorm room door. Ferran welcomed his parents to his room, and they stood just inside the closed door looking as if they felt out of place. "Hi again," he said.

"Ferran, *amor meu,* how are you?" his mother asked.

"I'm okay, Mama … and Papa," he answered. "It's just, you know, that I'm having some anxiety about this."

His father spoke to him gently: "We understand that, son. This is important. We wanted to come here to tell you something in person tonight. After that great game of yours, we went to dinner and we had a good talk."

"Well, okay. So is this is about Matt and me?"

Isabel was first to answer him: "Yes, it is, *fill,* We've had some time to reflect, and we want you to know that we deeply care about you no matter what."

"I appreciate that, Mama. I mean, I guess it is nice that you're paying attention to my life for a change. I've talked to you both about that before and you never seem to want to hear me. But, you've got to hear this: Now it's beyond just about whether or not you care, it's also about acceptance."

"Son, we understand that, we do," his father told him. "It's true that this news came as a surprise to us. But we are going to come to terms with it, and that's a promise."

"Trust me, it wasn't easy for me to accept it myself. Maybe if you'd been more interested in my life all along, I'd have figured out this part of who I am sooner. I get that it's difficult for you both, but Matt makes me happy the way I never knew I could be. I hope you can at least support me in that."

Isabel repeated to Ferran that he was still their son, and that they would still support him. "We are going to adjust," she insisted. "We just need your patience while we do."

"Mama, obviously it took some time for me to come to terms with my own identity." He fought back tears as he choked out the rest: "I just want to be sure — regardless of who I love — that you both still love me."

Both Ignasi and Isabel felt their breath catch. Their son didn't know if they'd still love him? They looked at each other, and then walked over to him together. Isabel wrapped her arms around Ferran and hugged him closely. "Of course, we love you!" she said, and gently rocked him.

Ignasi placed his hand on his son's shoulder. He felt he had to explain: "We love you without reservation, son. It's just that we had certain expectations for your life, and at first this news caught us off guard. That won't make us stop loving you."

"Thank you, Papa. But the truth is: before this, you two hardly knew my real life. You were too busy and preoccupied. So, now I am asking you to really see me. Life doesn't always go according to plan, does it? Matt and I are facing those challenges head-on, and it would mean the world to me if you both could do the same."

"Fill," Isabel said, choking back tears. "I am sorry that we didn't work harder to know you as well as we should have. You have always been a brave and determined young man. We admire your courage in being true to yourself, even when it's not easy." `

"Thank you, Mama. I'm just trying to really be me, and to have some happiness. I hope you can see that."

Isabel met Ferran's eyes and she told him honestly: "What I saw ... was the way you and Matteo looked at each other. Do you know what? That is the way that Papa and I look at each other. Ferran, everyone should have someone who looks at them like that."

The tears that welled-up in Ferran's eyes began to leak onto his cheeks, and he wiped them away with his hand. "Matt is amazing, Mama. He's just *so* amazing."

"And, let's not kid ourselves. That boy is truly and unfairly handsome," Ignasi quipped.

Ferran began to laugh. "Yeah, that too. For real."

"We support you, *fill,*" Ignasi assured him. "We are gonna do our best to fully embrace this new reality. Okay?"

Isabel gently touched Ferran's chin. "Okay?" she asked.

"Okay, Mama. Thank you. Thank you, Papa. I didn't expect things to change overnight. Just knowing that you are genuinely willing to try means a lot to me. It's a beginning."

Isabel and Ignasi shared a confirming look, and then nodded towards each other.

"We will always love you with all our hearts," his mother told him. "We are happy that *you* are happy in your relationship with Matteo."

Ignasi wanted to make sure that Ferran knew this: "Son, you have always made us proud. Your happiness is really what matters most to us. We will work on being accepting and supporting you every step of the way."

"Thank you," Ferran repeated again, and held out his arms. The three of them shared a group hug.

Isabel stated clearly: "Please be sure, Ferran. We love you. And we love you no matter whom you love."

"I really appreciate you for coming here and for trying to understand," he told them. "I love you both so much."

19

KINFOLK

And in the end
The love you take
Is equal to the love you make
— *John Lennon and Paul McCartney*

[Playlist reference: Mindy Gledhill — Hourglass]

Ekkheya

Giorgia Poulsen looked out at the dreary San Francisco morning from her kitchen window. She was washing the non-dishwasher-safe bowls that Clary, her five-year-old daughter, and Dave, her four-year-old son, preferred to use when they ate oatmeal for breakfast.

It was a work-from-home day for Noah Poulsen, and he had been watching the children until it was time for them to leave. They were picked up by the neighborhood carpooler for their trip to their respective preschool and kindergarten. Noah walked into the kitchen and sat down at the breakfast bar. "Giorgia," he said with an air of solemnity, "we need to talk about Matt."

From her station at the kitchen sink, Giorgia prompted him to give her his pitch. "Okay, Noah. What's going on? Is something wrong with Matt?"

"No, it's not that. I just called him to check-in and ask him how he was doing. And … he gave me a significant news update."

"What's that?"

"It's just ... he's finally in a relationship. And it's with another boy."

"Oh, I see," Giorgia noted. "You okay?"

"I'm okay."

Over the past six years, Giorgia had grown fond of being a so-called "stay-at-home mom." The nomadic married life of a couple of high-powered strategists for Eco-social Impact Investing had worn thin for Giorgia. It also seemed as though it had negatively impacted Matt's ability to build long-term friendships.

Giorgia had also become disillusioned with her work — with the whole idea that green capitalism could be a long-term solution. So, when Noah was hired to take over the social investments arm of a major bank based in San

Francisco, he and Giorgia decided she would stay close to home, devote more time to political projects, and expand their family. She hoped it would also give her an opportunity to help Matt find himself.

"All right," she probed, "so, do you think he's gay now?"

Noah rolled his eyes and smiled. "No," he said, with some confidence "I actually do believe him when he says he's bisexual. I mean, I didn't *want* to believe he was anything but straight when he told us that over the summer, but I got over myself. I do think he really is bi. It's just that — you know — he's had dates, but he's never had a romantic relationship before."

"I know," she confirmed. "He was busy flying away to Neverland. I was hoping that would change."

"Well, now he's dating this boy at university. He's a freshman named Ferran Bosch — a soccer player."

"Ooooooh!" Giorgia giggled, with a little too much eagerness. "I know who that boy is! Do you remember? When we went to visit Matt, he dragged us to that soccer game. We saw Ferran play. He was that tall, dark, and handsome boy with all the moves."

"I think I recall."

"Matt did seem enthralled sitting there on the field, Noah."

"Yep," he said, popping the *p* for emphasis. "I thought I might be noticing something."

Giorgia turned to Noah and smiled devilishly. "Can't say I blame him," she confessed. "That is one strikingly handsome young man. And those legs on him!"

"Giorgia!" Noah replied in mock horror. "Now listen lady, you should not be drooling over an 18-year-old soccer player's legs."

"Well, not just his legs. I was looking a little higher on his backside, too."

"You are a mess! Stop lusting after your son's boyfriend," he teased. "And maybe you're the one who should be giving my best to Peter Pan."

Giorgia brushed that off and tried to throw her best shade. "Maybe this will make my son stop being such a man-whore,"

"Giorgia!"

"Noah, come on. He's a babe magnet. He's been through a string of girls, and I'm sure guys as well. It's a pretty good assumption he's having sex. I saw Descovy in his medicine cabinet over the summer."

"What's that?"

Giorgia's years of social justice and environmental advocacy had kept her up to date. "It's a daily HIV prevention pill."

"Due diligence," Noah hummed. "That's my guy."

"I was glad to see it. I was even going to suggest we send him to Planned Parenthood for a vasectomy? But honestly, I'm happy he's finally dating someone. In an actual relationship, you know?"

Noah agreed. "He sounded very wistful when he told me about it. I think he's come down with a serious case of Ferran Bosch."

"Then I think it's time we finally adjusted to this, baby. When he came out to us last summer, I hadn't seen the bisexual thing coming either. But there it was. And he was bound to find someone to actually date at some point."

"I know. And don't bite my head off, but it is still a bit for me to take in. I think I always imagined Matt marrying a girl someday and starting a family."

Giorgia reflected: "I guess I had that expectation, too. But we can't let our expectations limit who he loves, can we? Or limit what kind of family he decides to create."

"True."

"He deserves his pursuit of happiness, Noah. I feel like we have to support him. I mean, regardless of their gender — loving someone is what matters."

"Yeah, of course. I'm just worried about how other people will treat him. You remember how those jerks and tourists harassed and bullied him at his stupid Pier 39 summer job..."

"Yes. I wish I didn't remember, but I do," she answered firmly. "That's why he came out to us. But can we really let our fears about *the deplorables* dictate all our actions? It isn't as if there is a shortage of loud and pushy fascists in the world today. Are we going to teach Matt that he should walk on eggshells to appease those kinds of people?"

"Hell, no."

"Exactly. Matt's got strength of character. And he deserves love and acceptance from his family."

"You're right. I do want to show him that we're okay with this. That we really love him, whomever he loves."

"I agree. And I think we need to make it an honest and open conversation with him. We have to let him know that we support him *and* his relationship. He needs to know that he's not alone — that we're here for him."

"What if we take them out to dinner?"

Smiling mischievously at her husband, Giorgia teased: "Does that mean I get to secretly stare at Ferran's glutes?"

Noah laughed and took Giorgia in his arms. "You are absolutely incorrigible, you old lady! What are you trying to do, be the MILF who stole your son's boyfriend?"

"An old lady can dream, can't she?"

"You are *not* really an old lady," Noah insisted. "That would be your mother," he said, grinning. "And, listen, I *might* be getting jealous."

"Awww, my Noah. You are the love of my life," she said, while nuzzling her head into the crook of his neck. "And maybe Matt deserves to have one of those, too."

"I'm on the same page, honey. We can't let our worries get in the way of Matt's happiness."

"With his unbelievably hunky soccer star."

"You know," Noah reminded her, "Matt is not exactly an ugly duckling. And he's smart as a whip."

"That's true. And he's very loving." Giorgia gave Noah a tender kiss, and then led him to sit down at the kitchen table. She suggested they invite Matt and Ferran up one night so they could take them out to Berber Restaurant for dinner.

"Oh! Yeah, I love that place!" Noah chirped.

Then Giorgia spelled out a plan. They'd invite Matt to bring Ferran to dinner and they would get to know him better. They hoped that by doing that — and seeing how Ferran and Matt were with each other — it would speed along their own adjustment.

Noah asked if they should bring their younger children, Clary and Dave.

"Sure!" Giorgia responded with a laugh. "If those two fine young men can handle dining in a restaurant with a four and a five-year-old, maybe they'll be able to raise kids of their own someday."

"*Åh mine guder!*" Noah exclaimed.

"I know you're on overload when you start pulling out the Danish exclamations."

"Just give me time to wrap my head around it all."

Giorgia assured him that, all together as a family, they could become fully accepting.

Noah looked at her adoringly, remembering again why he fell in love with her. "How would I ever get through life without you, Giorgia?"

"I'm glad we're on the same page on that!"

"Which part?" Noah asked with a smile. "Me wanting and needing you in my life? Or our bisexual son and his Sporty Spice boyfriend?"

"Yes."

"He's our kid. He's a good kid — a *really* good kid. Whatever challenges come our way, we'll face them together." Noah acknowledged that he knew that their love and support could make all the difference for Matt.

Georgia took Noah's hand in hers. "I could not have asked for a better partner on this journey. If Ferran's half as in love with Matt as I am with you, they are going to be just fine."

"That's my hope."

"Have you seen them look at each other?"

"At the soccer game?" Noah asked, sheepishly. "I shouldn't have been watching, but it was hard to miss the lovey-dovey eyes."

"I think there's probably a photo of them next to the definition of 'soul-mates' in the dictionary."

"All right, I know. Let me adjust to that."

"Okay, grandpa. Let's just make sure Matt knows he's loved and supported. That's what really matters in all of this."

"Yes, it is."

20

AWAY

"A flower knows when its butterfly will return."
— *Sanober Khan*

[Songlist reference: Gabrielle Aplin - Waking Up Slow]

Ferran

This day was definitely *jersei* weather. I was on my way to meet up with Matt at McHenry Library again, but I was going to have to give him some news that I wasn't happy about. As I walked up the path towards the entryway, I saw my beautiful boyfriend sitting outside on a wall, looking off into the woods.

I greeted him with: "Hey, handsome," and caressed the back of his head. He leaned up and kissed me. "Can we talk for a minute?" I asked, sitting beside him on the wall. "I gotta give you some news about my calendar."

"Your calendar?"

"Yeah," I answered, sadly. "You know I have an away game this weekend, right?

"I remember you mentioning it. What's up?"

"It just really hit me that this is gonna be the first full weekend we'll spend apart since we started dating."

"I know," Matt sighed.

"I don't want to be away from you. I'm sort of dreading it. I've never been so lonely on my own, and it shows."

"Ferr, you're such a sweetheart. But it won't be very long at all. I understand you don't want to be apart, but sometimes it's necessary, you know? It's a new thing for us, I know. But this is something you've done with people you care about a million times, right?"

"Never with you before, Matty. Never before knowing what I know now."

"I understand; I do. But playing soccer is your passion. You shouldn't give that up just because we'll have to be apart for a few days."

"I know, but it's hard. I don't even like going to the gym without you. That's why I'm really glad we work out together."

"Oh? Is that the *only* reason?"

"You *know* it isn't."

Matt winked at me. "Bad boy."

"I don't know why we can't always just go for a walk or watch movies in your room and be together," I told him. Matt nodded in agreement and said he wished we could.

The Vice Chancellor for Student Affairs and Success approached us just then. "Hey, troublemaker," she said, looking at Matt and smiling at him. Over the past year, she and Matt had shared several committee assignments together, and they'd personally negotiated the parameters on some student demonstrations to make sure everybody would remain safe. "Hello, Your Grace," Matt said with a slight bow. They enjoyed lightly teasing each other and genuinely liked one another.

"I'm glad to see you give your elders proper deference, Mr. Poulsen," she said, laughing. "But I saw you both out my window and I'm actually here to give *you* some news, Mr. Bosch."

"You know you can call me Ferran."

"Well, thank you Ferran. But I wanted to let you know I was just on the phone with some recruiters from the Earthquakes. They wanted to come here and take videos of you playing, and they were wise enough to call me to be sure they did it with minimal disruption. I told them the team has an away game this week, and that they should start with taking videos there. I just wanted you to know they're sniffing around. I can tell them we'd consider them intrusive if you'd like me to, but I wanted to tell you to see if you'd rather give them the go-ahead."

I took a deep breath. Then I blurted out: "Whoa."

Matt enthused: "Ferr, this is great!"

I felt wary about it. "It's a lot, Matty. I think maybe I'm okay having them do that at the away game, but I don't want them disrupting us at home. Besides, I want my focus during home games to be on the pitch … and on you."

"Noted," said the Vice Chancellor.

"So, Your Grace, I wanted to tell you some news about Ferran and me," Matt said, smiling.

"Oh? Well, I might be able to guess. Please correct me if I have this wrong, but are you two … together?"

"Yes," Matt said. "Officially boyfriends."

"Finally," the Vice Chancellor sighed.

"Stop," I told her, chuckling.

"Now, *this* is a team," she said. "If you don't mind, guys, I want to capture this for posterity. Will you let me take a photo of you two?"

"O my gods, are you kidding?" Matt said, with a quiet laugh.

I urged her on: "Do it!"

Matt and I posed for her to take a photo with her smartphone. "I have to put it on social media, right?" she asked us.

"You are impossible," Matt said, but he gave me a questioning look, and I nodded yes. So, we both gave her permission. She posted it to her official and personal accounts with the tag line: "Power Couple."

Then she smiled at us and said, "Thank you, men. Ferran, I will make sure to tell the recruiters your boundaries and make clear to them that campus security is prepared to enforce them. All right, sirs. Back inside for me." The Vice Chancellor turned to walk back to her office, and I called out my thanks to her as she left.

I looked back at Matt and shared my feelings with him. "I just wanna be with you, Matty. I really *like* spending time with you. It's gonna be strange not being able to see you or be with you for a few days. I'm gonna miss you."

"I'm going to miss *you!* Believe me, I completely get it. But things are happening for both of us. You know we have a lot of stuff going on and we have to show up for it. Seriously, I don't want to be apart from you either, but you know we'll still be connected even if we're physically apart."

"I know. You're right. But I can't help feeling like I'm gonna miss out on something while I'm away. What if something happens and I won't be there for you?"

"Oh, come on, Ferr. I think we might be able to muddle through."

I huffed.

Matt reached out and took my hand. He spoke to me softly: "Look baby, don't worry. We have texting and phones and video calls, remember? We can still check-in with each other. Plus, come on, I'll be just fine."

I felt my head tilt like an inquisitive puppy. I had to ask Matt if I heard him correctly. "Um … 'baby?'"

"I'm sorry," Matt said shyly, "Was that bad?"

I was a little surprised, and my voice was flat when I repeated it: "You called me, 'baby.'"

Matt seemed apologetic: "I wasn't planning that. I'm sorry." Did he think I was bothered? Oh, no, I wasn't bothered; I was feeling giddy.

"Matty, I *like* it!" I told him. "Please don't be sorry. I think I might like it even better than the when you call me

'Ferr!' Well, that is, I like it as long as it's *you* calling me 'baby.' I don't think I'd like it as much from anybody else."

"You are a big, charming hunk," Matt answered, leaning in again to give me another kiss.

"Am I just being silly?"

"I don't think there's anything wrong with that," Matt reassured me. "I kinda love it, actually. I think it's completely understandable to feel this way. I mean, our friends do say we're like magnets for each other."

"We are like that, aren't we."

"As long as we remember that we both have things we love outside of our relationship, too. And that isn't gonna make us any less devoted to each other. We're *us*, baby."

"When they think we're not listening. They call us 'Ferr and Matty" — like it's our team's name. Did you notice that?"

"We *are* a team, aren't we?"

"Ha! Yes! I guess we are."

I looked off into the woods, musing for a little while. Matt joined me in quiet reflection. I really loved just being present with him, and he seemed to love just being with me.

I felt it was time to explain some stuff to him. "Matty," I said, "I feel like I need to tell you something."

Matt gave me a concerned look and answered, "Uh-oh."

"No, it isn't bad," I was quick to let him know. "I was just thinking over what you said about the things we love that are outside of our relationship. I mean, I know I need to keep focusing on opening up and developing my life. All those years I spent acting and curating an image gave me a lot of time to ponder who I really wanted to be."

"And then you and April broke up."

"Hear me out. April and I had a polished image in public and some great sex in private, but there was never any romance between us. There was no passion. There was no being in love. The most important thing — for her and for me — was the deep friendship. That was the secret story and love that we *did* share with each other. And we each used that bond to have each other as a confidante, and to keep pushing each other to grow."

"I'm trying to digest that," Matt responded. "It seems like a pretty radical path to get growth from."

"My point — and I do have one — is that I already figured out who I am *without* you. I know what makes me tick, and what was an act. You didn't short-circuit my world, Matty; you helped turned on all the lights. So, it makes sense to me that I don't want to lose you, because I like who I am better *with* you than without you."

I saw Matt's eyes starting to glisten as tears welled up in them. He gave me the biggest smile, and said, "That may be the most intimate thing anybody has ever said to me."

Now I was choking up, but I kept going. "I mean it," I assured him. "I've even got some of my friends on the soccer team, like Bakari, and Cameron, and Ahmed … and they … well, they claim that we're sickeningly adorable and they tease me by calling us *The Ferr and Matty Show.* And I don't get bothered that they call us that at all; I *love* it. I love that when people think of me, they think of *us.* You and I have a deep friendship; we know that. But we're also definitely having a romance. It isn't about upholding some image; it's *passionate.* "

"Definitely passionate."

"The romance doesn't make me forget who I am, is what I'm saying. It is *all* about stretching my life. And I've felt I could do that better because you're here with me."

"Baby, I'm not going anywhere. We can each be our own person and still be totally connected — and still be *us*. Even if your whole team thinks we're gonna put them into a sugar coma."

"Not the whole team," I confided. "There were two guys on the team — *only* two guys — who had anything bad to say, and I made it clear to everybody on the team that I wasn't gonna tolerate that crap."

"So, you're a cheesy romantic and my hero all at the same time? I think this is the part where I swoon, right? You definitely can't give up on soccer now, mister."

"You helped me to remember that. And you're right that I shouldn't let my clinginess to you get in the way of pursuing other things that make me enthusiastic."

"Didn't people say *I* was the clingy one? Believe me, Ferr, you can cling to me anytime you want. And when you're at away games, you know I'm going to be patiently waiting back here like a good little soccer wife for you to come back to me."

I couldn't help laughing. "You're packing a lot of pipe for a 'little soccer wife,' my man."

"Okay, I'm not little everywhere," Matt admitted. "What a sweet talker, you are."

"You like it."

"I do. And listen, baby: soccer might be your favorite sport, but you're my favorite person. I wouldn't want you to give up your favorite thing."

"Matty," I said as I kissed his cheek, "you're my favorite person, place, *and* thing." Matt blushed and looked intently at his feet as I continued. "I've loved soccer all my life, and you care about my soccer playing. That means a lot to me, and I'm grateful for the encouragement you're always giving me."

He looked up and me through his long eyelashes, and my heart thumped. "I know you love the game," he confirmed.

"Thank you for being so supportive. You're so good to me."

"You go kick some butt out there this weekend, boyfriend. I wish I could be there, but I'll be cheering you on from here."

"I'll do my best," I affirmed. I could look at Matt all day long, but my eyes caught the time on my smartphone clock. "Oh! I'd better go. I'm gonna be late to class." I gave him another soft kiss. "I'll text you tonight before bed, okay?"

He smiled at me and said, "Please do."

21

UNASSUMING

"Simple truths are a relief from speculation."
— *Luc de Clapiers*

[Playlist reference: Fohkus — Open Mind]

Ekkheya

Walking in the crisp air through the Baskin Visual Arts studios on his way to the Music Building, Jake found Cameron sitting in the courtyard outside the Eduardo Carillo Gallery. Cameron was one of Ferran's teammates on the men's soccer team and an occasional volunteer on the campus farm. Along with Arjun, he was also one of the strongest supporters of Matt and Ferran to the rest of the team.

You couldn't miss Cameron. He had a penchant for making and wearing fashion with brightly colored feathers, as well as for creating art in several other media. He was also tall, fit, and fair skinned with shockingly bright red hair and amber eyes. He'd developed a sort of cottage industry out of making art and fashion with feathers, and was now the toast of local boutiques and regional comic-cons and similar conventions.

Cam also happened to be dating Matt's housemate, Ayesha. For Jake, it seemed especially brave for Cameron to be dating a transwoman. As he got closer to him, Jake could see that Cam was drawing on his sketch pad. Jake wanted to praise him. At least, that's what he told himself. But Jake was also voraciously inquisitive, and his larger motivation was to get Cam to spill some tea.

"Cam," Jake said, hovering above him. "Sorry to interrupt you, man. We haven't spent as much time together this quarter as we did last year."

"We should fix that," Cam replied.

Jake plodded on trying to make his point and fish for information. "You know I'm really good friends with Ferr and Matty, and I just wanted to tell you that I think it's awesome how accepting you are, and it's cool how you've corralled the guys on the team to be more accepting. Good on you, man."

"I appreciate that, Jake. Thank you. People really don't have any good reasons to be judgmental or closed-minded. It's a lot of useless baggage."

"We've gotten some good challenges to all that baggage. Like when the Vice Chancellor tags your same-sex couple friends as a 'Power Couple' in her social media post."

"Did you see all the likes? And the comments?"

"I saw a lot of people with ugly baggage they love to drag around," Jake remarked. "I guess we all have to ask ourselves if we believe our stories or if they're lies. But the upshot? Hundreds of likes and only twenty or so trolls is a helluva thing."

"Agreed," Cam confirmed. "And love is love, you know? Obviously, I don't believe in keeping anyone from who they love. You know I'm dating Matt's housemate, Ayesha, right?"

"I *do* know that and I admire your openness there, too. But I mean, you did have a little competition from Bakari."

"What to do there was up to Ayesha," Cam told him. "She made it clear which way she wanted that to go. And it hasn't made a dent in being friends with Bakari."

"Congrats. You and Ayesha doing well?"

"We're doing great. Ayesha's incredible, and we connect on so many levels. But I wasn't performing some kind of good deed when Ayesha and I decided to date — I wasn't trying to prove anything. Fact is, I just really fell head over heels for her."

"I get it, man. I'm kinda that way with Maura. You're both being true to yourself and your feelings, and not letting some people's stupid moralisms keep you from each other. That's why I think it's so great."

"Like I'm gonna let rude, egotistical, transphobic fossils dictate what genders there are and whether I can love them."

"Trans-exclusionary retrograde asshats."

"Yeah. … And I appreciate your fine words for Ayesha and me, Jake. It isn't always easy, but I want to be honest with myself and with others. So anyway, while we're oversharing and I'm being so honest, here's some more news."

"I'm all ears."

"You kinda are."

Jake smiled. "Shut up."

"So … Ayesha and I have met someone — a man we both have strong feelings and attraction for. It's Braden River, and we've decided to become a triad."

"Braden River? The trans guy from Oakes College and Ultimate Frisbee?"

"Trans men are men, Jake. But yeah."

"So does that make you…."

"Queer, Jake," Cameron said, in a matter-of-fact tone. "It means I'm queer."

"Oh. … Well, wow! That's amazing!" Jake gushed. "Congratulations, man!"

"Thank you! So, both Ayesha and I are polyamorous. And we found out that Braden is poly, too. And then Ayesha and I kinda realized that we both had a thing for him, so we talked about it and we decided to ask him out on a date. And the rest, as they say, is history."

"Seriously though, this is the kind of thing I've always admired when it comes to your open-mindedness, Cam. Not everyone can handle someone in their relationship being in love with someone else."

"But in our triad, everybody's in love with everybody. And that makes it a lot easier."

"Man," Jake marveled, "it's always the quiet ones, right?"

Cam laughed. "I guess so. But honestly, love can be a beautiful thing when you approach it with openness and respect and trust, with honest communication and good ground rules."

"And with a good calendar, I'm guessing."

"That, especially," Cam said, smiling and nodding. "But we're all really excited about this new chapter, and I'm grateful to have both of them who are on the same page."

"I know other folks who are doing this, and it takes a lot of guts to get into the kind of relationship that other people might find weird. And you three are making the effort to navigate it all. I'm happy for you."

"Thanks, man."

"I should probably get going to see my music coach," Jake said, sensing the time that had passed. "Nice hat, but the way; I like the blue feathers."

Cameron chuckled. "Thank you. And I hope I've given you enough news to chew on. Maybe us quiet ones have a lot more going on beneath the surface than you'd guess. But thanks for the props, man. I hope you enjoy your lesson."

"Thanks. I do, too."

Jake then continued to make his way down the path to the music building.

"Ain't *that* some shit," he muttered to himself, happy at discovering the surprise.

22

SHEAF

"When the world wearies,
and society ceases to satisfy,
there is always the garden."
— *Minnie Aumônier*

"Then Jesus went through a circuit
of all the towns and villages.
He taught in their synagogues and proclaimed
the good news of the Divine realm.
He brought healing to their diseased bodies —
freely, to their bruised and afflicted lives.
When he looked out over the crowds,
his heart broke.
So confused and aimless were they,
like sheep without a shepherd.
Then he told his disciples:
'The harvest is plenty, but the laborers few.
Set your intention that the genius of the harvest
will manifest the field workers
that the harvest needs.'"
— *the Gospel according to Matthew,
chapter 9, verses 35-38*

[Playlist reference: Wasia Project — My Vine]

Matteo

The shorter autumn days had definitely set in, and regular and special events were underway at our campus farm. Their farmers' market — called the Farmstand — took place weekly in the Haybarn. Some of Ferran's and my work duties included staffing it.

After breakfast that morning, we were kissing at the dining hall exit.

"You taste like coffee and maple syrup," Ferran purred.

"Uncanny. How do you suppose that happened?"

"You're a beautiful smartass," Ferran replied, bopping me on the tip of his nose. "So, what's next for you?"

"I have section for US and the World Economy up at John Lewis College, in Social Sciences Unit I."

"Oh, that's a hike! I have Survey of Classical Lit. It meets at the Earth and Marine Sciences unit, of all places. I can walk you to the shuttle, though."

"Okay. Also, on Thursday, I have to work the Farmstand and my shift is from noon to six. But I have a lecture in the morning at nine that goes until twelve-thirty, and then I have to get over there. Could my sexy man cover me for the first part of my shift, until one o'clock?"

Ferran teased me: "You found a sexy man to replace me already?"

"That is not gonna happen, you goof. So, can you cover for me?"

"You got it, baby. I was supposed to start my shift at one o'clock, so I'll just go in early."

"How late are you staying?"

"Until five, and then I have to go over to soccer practice."

"Then, this Thursday we can meet at the gym at quarter to seven?"

"Done deal, handsome."

"You're making me wanna kiss you again."

"Nobody's stopping you," Ferran seductively replied. So, I very eagerly kissed him again.

" I'm okay starting early," Ferran noted. "It'll give me a chance to sell more of all those carrots and beets we've been digging up."

"Can you meet for the gym *today?*"

"I have eleven a.m. to one p.m. open. Will that work?"

"That works. I can meet you back there at a little after eleven."

"You've got your stuff in your bag, Matty? I have mine."

"Yeah, I do."

"Okay, let's walk.

Ferran

As we strolled towards the bus stop, I was thinking about some of what we had been learning at the farm.

I was especially interested in using alternative means of exchange for food. I bounced an idea off of Matt: "I really wish we could move faster to 'non-transactional' at the Farmstand, the way we have at the Cowell Coffeehouse. Do you ever think about how we're gonna make the money-free Star Trek world happen? Like, to have the value come from democratic management of the land and the labor?"

"Working that out in my head all the time," Matt said.

"Gotta feed the people," I reckoned. "How's the poem go? 'Come eat and drink; buy without money or price.'"

"Watch it," Matt snarked at me, gently poking me in the ribs. "You keep quoting an old commie prophet like Isaiah, and you're gonna sound all Jesus-like. Then you *know* the Christian Nationalists will be sure to make you 'an illegal' for it."

I shuddered, and I said out loud what I was actually thinking: "If they spent more time trusting in love and doing the works of mercy like Jesus *told* them to, they might not be losing people in droves."

"True. So, I've got another quote: 'The harvest is plenty but the laborers few.'"

"Well, there it is, right? That, right there, begs the question. And that makes you look at difference between people who just wrap themselves in his brand, and a bunch of witchy people like us who actually take the stuff Jesus said seriously."

"Amen to that," Matt chuckled.

We arrived at the bus stop and I heaved a sigh. "I am so glad you're my boyfriend."

"Right back at ya, stud."

I tried to be witty: "I guess we can't easily do loaves and fishes right now, since the system isn't in place yet to have a Star Trek, money-free process every Thursday."

"We are miracle-deficient, alas."

"I'm not kidding, though. We need more programs like the Basic Needs Transfer to cover the cost of the means of production at the field site. That's how we get the curated boxes for the Produce Pop-ups and for the Cowell Coffeehouse to be free at point-of-service."

"Just the way abortion should be: legal, accessible, without apology, on-demand, and free at point-of-service."

I grinned at my truly remarkable boyfriend. "That's my lovely short king, the socialist feminist."

Matt took a small bow. "Thank you, thank you," he said, mimicking a Las Vegas lounge singer. "I'll be here all week. Don't forget to tip the piano player."

He got a laugh from me, I'll admit it.

"At least we have some transaction-free stuff set up," I ventured, "and it's starting to help people see that money is really a big, make-believe exchange process to keep control of the value and the supply of it in the hands of the few."

"I hope they do. 'That's one small step for a man; one giant leap for mankind,' baby," Matt said, again finding just the right quote. "But we have to take small bits and be real."

I lamented: "I just want it to move faster, is all."

"In that arena, faster would be better."

"Yeah, and anything probably moves faster than these shuttles," I grumbled. "I have to get walking over to Earth and Marine Sciences. One more kiss for the road?" Matt looked up and gave me a soft and tender kiss.

A woman standing near us at the shuttle stop turned to her friend and moaned: "It isn't fair."

I grinned at her. "What isn't?" I asked.

"The two of you being so freakin' hot and then being with *each other,*" she said. "I feel deprived."

"Thank you, I think?"

"Yeah," Matt said, "That deserves a 'thank you.'"

We kissed once more, quickly.

"Bye, baby."

"Bye."

I crossed the street to walk to class.

Ekkheya

Ferran and Matt stopped by the farm to check on a project a day later. They were working on a group of vanilla orchids that a professor had planted around the roots of an oak tree. It was two weeks since the orchids budded, but they still weren't open. That meant the guys couldn't collect the vanilla pod stamens, which frustrated them.

"I wish I could wave a magic wand and make them open," Ferran grumbled.

It was as if a lightbulb turned on over Matt's head. "That gives me an idea. Are you up to try an experiment?"

"What, me?" Ferran snarked, "Experiment with you? Oh, that never happens."

"And you said *I* was the smartass."

"And you are."

"Okay, look. On one of our first walks, I talked about magick as metaphysics, and you said it was physics that hadn't been well documented yet. So, I thought we could try to set an intention, and channel energy from the five elements to encourage the buds to open."

"Matty, baby. I've had fun joining in the rituals with you and some of our friends, but I'm not sure that kind of manifesting can be done."

Matt rolled his eyes. "Then, in this limited instance, what's the harm in trying?"

"None, I guess. All right. What do you want me to do?"

He had him there. "First grab a cup and fill it with ice from the cooler right there."

Ferran gathered a cup full of ice and brought it over. Matt got down on his haunches, close to the plants, and beckoned Ferran to do the same. Some of the moss and soil had scattered away from the plants, so he carefully gathered them back to the roots. He placed the ice cubes on and around the roots of the orchids so they'd slowly melt and safely feed them. Then he looked over at Ferran and asked, "Ready?"

"Sure, what's next?"

"Just try this. Let's close our eyes and visualize the sun filtering through the oak leaves and firing up the photosynthesis in the plants. Feel the light pouring down into the orchids. Can you see it in your mind's eye?"

Intrigued, Ferran said, "I actually can."

"Okay, so we've brought energy to the orchids from earth, water, and fire. Now we need to give them the air and etheric energies. So, visualize subtle energy gathering from all around us into our hands. … Are you doing it?"

I figured that was my cue. I helped to gather the etheric energy and move it into the subtle circuitry in both sets of their hands.

"Bizarre," Ferran commented with surprise. "I can actually feel my hands heating up."

"Good. Now let's open our eyes and point our palms towards the orchids. And on the count of three, let's blow air together toward the plants. Ready?"

"Ready."

"Okay! … One … two … three."

They both leaned forward and blew a breath of air onto the plants. As they kept their palms open towards the orchids, Matt also could feel his hands getting hot. They stopped blowing air, and everything stayed still.

And then, the buds moved very slightly and began to open in front of their eyes.

"What the actual … ? Matty, it fucking worked!"

"I guess it did. Wow."

"Damn right, 'wow!' I am definitely going to have to study more about doing that!"

Matt broke into a gleaming smile. "We can study it together."

"Yes!" I exclaimed, loudly enough to shake glass. I was hoping the vibrations would make it through the dimensional veils so both of them could hear.

Matt was startled. "Did you hear that?!"

"Yes?" Ferran asked, mystified.

"I …" Matt was at a loss for words.

"Yes, I did hear it." Ferran confirmed. "Maybe we have a helper."

And that warmed the jaded old "heart" of *this* member of the *lares*.

***

Over the next several days, Ferran and Matt put in time at the farm to prepare for the Annual Harvest Festival.

The festival served as a way to get members of the community and the media up to the land to witness and learn about agro-ecology techniques and public policy, as well as to buy and sample organic produce. Another major draw of the festival was the array of "Fall Fair" activities on offer, which made parents and their children happy. The Harvest Festival this year was set to feature live music, some guest speakers, an apple pie baking contest, hands-on gardening workshops, and games and activities for kids.

There would be honey tasting, face painting, apple pressing, pumpkin painting, and even biodiesel tractor rides.

It was wholesome enough to be a 1950s sitcom, except with actual people of color in it.

Local eateries were also going to be on hand to sell some of their fare, at least some of which would be made with items from the farm. It really was structured to be a fun way for people to connect with students and local community members.

Giorgia Poulsen burrowed her way onto the planning committee, working to secure a spot for a keynote speech by a UCSC alum who was one of her favorite prominent social justice and environmental attorneys. She was also able to find a young, gay, political internet personality to introduce the speaker. This online influencer loved the idea that he'd get to spend a long weekend in San Francisco and Oakland after the gig.

***

As a crowd gathered, social justice lawyer Kathleen Bryson and social media influencer Jonny Baronessa were standing behind the speaker's area. They chatted before making their appearances. I read your stuff," Kathleen told Jonny. "Practically daily. And just to let you know: if I had to choose, I'd pick queer men over straight men any day. Straight men are a lot of work."

Jonny laughed. "I think I'd have to agree with you on that one."

"You're up," Giorgia Poulsen told him, as she ushered him toward the podium. Giorgia and Kathleen had known each other for thirty years, and Giorgia had been absolutely determined to get the Harvest Festival committee to ask her to speak. As was often the case, Giorgia got her way.

Jonny took the podium to introduce Kathleen. "Hi. I'm Jonny Baronessa, and I'm an internet influencer. That's *one* of the things other internet influencers call me, anyway." Some members of the audience quietly tittered. "I was invited here today to make an introduction of your well-known keynote speaker, a UCSC alum from the Stevenson College class of 1987.

"I was asked to come here to talk about how my generation is pushing action on positively addressing climate change and social justice," Jonny continued. "But let me tell you something: You shouldn't put my generation on a pedestal or say we're the answer. Because it's not true. Some Baby Boomers fought to promote social, economic, and political equality. Some in Gen-X fought to advance diversity, independence, and modern organizing. Some Millennials fought to combat climate change and push forward freedoms for everyone. And now, Gen-Z folks have grabbed that torch — and we're sprinting with it, but we're not alone. We're *all* the answer. *If* we choose to be. Our generations are in this together. So, without further ado, please welcome human rights and environmental attorney Kathleen Bryson."

To applause from those gathered at the event, Kathleen walked up to the podium and gave Jonny kisses on both cheeks, European style. Then she took the microphone.

"Thank you, Jonny. And thanks for that reminder that we're all in this together. And I want to say a special thank you to Giorgia Poulsen and her son, Matteo, for wrangling this invitation for me. Giorgia seems to be able both to be an amazing mom, and also to have a strong hand in making good things happen for people and the planet. And Matteo, thank you for following in her footsteps."

Giorgia and Matt smiled brightly at each other.

Kathleen continued speaking. "I've come to the Harvest Festival today to remind all of you how important this work is at the UCSC Agro-ecology Farm and Garden project. The techniques that are being launched and implemented here have the potential to transform the way we live and eat and heal. To do so in ways that create a healthy bounty for everybody, and that restore rather than destroy the ecosystem."

Kathleen's face became more serious. She pressed on: "But, there are forces that continue to get in the way of progress. They are the corrupt and authoritarian forces of those who hoard wealth and power, who enforce their control with overbearing police tactics, and who violate the human and overall natural ecosystem to satisfy their greed." Storytelling was a strong arrow in Kathleen's quiver. She was about to paint a compelling word picture to draw in her audience.

"I do a significant amount of work with small cannabis cultivators who were drawn to the work in order to nurture plant medicine and sustainable ecology. They wanted to celebrate the powerful female flower that, now, certain clusters of rich white men view as a goldmine. Environmental and social politics have surrounded the plant since it first made its way to our hills — from the first hippie who planted, to the last 'corporate' farmer. In the early days, these flowers represented freedom. As cannabis grew in exchange value, it meant that families could lead a rural, off-the-grid lifestyle, but still afford dental care, transportation, food, and that new roof for the house… and, most importantly, biofuels for the winter!"

With visions of a wintry homecoming now settling into people's minds, Kathleen honed the message. "As with the defense of all freedom though, it comes with a cost. Where I live, the War on Drugs made our simple homes into targets. For us, homeowner's 'insurance' — in quotes — meant stashing piles of cash to pay corporate defense lawyers, who then became rich and arrogant. There were yachts and private planes and wealthy homes for them … with *their* toys never getting seized by police…"

As Kathleen continued her vivid description of the heinous economic injustices, human rights violations, and destruction of the ecosystem being wrought by vulture capital and its enforcers, Noah tapped Matt and Ferran on their shoulders to point them toward his younger children, Clary and Dave, who were sitting on stools waiting to get their faces painted.

"Are we on face duty?" Ferran asked.

Noah grinned and advised them: "They're not gonna have it any other way."

"Mum's enthralled with Babs's speech."

"Babs?" Ferran asked.

"That's Kathleen's nickname. She first got it here at UCSC. And Babs and my mum are old friends," Matt said, filling in the blanks.

"Oh, cool. And you call your mother, 'mum'?"

"Yes, I do. She's Italian-American but she spent a lot of her school years in London, so she kept hearing mothers called 'mum,' and it stuck."

"Got it. So, which one are you taking?" Ferran asked Matt, indicating the kids.

"If you can deal with Dave's squirming, I'll take Clary."

"You got it"

"Okay, boys," Noah said, beginning to walk toward the pumpkin painting table. "Time for me to go help Cam on pumpkin painting duty."

"Ferran!" Dave called, loudly. "Make me a clown!"

"Ferran!" Clary yelled.

Matt smiled and looked at his boyfriend. "You're the favored brother-in-law," he joked.

Ferran grinned at Matt. "I do not mind you making us practically married, baby."

Matt blushed and smiled.

23

BAPTIZED

"The ocean makes me feel really small
and it makes me put my whole life into perspective…
it humbles you and makes you feel
almost like you've been baptized.
I feel born again when I get out of the ocean."
— *Beyoncé Knowles*

*[Song reference: Silk City, Dua Lipa,
featuring Diplo & Mark Ronson — Electricity]*

Ferran

Sixteen days into November, it was an unusually hot day.

"Climate change," Matt observed.

I answered him with sadness: "At least it means we get some time here at Bonny Doon."

Some of our crew — Matt and me, Janaya, Alicia, Alex, Jake, Maura, Emily, and Stu — came to Bonny Dune beach at sunset to bring a bunch of Hershey's Roasting Logs and build a bonfire — which was illegal, of course — and to share some cheap boxed wine. With the majority of us being under 21, that too was illegal. Jake was the designated driver, so he was going to skip the drinking.

We procured our illicit booze — and some Italian soda for Jake — by way of Alicia, who was 21, and Janaya, who was 26. Our other crew members — Arjun, Bikari, Garrett, Cam, Braden, and Ayesha — had begged off coming with us in order to bury themselves in homework.

After we all trekked to the far end of the beach near a rock wall, we started to build our bonfire and lay-out our blankets and towels. Maura sat down close to the fire with Jake beside her, and rested her head in Jake's lap as he looked at her adoringly. Stu and Emily were telling really bad Dad jokes in tandem. Alex and Alicia were roasting marshmallows, and Janaya was casting Tarot card spreads on the blanket in front of her.

Janaya suddenly appeared startled, and spoke up about the Tarot spread she'd just thrown. "Yikes! All kinds of major arcana about death, and revolution, and transformation."

"Geez," Maura grumbled, "what question are you asking?"

"Climate change. And this layout says there's a rough fight ahead."

Depending on how you look at it, Stu waxed either philosophical or dire: "Remember what Thomas Jefferson said. The tree of liberty must be refreshed from time to time with the blood of patriots and tyrants."

Janaya obviously got a shiver from that. But then she shared a story with us: "That reminds me of a story in the Ramayana. In one of the great battles between good and evil, Rama and his comrades slay Ravana. After that, Rama requests that Indra, the leader of all the Devas, restore the lives of all the monkeys who died in the great battle. So, I'm thinking: Maybe that's what's ahead? A restoration?"

"Hmm, monkeys. Well, we did come from a bunch of apes," Jake noted.

***

Ferran

I was thinking about going for a walk with Matt so we could have some alone time on the beach. I caught his eye and tilted my head to point away from our bonfire. We traded silent looks and it seemed we were on the same page.

We both stood, and I told the crew we wanted to take a walk along the water. Matt grabbed a couple of towels — just in case we got splashed by a big wave. Then we excused ourselves to take our walk down the beach together.

Since the sun was setting, it was getting darker as we walked. I was trying to adjust my eyes to the waning light just as Matt told me that he was, too. "Should we keep walking this way?" he asked.

I answered, "Yeah." Then I told him something I'd been pondering. "Matty, I have something I want to ask you. I've been thinking about it for a while."

Matt questioned me gently: "What is it, Ferr? You seem like something's different tonight." I had been very quiet on the drive out to Bonny Doon.

"It's just … I've been thinking a lot about our relationship. About how much I love *us*. About how much we mean to each other."

"I'm always thinking about that, baby," Matt said, softly. "You know, you make me tingle — no amount of electricity could compare. You mean everything to me."

"And you mean everything to me." I reassured him. I hesitated a moment, but then I launched again into what I wanted to tell him. "There's something I want to explore with you — it's something I've actually been longing for."

Matt was now very alert. "You know you can tell me anything, Ferr. What is it?"

I felt lucky that, in the dark, Matt couldn't easily see my beet-red and overheated blushing. "You know…" I said, haltingly. "You know that … when we've made love, I've always been the one to do the, um … you know…"

"Yeah, I do know," Matt said. "I love it — every second of it. I love feeling you inside me."

"Well, what I've been thinking about … is that I want to feel you inside *me.*"

"Oh!" Matt answered, surprised. "I wasn't sure if and when you might be ready for that. Especially given the … um … the size challenge."

I stopped walking, and then so did Matt. I turned to face him to reach out my hand, and I gently stroked his face. "I want you to make love to me. On this beach, in the sand, under the stars."

Matt began to answer, but his breath caught. With his eyes wide, he tried again: "Ferran, I…" Then he shook his head. His handsome ginger tresses shone in the glow of the rising moonlight. Then he let out a soft laugh and looked at the ground. "Wow," he whispered, "way to catch me off-guard, baby."

After a few beats, he looked up at me and nudged me. "I didn't know you felt that way. And I'm kinda turned on that you do. Like, *a lot.*"

"Oh, good!"

"And you want to make love right here on the beach? With our friends 150 meters away? You're a *bad, bad man.* And it's *so* hot."

"Will you?" I asked him, plaintively.

"Uh, YEAH! I'm *certainly* willing to give it a go. But are you sure? I don't want to hurt you."

"I am well aware you'll be using the longsword … as it were."

"As it were."

But I was determined. "I've thought about it a lot, baby. *A lot!* And I've practiced!"

"Oh yeah?"

"And I'm ready. I really want this — I want to bond with you … on an even deeper level."

"You big stud. I love that so much," Matt said, smiling up at me. "And it will definitely be *deep.*" And that got a laugh out of me.

I made what I wanted even clearer to him: "Listen Matty, I do *not* want you to be too gentle. I'll tell you if I can't take it."

"Really?"

"Really. I want my man to *take* me. You're my gentle beauty, but I want you to give it to me *rough.*"

"If that's what you really want, I hope I can make you feel the kind of ecstasy that you make me feel. … Fuck, you are making me hard as a rock, baby."

"Glad to hear it. Also … you can… um…. kiss me all over… like, everywhere."

"Everywhere?"

I chuckled. "Well, as long as we don't get sand in your mouth. So … could we look for the right spot?"

"Yeah, I think *so.*"

I clasped Ferran's hand and we resumed walking further down the beach, searching for a perfect spot. Off in the distance, I could hear our friends continuing to chat and laugh by the bonfire, hopefully oblivious to what we were about to do.

Maura

Janaya's cold Tarot reading when she first sat down and cast the cards had left her dismayed. Now she was aiming for lighter fare, I guess. She was giving Jake and me a Tarot reading, while all of us around the fire broke out into intermittent laughter. After a good while, we all started to wonder aloud what had become of our "Ferr and Matty."

"Those boys have been gone awhile," Janaya noticed. "It's dark."

"We've all been to this beach more than a hundred times — like, since we could first drive." Alex said, dismissively. "They can find their way,"

That was my cue, I think. I placed the back of my hand on my forehead, and intoned melodramatically: "They only get lost in each other's eyes." Chuckles erupted around the bonfire.

"Stop," Jake said. "They're so *cute* together."

Emily related the story to us that when Stu told her about Matt and Ferran coming out to him, she and Stu had literally laughed out loud. "Like, how could you be constantly hanging out and looking at each other that way, and think people wouldn't eventually figure it out?"

Emily agreed. "They're so in love with each other I can barely watch the sweetness sometimes. I'll wind up giving myself diabetes."

The sweetness factor had not kept the bigots and the Tankies from trying to make Matt's and Ferran's lives crappy, Jake observed.

"But they didn't put up with it," Janaya reminded us. "They really took control of the narrative. You know Matt was already partially out, but Ferran brooked no bullshit from anybody. He even called the team together in the locker room after we won a game, and told them that he scored the final goal because his boyfriend was cheering for him off the field. "

"Oh, *hell* yes!" Alicia exclaimed. "I didn't know he did that!"

"Yeah," Janaya told them. "And a couple of the guys started saying it was gross. And I'll never forget the way Ferran handled it. He got up closer to them, and said that the whole reason he was telling them about it was because he was tired of feeling like he couldn't bring Matt to team hangouts, when their girlfriends would be slobbering all over them. Then he got right in their faces and said: 'And that stops *today*. He's my boyfriend, and from now on he's part of the squad just like your girlfriends are.' And he told them if they didn't like it, they could meet him outside."

Emily was enthralled. "What did they do?"

"The two jerk-wads folded like a lawn chair," Janaya answered, with a grin. "And then a bunch of the rest of them were saying they *knew* there was something between Ferran and Matt. And Cam and a couple of others said they'd seen them making out near Porter. And several of the guys started slapping Ferran on the back and just talking about the game. That's when Bakari told Ferran that he and Matt are sickeningly adorable."

"Well, they kinda are," Alicia agreed. "But good on the guys on the team, except for the two idiots."

"So," Alex began. "… This is a total *non sequiter* …."

"Oh, you *never* do that," Alicia said, with an eye-roll.

"Shush, you! Did any of you know that Ferran was with April for *six years?* And even though the two of them looked like gods, they led this whole 'Every Body Has Worth' body-positivity campaign together to combat body dysmorphia in our high school?"

"Oh, *that's* cool!" Janaya answered.

"So, like, I wanna say," Alex went on, "that April and Ferran did all the right things. They also went to all the right parties and everybody was envious of their sex life, and even with their body acceptance campaign, everybody just wished they looked like them."

Alicia lamented: "It really isn't fair."

"I wonder if there are people who look at Ferran and Matt and feel despair," I pondered, "because they tell themselves they'll never be so gorgeous."

"Yeah! I'm one of them," Jake grumbled.

I reached up and touched Jake's chin. "You are very handsome, Jake."

"Thank you?"

Alex continued his story: "But, listen: despite all that, there was never once in those six years that April and Ferran were together — never even once — that I saw either of them look at each other the way Matt and Ferran look at each other." All of us were quiet for a moment. "I *know* Ferran. When he looks at that man, it's like he's worshipping him."

Stu spoke up: "Come on, Alex. If you weren't straight, wouldn't Matt be someone you'd worship?"

"Yes, I would. But I *am* straight. And they're *still* both my celebrity man-crushes." That sparked a fair bit of laughter and agreement around the bonfire.

"Seeing them with each other is kinda magickal," Jake added. "I mean, come on. You know if people were trying to make a case that soulmates are a thing, they'd point to those two."

"I agree," I admitted.

"Everybody," Alicia declared, "deserves to have at least one person in their life who worships at their altar with abandon."

I raised my cardboard wine cup and announced: "Cheers to *that,* girl."

Jake looked down at me and quietly and told me: "I worship at yours."

"Jake, you sweetheart. I'm really beginning to believe that. I should have asked you out sooner."

Alicia teased us: "That was another chapter of 'When are they gonna figure it out?'" Alex told us he was really glad we were so happy together. And at that moment, a very loud noise that sounded like a combination of a full-throated growl and a long, low moan pierced the air, even rising over the sound of the waves.

It startled Emily. "What the hell was that?" We all turned in the direction of the sound.

I looked around the bonfire and asked, "You don't think they …"

"I'll bet they did," Stu piped-up.

Jake just sighed and said, "Fuck."

"Yeah, *that,*" Alex agreed.

"I'm just sorry I didn't get to watch," Alicia said, with take-no-prisoners honesty.

Jake's eyes got wide and he sputtered: "O. my. gods."

"Well, it's the truth!" she insisted.

24
WORDS

"In the beginning,
what existed alone was *Being,*
one without another.
But its own word itself invokes life,
and the breath of life is its twin flame.
This is a pair indeed;
and the word and the breath of life
are the locus of the call, and of the relationship.
This pair is joined together in what they emanate,
and when this couple is joined together,
each fulfills the longing of the other."
— *The Chandogya Upanishad*

"Immature love says: 'I love you because I need you.'
Mature love says "I need you because I love you.'"
— *Erich Fromm*

[Playlist reference: Fly By Midnight — Infinitely Falling]

Matteo

The rain was going to come down any minute.

We were walking down from Elfland in the direction of Stevenson College, and I could tell that we were about to get drenched. In Santa Cruz, just before the rain pours through the trees in the forest, there is a fragrant aura that emanates like an incense. It's a blend redolent of intensive redwood, cedar, and oak, of old, wet leaf mold and moss, and the suddenly sharper scent of the sea.

That distinct scent was filling the air, and Ferran was grumbling about him being an idiot for failing to bring an umbrella. "Ferr," I told him, "These days, who knows what the rainy season is gonna be. Neither of us remembered to bring an umbrella. The rain isn't gonna make us melt like the Wicked Witch of the West."

He frowned. "Are you sure about that? Maybe the five elements are conspiring to drown us because we're too sweet for our own good."

The first droplets that I could feel began to fall on us. "Here it is," I said. It took barely thirty seconds for the drizzle to become torrents. A minute later, we were looking at each other and laughing.

"It's a bit cold," Ferran replied, "but it's not so bad,"

"I can't think of anybody I'd rather swim with to Stevenson College than you," I joked.

Ferran and I had a deep friendship —a friendship that had been nourished by shared interests, passions, and a mutual understanding that transcended words. It had grown deeper with every passing day, but it wasn't until our lips met for the very first time that the fireworks of our connection lit-up the truth for us. We both had been trying to maneuver around that truth, but we'd fallen for each other. It shattered the confines of my understanding of intimacy and of Ferran's understanding of his sexuality.

He reached out for my hand and stopped walking, which also brought me to a halt in the downpour. Then he took me in his arms and kissed me. He did it with such a tender passion and aching urgency that my knees nearly buckled. The trees were continuing their protest against the wind and rain, but in that kiss, we were in a free-fall of submission to each other.

When we broke the kiss, we both stood there with our clothes soaked and our hair dripping. I wondered what had come over Ferran. I looked up longingly into my boyfriend's eyes and asked, "What's on your mind?"

"You know how much you mean to me, right?" he asked. "How much I care about you?"

"I think so," I answered. "I hope so. My heart tells me so."

"You've shown me a world beyond soccer, and appearances, and burying myself in the classics, Matty. A world where I can stand for what I believe in with my partner by my side. I feel like we have so many dreams to chase, and I'm glad I get to chase them with you."

I felt a wave of emotion wash over me. "You know I feel the same about you. Being with you makes me *so* happy. I can't imagine my life without you, Ferr."

Ferran took a deep breath, and then he said the words: "I love you."

Hearing Ferran say it, I was so happy I thought I might explode. Reveling in the moment of delicious pleasure, I gushed back: "I love you, too!"

Ferran looked at my exceptionally wet forehead. He leaned down and kissed me on it. He said, "I wasn't completely sure how you'd react."

That struck me. "Ferran Bosch!" I exclaimed. "I've been *hoping* for this moment. The words were sitting on the tip of my tongue, and I thought I'd be the one to say them first."

"I didn't think it was possible for you to be more beautiful," Ferran told me, looking deep into my eyes. "But the rain did it. It made you look like you needed me to hold you and keep you safe. Then I knew in every fiber of my being, and I couldn't keep the words inside."

I couldn't help letting out a little moan, and I answered him: "Ever since I met you, I've been falling deeper and deeper in love with you. You make me feel things I never thought were possible."

"I finally think I understand what love is because of you. And *home* is wherever I feel love and have love. You certainly rocked *my* world, Matty."

"I guess I did, but you've rocked mine, too. I feel home with *you*. You're everything I dreamed of."

"Every day, I'm grateful you're in my life."

"I love you," I repeated.

"I love *you,*" Ferran agreed.

I smiled at him as the pouring rain continued. "Now, could we keep walking to your room? So we can get dry?"

"Just so you know," Ferran insisted, "this was not a ploy to get you naked and take you into a hot shower with me."

I had to laugh. "Oh, I hope we can do that, too."

I clasped onto Ferran's hand, brought it to my lips, and kissed it.

Ferran moved our clasped hands over to himself and kissed mine as well. Okay, then, let's march forward," Ferran said, smiling.

I assured him: "Baby, I think that's exactly what we're doing."

25

CHOCOLATE

"Many of us learn as children
that friendship should never be seen
as just as important as family ties.
However, friendship is the place
in which a great majority of us
have our first glimpse of redemptive love
and caring community."

— *bell hooks*

[Songlist reference: Pink — Trustfall]

Ekkheya

On a cool evening, the friend group gathered at Bakari's apartment on Younglove Avenue for dinner. Since the crew had decided to get solidly behind the idea of trying to eat more plant-based meals, they were all eager to participate in experimenting with new dishes. The crew also increasingly liked hanging out together when they could.

Bakari promised to build a feast around his new vegan version of lasagna. He felt it more than rivaled his grandmother's traditional meaty version. Making a great meal together and having a night of board games was reason enough for this crew to get together.

On this night, their disappointment was that Matt and Ferran would not be joining them. Matt had a miserable sinus infection, and Ferran was tending to him. Sort of insufferably, if the occasional texts from Matt were any indication.

All the rest of the crew gathered around the dining table: Bakari, Stu and Emily, Jake and Maura, Cam and Ayesha and Braden, Alex, Arjun, Garrett, Alicia, and Janaya.

The table was covered with ingredients, and they were all working to prepare them — slicing and dicing vegetables, and mixing nutritional yeast and various sauce ingredients for a delicious vegan lasagna. They were also chopping ingredients to make an enormous salad, along with mixing up a fresh balsamic vinaigrette dressing. Their conversations and laughter filled the room.

In the midst of it, Braden nudged Bakari, and asked, "You really think it can match your grandma's meaty masterpiece? That's a bold claim, my friend."

"Oh, it's more than just a claim. It's a full-on taste bud revolution! Trust me, you won't even miss the meat."

Janaya pointedly encouraged them to pick up the sous chef pace: "Let's keep the momentum going, people! The more we pitch in, the sooner we eat."

"Ooooh," Bakari cooed, "Coach be coaching!"

"You be grateful you have my skills at your disposal, young man," she reminded him. "If I were a faculty member instead of a staff coach, I probably couldn't be such close friends with all of you."

"I'm actually glad this whole group is together," Arjun admitted, "because you people have become my closest friends. I mean, some of us met last year. But this year we've had the Ferr and Matty Show, and this has really become like a family. You all mean a lot to me."

Ayesha confirmed that, adding: "*Found* family."

And Cam emphasized it: *"Chosen* family."

"I like that," Emily said. "But speaking of the boys, I'm bummed they aren't here with us. It's sad they had to stay home. Do you think they'll actually *survive* without us?"

Stu chimed-in: "You know they're holed-up in Matt's room because Ferran insisted on nursing him back to health."

"He got that sinus infection right after they went out and got soaked in the cold rain," Maura complained, adding an audible *tsk tsk.* "What did they expect?"

Emily reminded her that it had been a big day for them. "They said, 'I love you,' for the first time to each other in that rain."

"That is so totally romantic," Jake gushed. "O my gods, they kill me."

"Let's hope it doesn't kill Matt," Stu noted. "The sinus pressure triggered a migraine before he could even start taking his antibiotics."

Braden told us Ferran had texted him that Matt was in a world of hurt. According to Stu, Ferran had gone into total Florence Nightingale mode. "He rushed out of our dorm room armed with a witchy first aid kit. I kid you not. He packed tea, wild honey, a bottle of elderberry Fire Brew, silver-zinc nasal spray, and a jar of Vicks."

"When you break out the Vicks, you mean business," Alicia remarked.

"Remember, his parents are Spanish and Catalan," Alex noted. "Vicks Vaporub is their prized magick cure-all." Janaya assured us that she, too, was a firm believer in the stuff — she claimed it would indeed work on a lot of things.

"In any case, I'll tell you what," Arjun said, offering an observation. "That man is hopelessly devoted to Matt."

Emily concurred: "And vice versa. It's hard to believe they've only been together a few months. I can't imagine them apart."

"I don't think any of us can, really," Bikari added, while whisking the non-dairy cheesy concoction that was in the bowl in front of him. "It's like they were literally made for each other. I'm just really glad they were the magnets that pulled us all together."

Maura voiced her emphatic agreement with Bikari, and thanked him again for playing host. Her reputation for figuratively stirring the pot was well-earned, and there she was, literally stirring the pot of Bikari's homemade marinara sauce on the stove. The others had the sautéing and cooking and layering of lasagna noodles underway.

Alicia offered to set up Scrabble and Yahtzee on the game table to play while the prep was getting finished and the lasagna was baking.

"Well, now, while the lasagna is in the oven," Maura announced, "I'll be getting the stuff ready for the dessert."

That prompted eagerness from Ayesha: "I heard it's going to be a very special one,"

"Chocolate Madness," Maura confirmed. "So, I made some chocolate mousse to go with the brownies that Jake freshly baked earlier. Not vegan, but vegetarian at least."

"O my gods!" Janaya gushed excitedly, "I love Chocolate Madness."

Cam grandly proclaimed to them all: "We've had a lot of sappy talk here, so of course I have a Willy Wonka quote to match."

The rest of them sent up an audible groan, but Bikari encouraged him: "Go ahead."

"If you want to view paradise, simply look around and view it."

They all groaned again, but Bikari riffed off of the quote: "A Chocolate Madness is more than pure imagination."

Yet more groans ensued.

Alex asked Janaya what this storied confection was about. She explained that it was an incredible dessert that used to be served at a since-closed Santa Cruz restaurant called Saturn Cafe. "My family loved it," she said, "so, when they closed, I started making it myself."

"That's how I learned, too," Maura confirmed. "It has McConnell's Dutch Chocolate ice cream, homemade chocolate mousse, fresh baked brownies, intense hot fudge, whipped cream, and dark chocolate chips."

Alex joked that it would probably put them all in a chocolate coma, but it would be totally worth it.

Then, wondering about their upcoming plans, Janaya asked the crew if Matt was still wanting to host everyone for Thanksgiving.

"Of course!" Ayesha responded. "It's only a few days away. It's all of us at our house who are hosting, and we already have a bunch of supplies."

Janaya suggested she put a grocery list on their group chat so they all would know what to bring, and Bakari agreed.

"You got it," Alex answered, "we can all help."

26

CREW

"You could be the captain of your soul.
But you have to realize that life is coming from you
and not just at you, and that takes time."
— Timothée Chalamet

"There are no passengers on spaceship Earth.
We are all crew."
— Marshall McLuhan

[Playlist reference: Jason Mraz — Song for a Friend]

Maura

A few days later, as the weather apps were predicting the likelihood of more rain, our online group chat lit up and we all decided we were in desperate need of a study break. We agreed to meet at Mr. Toots Coffeehouse. It was a place in Capitola Village that was a short hop from Matt's house on Pleasure Point.

Matt and Ferran were sitting at a makeshift extended table in the coffeehouse with our crew. We were all gleefully chatting and I felt like we were bonding even more closely. The boys were back with us in our circle, and we were all definitely happy about that.

Matt's vibrant, 80-something, maternal grandmother, Anna Gravina, also happened to be one of the co-owners of Mr. Toots. She was working in the back office. Those of us in the crew who'd already met her knew she had a delicious flair for the dramatic.

Mr. Toots had become locally famous for its signature large coffeehouse drinks, which arrived to the table in huge goblets. They were decadent, and we'd all ordered our favorites. Some ordered the Café Borgia, an orange mocha with whipped cream. Some ordered the Café Cinnamon, which was covered in shaved milk chocolate. Others ordered the purist's Ghiradelli Hot Chocolate. A few others ordered the Mocha with extra chocolate. Without a doubt, we were a crew who loved our chocolate.

Sipping his Borgia, Bakari announced that we were giving him the chance to have the study break he needed. I joked that we were all just using it as an excuse to score another chocolate high. "We're a bunch of Chocoholics," Alicia confirmed, noting that we'd binged on Chocolate Madness the other night, and here we were getting another fix at Toots.

Can't blame us," Jake said, "Chocolate is basically the eighth wonder of the world."

Arjun, ever the philosopher, noted that in some cultures it is called the food of the gods. He said he found irony in that, because some big industrial farmers who play god might be killing the environmental future of the cacao plant. There was no mistaking that this was a table full of Santa Cruz university students with this kind of conversation.

"We talk about Deep Magick, and I don't think it's only personal. The blood of mass extinction events and genocides is calling from the ground," Matt said, dryly and politically — no big surprise there.

"Yeah, I agree. But what do you think we should do about it?" Ayesha asked.

"Alicia, isn't the saying that the quality of your relationships determines the quality of your life?" Matt asked.

Alicia confirmed it: "That's what the peer-reviewed psychological evidence says."

"So, I think that a life of true quality doesn't seek to reap such ridiculous quantities from the Earth that it destroys the human habitat in the process," Matt declared.

"Okay, I get that. I'm definitely picking up what you're throwing down," Ayesha agreed.

Arjun related *another* philosophical story to our table of friends. "There's a myth in the Puranas, where Shiva attacks the demonic exploiter, Andhaka, with a trident. But every drop of Andhaka's blood that falls to the ground spawns another demon like him. So, Shiva decides that to keep that from happening, new agents would keep having to come into being in order to transform the way that the Earth is kept. They'd have to build that new way by consuming the blood that Andhaka leaves behind before it can take root in the ground."

"So … what?" Ferran wondered. "How's that relevant?"

"When we serve hot chocolate or golden milk in India," Arjun answered, "some households serve them in special cups that have scenes from that myth carved or painted on them."

"So, let me see if I'm following all this ponderousness. The blood from Andhaka could be a metaphor for chocolate? We transform it from being bad to being food for the journey?" Ferran asked.

Arjun nodded. "Pretty much."

"That's intriguing," Ferran said, contemplating. "There's a lot of evidence that the abundant flavonoids and antioxidants in cacao are brimming with health benefits, from lowering blood pressure and inflammation, to reducing the chance of heart disease, diabetes, and even dementia, to treating depression and increasing libido." Then, he laughed. "Maybe that's why this crew craves it so much! And maybe the Aztecs weren't kidding when they called it the food of the gods."

Ayesha mused, "There's some kind of tale about this in pretty much as many cultures as have myths, you know. They always tell a story about a band of rebels and a leader who take on the struggle. And as the myth goes: there are those who will choose to commit no treachery, and if any of them will give themselves willingly to the cause of justice for the people and the Earth — even if it will mean that the undeserving also get freed from destruction — then their sacrifices will crack the death spiral and reverse it."

"Dramatic!" Jake declared. "But honestly, I wouldn't be surprised if that's why this group has come together."

"I'm gonna have to reflect on that one for a while," Matt acknowledged, "but fewer and fewer things surprise me these days."

"I dunno, but this is *way* heavy," Braden said, "and I brought a box of edibles if anybody wants to lighten the mood a little." There was laughter around the table, but only Ayesha took him up on the offer.

Since Braden had been a wake-and-bake kind of guy that morning, he already had been especially giggly. Cam teased him about it, and Braden responded: "Smoke the greens, make the memes, seize the means," which had everyone laughing.

Ferran smiled. "We're not gonna partake of any bud, but now that the patient is back to his old self we can help you indulge in some of this chocolate-fueled debauchery. I'm really happy that this time we could hang out with all of you."

Matt rested his head on Ferran's shoulder. "You were a complete nag, and if I'd had more energy you'd have made me crazy, but you did far more than the antibiotics did to get me up and running again."

I had to give them grief for that treacly sweetness. "O, gods," I muttered, rolling my eyes at them.

Matt laughed at my snark. "You love us."

"I do," I confirmed.

Matt also informed our crew that he had now learned how to use Vicks on his pressure points to help soothe a migraine.

"See," Ayesha proclaimed, "Vicks really is a miracle cure!"

"Cheers to that," Emily said, raising her Café Cinnamon in a toast, "and cheers to getting our cravings satisfied."

"Hear, hear!" cheered Garrett, as we all clinked our goblets together.

"I've been craving the Thanksgiving feast you all are going to have together," Braden told us, "But I have to go spend it with my grandmother, so I can't make it this year. This might be her last Thanksgiving. I have to go."

Ayesha and Cam put arms around Braden's shoulders, and assured him that even though he'd be missed, he was doing the right thing. "She's always been more open and supportive than the rest of my family of origin," he said. "I just want to spend this time with her."

"And you're right to do it," Matt agreed. "We'll still be here when you get back, man." Matt told all of us he was glad to just be present with us, right there and then. "It's good to be feeling better finally, after that sinus infection and migraine. It felt like hell to go through it and to miss out on dinner with all of you. I didn't think I'd miss it so much, but I did."

"We missed you, too," Bakari assured him.

Ayesha smilingly looked over at Ferran and quizzed him: "What's a ginger with a sinus infection look like?"

Ferran chortled. "Like a red nosed reindeer," he answered, "with a very shiny nose."

"Mean," Matt muttered.

Ferran nuzzled Matt's ear. "I couldn't possibly be more in love with you, Rudolph."

Matteo

Anna, my grandmother, approached the group with a mischievous smile on her face. Ferran and I had only informed her of our romantic relationship within the past few days, but she couldn't have been more thrilled. "Oh, my darlings!" she gasped dramatically at both of us. "You boys have made me the happiest matriarch in Capitola Village!" She was hardly able to contain her excitement, and she began to gush over us and make uproarious — and sometimes, superbly inappropriate — comments.

"What's got you so giddy, *Nonnina?*" I asked.

"Boys," she answered, placing a hand on her chest, "just discovering that you both have joined the bi brigade is *divine!* I need that energy in my life! Plus, the fashion tips!"

Ferran rolled his eyes and laughed. "I think that may be my department."

"You do seem like you could pull off being a dapper hunk, my dear."

Ferran chuckled.

"I'd honestly rather be naked," I offered.

"Well, Matteo," my grandmother commented, "I can empathize with that, but it really doesn't work everywhere, darling. Especially if you're built anything like your grandfather in the major tools department."

"O my gods," I groaned, blushing.

She winked and waved her hand. "Oh, don't you worry your pretty little head, darling. Or big head. Whichever."

Ferran — and the rest of the crew at the table — laughed, heartily.

"Well, I guess that's out in the open, then," Ferran smiled.

"Or it isn't, darling. Right?"

The rest of us at the table laughed again. *"Nonnina,"* I said, "you always have a colorful way of putting things."

"My darling, if life isn't colorful then what's the point? Besides, you're both so blessed. Being able to love more than one gender means you have so many options! Quite envy-inducing, if I do say so myself!"

"It can be!" Jake interjected. "And those two aren't the only ones in this crew. We've got a few more."

"Are you telling secrets out of school, dear?"

"No, ma'am," Jake answered, "it's all out in the open!"

"My dears! This is a delightful little chosen family you have!" my grandmother told them all.

"I never really thought about me being bisexual as having a sort of buffet of options," Ferran said. "I just wanted Matty. And that surprised the heck out of me because it was so different from what I was used to. I really don't want to see anybody else; I don't know if I ever will."

"That goes for me, too," I noted.

"Oh, my sweet boys," my grandmother said, grinning mischievously, "there's a whole world of possibilities out there waiting for you to explore. And don't worry, you can be there to hold each other's hands through it all."

"I think for us that's something for way in the future, if ever," I said.

"I'm going to have to agree with Matt," Ferran added "I'm just so happy to finally be together in a relationship with him — like, a passionate one. It makes me really happy."

"And about time, too!" my grandmother quipped, clapping her hands. "Love knows no bounds, my dears. Two handsome, intelligent young men like yourselves deserve nothing less than an extraordinary romance!"

Around the table, the members of our crew voiced their agreement in feeling that Ferran's and my relationship was pretty extraordinary.

"We were lucky to find each other," Ferran suggested, looking at me with sparkling eyes.

"Luck has nothing to do with it!" my grandmother insisted. "It was written in the stars, I tell you! Everything has aligned and brought you two together."

Maura agreed with my grandmother's sentiment, too. "They're like the definition of soulmates, aren't they?"

I felt humbled, and from the blush on Ferran's face, I could tell that he did, too. But I also felt gratified to hear the agreement around the table.

"Nonnina," I asked, "are you trying to set a record for embarrassing me in front of everybody?"

She raised her eyebrow. "Oh, my sweet Matteo, there's nothing outrageous or embarrassing about speaking the truth. And trust me that my reading of you two, and my compliments, are as fabulous as *I* am."

Ferran grinned. "We can't argue with that, ma'am."

"Ferran, I told you that you could call me Anna!"

"I'll try to remember that, Anna."

Sitting down beside Ferran and me, she offered us some grandmotherly advice. "Now my boys, I can assure you that this old Bundle of Fabulousness is one hundred percent in your corner. But it looks like all your friends here are, as well. Do you know how important it is to have that?"

"I hope we do," I answered.

"When you're around me, feel free to be as openly smitten with each other as you want," she assured us. "Don't be worrying about any judgment from me. Besides, I have a reputation to uphold. Being fabulous and supportive takes practice, you know."

I squeezed Ferran's hand. "Anybody would be lucky to have you, *Nonnina.*"

Ferran smiled widely. "Truly, Anna, you're the best."

"You two are going to make this old diva weak!" my grandmother declared, dramatically placing a hand on her heart. "Now, you haven't told me the whole story. How did this beautiful romance blossom? I know this is going to be swoon-worthy. Tell me everything!"

I think Ferran and I knew our love story could be one for the books. Actually, we couldn't wait to share it with my grandmother. But we exchanged a look, sharing a silent understanding that we didn't want to detract from our time with the crew. As if reading our minds, our friends chimed-in just then to tell us to tell my grandmother the full story.

So, we settled-in as the sun started to set, telling our tale of unexpected love. My grandmother readily gushed and sprinkled her own sassiness throughout the conversation. Our friend group helped by adding even more details. After we wrapped up the story, we both hugged her as she had to leave to go back to work.

***

As my grandmother walked back to the office, Alex patted me on the shoulder and his face got serious. "We all missed having you around, Matt. It's good to see you back in action. And the whole story of you and Ferran gets me kind of emotional."

I remembered Ferran's stories that Alex and April used to be at odds constantly. "I'm glad you and I never bicker," I told him, "I guess I'm not as much of a threat."

"Or maybe," Alex offered, "I just got over my insecurity about what it means to be a best friend. Let me tell you, Matt: Ferran looks at you more adoringly than he ever looked at April. But I love you guys, and I don't feel like you compete with me. I feel like you're my brother-in-law."

Ferran looked at both of us and said, "Alex, that's intense."

I took Alex's comments with a special warmth. "I love every bit of what you just said to me," I told him. "Every bit of it, man."

"Me too" statements went around the extended table.

"Maybe 'brother-in-law' was a wee bit premature, but you two *are* 'Ferr and Matty'." Cam told us. "You're both good guys, and I can see how happy you are together."

"I appreciate you saying that, Cam. Don't get me wrong: I know he can be challenging," I said with a chuckle. "But he makes me look at the world differently. He makes me smile when I don't feel like smiling. He's strong and kind, and entertaining and infuriating."

"Hey," Ferran griped, giving me side-eye.

I continued: "He's my special person. Sometimes I think I'd prefer him bound and gagged, but I don't know what I'd do without him."

Ferran grinned and winked at me. "I don't even know where to start with that".

Arjun wagged his finger in the air emphatically and declared: "I say they're soulmates."

"Signs of a lifetime," Stu agreed.

Janaya looked at us softly and smiled. "And here I thought soccer was the only end-game we had in common."

I could see Ferran get choked up about that, and a tear began to trickle down his cheek.

"You guys," I said to all of them, "you're amazing."

27

THANKSGIVING

"Bearing faith is the substance
of the things that we hope for.
Trust is the evidence
for the realities we have not yet seen."
— *Paul the Apostle, Letter to the Hebrews,*
chapter 11, verse 1

[Playlist reference: Kenny Loggins — Celebrate Me Home]

Ferran

Thanksgiving Day showed up sunny and slightly warmer than usual, and Matt was excited to have our crew all together for the feast.

A well-known Kenny Loggins song was softly playing over the sound system. I kissed Matt on the tip of his adorable nose and he asked me: "Are we gonna turn on every love light in the place?"

"I think you have the power to do that, with or without my help," I answered, "but I definitely wouldn't want to do this without you."

We'd discovered that our collection of friends all had some witchy ideas in common, and we'd been learning and celebrating that as we got closer to each other. When we were hosting our friends together, I could see in the way Matt behaved that he could feel the bond between him and me even more strongly.

That bond meant home and family to both of us. I don't know why we'd both told each other of those feelings, or how it had happened so quickly, but I was glad. Still, there were still moments I worried I couldn't trust that I'd found it.

Our friends were already mingling in the combined living and dining room, loosely gathering around the extended table. They were already delving into intellectual banter, and I could tell it was going to be one of *those* days — of stereotypical university student kinds of conversation. With this crew, it was usually entertaining, so I didn't mind.

At the of a large table extension, Matt and I had staked-out seats at the corner of a curved leaf we added for the gathering. Around the board were seated Cam and Ayesha, Garret, Arjun, Alicia, Bakari, Alex, Jake and Maura, Emily and Stu, and Janaya. Most of us were meeting our one new guest — Janaya's friend, Laleh — for the first time.

Laleh hailed from a wealthy Persian family and was a third-year student at Kresge College. She and Janaya had been close friends since they first met at the start of those three years, on the front porch of an off-campus party. Over that time, Janaya learned that, for practically any event during which a family presence might be nice, Laleh would most likely be left orphaned by her parents.

"Thank you, people!" Matt said to all of us as he and I took our seats around the feast. "Thanks to all of you for coming here to join our house in celebrating the Harvest Thanksgiving together. You know I am so glad to have all of you in my life."

"I am lucky that I get to be a co-host of this dinner and that it means *I* get to speechify, too," I joked. "But seriously, I think it's a beautiful day for the first Thanksgiving that we're all spending together. And I wanna say how proud I am to be in this circle, because of all the love that's here."

Around the table, people nodded.

"The love at this table is magick," I said, "it's a power. For me, meeting you all and getting to know you has reinforced that we're worth fighting for. I am really thankful for you all, and I'm *especially* thankful for my Matty. I have a hope and a wish for all of us: That all the love around this table can deepen our understanding and empathy, and that it can fuel our efforts for people and the planet."

Affirmations of agreement went around the table, except that Janaya's friend Laleh was rolling her eyes.

Maura spoke up: "Well, I'm especially thankful for my Jakey Wakey," she cooed, trying to be as saccharine as possible.

Jake looked at her with mild embarrassment. "Jakey Wakey?"

I quickly sealed it: "I approve of this nickname!"

"O my gods," Jake said, shaking his head. Maura giggled.

There were a few full bottles of chardonnay on the table near Laleh. She took hold of one of them and immediately set about pouring into her glass. She gulped from it and repeatedly topped it off as if it was from her own personal bottle.

Matt decided to just continue: "And you're all our crew, after all. Except our special guest, Janaya's friend Laleh."

"Hi Laleh," Alicia piped up, "It's nice to meet you."

"Yes, a pleasure," Alex affirmed.

"Yes," Garrett added. "Welcome to our house."

Bakari joined in, commenting, "I'm glad I'm considered crew."

I claimed him: "You and Cam are my soccer besties! Of course, you're crew!"

"Especially since you were at the bonfire with us at Porter and we found out you could fire dance," Matt reminded him. "That was impressive, especially while you were singing *Rise With the Fire.*"

"Kinda gave myself away with that, didn't I," Bikari replied, mischievously.

"As far as we were concerned," Garrett told him, "That's what sealed the deal for all of us wanting to get to know you better."

"Well, I didn't know I'd have to be here to make up my astronomy exam over Thanksgiving break, so I'm really glad you all extended the invitation," Bakari admitted.

"Glad you could be here, brother," Cam said, patting him on the back.

"We really do love to have this whole crew together, especially here at our house" Ayesha reflected. "I'm just sad that Braden couldn't celebrate with us. But it was important he head to his grandmother's house this year."

"It won't be for long," Cam told her, petting the back of her head. "He'll be back with us soon."

Arjun said that since Matt and I were camped out there at the Live Oak house for the break, everybody would just have to settle for getting their cuteness overload from having to watch us being lovebirds.

"Will you leave them be?" Janaya chided him. "They can't help it they're too adorable and romantic to bear."

"I'm happy to be a romantic, and I'm going to have to start hating you all," I joked. "Except maybe you, Laleh. It's really an honor to have you join us. Thank you for coming."

Laleh looked over at me archly. "Well, thank you, Ferran," she said with strained politeness. "It's a thrill to finally meet you. Matt was just telling me so much about you."

Geez. What did I ever do to her? "Hopefully, he only said good things," I answered calmly.

"Of course, I did," Matt insisted, grinning. "I'm a romantic, too. You know I would never tell about your 'bad boy' side."

That got a wink from me and eye-rolls from the rest of our friends.

"Listen to all that mushy romantic noise," Laleh groused with a bit of disdain, and she took another gulp of wine. Then she peered over at Matt and me. "And don't the two of you look like a homosexual wedding cake topper. How whimsical."

"We're both bisexual," I said, correcting her.

Matteo

Although Laleh was a new guest, I could tell from the look on Alicia's face that she was starting to feel antagonized by her.

Alicia posed a question to her: "What's your problem with romanticism? I don't see anything wrong with it — visionary ideals, adventure, mystery, experiencing emotional depth. I don't see anything wrong with the whimsy part of it, either, for that matter."

"It seems to be such an easy illusion for people who just love the way things *look* to other people," Laleh pontificated. "I mean, think of how this looks: Ferran's snagged himself a boyfriend who lives in *this* house, and this is almost palatial for Santa Cruz." She turned to Matt and gave her opinion with a grin: "Your parents must be doing well, Matt."

Was Laleh saying that Ferran was some poor brown boy who wanted to look good by having a rich boyfriend? If she was, she had no clue how completely off-base that was. Besides, she was being rude. I answered her flatly: "Enough of us live in this house to make it cheaper than living in the dorms."

I could see the rest of our guests bristling around the table. Ferran focused sharply on our wine-guzzling guest, and his body language said he was getting tense and annoyed. "I'm not sure what you're implying, Laleh," he said pointedly. "My desire to be with Matt turned out to be my ticket *out* of a manufactured image, not my incentive to start one."

"He's also white and privileged," she snapped.

Ferran's eyes narrowed. "Do you think that's why I got together with him? Matt's an organizer and a leader," he said in a measured tone, "and it's mostly for labor stuff and for intersectional environmentalism — and I think you're aware of that. *Both* he and I are eco-socialists — did you know that? And any privilege we have, we use to push the wedge to further open the door."

Perhaps because the alcohol was numbing her feelings, Lalah's reply was harsh: "It's very *convenient* for you to talk about eco-socialism and all your *other* romantic notions when you're a soccer jock and you have a rich boyfriend."

"You have rich parents," Janaya chimed in.

"And *I'm* actually focused on working for social justice," she snapped again, "not on trying to get myself noticed by a Jonathan Anderson or by some soccer franchise."

I drew a breath through my teeth and I could tell my eyes went wide. I stared at Laleh and began to sputter: "You …"

Ferran turned to me and pleaded: "Baby, please?" Then he turned back to Laleh and calmly explained: "Laleh, neither Matt's parents nor mine are rich, like *yours*. They're both sorta middle class. And I don't even pretend to be noticeable enough for any fashion houses."

Our other guests muttered some disagreement with Ferran on his being noticeable enough.

Ferran kept talking. "I'm not gold-digging from Matty, and I'm also not here on my parents' dime. And I didn't want to be. I'm here because I earned four soccer scholarships and a Classical Association of California Award. And even if my parents were paying, it wouldn't make what you call my *romantic* eco-socialism any less real."

Laleh's head began to bob slightly, and she quipped: "Or your ability to be a fashion plate, Studly Do-

Right. You know you make a noticeable splash, but I'll let you slide on that one."

I was afraid she was going to derail our dinner, so I tried to remind her of her own status. "I don't know why you are saying these things. Laleh, your parents have more money than God. They're giving you a free ride and platinum credit cards. My parents don't fund the bulk of my costs. I'm funded by the Broward Youth Award and three more financial scholarships for community and environmental sustainability."

"Yet here you are, in surfers' paradise, with all your longed-for romantic visions, pretending that romance is the ideal, and that your magazine cover of a boyfriend is the proof."

I wanted so much to derail her tirade, or at least to move her to stop talking. "Look, on a personal level, some people just *are* romantic and some *aren't.* That's why aromantic people exist," I told her.

"Romance is just a construct," she boozily declared.

This ping-pong game was definitely a discussion among university students, and I could tell it was likely to just get more and more jargon-y. I rolled my eyes. "What *isn't* a construct — in the physical world, I mean? Some constructs are more helpful and enduring than others."

Laleh reached for a bottle and topped off her glass again. "What do you think makes one construct more helpful than any other?"

"That gets into the same questions about why you claim you're motivated to pursue social justice," I noted. "So, why is it that you say you want that?"

"Because people deserve equity, and to live decent fulfilling lives," Laleh declared in an imperious tone. "And because we need a sustainable ecosystem to do that in."

Ferran jumped in with a classically rhetorical probe: "But as an example, then, why would you say that's any more important than seeing the world as a resource that, at any human or environmental cost, you should try to exploit to profit yourself?"

"Because doing that doesn't take the common good into account, or the flourishing of the human spirit, or the fact that the resource is finite in important ways! Doing that is evil," Laleh insisted.

"Evil?" Arjun interjected, philosophically. "You're going to make distinctions about good and evil? But wait. Aren't those just *romantic* notions based on your location and your perspective?"

Laleh reacted a bit loudly: "No, because people's lives matter!"

"Okay, let me ask it this way," Ferran debated further. "If there is no 'meant-to-be,' or no trajectory of consciousness — I mean, if all moral values and perspectives are equivalent and relative — then why *should* people's lives matter? Or, why would any of us choose to center our focus — and I do — on some people's lives as needing to be lifted up more than others?"

"You sound like some right-wing Evangelical Christian," Laleh intoned, her "s" sounds becoming more sibilant.

That was my cue: "The problem isn't that right-wing Evangelicals *have* values and priorities, Laleh. It's that they have *the wrong ones.*"

"Wrong ones?" Lalah asked in disbelief. "Saying that is like a reason people get into wars."

"Ultimately," Emily offered, "people really get into wars because some people fight for the privileges of empire while others fight for social justice. So, let's be real now: do you, or do you not want social justice?"

"I do," Laleh replied, a smile pasted on her flushed face.

"But it seems like, when push comes to shove, you wouldn't fight for it." Alicia probed.

Laleh demurred. "I didn't say that."

Then I dove into the eye of storm: "You didn't just argue that everybody has a perspective. When you dismiss romantic inspiration as 'just a construct,' it suggests that all the perspectives have the same equivalent value. You claim you want social justice, but how do you fight for that when your moral relativism, and your contempt for the art of the human spirit — which you reduce to calling socially 'romantic' — says it isn't more important than bigotry or greed?"

Laleh made an attempt to argue for her intellectual superiority: "It's just obvious. Look, I'm fighting for it, I've already written a paper on social justice, and it's getting published in a prominent humanities journal!"

"Don't you think you might be overly romanticizing your writing?" Emily asked.

"You can't change the world for the better with notions about love," Laleh sniped bitterly. "Your level of *feeling* doesn't mean that other people won't see you as just some ignorant, privileged white person who wants to take up space by using some romantic grand narrative about saving the world. You have to *strip away* all the narratives. Jumping on some bandwagon, without radically removing the *sentiment,* can do a lot of harm to understanding how *fake* it all is."

Maura seemed to be aggrieved, and decided to take a stab at quieting the pontificating guest. "I gotta say this. I'm a physics major, Laleh. I observe stuff in terms of how things work over long periods of space-time. So let me tell you: your postmodernist word salads *do* actually accomplish something. They passively criticize passion, and they try to tear down the ideas that endure for large swaths of space-time. Here on our fragile little planet, conscious beings we're aware of have given us those passionate ideas. And all the while you're busily deconstructing *for the sake of* deconstructing, you're allowing the Empire to roll along and crush the people and the planet. So, what your method does is serve as exactly what Jean Paul Sartre said it does: to be the last ramparts of the bourgeoisie."

"No, it doesn't!" Laleh insisted. "My writing helps people see that there are holes in their basic assumptions!"

I guess Ferran decided it was time to apply his classics knowledge with a heavier and wordier hand. "Come on, Laleh. Any critically and culturally literate person who has the ability to think outside the box can challenge basic assumptions. A person can develop a cosmopolitan meta-worldview and see why *some constructs are better than others* — precisely for the romantic reasons you said are why you want social justice: for the common good and the flourishing of the human spirit."

Maura took another swing. "But that isn't your approach, is it. With your approach, there's no social *reconstruction.* You're basically making an argument in favor of ever-intensifying alienation and atomization. So, there you are, being a privileged advocate for tearing apart all the enduring verities, and dissolving all the glue, and then you just want to have your glass of wine on the rubble."

Laleh dismissed the arguments with a dramatic flourish: "That's just your idea of it."

Cripes on a cracker. This was out of hand, and our gathering was sounding like a freakin' philosophy class.

"Some ideas are better than others," I brusquely proclaimed. Then I looked across at Janaya and nodded at her subtly. "And speaking of romance," I said, trying to change to focus back to the grateful feast we were all about to share, "Janaya, shall we do the honors now?"

At last, Laleh fell silent.

Janaya stood from her seat and grabbed her wine glass, filled with a small amount of Chardonnay. I stood-up from my seat and similarly grabbed my wine glass. For those who would recognize the poem, we began the time-honored volley of verses. Except, although it sounded like poetry, it was really a witchy incantation that is often used to bless food and the company around a feast, to draw up a positive intention.

As we held up our glasses, Janaya and I recited it in tandem.

May the Circle be open …

But ever unbroken.

May Her peace, and His …

Be ever in our hearts.

Wassail at the Harvest!

Merry Meet, and Merry Part, …

And Merry Meet again. So mote it be!

Everyone except Laleh raised their glasses at that line, and added their own: "So mote it be."

Laleh looked around the table, befuddled.

"What in the world was that?"

Ferran

I wasn't sure how much to tell her, since she seemed tipsy, obnoxious, and shocked. "It's ummmm…."

It's an old Harvest blessing," I said, taking another small sip of my own wine.

"How long have we been friends," Janaya asked Laleh in disbelief, "and *how* long you lived in Santa Cruz?"

Laleh seemed confused. "Should I have heard this thing before?"

I think Alicia was hoping to avoid adding religious disagreements to the cloud that was already hanging over the feast. "Well, maybe," she answered, "or maybe not."

"Okay now, everybody" Matt proclaimed, moving along. "Let's dig-in."

Everyone began to serve up the abundance of delicious foods. Released from the intense back-and-forth that Laleh had ignited, and largely ignoring her, we moved on to engage in friendlier and livelier conversation. She didn't seem to notice, as she poured herself more wine. I told Matt that all the food looked amazing and kissed him on the cheek, which made Matt blush. I loved when I could make him blush.

"Thank you, baby. I wanted to make sure everyone had a great Thanksgiving feast."

"Oh, Matt, another romantic construct," Laleh said, grimacing.

I don't think he was in any mood to indulge her further. "What have you done lately to empower indigenous peoples?" he snapped. "Or do you just enjoy ruining the loving associations people place on a holiday, when they're wholly unrelated to its mythical origins?"

Alicia again tried to calm the storm. "I feel like we should be thanking Matt for being an amazing lead chef," she said, looking at Matt with pleading eyes.

"Well, yes Matt! You're such a talented chef! I can't wait to taste… well, *everything,*" Laleh said, suggestively.

I wasn't sure what I'd just heard, but I tried to give Laleh a friendly smile and offered: "You'll love it, Laleh. Matt and Jenaya have been working on these recipes for days. Everything was chosen for being environmentally friendly."

"Well, I can't wait to be a taste tester for Matt, then," Laleh quipped.

Jenaya nervously tried to explain to me that Laleh and Matt had previously met. "Oh, I was meaning to tell you, Ferran. Last year we were at a party at Merrill, and that's where I introduced Matt and Laleh."

"You know, we just had an instant chemistry," Laleh commented, before she took another gulp of her wine.

Matt seemed startled by her assertion. "We did? I don't really remember that."

"He was so into me at that party," Laleh added, apparently trying to flirt.

I felt myself grow cold and pale. Deep inside, I began to feel a pang of fear — that this was my biggest worry coming true — and with the most awful of competitors. My experiences with my parents and with April still haunted me, and I'd never wanted anybody the way I wanted Matt.

Sweat started to form on my brow. My body kicked-in with hyper-vigilance, and my head started telling me that what Laleh was saying must mean that eventually Matt was going to abandon or betray me. Trying to shake it off, I just muttered, "Interesting."

Matt shot me a look. "Not really," he said emphatically.

Laleh persisted, though. "Come on, Matt. We had so much fun that night. Don't you remember?"

Awkwardly, Matt replied, "It was a year ago, Laleh. It was just a fun little party. Maybe you felt I was especially into you, but I was flirty with everyone and you were pretty tipsy. There wasn't much else to it."

Bakari looked at Alicia. "Some people will always abuse magickal power when it's put at their disposal," I heard him tell her quietly, "but it always backfires on them."

Alicia replied quietly near Bakari's ear: "It's better when they don't try to make it explode on everybody, though."

Laleh was taking a long swig of her drink, with her gaze fixed on Matt. Playfully tapping his arm, she probed: "So, this house you all are leasing really *is* beautiful. Mind showing me around later?"

"Uhhh …" Matt looked to me with his brow raised. "Okay, I guess." He still seemed nervous from all the awkwardness. "Maybe we can do a little tour after dinner."

I saw Arjun stare daggers at Janaya, who was about to say something to Laleh when Emily jumped back into the conversation in an attempt to release the tension. She lavishly praised Matt for beautifully decorating the house for the season. "And it's a perfect setting for a warm, cozy Thanksgiving dinner. Those views of the Bay are amazing."

"Right?" Matt agreed. "Thank you! We tried to make it a welcoming atmosphere for everyone."

Jake then tapped his knife on the side of his glass, and then raised it: "Here's a toast to a day of friendship and gratitude. Cheers!" The rest of our friends also raised their glasses and repeated a "cheers."

I could hear that Bakari and Alicia, seated at the far end of the table from Laleh, were quietly sharing their observations of her imbibing. "That doesn't look … sustainable," Alicia commented.

"Nope," Bakari agreed. "And who lives such a sheltered life for three years in a place teeming with witchy people that they've never heard that spell?"

Alicia nodded and suggested that maybe all the wine had kept Laleh from noticing.

Matteo

After we all had our fill of dinner, most of our guests helped Ferran and me clear the table. Then they made their way over to the couches and chairs in the living room for desserts and coffee and more conversation.

Laleh trapped me by the drinks table and was attempting — unsuccessfully — to be enticing, while continuing to drink wine heavily.

"Well, Matt," she said seductively, "I've been enjoying your company tonight. You know, I've always had a thing for you. You're so sexy, and so different from the guys I usually date."

"Maybe you don't date bi guys," I answered flatly.

"That just makes you more of a challenge. And listen, hottie, I've noticed that Ferran seems sort of possessive of you with his body language. How are you handling all that *machista* crap?"

I was somewhat taken aback, and I was losing all patience with her. "Look, Laleh," I said, "I don't really think that's an issue for Ferran and me." I paused for a moment to try to regain some calm. "I appreciate your attraction, but I'm not sure what you're imagining. Do you think I'm just some horned-up bi guy playing hard-to-get for a challenge or something? Ferran and I have really clear communication about our relationship agreements, and we trust each other. We've talked about all our boundaries and expectations. I don't feel like he's a captive of the whole *machista* thing."

"Oh, you don't? Look at him. All that dark Catalan fire, and all those muscles." She began lightly slurring her speech, "He's like some swaggering swashbuckler on a Spanish galleon."

"Well, yeah," I agreed. "It's hot as fuck."

"But, Matteo … You're zo exshquisitely handsome. You might look like a Danish ginger, but I hear you're part Italian stallion."

"Jesus, Laleh," I groaned, rolling my eyes.

"Don't you get tired of being tied down to him? Eshpeshally since you don't get many chances to have some fun with women? Sometimes you jushh need a little excitement, you know?"

This was making me very uneasy. "Laleh," I told her firmly, "I am not open to any extracurricular excitements. I'm not even looking for that now, and neither is Ferran. We're not in an open relationship. And if Ferran and I ever want that, we'll have already talked about it and established clear ground rules and ways to do teamwork around it."

"Oh, pffheh," she muttered.

I reinforced my point: "I'm in love with Ferran and I'm committed to him. I'm not going to do anything to violate his trust. So, I am not gonna go down that path with you, okay?"

Laleh looked at me with pouty lips. "Suit yourshelf, Matteo," she slurred. "But trus' me, you'll regret not taking a chance. You should *live a little.* Life's too short to be so … *cuffed.* This could jushh be our little secret. Come play with the Perzhin prinshess, jus' for tonight."

This was getting me deeply uncomfortable. Laleh just kept drinking and was coming on to me shamelessly. I noticed that the other members of our crew were watching it unfold, and they seemed to be getting annoyed.

Ferran seemed to be seriously triggered, though. He made his way to the drinks table and asked in a gruff tone if anybody needed his help with anything. "I've got all I need," Laleh quipped in a boozy cloud.

I looked up at him with a quiet plea: "I can handle it. Let me take care of this." So Ferran walked back to the others. He did not look pleased. I tried to escape Laleh by moving into the kitchen for cleanup. Out in the living room, Laleh stared out at the Bay and kept drinking.

***

An hour later Laleh wandered, wobbling, into the downstairs master bathroom — just at after Ferran had gone outside on the patio with some of the others. She called out to me that she needed help.

Frustrated, I sighed and rolled my eyes. But I was worried she might be so drunk that she'd hurt herself. So, I went to see what was happening, and walked into the bathroom. Laleh swooped by me and quickly closed the door to get us alone.

I was confused, but far more annoyed. I tried to maintain my composure. "Laleh," I demanded, "why did you call me in here?"

Trying again to be seductive and working very hard at making her "s" sounds less sibilant, a very tipsy Laleh announced: "I thought a little privacy might be nice. No one will even know we were in here."

She attempted to lean in and kiss me, but I grabbed onto her shoulders and moved her away, just after her errant aim had left a lipstick smear on my chin.

Realizing her intentions, I demanded that she stop immediately. "This is completely wrong," I snapped at her. "I told you, *no*. Ferran and I have a commitment. You don't get to just trick me into giving you what you want."

Laleh ignored my words. "Come on, Matt, let's play. Ferran doesn't have to know."

Firmly and strongly, I told her again: *"No.* I am not gonna do this. How many times do I have to tell you? I'm in love with Ferran, and I am not gonna betray his trust."

Just at that moment, Alex jiggled the bathroom handle and the door opened. He immediately saw me holding Laleh's shoulders, and then spotted the lipstick smear on my chin.

"Um…," he said, his eyes widening, "Well, I didn't mean to interrupt."

I looked up at him and told him he hadn't.

"Shurrr, you did," Laleh slurred, again trying to sound alluring.

"Buddy, I hope you have a really good reason for all this," Alex commented, seeming mystified. "That's my longest-running and closest friend out there whose heart you're gonna break."

Ferran

I heard a commotion going on in the bathroom near the front door, so I walked over to see what was going on. I peered over Alex's shoulder into the open doorway, and took-in the startling scene in front of me. Could this be happening? I felt my blood boil: "Can someone tell me what the actual fuck is going on here?"

Matt looked like a wounded deer caught in the headlights. He answered me insistently: "There was nothing even close to an actual fuck."

Lalah slurred as if she was speaking through a thick surgical mask: "See, honey? I told you he was all *machista* possessive!"

Alex looked back at me. "What were you doing in here?" I demanded.

"Ferran … I just found them by mistake."

I looked at Matt in pain and rage, and my eyes filled with angry tears. "Is this 'handling it'? I can't even believe this!"

"Ferr," Matt pleaded, immediately trying to defend himself, "this is not what you think. I would never do something like that to you!"

Alex calmly and genuinely asked him: "So, what the hell is it?"

Alex's question set me off even more. It might sound like an accusation, but I had to ask: "Did you … did you have a bathroom quickie with this …. this *drunk*… at our first Thanksgiving together?" As soon as the words left my mouth, I wanted to take them back. But I was already blinded by emotion — maybe triggered by my too many experiences feeling like this in my past. I felt taken for a fool, and I didn't know what else I could do but demand an answer.

Matt seemed stricken. Maybe it was my tone, or my question, or both. Sure, he seemed to be getting upset, but I already felt like my heart was yanked out of my chest. He asked me sharply: "How could you say that?"

"How could you do this?" I shouted, my head feeling like it was going to explode. My words were tumbling out of me, and I didn't feel like I had control of them. Everything in my body was telling me I was getting abandoned and betrayed again by someone I desperately wanted and needed. "What are you even doing?"

"Nothing!" Matt yelled back. "And there was absolutely no sex going on here! I wouldn't even let her kiss me when she tried! I love you! I love you *so* much! We're a team, and we made our rules; I would never, ever betray you. How could you think I would?!"

At that point, Laleh began to topple forward in her severely drunken imbalance. She peered out at me through her alcohol-clouded eyes. With an inebriated fanfare, she slurred: "Drama queen!"

That was more than enough out of her for me. "Piss off!" I snapped at her.

Alex was apparently thinking the same thing, and I'd barely finished saying the words, when I heard his echo: "Piss off!"

Just as Alex finished, Matt glared at Laleh and shouted: "Piss off!"

She collapsed onto the bathroom floor and sloppily put her head between her knees.

I gaped at Matt though agonized tears, and I asked him plaintively: "How can I trust what you're saying, when Alex found you in here alone with her and I can see her lipstick near your mouth with my own eyes? And she's been hitting on you all day?"

Matt let out a frustrated grumble and argued his point: "She's drunk! I didn't do anything, Ferr. I love you. I would never mess with what we have. Why would you think I could ever want anything that would jeopardize you and me?" Matt had grown pale, and a tear was running down his cheek. Maybe I'd hurt him, or maybe he just was sad for getting caught. He looked bewildered, and Alex was looking rattled and shaking his head.

My mind was spinning in panic, and I could feel that my weeping was making my whole body shake. I felt embarrassed by the whole scene — triggered and in pain. I had to get out of there, to get away from the whole mess. I turned and walked to the coat-rack in the foyer and grabbed my coat, then opened the front door, walked out, and slammed it behind me.

Matteo

After the door slammed, nobody spoke for what felt like the longest twenty or thirty seconds of my life. Alex finally broke the silence: "I don't know for sure what went down Matt, but this is bad. You and Ferran have got to fix this."

By this point, tears were pouring down my face. I was hurt and I was angry. I begged Alex: "How could he think I would violate his trust?"

Alex reached out his hand and rested it on my shoulder. "Matt … Matt, breathe. Just count to ten, okay?" he said, trying to calm me. "Don't forget what's gone down between you and Ferran. You rocked his world, man; you've become like the air he breathes. He loves you so much, and I think he freaked out. I think this might have looked to him like his world just came to an end."

I could barely keep standing. I wrapped my arms around myself, and I couldn't control myself enough not to start rocking back and forth. "I would *not* break his faith," I said, choking on my tears. "I love him! I love him more than anyone or anything!"

"I know, buddy. I know. This just looks bad is all. And I think it's his biggest fear."

From her crumpled position on the bathroom floor, Laleh apparently decided someone cared to hear her speak. "I told you he was a possessive *machista* pig," she slurred.

The fury overtook me and I screamed towards Alex to handle her before I had to: "Get her the fuck away from me! I want her out of my house! Tell Janaya to take her lousy, drunken, trashy friend and get her the hell out of here now!"

28

IMPERATIVE

"Remember that just because you hit bottom
doesn't mean you have to stay there."
— *Robert Downey Jr.*

[Playlist reference: Coldplay — Clocks]

Ekkheya

Laleh got herself into a drunken stupor, and it brought out some of her worst behavior. I had good reason for my attentiveness to this band of young people who had Ferran and Matt at their center. But they were all reeling from the shenanigans of Thanksgiving night. Ferran and Matt were feeling devastated, as if torn apart by a mean-spirited trickster.

In case you didn't know, there are other guardian and messenger spirits like me all over the planet. Some of them are tricksters, but most are not mean-spirited. Laleh isn't one of them in any case.

Each of us has a place to watch over, and we're actually a kind of family. Just as with human families, some of us are closer than others. Sometimes, although not always, family of choice overlaps with family of origin. That probably describes why I'm closest to my brother, Wisake — pronounced, whih- SAH-kay.

I'm not much of a trickster, but he is. Wisake tends to hover around Evanston and the northern parts of Chicago in Illinois. He likes the vibe of a coffeehouse called *Loaves and Witches* in Edgewater. He'd also admit to having a particular fondness for hanging out at Malliway Brothers' metaphysical supply store in Rogers Park. He thinks the staff are cute. Since he's about four thousand years older than they are, I tell him he's a cradle robber. But I digress.

Way back when, some of your ancestors wrangled his name into English to come up with the word, "whiskey." That ought to tell you a lot.

Some wild stories claim he helped create the world; my guess is he just found some considerably inebriated folks and corralled them into their storytelling. That kind of thing was mostly harmless. Laleh's drunken behavior, on the other hand, was not the kind of thing my trickster brother would approve of.

Her behavior not only triggered past trauma for both Ferran and Matt, it also had a painful impact on the chosen family they were developing.

My brother grimaced as I told him about the emotional roller-coaster Laleh's actions had unleashed. "Talk about a disturbance in the Force," he quipped. "We can say that, right?"

"This is not time for levity," I grumbled.

"Honey, levity is the only thing that gets me through with these humans a lot of the time," he observed. "So, what's to be done?"

I knew that Janaya was suffering in her sympathy for her friend, so I asked Wisake to help me — once Janaya could get to sleep —to present some dreams to her that would provide her with options for her emotions.

Emily and Stu contacted her to set up an in-person chat near the Wave sculpture on campus. They felt it was time to offer to help Janaya deal with her friendship with Laleh, if she wanted it. They also felt like they could all use some fresh air away from any prying ears.

The day was somewhat windy, and they were dressed warmly as they waited under the sculpture for Janaya to arrive. She got there wearing a hoodie and a blanket, plopping herself down on the ground. She looked as if she'd barely had any rest.

Stu was the first to speak. "Thanks for coming up here, Janaya. It's good to see you away from that whole mess."

"I look like hell," Janaya groaned. "I had the weirdest, most vivid dream last night. But it told me I had to resolve some big issues."

Wisake and I took that as a win.

Emily spoke-up: "I don't think any of us have slept well, so I'm really glad you agreed to meet with us. We know she's your friend, and we hate to see you hurting because of Laleh's actions. When you took her and left Thanksgiving dinner yesterday, you looked mortified. We were worried about how you might be handling what happened."

In her fatigue, Janaya unloaded: "I appreciate both of you for your concern, I really do. It's been a tough time for the last few months dealing with her. I've talked about it with my therapist and I feel like I'm drowning in my codependency with that girl. I just want to help her, but I know I also need to take care of myself and set some healthy boundaries."

Stu placed his hand on her shoulder, trying to comfort her. "Look, we understand. It's not easy when you care about someone who's dealing with addiction."

Emily agreed. "Absolutely the truth. But you have to remember that you can't fix Laleh. Only she can do that for herself. You can be there to support her, but you can't do it all *for* her."

Rubbing her face, Janaya acknowledged that she was aware. "It isn't just a saying. Her heart really *is* drenched in wine. It's just so hard to accept. I've been trying to help her for so long, but I'm realizing that she needs professional help, like drug detox. And, clearly, I can't provide that."

"Setting boundaries is crucial," Stu urged. "If Laleh isn't willing to seek the help she needs, then you have to prioritize your own well-being. You can't let her drag you down with her."

"Exactly! You've been a pillar of strength for both Matt and Ferran, and we don't want to see you lose yourself in this mess with Laleh. It's important to take care of yourself, too."

"I appreciate your perspective, and I want to be sure you both know that," Janaya told them. "It's just difficult when there's so much history between the two of us. In her first year here, she was like my best friend. But as she drank more and more alcohol, that changed. I mean, her parents are really a piece of work, and it shows. I know I can't solve that for her and that I need to prioritize my own mental health and happiness."

"You deserve to do that," Stu assured her. "And remember, we're here for you too. We'll support you through this and help you stay strong if you want us to."

Emily reaffirmed what Stu had said, and assured Janaya that they considered her family. "We want what's best for you and we'll be with you every step of the way."

Janaya told them she knew there was a tough road ahead, and she thanked them for being so supportive. "I hear you both," she acknowledged, "and I probably need an Alanon meeting. I'm determined to take care of myself and maintain healthy boundaries with Laleh."

Stu assured her that he and Emily had faith in her, and that they believed she would find the strength to overcome the grief she was feeling and move forward. They both assured her they'd help her get through it. "Remember you're not alone," Emily urged her. "Lean on us whenever you need to."

"Thank you for being in my corner," Janaya told them, "It means a lot." She said she would be speaking to Laleh's parents about sending their daughter to a Hazelden-Betty Ford center for detox and recovery.

"Where even *are* her parents at this point?" Emily asked.

Rolling her eyes, Janaya filled them in: "She told me they flew from work in Dubai directly to some holiday in Cancun — typical *nouveau riche* and tacky. Can you believe they like Cancun? Anyway, they decided they didn't need to stop back home because — you know —

why would you bother seeing your pesky child when Cancun is calling, right?"

Stu muttered an "ugh."

"But I have their mobile numbers. We've talked before about the direction that Laleh's been going. They're not exactly overflowing with a capacity for empathy, but they'll send money."

29
PINE

"Give a man the world and he's pining for the moon."
— *Susan Howatch*

[Playlist reference: Tyler Childers — In Your Love]

Matteo

The afternoon was approaching evening, but all day the sky had been gray.

I was a few hours clear of a micro-dosed mushroom trip that had given me no relief at all. It had, however, made abundantly clear to me that I could see the signs of a lifetime with Ferran. I collapsed onto my futon and made a video call to Alex. When he answered, I know he must have thought I was babbling, so I tried to collect myself.

"Alex, I need your help," I said, voice shaking. "I don't know what to do. He won"t talk to me and I feel like my heart is shredded. This can't be the end."

Alex took a deep breath and answered me. "I know, Matt, I can tell how upset you are. But you know I got a look at that scene before he did, and it even took me a few minutes to figure out what she'd done to you."

"I tried to explain!" I protested.

"I think Ferran could only see the surface. And he got into such a state when he saw it that he just went completely off."

"I've never seen him lose it like that."

"Look … Matt … You're right, he lost it. He isn't in his right mind."

I wanted to understand. "I don't know what was going on for him."

Alex attempted an answer. "Try to think of where he's come from with all this. April was with him for six years. You and I both know the truth about that: besides being girlfriend and boyfriend, they were each other's most intimate friends. And even though we know it wasn't really a romance, I think it wrecked him when she broke up with him."

"Yeah."

"I think she was right to do it — she absolutely did it for the right reasons. But he still felt left behind and hurt, and that was the wound that was still really sore when he met you."

I moaned, thinking about Ferran's pain. "I know. But Alex, I wouldn't betray him. I don't want to break up with him, *ever.*"

"I really do understand and I love you for that buddy," Alex said, and then took another deep breath. "But you have to keep something in mind. Literally, this man only realized he was bisexual because he fell head-over-heels in love with you."

I felt my stomach drop. "I…" My words caught in my throat.

"You two are in each other's hearts far more than any ordinary couple I know of. You belong together and everybody can see it. Except maybe Laleh. I think she was trying to get what she wanted by creating that whole scene. And I think when he saw it, he had a reflexive reaction. I feel like he must have thought you were abandoning him, too. And he must have felt sheer terror."

"Has he told you that?"

"Not in so many words. But, from everything he *has* said, I'm certain that what's going on."

"Alex, I would never abandon him. *Never.*"

"I know."

"He's the one who — Alex, he just left me there and walked out."

"I know that too. He was a mess, and he's still a disaster."

"That's no comfort for me."

"Look Matt, you know I really like you and that I like you guys together even more. Hear me out on this:

Ferran is just in his own way right now, so please don't give up on him. I've never seen him like this, and we've been friends since we were twelve years old."

"Giving up on him is the last thing I want to do. Alex, I know what the hell I'm fighting for. I'll wait for him."

"That's right. I support you in that. Stand your ground, man."

I felt like I'd been duped. "I was just trying to help her out and make sure she got home safely," I argued. "She was staggering drunk and she'd been bothering me all day. You know that's the exact moment that Ferran walked in and jumped to conclusions."

"You're right, Matt," Alex reassured me. "He absolutely misunderstood, and I'm not excusing his reaction. I know it's hard to believe, but even though Ferran knew he could be putting everything on the line for you, he wanted you with all his heart. And he was strong enough to actually do it, because you were there to support him. I know he loves you *so* much."

"I wish he understood how much I love *him.*"

"He was already on edge because Laleh was trying to pick fights and seduce you all day. I think anger and fear quashed his rational thinking, and that's why he got it all wrong."

"That's exactly what I've been trying to tell him, Alex, but he won't give me the chance. That night she was acting-out was a disaster, but I absolutely *did not* cheat on him. You know I wouldn't, don't you?"

"I believe you never would, Matt."

"I think he saw Laleh's damned smeared lipstick on my chin and he just assumed the worst. You watched him, and you heard him accuse me of cheating and then storm out of my house."

"I saw it, and I wish I never had. I can only imagine how much pain and anger you must be feeling."

"He's everything to me," I said, the tightness in my throat bringing more tears to my eyes. "This really can't be the end."

"You two just really need to talk this through, Matt."

"I've tried to call and text him, and I've sent him countless direct messages. I've poured out my heart, Alex. I've tried to make him understand what really happened and I've begged him to let me come over. I've even considered sending a letter by snail mail. But I think he's blocked me; he hasn't responded to anything I've sent. It feels like he's completely shut me out of his life."

"Believe me, I've tried to get him to hear the truth. I can't defend him; he's acting like a fool. I'm really sorry, buddy, but he's like a wounded animal right now. I told you I think of you like you're my brother-in-law, and I know this must be incredibly rough for you."

"I feel like my world is falling apart."

"I wish this wasn't happening. Have you tried asking Stu if you could go to their room and see him in person?"

"Yes, I texted Stu. He said if Ferran wasn't answering me, he didn't think that me coming to the dorm room would be good. He said Ferran might feel ambushed."

"Just fucking hell," Alex said, in exasperation. "Fuck, fuck fuck! I just … Look, have you considered giving him some space and time to process everything?"

"It's been more than three days already, Alex, and I'm getting scared. I feel like cold death, and I've actually been counting the hours. We're up to eighty-nine, and I can't stand it. Eighty-nine hours of complete hostile silence from the love of my life. I can't bear the thought of losing him — over something that *never happened,* in a situation that wasn't even my fault!"

"I have to say this to you, Matt. You were wronged — no question. I hope you can forgive him for it. And I really understand your desperation, but sometimes people need time to process their emotions. It might be hard, but try to be patient with him. I've known him for so long and I know he's miserable. I am going to go talk with him again."

I was choking on my tears. "I can't let him slip away without fighting for us, but I don't know what to do."

"Breathe."

I tried to take some deep breaths and steady myself. I thanked Alex for taking time to talk with me and for being there for me during this mess.

"Man, you're chosen family," Alex assured me. "I hate seeing you in pain, and I hate seeing Ferran in pain."

"Thanks, and thank you for wanting to go talk to him again. I'm just holding on to the hope that Ferran can remember how much I love him, and that he'll have enough faith in me to hear what really happened."

"He needs to get over his cheap self, and remember where his worth is — and yours."

"I think I'm gonna go up to the soccer field. I don't have anything else Alex; I feel lost. Just being there where his energy has been is what I need right now."

"I'll give it my all, Matt."

"Okay thank you again," I said. "I'll text you later."

30
RECTIFY

"Compassionate non-attachment is not indifference.
When you are indifferent, you don't look at a person.
You are walking along the street
and somebody is dying of thirst,
but you will not look at him.
If you are non-attached, your inner being
will compel you to give him a glass of water.
But if he doesn't drink it, you will not feel sad or angry."
— *Sri Chinmoy Kumar Ghose*

"The rain falls equally on all sides,
both the just and the unjust.
It is a great cloud rising above the world.
It is not for your heart to bear
the burden of trying to decide
who is deserving and who is undeserving.
Rain your loving-kindness equally on all."
— *The Buddha Siddhartha Gautama,*
Prince of the Shakya Tribe, in the Lotus Sudra

"I am giving you a new commandment: Love one another.

The way I love you, you must love each other.

This is the way anyone would know

that you are my disciples,

that you show love for each other."

— *Jesus the Nasorean,*

in the Gospels according to Thomas and John

"May love lead your hands to help others."

— *Matshona Dhliwayo*

[Playlist reference: Norah Jones — Don't Know Why]

Ekkheya

It was just before sunset, and the day was bright enough that the dining room at El Palomar was still flooded with light during the lead-up to the suppertime rush.

Janaya called and asked Laleh to join her at the restaurant. She was going to make a last-ditch effort to point her friend toward help. They got seated and decided to order one of their favorites, a *Plato de Mariscos* with chips, and they asked the waiter for hot tea to start.

Janaya jumped right in. "Laleh, we have to talk." Oddly, Laleh seemed mystified as to why. But she went along, because Janaya was like a big sister to her.

"Look," Jenaya began, "I wanted to talk to you about what happened at Thanksgiving. I have to be honest with you, your behavior was really … *contemptible.*"

"What are you talking about?" Laleh protested. "I only did a little flirting with Matt. All I did was try to have a good time."

Janaya shut down that take: "It was most certainly *not* a good time, Laleh. It was reckless and disrespectful."

Laleh confessed to being unable to remember much more than eating organic turkey and squash, and asking Matt for a house tour. "I don't see what was so bad about anything I did," she claimed.

"Really? So, were you in a blackout? I'm not surprised I guess."

Laleh shot back: "Rude!"

"Me, rude?" Janaya snapped, annoyed. "Let me refresh your addled mind and fill you in on *rude,* lady. You got yourself extremely drunk and you threw yourself sexually at Matt, *against his will.* He rebuffed you, but you wouldn't let up. You even lured him into the bathroom on false pretenses, and trapped him there while you tried to force yourself on him."

"What?!"

"Laleh … It was heinous!"

Laleh dismissed the story as exaggeration. "It can't be as bad as you're making it sound," she insisted. "Maybe Matt should have made things a lot clearer if he didn't want it. Besides, Ferran worships him; he'll understand."

Janaya was clearly angry by this point, but she tried to remain measured. "No, Laleh." she answered in a steely voice. "Matt shouldn't have to make his 'no' any more loud-and-clear than he actually did. He told you that they're not in an open relationship, and he told you his boundaries and you should have respected them. And don't assume that Ferran will be so understanding; you don't know what damage you might have caused."

"Oh, what *drama,*" Laleh chortled.

Janaya hit back hard: "Laleh, you tried to assault Matt."

"This is ridiculous! I can't believe you're blaming me for everything."

"I'm not blaming you for everything," Janaya told her clearly. "I'm holding you accountable for what you actually did, and your actions were extremely disrespectful. Some part of you also must have known that if Ferran saw your little trap, he'd be likely to get the wrong idea. It seems like you hoped it would start an argument. And now it appears that all your melodrama might have actually succeeded in breaking them up."

"That can't be true."

Janaya's face became hard and serious, and she laid down the law: "If that happens, Laleh — if those two soulmates are torn apart because of what you did — I guarantee that *you will be shunned.*"

"O my God!" she replied, exasperated. "I don't even remember doing that. I'm just a crazy girl when I get a little boozy; I didn't mean to cause any problems."

The waiter appeared, asking the two women if they were ready to order. Janaya informed him that they needed to finish some business and would need some more time — perhaps ten more minutes.

Janaya turned back to Laleh when the waiter left them. "I understand that addiction can cloud your judgment," she told her, "But your actions certainly gave the appearance of being malicious."

"I don't think I'm a malicious person, Janaya."

Janaya pressed ahead, emphasizing the importance of Laleh taking responsibility for her own actions. She gave Laleh the rundown of the ways she had already attempted to help her: "I have tried doing things for you. I've tried covering for you. I've tried Harm Reduction with you. I've tried Motivational Interviewing with you. But you just keep sinking into your addiction, and treating people horribly. This incident is just another example and it's time for you to seek help."

"What do you mean, seek help?"

"I think it's time for you to admit yourself to a detox and get the help you need. Your addiction is affecting not only your own life but also the lives of others. Your behavior at Thanksgiving should be a wake-up call, and the next step should be rehab."

"Detox? Rehab? That seems pretty extreme," Laleh protested. "I can handle this on my own."

"Obviously, you can't. Are you gonna wait for your life to get good again before you start being a better friend — to yourself and to me? Look at how it's affecting your life and the people around you. You're failing at school, your parents 'relationship with you gets worse by the day and you're not in therapy for it, and now you're ruining friendships and trying to break up two bi guys who love each other. You need professional help, Laleh."

"I don't need rehab," Laleh insisted "I just need to cut back a little."

Janaya was exasperated, and told her emphatically that she was actually trying to be real with her. "This news doesn't seem to be getting through your thick skull, Laleh. Your behavior at Thanksgiving was absolutely disgusting. Not only did you make a fool out of yourself, but because of your unwanted advances you may have jeopardized one of the most beautiful and loving couples I've ever seen."

Laleh gave Janaya side-eye. "Harsh."

"I care about you," Janaya continued. "You know I've been your friend these past three years while your parents have acted like they're too busy traveling to even check-in on you. I want to see you overcome this addiction — I do. But I have to detach with love from your mess. If you refuse to seek help, I can't continue to stand by and watch you treat everyone so ruthlessly. It's time you faced the truth."

"What truth?" Laleh asked defiantly.

Janaya broke it to her: "If you don't make an effort to get better, I'm done hanging out with you. And if you truly care about salvaging *any* of your relationships, it's time to get help."

"It sounds like you're threatening me."

Janaya sighed wearily. "Do not try to play the victim here. You're doing major harm to yourself, and your behavior toward Matt and Ferran was reprehensible."

"Reprehensible? That's a really strong word."

"I'm being *gentle.*"

Laleh's face slowly changed from one of anger to one of defeat, drained of much of its color. She sunk her head down into her hands.

Eventually, Laleh spoke. "I'm sorry," she told Janaya. "I didn't realize it had gotten so bad. I don't want to lose you as a friend."

"Laleh, I don't want to lose you as a friend either. But your addiction has taken power over your life — you've lost control. And you can't overcome the trauma from your parents if you're just gonna keep trying to drown it in alcohol and other drugs. You deserve to be happy and to make a better future. If you go to rehab and get the support you need, you have a chance to turn things around."

Still peaked, Laleh seemed afraid. "Okay, maybe I do need to consider this. I don't want to keep hurting people. But my parents won't pay for it, and I certainly can't pay for it myself."

"No," Janaya informed her. "Your parents *will* pay for it. I've already spoken with them. They're not motivated enough to come home from Cancun to lend their support, but they will foot the bill."

Laleh was surprised: "You talked to them? This is just too much; how could you do that?"

Janaya reminded her that it was because she was her friend, and hated watching her destroy herself and hurt other people. Then, Laleh began to cry. She looked up and asked Janaya for help in finding a good rehab facility.

"Your parents already said they'd cover a stay for you at Hazelden-Betty Ford, in Palm Desert. They'll even get you a plane ticket. Most addicts don't have that luxury, Laleh. You have access, so don't pass it up."

Laleh began to look frightened. She said she had to tell Matt and Ferran that she was sorry, and that it was her fault, not Matt's.

"You have to save that 'til later when you've more time and tools to get stabilized," Janaya told her firmly. "Getting involved with them right now won't help them or you, it'll just make the mess worse. You have to focus on recovery."

"If I go, will you still be here to support me?" Laleh asked, timidly.

Janaya reassured her: "Of course I will, if you are willing to get help. I will fully support you. You're not in this alone."

"Okay, thank you. Thank you for being honest with me. I do appreciate your support; you're being a good friend."

The waiter returned to their table.

Janaya asked a teary-eyed Laleh if she would be able to eat. Laleh shook her head no. Apologizing to the waiter, Janaya told him they'd received some rough news. She handed him a $20 bill, and thanked him for being so attentive.

"Come on," Janaya said, helping Laleh from her seat. "I'll give you a ride home and we can pack for your flight."

31

PRIVATION

"To love. To be loved.

To never forget your own insignificance.

To never get used to the unspeakable violence

and the vulgar disparity of life around you.

To seek joy in the saddest places.

To pursue beauty to its lair.

To never simplify what is complicated

or complicate what is simple.

To respect strength, never power.

Above all, to watch. To try and understand.

To never look away.

And never, never to forget."

— *Arundhati Roy*

[Playlist reference: Lewis Capaldi - Someone You Loved]

Maura

Several days had gone by since Laleh elicited disaster on the night of our Thanksgiving dinner. Alex had texted me that, if we were going precisely by Matt's count, ninety-one hours had passed. That heartbroken ginger was literally counting minutes and hours.

Janaya also direct-messaged me that she intervened with Laleh. She'd insisted that Laleh either go to a detox, or else not bother trying to talk to her again. Texts and DMs were flying between everybody, but Ferran was shutting-out all of them.

I was not going to let that get in my way, and I decided to go over to Stu and Ferran's room to give Ferran a stern dose of Irish admonishment. Stu didn't seem interested in being shut-out, either. He was sitting on his bed, stone-faced, when I arrived at their dorm room. He motioned for me to come sit beside him, and we watched Alex try again to reason with Ferran.

Alex was like a brother to him, and he was making it clear that Ferran couldn't escape hearing him out.

"He was totally distraught when we ended our video call," Alex continued to argue. "Matt was on his way to drive from his house up here to campus. So, I know that, at this moment, he's sitting at that soccer field where he *devotedly* watches your games. And why? Because he needed to be somewhere that felt like even the *energy signature* of your efforts would be there."

I knew that Alex had already tried several times to talk some sense into him — to get him to hear the truth and to stop sabotaging himself and his relationship — but Ferran was being strangely stubborn. I could see Alex working hard to remain calm, even though he was becoming extremely frustrated with him. I decided it would be better for me to get him out of there for a breather before another of Ferran's relationships broke apart. "Come on," I said, taking hold of Alex's shoulder and shooting Ferran a disapproving glare, "Let's go for a walk before you get even more angry at him and cross the line."

With all the kindness he could muster, though, Alex delivered a warning to Ferran as we were leaving: "This cannot possibly be the end, Ferran. You will regret this for the rest of your life. You were lucky enough to stumble onto your soulmate, and if you make this the end, you will never forgive yourself."

Ferran

I was caught off guard when Alex and Maura left our room, because it was Stu who completely lost his temper with me.

"Ferran, *what the hell?*" Stu shouted. "Maura came over here to talk to you and wound up having to take Alex out of here before he got too angry with you! Alex is your longest-running friendship, and he just *begged* you to go down to that soccer field and fix this. You are tearing Matt apart!"

This degree of fury was completely out-of-character for my roommate. In a voice that shook me with its depth and volume, Stu called me out in the most florid terms. As he hollered at me, it seemed like he kept gripping the back of a chair until his knuckles turned white so that he wouldn't take a swing at me. I had never seen him so angry.

Stu's yelling reached a bitter crescendo: "You'd better suit up, show up, and get your goddam fractured sense of self out of the fucking way, Ferran!"

My skin had gone cold and clammy, and I was actually shaking. It wasn't until Stu flew into this rage at me that I felt the walls break apart inside me — the fortress of my fears about loving and losing Matt. I tried to speak, but Stu immediately cut me off.

"*I'm* talking right now, you jackass! Alex was absolutely right that this can't be the end. Do you even realize what you and Matt have? Do not throw this away! That man is, like, *the love of your life!* You know that Matt loves you more than anything in the world. You know he's gotta be sitting out there on that field with his heart being ripped into pieces because of your stupid jealousy. Get your sorry ass out there and make-up with him!"

I felt myself shudder, and I know I must have blanched. My throat was parched, but I managed to speak: "I didn't mean to hurt him, Stu. I just... I couldn't handle the thought that he would cheat on me. The idea he would ditch me and I'd lose him totally — it wrecked me."

Stu's eyes were fiery, and he looked like he was trying very hard to bring his level of rage closer to the ground. He breathed deeply, but then he still spoke sharply and loudly. "So, you just didn't bother discussing what was going on, and you stormed out without having a real talk with him! You are a gutless *prick!"*

My protest was weak: "I just saw red."

"He did *not* cheat on you!"

"Stu …," I said, as my throat was closing up. "I feel like my whole world is falling apart."

Stu answered me in a lower volume. "For gods' sakes then, Ferran, put it back together. Look at the pain you've caused Matt. Look at the pain you've caused yourself! It's time to put your stupid ego aside, man. Go down there and make things right with him."

"I don't know if I *can* make it right. What if he doesn't want to see me? What if it's too late?"

"Stop making excuses, you idiot," Stu scolded me. "How could he hate you? The two of you live and breathe each other. Everybody else can see that you two are soulmates; why can't you? The only way to find out how to fix this is to go down there and face him."

I was shivering and I felt like there was a lump in my throat the size of a grapefruit.

Stu's posture began to soften, but he pressed on. "Come on, man. You know what you usually do on that soccer field. You break through the fear, and you do what needs to be done, and you *win*. Go do that with your man, you fool, before I have to punch you out."

"All right, Stu," I replied while nodding. "All right. I'll go down and try to talk to him. But what if he hates me? I'd deserve it."

"Then you will have to deal with it, Ferran. You overreacted to the manipulation of a drunken princess who threw herself at him. You made this mess, and it's about time you clean it up. Now go!"

I was scared. But I took a deep breath, and turned around and grabbed my coat. Then, I set off on the walk down to the soccer field — to the place where Alex told me Matt would be sitting. On the way, I went into the contact list in my smartphone and unblocked Matt — because I was a jerk and I had blocked him

***

I caught sight of Matt on the field, and my heart broke all over again because I could tell he was in deep pain. He was sitting there on the ground sobbing, his eyes flooded and overflowing. I pushed myself to keep walking towards him, and he looked up at me through his tear-soaked lashes as I approached.

I was ashamed of myself, and I couldn't stop shaking. My eyes were stinging, and I tried to take-in a breath. I felt like I was choking on it, but I made the effort to speak.

"Hi," I muttered.

"Hi."

"Stu told me if I didn't come and make up with you, he was going to punch me out."

Matt sniffled. "Is that the only reason you're here?"

Then tears began to stream from my eyes as I answered him: "I came down here because I'm so in love with you that I think if I didn't, I might forget how to breathe."

"Ferran, listen to me, *please.* I would never lie to you about any of this."

I tried to form words to respond, but I couldn't.

Matt continued anyway: "I would never hurt you like that. I love you so much I don't even have the words, and it kills me that you can think I would ever cheat on you."

Matt looked at me with such sad eyes, I felt even more broken. By this point, I was heaving as I cried. When I could steady myself, I said: "Matty... I'm *so* sorry. I never meant to hurt you like this."

"I thought you understood how much you mean to me," he told me, his voice strained. "I let my guard down for you, and then you pulled the rug out from under me."

I nearly fell as my knees weakened, and I sat down on the ground, facing Matt. I tried to explain why I had acted so stupidly. "I was scared to death," I insisted. "I thought you were done with me. I thought I was going under, and there was no one there to save me. I felt like my heart was ripped out."

Matteo

"That's how I felt," I answered him in the steadiest voice I could manage. I was aware that I had started to glare at Ferran, but I tried to keep myself in check.

His confession spilled out of him. "I completely shut down and I shut everybody else down. I'm sorry, Matty. I'm so, so sorry. I saw Laleh coming-on to you the whole day. Then I saw the two of you in that bathroom together, and you were blushing. And I saw you had her lipstick on your chin, and I lost it. The first thought that took over my mind was that you got tired of just being with me — of only having a guy when both of us are bi. I thought I was losing you, and it made me crazy."

I was perplexed, so I asked him: "Have you gotten tired of me because you don't get to play with women?"

"No! It isn't about that," he sputtered. "It's about … it's that I *love* you! I don't want *anybody* else, of *any* gender! I don't need everything at once in order to be bi. The reason I realized I'm bi is because I wanted *you!"*

"So … why would you think it would be any different for me? Because it *isn't,* Ferr — it isn't any different. You're my person."

"You're *my* person."

Ferran's eyes searched mine. I said, "You once told me that you were willing to put everything on the line so we could be together."

"I meant it."

"Then why not everything on the line to *trust* each other?"

Ferran wrapped his arms around himself and began to rock slightly. "Because I thought I *had* put everything on the line and then *lost* it, and lost you. I thought you might walk away from me for that woman."

I ran my hands over my face and wiped some of my tears away. Then I pulled my hair back with my hand and scrunched my eyes closed, trying to relieve some tension. I opened them again and slowly lowered my hand.

As he gazed down at the ground, I spoke: "Ferran, listen to me, and I need you to hear this loud and clear. Just like you, I'd still be one hundred percent bisexual whether I was with one gender, or two, or several. You know that. And I need you to know, without a doubt, that if we were ever going to try playing with other people, it sure as hell wouldn't be at this stage of our relationship when we're still bonding with each other. For sure, it wouldn't be without us working out all the agreements together *in detail.* Okay? And it isn't even on my radar."

He answered me, sniffling: "Mine either."

"Good."

"I let my fears control me," he blurted, wiping his eyes with his coat sleeve. "I lost sight of what's real. I love you, Matty. And I really don't want to lose you."

I wanted to save our relationship, too. I pleaded with him: "Would you give me a chance to make things right? I'm willing to do whatever it takes to earn your trust again."

Ferran spoke assertively for the first time since he arrived on the field. "Matteo Poulsen," he declared, "I think I'd better strongly correct that idea right now. You don't need to earn my trust because you didn't violate it. *I Am The Asshole.* I let my jealousy run wild, and I wouldn't listen and hear."

That just led me to feel sadness. I was confused, though, and I had to know the answer. So, I asked: "Why did you shut me out?"

Ferran took a long moment before he tried to reply. "I think I decided that if I just cut ties, I'd be the one harming myself first, before you could do it."

The awful picture was coming into focus for me. Ferran had been so fractured as a kid by the people he needed the most, he was sure that all he deserved was to be abandoned or humiliated. He was always on the lookout for the next thing that would reinforce that message. He loved me, so he was sure I'd be willing to hurt him. He decided he would harm himself first, so he could tell himself that at least he was the one in charge of it. I covered my mouth and fought back more tears as the realization swept over me.

"I was so stupid," he said angrily. "I was so afraid of losing you that I actually hurt *you*. And I was such an idiot to let myself get manipulated by the wreckage of an untreated alcoholic."

For a moment things were quiet, until I spoke.

"You just left me there."

Ferran

Those words fell like a bomb — one that was sending shrapnel into every corner of my mind and body. The words ran through my mind on repeat:

I just left him there.

Sometimes people use the term "shook" to describe their whole world being jolted, but that term fell far short of the upheaval I felt at hearing Matt's words. The thing I dreaded most — the very abandonment and humiliation I feared so intensely — was exactly what I inflicted on Matt. On the one person in the world I care for the most.

The realization of what I did, and why I did it, set my entire worldview on edge. A wave of raw, despondent emotion overwhelmed me. I thought if there was such a thing as perfect contrition, it would feel like this. My heart felt like it was squeezing in my chest.

"Matty, I am *so* sorry," I sputtered with a quavering voice. "I will *never* do that again. If you let me, I will make this up to you *every day*. Please forgive me."

He reached out his hand and cupped my cheek. I felt his warmth there, and for the first time in days I didn't feel like the walking dead. He locked eyes with me and proclaimed exactly the words I needed to hear: "I have never felt about anyone in my life the way I feel about you. I don't want to break up with you, Ferran. I don't want us *ever* to break up."

I must have been ugly crying, because he pulled me into his arms. I buried my face in the crook of his neck, but still managed to answer him. "I don't want us to ever break up, either, Matty. I love you so much that just seeing you in there — with her and her damn lipstick print — I panicked at the fear of losing you. My stupid insecurities got the best of me — that the pain would kill me."

"I'm sorry."

"You have nothing to be sorry about. I fucked up. You were trying to help her, and she was being a drunken mess and just trying to get into your pants. *I'm* sorry. I really *hate* being apart from you."

More tears leaked from Matt's eyes. "Ferr, I gotta be honest, it made me really frightened."

"I'm *so* sorry. I've never been totally in love with someone before. I don't know how to do this."

Matt stepped back, but reached down and took my hand. "Ferr, I've never been totally in love with someone before, either. We're bound to mess up. I think we've really got to listen to each other whenever we might not be seeing what's really going on."

"I'm an asshat, and I probably need therapy."

"You're a wounded warrior, and so am I. We both probably need therapy. We don't have the luxury of having any presumptions about each other — we haven't been together long enough. We're going to have to actually communicate instead of assume."

"I can do that."

"I know if we work together, we can work through anything. I don't want anything to come between us. Ever. Ever. Ever."

"Me neither, Matty. I'm *really* sorry for ever doubting you."

"Promise me we will talk out anything and everything if we're ever this hurt or angry again?"

"I promise, Matty. I promise with everything I've got."

Matt's lower lip began to tremble. "I'm sorry I haven't made you feel safer and more secure."

I pleaded with him: "Baby, please. I'm the one who's been ridiculous. Can we stop doing this now? I love you more than anyone, and I don't ever want to be without you."

"I love you, too," Matt said, tightly grabbing onto me again.

32

HYGGE

"This world would be a whole lot better
if we just made an effort
to be less horrible to one another."
— *Elliott Page*

*[Playlist reference: Rita Sawayama
(featuring Elton John) — Chosen Family]*

Ekkheya

Emily's birthday evening was chilly, but that was ideal for the crew to gather together for a night of delicious foods, birthday cake, coziness, and watching *Interview with the Vampire*. "Cam, I love our *hygge* nights. Thanks again for hosting us all here," Matt offered. "I'm glad this time all of us could make it."

Cam was excitedly trying to arrange people in his living room. "Okay everybody" he called out, "grab a spot on the couch or on the pillows and get ready for the cuddle piles!"

Ayesha stretched out her arms towards both of her boyfriends. "You and Braden better be over here!"

Ferran walked into the living room bearing loaves of warm, freshly baked bread, announcing: "Now *this* is the best way to spend a cozy evening. This is my homemade sourdough, people. Cam helped me with it a couple hours ago and it's fresh and warm from the oven."

"Yum!" Braden declared, back on his feet immediately. "That's what was making that amazing smell. I need some of that."

"And look!" Alex joked. "He bakes, too!" He turned to Matt, and said for everyone to hear: "My BFF can be an idiot sometimes, Matt, but please keep him around. He's a man of many talents."

Matt's response was emphatic: "He's not going anywhere if I have any say in the matter."

"Baby, you have *all* the say in the matter," Ferran answered.

Alex looked back and forth between both of them. "Listen up, you two. It might be bad manners for me to tell you this, but we all were feeling pretty devastated when you two were fighting. Or I should say, when Ferran was being a dick."

"I will cop to that," Ferran noted.

"Please try not to do that again, guys."

"Alex, as long as he'll let me stay with him," Ferran replied, "I'm never letting him go."

Matt's emerald eyes welled up and glistened. In a rough voice, he just said, "Baby."

"O my gods," Emily groused, "you guys are killing me with the sweetness."

Ferran and Matt responded at the same time: "Sorry, not sorry."

"Geez, you even snark like soulmates," she said with a smile.

Stu sat down between Emily and Ferran, and turned to put his arm around Ferran's shoulders. "Buddy, I gotta tell you something. I know I should have apologized sooner for losing my temper with you when you wouldn't talk with Matt."

"I don't think I'd have woken up if you didn't."

"I'm just sorry I got so angry and yelled at you, man. But you have to know how important you two are to the rest of us. Your fight gave us all a chance to check-in with each other about how bent out of shape we all were about it." There were murmurs of agreement around the room, and Stu went on. "Honestly, you two have been the catalyst for our whole group becoming such close friends. Maura may be our cruise director, but you guys are our glue."

"Can't I be the Irish yenta?" Maura interjected.

"Po-tay-toh, po-tah-toh," Jake said.

But Stu pressed on. "Listen, when you weren't communicating, we all got a chance to see how much we really love this weird little power pack of people, and how much we depend on you two to draw us together. Do you realize how you shine for us all? We do. We realized we all look to you to lead us, and we like it that way."

"You're like double stars pulling us into orbit," Maura added.

Matt gave a small protest: "I think you give us too much credit."

Cam nipped that protest in the bud. "I don't think so. Stu and Maura are right. Maybe you had to go through this mess with each other to see what the rest of us can see. We were thinking of you two as our Invincible Sun, and that's been kind of an irresistible thing. This crew became like a family because of you two, and we all got a chance to realize it when we thought we'd lost our north-star."

Matt and Ferran looked to each other and they both seemed choked-up.

"Okay, this is getting *way* serious," Jake croaked. "I'm glad you guys are together, but I'm gonna cry if this keeps up."

Emily tried to break the tension: "It's my party and I'll cry if I want to!" She made a show of reaching to grab a slice of smoked salmon. "If we're going to talk about what's irresistible, I think we could be talking about all this amazing food instead of all winding up crying again."

"Okay, darlin', you're right," Stu responded, switching from the arm around Ferran to place his other arm around Emily. "I felt like they had to hear it. So, to your point, I just want everybody to know that all the fish and meats on the table are from local, sustainable farms because we're cool like that. And Emily: Matt and I made a carrot cake for your birthday. From scratch. We'll bring it out to you after the movie, okay?"

"You guys! From scratch? You know carrot cake is my absolute favorite."

Then Bakari reached out for the coffee table, as well. "Hey — right now though, peep this. These charcuterie boards are looking pretty damn delectable. And they're making me *hungry.* And the food's part of *hygge,* right? By the way, Matt, a big thank you to your father's Danish background for giving us this concept. Love that!"

Maura also sang the praises of the abundance of good smoked salmon while Jake went for the bread, acknowledging that fresh hot breads were his favorite part of any meal.

Braden wrapped his arm around Garrett on one side, and Ayesha on the other, and then suggested the group could play Scrabble or Rummy 500 instead of seeing the movie, if they wanted.

"Oh, no, no, no," Jake insisted. "Not cards. You all are card sharks! I am not getting crushed in a card game again. Besides, you're just afraid to watch a horror movie."

Cam smiled and pointed at Braden: "He gets spooked easily."

"I can watch horror movies!" Braden protested.

"Aw, honey," Cam cooed. "Scoot closer to the infrared fireplace. You can stare at the electronics if you have to hide your eyes from the movie." Braden called Cam mean, and then kissed him. Then he leaned over and also kissed Ayesha. "Yeah, you love us," Cam teased.

"You know you do," Jake agreed.

"All right," Braden admitted. "I definitely do."

"And we love to see it," Bakari acknowledged. He grabbed a handful of mixed nuts, then looked out at the group and asked, "Next time, could we do a hot tub for our cozy night?

"You mean at like the Tea House? The giant hot tub?" Alicia asked.

As Arjun sat down with a bowl of fresh popcorn in hand, Garret said he liked the hot tub idea. "Okay now, people," he announced. "Ready for some *Interview with the Vampire?* "

Janaya snuggled up next to Matt and winked at Ferran. "Perfect timing," she said.

33

MYCELIUM

"Love transforms us.
The deeper the love, the deeper the transformation."
— *Laura Livia Grigore*

"You have to act as if it were possible
to radically transform the world,
and you have to do it all the time."
— *Angela Davis*

[Playlist reference: New West — Those Eyes]

Matteo

The morning sunlight began to reflect on the Bay and dance through my bedroom window as Ferran and I were waking up in each other's arms. "Hello, beautiful," he mumbled, with his face buried at the crook of my neck.

"G'mornin' Ferr."

"Kiss me."

"Ferran, I must have gross morning breath. I'm going to go brush my teeth."

"Seriously?" Ferran grumbled. "You're going to stop letting me hold you so you can get cozy with a toothpaste tablet?"

"You can hold me after you brush *your* teeth, baby."

"Cruel," he griped.

We both climbed out of my bed and made our way to the bathroom, bumping into Arjun in the hallway.

"Jesus," Arjun said, somewhat exasperated and unable to avoid looking at Ferran's considerable endowment — and my even larger package. "I don't mind nudity in the house, but you guys could put out people's eyes with those things."

I laughed, but Ferran was apologetic: "I'm sorry, Arjun. We just hopped out of bed."

"Obviously," Arjun grunted, as he disappeared down the hall.

Ferran looked over at me. "Is he angry?"

"I don't think so. Just surprised."

"Okay."

We went into the bathroom and each grabbed our toothbrushes. After our joint toothbrushing session, we bounded back to my room and dove back into bed."

"I get kisses now, right?" Ferran pleaded.

"Yes, please."

I think we both loved to kiss. I know we kissed each other with an unreserved joy. Then I nuzzled into Ferran's furry chest. "I love you," he purred, "and all the small things that you do."

"I love you too, baby," I told him. But my conscience had been bothering me and I felt like I needed to tell Ferran what I'd been ruminating about. I hesitated in a brief silence, but then I voiced it.

"Ferr, something's been weighing on my mind since we reconnected on the field after Thanksgiving. I just think it's right for me to tell you about it."

Ferran raised his head to look at me. "O, gods," he said, nervously. "Did I do something wrong?"

"No, Baby, no," I reassured him, raising my head and looking back at him. "This is about me being stupid while we were apart."

Ferran looked deeply into my eyes. "Whatever it is, Matt, it'll be okay. Just tell me. What happened?"

I put my hand on his chest and gently laid him back down on the bed, and then rested my head on him. Ferran began running his fingers through may hair, which felt amazing. I began to explain: "It doesn't involve anybody else, okay? It's about me, and I feel like I shouldn't keep it from you. So … I know you're not a big fan of alcohol, and it's probably worse after watching Laleh be a total mess. And I know you don't do any party drugs or psychedelics or anything. But I have tried psychedelics before and…"

Ferran cut in: "Did you drop acid while I was being an asshole?"

"No," I clarified. "I had a small amount of magick mushrooms stashed in the back of the freezer from this summer when I last used them. The last time I used them, I basically laughed for four hours. Anyway... I know it may sound idiotic, but I thought using them might help me get perspective and find some calm, because you gotta know: I was *anything but calm.* Baby, I was in so much pain during that time we spent apart. I was feeling really lost and heartbroken, and I'm really sorry if I disappointed you."

"Matty, you did not disappoint me," Ferran insisted. "It's just ... I'm a little worried about you taking drugs so you didn't have to feel your feelings."

"But that was the point, baby. I *wanted* to feel my feelings. I wanted to see them and get the big picture about them."

"Then I guess if you did, that's good."

"Well, yeah. It did turn out to be good. But I want to be up front with you about *why* it was good. During that whole experience, all I could think about was you."

"What do you mean?"

"I mean I was tripping, but what consumed my thoughts was how much I wanted to be with you instead of being caught up in the effects of the mushrooms. I could see the scenes of all the moments we'd spent together in my mind's eye. I realized I want it all with you, Ferr — I want a life with you. And here's the irony I got out of using the 'shrooms: I don't want to artificially escape my feelings anymore. Feeling everything means I get to love you as intensely as I do, so I want to feel everything."

"Matty, listen to me: I'm not upset about it at all."

"Really? You're not mad?"

"Not at all. Look, I've never been into drinking or drugs because they could affect my performance on the soccer field. But everyone has their own path with this stuff. I understand you were hurting and searching for answers."

"I wanted to pry the door open in my mind."

"I hear that, baby. You were ready to feel all your feelings, and I wanted to shut off all of mine. I get it. But I need to ask you something, okay?"

"Yes, sure!"

"Just … in the future, I want us to communicate about anything like this ahead of time. Is it all right if we do that? We're in this together, Matty. When it comes to something as intense as you using mushrooms, I hope we can make that decision as a team."

"We definitely can. And I was able to see how powerful and important these substances are. They require a lot of guidance."

"Then I definitely want us to work it out beforehand."

"All right, Ferr. But here's the thing about my psychedelic experience: I don't feel like I have any use for them anymore, so I don't want them. While I was tripping, I got clarity. Every thought, every visual, every feeling — it all led back to you. Even when my mind was altered, my feelings for you were my touchstone. That was a revelation I couldn't ignore."

Ferran

Before meeting Matt, I was never one to cry much. But lately, I felt like I could laugh and cry with an ease I never used to have. And here I was, about to cry again. I let myself be vulnerable and I asked him to tell me again: "You were thinking about me the entire time?"

"Yes, I was. That's what I mean: I was thinking about you so much I wished I could get un-high right away, and go see you face to face. And when I was finally down from the trip, I made a video call to Alex to beg him to talk with you again."

"He did, Matty. He tried to talk to me a bunch, but I was completely just shut down. He was trying to reason with me. That last time, he and Maura got so frustrated with me they left. I refused to hear anybody until Stu flew into a rage at me about it."

Matt picked up his head from my chest and looked into my eyes. "Stu didn't just yell at you? He actually flew into a rage?"

"Scared the fuck out of me, Matty. I literally felt like he was *not kidding* — like he was really gonna beat the crap out of me."

"Our mild-mannered Stu who tries to be your big brother?"

"One and the same. He said what they were all saying: that you were my soulmate, and the love of my life, and you didn't cheat. Stu just said it a lot more loudly and angrily. He told me I was being a fool. And he was bitter when he reinforced what Alex had said: that if I kept being an ass and I ended things, I'd never forgive myself."

"Ferr, maybe it's crazy, but I feel like you really are the love of my life. That was never so clear to me as when I was stuck tripping on those 'shrooms but I was ready to be down from the high."

"Do you feel that way when you're sober?" I asked him.

"Yeah, Ferr. Completely, And I *do* feel like we're soulmates."

"I do, too, Matty. I really do," I assured him. "It feels like there's some network that connects us that runs underneath everything."

Matt laid his head back onto my chest, and I could feel my heart beating against his cheek. "I think this is the last time I'll ever do those kinds of substances," he said. "I don't plan on using psychedelics again. I just wanted to be fully transparent and honest with you. That's what I want between us."

"Thank you for telling me. And I want that honesty between us, too. Always."

Matt promised he would give me that, and I echoed that promise for him.

"Thank you, Ferr. I was worried you'd be really angry at me, or disappointed."

Finally, after this heavy conversation, there was a chance to tease him. "Well," I purred, "I have to admit that it was an interesting choice: using a psychedelic as a gateway drug to get me to cuddle in bed with you."

Matt groaned. "Now I'm just gonna have to spank you," he warned.

I nudged him. "You would never."

"Just you wait, you big goof," he teased me.

"I love you so much, Matty."

"I love you, too."

34

PUPPY

"Life has taught us that love
does not consist in gazing at each other
but in looking outward together in the same direction."
— *Antoine de Saint-Exupéry*

[Playlist reference: Sara Bareilles — Many the Miles]

Matteo

The air was a bit cooler and the days were getting shorter. It was very early evening and the sun was already setting as Ferran and I brought cafeteria food back to his room. As we set down the food on Ferran's desk, I flipped-on the electric kettle to make tea for both of us. "Ferr," I said, "I have a little news for you."

"Is everything okay?"

"Yeah, everything's fine," I assured him. "It's just that... I have to go to this community organizing training in Los Angeles from Thursday morning until late Sunday this weekend."

Ferran told me he thought it was great news since I loved that stuff. He asked me if it was part of one of my Politics classes. I let him know it wasn't, but that if I wrote up a synopsis, I would earn some practicum credit for it.

I elaborated: "It's just a skills-building thing so we can apply it in local issue campaigns and stuff. The conference is being put together by one of the training groups that Jane Fonda and the late Tom Hayden and a bunch of others helped to create."

Ferran mentioned that he loved Jane Fonda.

"Anybody with more than half a brain loves Jane Fonda, baby. I've been lucky enough to know her since I was four years old. She's friends with my parents from back when we were neighbors — when we lived down in L.A. for Dad's bank.

"That's so cool!" Ferran nearly squealed. Then, I guess he saw the sad look on my face. "Matty? You don't seem like you're very happy at all about heading down there. What's really going on?"

I reminded him that it would be the first time since we became boyfriends that it would be me who had to go away for the weekend. "And, it's just for this stupid conference," I grumbled.

"It is *not* stupid," Ferran insisted. "*You* were the one who charged-up all those people and got the books back into that Sierra school district after the MAGA fascists banned them, Matty. *You* were the one who got the workers at the Starbucks by your high school to form a union and to help with boycotts. *You* were the one who got high school students to join the picket lines at Tartine. You're a leader, and you're brave and caring, and this is the stuff that really moves you."

I have to admit, I was surprised at my boyfriend's fervor about this. "Ferr! You are just *so* amazing to me! And it's true: I really do believe in what I'm doing, and there are still too many things I haven't done yet. But if I'm being honest, I really don't want to be away from you at all."

"*Puppy...*" Ferran said, opening our food containers and putting some serving utensils in them. "I feel the same way. Remember when I had to spend that weekend playing an away game a few weeks ago? We both missed each other a lot, and it was rough."

"Exactly! I hated having you away from me, and now I have to do the same thing." Then it hit me, and I looked up at Ferran. "Wait... 'puppy'?"

Through a cheeky grin, he suggested: "Poodle?"

"Don't you dare."

"'My sweet, gorgeous cocker spaniel with the luxurious, flowing red hair?'"

"Cringe!" I shuddered. "Gods! All right, then. 'Puppy' will be acceptable."

"Thank you."

We sat down to eat, and I sighed. "It's just hard, you know? We're like in each other's field of gravity. I just find it difficult to be apart."

He told me it didn't mean we cared about each other any less. Then, he said: "Matty, we both have our own interests and passions, and sometimes that means we have to be apart for a minute to pursue those."

"It is a *lot* of minutes, thank you," I complained. "A whole four-day weekend training. …"

"Puppy."

"Okay, I understand what you're saying. … And you know I want to be supportive of your passions, too. It's just that even though this training means a lot to me, I don't want it to affect *us.*"

"It's not going to. I'm here for you, Matty. I support you in everything you do. And I want you to grow, and to be the best version of you."

I scooted over and rested my head on Ferran's shoulder, and he kissed me on the top of my head. I looked up at him and smiled. "What if you find some other ginger to make you obsess?"

He laughed. "Oh, is *that* what this is about? My baby's a little jealous? Are you worried that the second you're gone, I'll run off with the first hot girl I find?"

"Or guy?"

Ferran smiled and gave that some acknowledgement: "Or guy, I guess."

"What if I *am* jealous?"

Taking me in his arms, Ferran held me close. "Matty," he said, "there is no competition for you." He gently pressed his lips to mine. Then he said, "This weekend, you go focus on your training, and remember that I'll be here waiting for you."

I really needed that reassurance, and I told him as much. I thanked him again for being so understanding about it.

But then, Ferran asked me nervously: "What if you find some hot activist down there and you want to have a hotel tryst?"

I wanted to address that question in all seriousness. "I don't think either of us is anywhere near ready for something like that, if that's ever even on the table."

Ferran exhaled: "Woah." Then, he made a confession: "Maybe I shouldn't admit this Matty, but I don't think I've ever in all my life had a feeling like the one I just had in the pit of my stomach."

I leaned over to kiss him again. "Baby, we're gonna get to a place where we're not so afraid," I reassured him. "But you don't have to worry; I'm barely able to leave your arms. I'm not going to go hook up with anybody."

"I really did learn my lesson to have complete faith in you," Ferran promised. "But I wanna be sure that if you ever want to do that… Please Matty, we'll talk honestly about it first, right? We're a team, and we'd figure it out… Promise me?"

"I promise you. And I don't want to do that anytime soon, if ever."

Ferran relaxed. "I'll be counting down the days until you're *back* in my arms, you know."

"Me, too."

35

DRIVE

"Morning without you is dwindled dawn."
— *Emily Dickinson*

[Playlist reference: Kina Granis — Beyond the Sea]

Ekkheya

A temperate Saturday night settled-in on the conference in Los Angeles. Actually, it was technically in Santa Monica — at the Fairmont Miramar Hotel, to be exact. I was glad that Matt was there for a couple of reasons.

Not surprisingly, my first priority was that he was growing some of the skill sets that would make his work have an exponential impact — part of the magick that he and his band of friends would be bringing to each other and to the world. My next concern was for Matt and Ferran to have a little rancor-free distance from each other. If absence would make their hearts grow fonder, this was a perfect chance.

Yes, I admit I had an agenda — one in which I saw those two playing a pivotal role. But that isn't news to you. Nor is the fact that I'm a sentimental old spirit. So how could I fail to be in love with their love for each other and for their chosen family?

Matt looked over the Sunday schedule. He pondered having to sit in the union-building strategy and tactics workshops the next morning, followed by having to drive back to Santa Cruz in traffic. He groaned. The truth was that Matt had already been through the Sunday workshops before. And he'd also actually done the strategies and tactics for real, on the ground.

On top of that, he was missing Ferran so much it was painful. Part of him wanted to provide an example to the other young organizers. Part of him felt like there was a homing device inside him calling him back to the man he loved.

He was craving a slushie, and had decided to wander out of the hotel in search of one. Should bad come to worse, he knew there was a 7-11 store on Wilshire at 7th Street. He reasoned that if he had to walk that far, it might help to clear his mind.

Matt made his way down to the lobby. As he exited the elevator, he caught sight of Jane Fonda and Ted Danson having a huddle. They were among the celebrity activists who were co-hosting the conference.

Jane looked up from the conversation and spotted Matt right away. She waved her hand and called out to him: "Matteo Poulsen! How is your mother? Are you down here doing this with the Sunrise Movement?"

"Hi, Jane!" he answered sheepishly. He walked over to them and looked up at Ted Danson, who smiled broadly as he greeted him. "Hey, kid. Still presenting the best of your parents' features, I see."

"Thank you, sweet talker. How's Mary?"

"She's good. At home exhausted from doing an actual music tour around LA, if you can believe it."

"Music tour?" Matt asked, surprised. "I'll have to read up on that. Please give her my best. But let me answer your questions, Jane: My mom is fine, it's just that having two kids running around all the time is a lot. I'm sure you both remember that from experience. And as for Sunrise, I love them, but I'm not directly working with them this time. I'm just a free agent for this particular conference; I'll get credit if I write it up for one of my courses at UCSC."

Jane took a good look at him, and smiled broadly. "I'm so glad you're here," she said. "May I have a hug?"

"Honestly, I'm sort of emotional right now. If you hug me, I can't promise I won't cry."

"Woah. I heard that," Ted chimed in. "Better give him a hug, Jane. Sounds like he needs to let out some feelings."

So, she did just that, and Matt *did* begin to softly cry on her shoulder.

Jane was concerned. "Matteo, what's going on? You don't have to tell us, but you know you can if you want."

"I think maybe I'm just being a giant baby," he told them. "I've already done tomorrow's workshops before, both as trainings and in real life. And if I stay, I'll be driving back in Sunday afternoon traffic. But more than anything, I miss my boyfriend so much I think I'm gonna break."

"Boyfriend?" Ms. Fonda asked in mock incredulity, pretending to grasp pearls. "I thought you were Young Mister Heartbreaker, with whatever gender you were playing with at the time."

"You make it sound *so* dirty," he teased.

"Matteo," she chided, "I have known you since you were four years old. I'm allowed to give you some shit."

"Okay,' Matt said, misty-eyed, but laughing.

Ted then decided an inquiry was in order: "Now, Matteo. Do I have this right? This boyfriend is so important to you, that you — Mister Dedicated Organizer — are at a policy conference, but you're *pining* for him? Is he more important than your goals?"

"Not *more* important, Ted. *As* important."

"Now, *that's* a good balance for you," Jane observed.

"If you're aching this bad, kid, I think you can skip repeating the workshops tomorrow," Ted offered.

"Matteo, please listen to me," Jane told him gently. "You're 19-years-old. You're a devoted organizer with a passion for this work, but you also get to have a personal life. And from what I can tell looking in from afar, you haven't allowed yourself much of that. Go home and be with your man."

That sealed the decision for Matt.

Matteo

Those two — to other people they were celebrities, but to me they were neighbors who took care of me when I was a kid. And Jane and my mother were two peas in a pod. Her personal compassion was the encouragement I didn't know I needed, and it helped me make my move. I said my thank-yous and goodbyes to them and scurried up to my room.

After writing a note for the Earth Sciences dude from UCLA, with whom I was sharing the double room, I gathered my things into my rucksack, left the note on dude's bed, and headed out. I was grateful that the hotel had high-speed EV chargers. It mean't I'd probably only have to stop once on the way back for another high-speed recharge.

I packed-up the car, went to the 7-11 to grab a wild cherry slushie, and decided that taking the 10 to the 405 to the 5 would be the fastest way out of the Los Angeles Basin overnight. I calculated that it would probably take me a little over six hours to get home to Santa Cruz.

I was hatching a coming home plot, so I texted Mario, the night proctor at Stevenson, and asked him to help. Being a softy, Mario agreed. One important item remained; I had to text Stu.

**Stu buddy I have a big favor to ask -
I've been excused from the repeats
of stuff I've already done
so I can leave the conference early
I'm driving home overnight –**

**I want to surprise Ferran first thing in the morning
with coffee and a doughnut and me -**

I should get into Santa Cruz a little after 5:30

You're the key to it though buddy -
I would need you to be awake around 6 am
to let me into the dorm and your room when I text you -
And everything would have to be super quiet
so Ferran's still asleep - I'll owe you, man

I can stop by Ferrell's and get stuff and
then come up to Stevenson - I already asked
Mario if he'd let me park in his spot
since he doesn't even have a car

    A very long three minutes later, my smartphone
chimed as a text came in from Stu.

i want an apple fritter and no coffee
i will let you in when you text me
and then go to emily's and go back to sleep
like a reasonable human being
i already texted and she's in

you do owe me
and you are gonna help me figure out
what gift I can give emily for our anniversary
because I suck at figuring that stuff out
and you just seem to know

your heart will be here soon, matt

if this were anybody else but u 2
i'd tell them to go to hell,
but i have a soft spot for u 2 mawkish bisexuals

who both look like
you should be on a runway in milan -

**anyway don't get here and have sex all day long -
cos i gotta be back at 3 to prep for a monday class**
[purple heart emoji]

**Thank you... You are my personal
lord and savior of the month**

                                            damn right - g'night

***

    The next morning, Stu let me in. He grabbed his apple fritter and silently rubbed his palm over my head to mess up my hair. Then he took off as planned.

    I quietly set down the coffee and doughnuts, shook out my hair, and kneeled down on the floor next to Ferran's bed. He was asleep facing the wall, but he was near the edge of the bed. I leaned-in close to him, tenderly kissed him on the back of the neck, and whispered: "Surprise, baby. I'm back early."

    Stirring from his slumber, he turned to face me and rubbed the sleep from his eyes. He seemed to be trying to focus on my face through the surprise. "Matteo Poulsen," he quietly croaked. "What are you doing here, puppy? I thought you weren't coming back until sometime tomorrow night."

    I couldn't help my silly grin. "I couldn't wait another day to see your beautiful face, baby. So, I decided to skip the last workshops and drive here overnight to be with you."

    Ferran reached out and stroked my hair, looking at me with heart eyes. "I can't believe you drove all night to come home to me," he said in a raspy voice.

"'To come home to you,'" I repeated. "I really like the way that sounds."

He thanked me effusively and told me that it was a truly sweet thing to do. "This is another first for me," he said, "and you've given me a lot of firsts."

We both had a laugh about that. I also pointed out that I'd brought him fresh coffee and doughnuts from Ferrell's. Ferran chuckled: "Deadly but delicious."

"You know I aim to please."

"Oh, you please me," he confirmed, as he took a swig of coffee. He rated it 'mediocre but passable' and I reminded him he was a coffee snob. Of course, he agreed with that label wholeheartedly. He took another swig and swished it around in his mouth before swallowing.

"What are you doing?"

"Getting ready to give you coffee kisses," he answered, setting down the coffee and putting his arms around me. "I missed you so much," he told me, as he leaned down and gave me a soft, tender kiss.

I laughed gently. "The coffee breath is mediocre, but you are infinitely better than merely passable."

Ferran looked at me with wonder. "I still can't believe you're here."

"Ferr, I missed you so much. More than I have words to describe. I even ran into Jane Fonda in the hotel lobby and she kinda pried out of me what was going on."

"Yeah? What'd she say?"

"She told me to go home to my man."

Ferran laughed. "Nice! I told you I love her! But why did you decide to skip the workshops?"

"Because I literally couldn't stand to be away from you for another day. And the whole day today would have been repetitive for me, anyway, thanks to the work I put in organizing at Starbucks and Tartine. So, I realized that being here with you and making you happy makes *me* really happy. That's more important to me than attending yet another set of workshops on union-building strategies and tactics. And, besides: you're my person, remember?"

"I remember, and you're making my heart thump. And don't forget you're *my* person, either. But I'm also a little worried about you leaving that conference, Matty. Your leadership is the reason that my dedication to social justice organizing is growing deeper and stronger. I get strength from my connection with you and with all our friends. They do, too, I'm sure."

"Do you feel like I'm letting you all down?"

"Not at all! Damn, let me try that again. I don't think I said it right."

"Maybe I'm being dense."

"That's not it, baby. It's that I'm thinking about the big picture about the time we've had together so far. More than ever, it's taught me how precious every moment is and — right here in the present and for the future — how precious our lives are on Earth."

"Okay… keep going."

"I love you and I love our circle of friends, but that also makes me feel a bigger love: my responsibility to love the planet."

"I get that."

"Matty, coming home to me is the *best* surprise and I can't believe you did this for me. But I don't want you to give up the work for me; I want us to work on it together."

Ferran was so beautiful on so many levels, I wasn't sure what I'd done to deserve him. I reached up and stroked his shoulder as I spoke softly to him: "There's almost nothing I wouldn't do for you. And you know I'm committed to the work, baby."

"I love you so much."

"Look, I like clean food, water, and air, right? And I like my health. And I want social justice. I believe all of those things are human rights, and I want everybody to enjoy them with freedom, and equity, and solidarity."

"Yes."

"I'm kinda all over it, Ferr, you know that. But I'm also committed to you. If I wasn't so in love with you, I don't know how I'd sustain the power to do this stuff. And I certainly don't know how we would have made a family out of our friends — because you know they're just as dedicated as we are. And maybe just as strange?"

"Matty, I gotta tell you: I am pretty amazed every day by our little chosen family."

"Me too! And do you remember when you told me that you know who you are without me?"

"Yes, I do."

"Well, I know who I am without *you.*"

Ferran

Without me? I guess Matt's saying that shouldn't have put me on edge, but it did. I had to take a moment to beat down all that hypervigilance my body had become so used to reacting from.

Matt saw me take a deep breath, so he paused. I focused on him kneeling next to me, and on how it felt that he was touching me. Cautiously, I asked him to tell him more, and I listened closely to really hear what he was saying.

'I'm gonna quote lyrics from a musical. Is that gay enough for ya?" Matt asked with a grin.

"I hope this is good," I said, trying to smile.

So, this was his description: "There's this song in the musical *Hair,* where a character sings:

> Do you only care about the bleeding crowd?
> How about a needing friend?
> I need a friend.

And I think about those lyrics a lot. While I was growing up, I put together a life that was all about caring for the bleeding crowd, but not for the needing friend."

"What do you mean, puppy?"

"You know my family moved around all over the place when I was a kid. So, I never felt like I had real friends. And then, when I was fourteen years old, the first girl I ever went out with dumped me — for a boy who was *tall* — and it broke my heart."

"You're my short king, Matty."

"Yeah, but I wasn't *hers.* And on top of feeling isolated, getting dumped by her for something like that really stung. So, I threw myself into building my life by acting like a human *doing* instead of a human *being.* It was my way of not having to feel anything intimate — in case letting anything in-close might be really painful."

"Ah. That tracks. Now I think understand all your hookups from last year."

"Yeah. And in junior high and high school, I was also hiding in my closet about liking more than just girls. So, I threw myself even deeper into activism. That way, I never had to look at my needs. I didn't date, I just hooked up, and it got to be a habit. I got here last year and I just took that same life to the next level, even though I knew it wasn't who I was inside. At least being here, I felt like I could start to come out, so I guess there was that."

I was hanging on every word. "Did that help?"

"It was only a partial relief," he answered, and I felt my heart sink.

"Think about it, Ferr. Last year, I hadn't come out to my parents yet. So, coming out to some other people here at school? The only other help that gave me was to make it as easy to hook up with guys as with girls. Who was I? Besides being 'Activist Matt,' I was eighty percent machine, ten percent surfer, and ten percent ethical slut. Obviously, it was the machine part that was getting problematic. My life was all cool, casual, and political — and mostly uninhabited by the real me."

That made me so sad. I could only respond by voicing his name: *"Matty."*

"Do you understand, Ferr? You changed all that. I had no defenses against you and I didn't want any. You made it possible for the real me to walk out into the light of day. I *do* know who the real me is, and I am far happier being me *with* you than without you."

"Yeah?"

"Yeah. And if I don't absolutely *have to* be without you, why should I be? You inspire me, and I had to come home and tell you that."

I felt like my heart swelled, and I pulled Matt into a tight hug and kissed him with passion. When I broke the kiss, he was breathless. "You remind me how lucky I am to have you," I told him. "But Matty, please promise me you won't skip any more stuff for me that's super-important, okay?"

Matt smiled and held up his hand, like a Cub Scout taking an oath. "Okay, Ferran Bosch. I solemnly promise that to you. This time it was a special occasion, but from now on I'll find a balance between my political commitments and spending time with the man I love."

I could feel my face glowing with my smile. I took both of Matt's hands and put them together in mine. Then I lifted them up and kissed them. "That's all I'm asking for, puppy. Just like you asked it from me. But please don't take that as any kind of rebuff, because I am overjoyed that you're here with me right now."

Matt kissed my forehead. "I will grant your wish," he said, regally. "Now, could we just stay in bed today, and cuddle and kiss and nap? Obviously, I haven't slept, and Stu is coming back at three o'clock to prep for a class tomorrow."

"Oh," I happily questioned him, "you two colluded on this?"

"How else do you think I got in here?"

"Okay, baby. I think I can manage to skip the group project meet-up for my Greek class today. But I'm gonna have to start functioning around three o'clock, too. So, if you want, we can do that 'cuddling and kissing and napping' thing until then."

"I *want.*"

"I love you, Matty."

"And I love you. *So* much."

36

DINNER

"In any given moment we have two options:
To step forward into growth
or to step back into safety."
— Abraham Maslow

In a romantic partnership,
I imagine the only thing more cheerful
than knowing you would choose
your own parents as family
is knowing that you would choose
your partner's parents as family, too.
— Gwendolyn Brooks

[Playlist reference: Ms. Niki — Rainbow]

Ekkheya

The night was getting a bit colder outside the highly rated Peruvian restaurant in San Jose. Giorgia and Noah Poulsen had registered with the host and were standing just inside the entrance, waiting to be seated.

Isabel and Ignasi Bosch entered the restaurant and saw them. Smiling, they walked up to Giorgia and Noah. "Well, hello!" Giorgia greeted them. "You must be Ferran's parents?"

"And you must be Matteo's?" Ignasi asked.

Noah observed: "I guess it was a good idea that we exchanged selfies so we could recognize each other."

Ignasi and Isabel returned the Poulsens' hellos, and both sets of parents were expressing pleasure at finally getting to meet each other. Ferran and Matt opened the restaurant doors and a burst of chilly air swept inside. They walked nervously, hand-in-hand, towards their group of parents. "Sorry we're late, everyone," Ferran explained. "Traffic on Highway 17 was a nightmare."

Matt agreed: "We thought it might make us really late."

It was partially true. The guys had made a late start over the hill. There was something Matt insisted on accomplishing on his knees in front of Ferran, and something about Ferran needing to be bred before dinner, but I tried the best I could to focus elsewhere.

"No worries, boys. Your presence is felt whether near or far," Giorgia reassured them. Then, she turned to level some maternal worry: "So, Matt, did that Niro EV of yours make it up the hill okay?"

Matt rolled his eyes. "Yes, it did, mum."

Ferran figured this was the time to chime-in to help his boyfriend: "It did, Mrs. Poulsen. It has really good torque."

"Ferran, *please* call me Giorgia. And don't worry about timing; we're just glad you're here."

Isabel and Giorgia broke into broad smiles as they each took a good look at the other's son. They both sighed. Then, as if on cue, both of them simultaneously said: "Your son is *so* handsome!" And all four parents laughed. Matt and Ferran were embarrassed but grinning, and both of them lowered their heads and looked at their shoes.

Perhaps it was a way to distract from the fact that they'd both been ogling each other's very handsome sons, but Giorgia and Isabel *oh-thank-you'd* each other profusely. Ignasi simply noted that the boys obviously had excellent taste. Self-consciously, Ferran pleaded with them to stop, and Matt begged, "Please reel it in, you guys. I'm blushing enough as it is."

That was when the head waiter arrived to seat the group at their table. "Six for dinner? Right this way, please."

They all followed him into the dining room to their large round table and took their seats. Matt sat nearest to Isabel and Ignasi. Sitting at his side, Ferran was nearest to Noah and Giorgia. Another staff member poured water for each person at the table and handed them menus. He asked is any of them would like a cocktail and all of them demurred because it was a work night.

As the wait staff left, Noah announced that he loved Peruvian food.

"We found this place when we were taking visiting relatives on a tour of the Bay Area," Ignasi told them. "For all the ethnicities we have at this table, I don't think any of us is Peruvian. So, we'll all get an out-of-the-ordinary experience."

Giorgia smiled: "I thought out-of-the-ordinary experiences had become the new standard for all of us."

"Right?" Isabel confirmed. She turned to Matt and reminded him that they'd sat next to each other while watching several of Ferran's soccer games. She told him that chatting with him made the games much more fun.

"I'm glad you think so, because I love doing that, too," he answered.

"So," Ignasi asked, "how is university life treating you boys?"

Matteo

I reminded Ignasi and Isabel that I was in my second year as an undergraduate, so I'd grown more used to the grind than Ferran had.

Ferran shrugged his shoulders and grinned as he sighed. "I'm sure it won't come as a surprise to any of you that has been a whirlwind of a first quarter for me," he joked. "It wasn't only meeting and getting closer to each other, but also navigating our academics and everything else in the midst of that. It's been almost like an adventure ride at Disneyland."

"That's for sure," I agreed, "but we've also had fun. Ferran's soccer games, my campaign volunteering, going hiking together, and exploring new places. Plus, getting to know all of our friends, we've been able to have plenty of dinners, and games, and movies, and a *lot* of chocolate."

Isabel made a motherly observation: "I'm happy you could do all of that and your grades did not suffer, Ferran."

He beamed at me as he answered her. "Matty keeps me on my toes."

"That goes both ways," I insisted, and then realized what I'd said. "Just like both of us," I added, chuckling at my own words. Luckily, everybody at the table laughed.

I was anxious about this dinner before we arrived, but Ferran kept reassuring me it would be fine. As our parents chatted with each other more around the table, I was able to finally relax. Our waiter returned take our orders, and afterward the conversation remained lively. It continued as our parents bonded with each other over shared experiences and stories. It felt like they were bonding more closely with us as a couple, too.

I looked over at Ferran and felt more at home than I think I had ever felt before.

Ferran

I was worried about whether my mama was ready to meet Matt's parents, but she seemed to really enjoy talking with them. On the ride over, Matt told me he was anxious about how the dinner would go, but I did my best to comfort him — whether I believed my own calming words or not. I think having both our mothers act like cougars towards us helped to break the ice, even if it was a little embarrassing.

My papa summed up my own feelings about everything I'd discovered from being with Matt. "This has been almost five months filled with many new and wonderful experiences," he said, "and I'm glad we've had them."

"Me, too," Noah agreed.

Looking over at my parents, Giorgia took the subject another step. "Well, speaking of new experiences," she bridged, "do you have any plans for the upcoming holidays?"

Papa announced that he and Mama were thinking of going back to Spain for a visit. "A little time in Madrid and a little time in Barcelona," he told them. "It's been a good while since we've been back, and we also need a little couple time without work."

"And without your son there, putting a damper on your amorous shenanigans," I joked.

"That, too," Papa agreed.

Mama asked the Poulsens about their own plans.

"Well, we're still deciding," Georgia told her. "But I think a cozy family gathering might be in order. We don't always get to have everyone together for the holidays, and I love it when Matt and my mother can spend it with us. My mother is going to Mexico with a friend this Christmas, but we'd love to have Ferran visit with us if you'll both be away."

"What a lovely invitation," my mama replied.

"Ferran got to meet our little girl Clary, and our little boy Dave when he and Matt came up to have dinner. Then the boys did face-painting for them at the campus's Harvest Festival. And our kids absolutely adored him. They want him to come back as soon as possible."

I was about as happy and excited about hearing that as I could be. "I love those kids!" I nearly cheered.

Matt had heart eyes for me when I caught a glimpse of him beside me. Noah smiled at the two of us, and made the invitation specific. "We would love for you two to visit us over the holidays, guys. We know you could maybe house-sit for the Bosches, or maybe stay at your house off-campus, Matt. But we'd love some family time with both of you. And the kids love it when they get to spend time with both of you."

I asked my parents if they were going to board Adelina while they were away, and they said they planned to have her stay with Howard, the dog walker. I approved: "Oh good, she *loves* Howard."

"I want to meet her so much," Matt pined.

"Well, Ferran," Papa chided me, "you have to bring Matt over to meet Adelina!"

"Okay!"

Matt looked over at his mother and said, "I think we'd love to spend some time with you and Dad and the kids over the holidays, mum." He had a smile from ear to ear, but I know he didn't want to make the decision for me. So, he asked, "Can we talk about that when we drive home, Ferr?"

And I confirmed: "Absolutely."

Noah asked my parents how it had been for them since Matt and I had delivered our big news. Mama looked over and smiled at me with soft eyes. "Well," she said, "it was definitely a surprise for us when Ferran told us about his feelings for Matt. We hadn't ever anticipated it."

"Neither had I," I smirked.

"But you know, look at these two," she continued. "I think we've come to accept that they really do care for each other very much."

Matt turned to me and agreed: "That's true, I care about you a lot." I could feel my face heating, and I smiled.

"But how could we not see how happy they are together?" Papa said, joining in.

I gazed at my beautiful boyfriend and said, "He makes me *so* happy."

Isabel saw us locking eyes. "Look at that. How could we not support them in that?"

"That's really wonderful to hear," Noah said, smiling. "We went through a journey last summer when Matt came out to us as bi. We were really angry that he'd been bullied and harassed at work, and we wanted to make sure he had our support. We kind of had to get over ourselves and open up our minds fast."

"And I'm thankful you did," Matt added. "And also, that when I told you about Ferran, you didn't freak out."

I wanted to give Matt's folks their due. "Your parents have been great, Matty. Giorgia, Noah, you really have made me feel welcome, and I'm really grateful to have my own parents accept me."

"Me, too!" Matt agreed. "Dr. and Mr. Bosch, it means a lot to have your support."

"Please," Isabel said, patting Matt's hand. "We're Isabel and Ignasi for you, Matt."

Our group's plates arrived, and I was definitely hungry. We were all marveling over the wonderful aromas and the presentations of the foods. The conversation ebbed and flowed while we dug into our dishes and savored the deliciousness — all of it.

37

SOLSTICE

"You are full of unshaped dreams.
You are laden with beginnings…
There is hope in you…"
— *Lola Ridge*

[Playlist reference: Rihanna — Lift Me Up]

Matteo

We were finally getting some alone time, ensconced in the large downstairs guest room in my parents' house in San Francisco. The weather outside was growing colder, and we were cuddled together in front of a fire. I snuggled up closer to Ferran. "I'm gonna say it out loud so I can believe it's true," I told him. "We're having our first Winter Holiday together as a couple, and I couldn't be happier."

Ferran's giant smile made the corners of his eyes crinkle. "I *could* be happier," he responded, "if we have *all* our Winter Holidays together from now on, thanks."

I agreed I'd vote for that, and I started gently caressing his cheek. I also voiced my relief that we didn't let the Thanksgiving fiasco break us apart. "I feel like we've grown a lot from that experience, and because of it our relationship has become really different.

"Better," Ferran said, nuzzling against my chest, "and a lot more solid."

"In the best possible way," I agreed, kissing Ferran on his head, "I really feel that."

"See? The bump in the road only made us stronger."

"More like a pothole," I muttered.

"I agree it was a train wreck, Matty. But we learned important things about each other, and that allowed us to get closer. One way or another, I think we always push each other to be the best versions of ourselves. We found our way through it."

"With a crucial assist from our friends."

"Look who's learned some soccer terminology," Ferran chided. "We got closer to our friends because of it, too. It would be nice if there were no storm clouds, but at least we found the silver lining."

I grumbled. "I hope so. But that one felt like Hell on Wheels. Could we please not do that again?"

"I'm sorry I was a jealous idiot. Dysfunctional attachment reactions suck, but we've both got 'em. At least we know that about each other now, and we're each working on our stuff."

"Speaking of which, I have a video session with my therapist on the 27th."

"Me, too. But I can go use my smartphone in the car, and you can stay here and have privacy."

Matt rolled his eyes. "As much as Clary and Dave will allow me," he sighed, with a mini-smile.

"But, puppy, you know the fears that take over my head. You're so important to me that I get afraid sometimes that this wonderful, amazing dream will disappear. I promise you, though: I respect the trust that we have between us. I promise to tell you when I'm feeling that awful fear rising-up inside me. I promise we can talk it through."

"Baby, I know. And I promise I'll be honest with you about all that stuff too. I don't want to lose you, either, Ferr."

"Good!" he said, and leaned up to kiss me. He looked around the room, and then gestured to the fireplace and the festive decorations. "I admire your parents for doing all this," he observed. "They've made it really warm and magickal in here for us. At least, I feel that way. And the Winter Holiday music they've got playing in the background is like adding the perfect, cheesy Hallmark touch."

"Oh, they are definitely Christmas queens," I acknowledged.

"And Chanukah queens, and Diwali queens, and Ashura queens, and Solstice queens, and Kwanzaa queens, and …"

He had me laughing, but I kissed the next word out of his mouth to stop his litany. "Yeah, okay," I conceded.

"They want to celebrate *everybody's* religion. They say that Christmas makes them very eclectic when it comes to all the other winter light festivals."

"But they do remember what generation we're part of, right?" Ferran teased. "We're busy; we have a lot of manifesting to do, and neoliberal messes to clean up. Are they keeping in mind that we're more focused on the spiral dance between spirit and science than in following any organized religion?"

"Ferr, I know you're teasing, but we have to take that stuff slowly with them. Don't you think we've shattered their illusions enough for one year?"

He laughed: "You've got a point."

Ferran laid his head back down on my chest, and I caressed his hair as I reflected "They've only just got their heads wrapped around the queer part."

"I know, you're right. We should probably save the magick part for later."

I leaned down and lifted his chin with my fingers. I kissed him again, loving every opportunity I found to do it. "I might be actually looking forward to the winter quarter at UCSC," I suggested. "We could make it an adventure together."

Ferran didn't sound convinced. "That's certainly a rose-colored vision of school, Matty."

"Okay, Debby Downer. If you'd rather, I could talk instead about the workload we're gonna have. And the cold rain, and the mud at the farm. And not being able to go on as many walks, and feeling melancholy in the dark forest."

Ferran grunted. "Fine. I much prefer the adventure part." As he leaned up for another kiss, the booming sound of my giggling siblings echoed in the background.

"Sounds like my little sister and my baby brother are having too much fun."

Ferran grinned. "It's adorable how much your family celebrates. They must be excited for Santa's arrival."

I nuzzled his hair. "And don't forget they've got you here, too — that's everything. They love you. And *we* are family, baby. I mean, Ferr: we're *us.*"

Ferran

Matt's sister and brother found a way to open the locked door and bounded into our room, giggling and jumping onto the bed. That startled Matt, and he asked them how they got the door open. "We have a ghost key!" yelled Dave, Matt's four-year-old brother.

"Do you mean a skeleton key?" I asked him.

"Yeah, that," Dave confirmed.

Clary, Matt's five-year-old sister, obviously was hiding something in her hand. Matt held open his own hand in front of her. "Give it," he said, in a tone that left no room for argument.

Pouting, Clary handed him the key, but told him he was being mean. "You love me," Matt told her. She gave him hardcore side-eye.

Dave began to jump on the bed again, chanting: "We wanna wait for Santa with you guys!"

"I think your parents might get cross with you if you stay up and make noise," I answered him, trying to sound reasonable. But Dave was nonplussed.

"You'll protect us, Ferran!" he declared. "You're big and strong!"

Even as she was cuddling up next to Matt, Clary gave us an order in her best lecturing voice: "Don't be Grinches, you guys."

Matt patted her on the head. "We not being Grinches, Clary We're *saving you* from the Grinches."

I gave Matt a gentle shove at his shoulder. "Puppy, Noah and Giorgia are *not* actually Grinches."

But Clary was ready with a very surly retort: "I *think* that that depends on their mood, Ferran." I gave Matt an amused, wide-eyed look.

"She takes after her big brother," he shrugged.

I bopped her on the tip of her nose with my index finger. "Both of you are troublemakers," I pronounced.

"Okay," Matt said, trying to corral both children, "you kids are up *way* too late."

"It's early!" Dave declared. And Matt told him he should know better.

Dave yelled, "I want a hug from Ferran!"

"Me, too!" Clary agreed.

"You can both get hugs if you'll go back to your rooms and go to sleep, so Santa can get here," Matt told them. Clary told him he was no fun. "Okay," Matt rejoined, "you can go without hugs from Ferran if you really want to. More for me!"

"Noooooo!" Dave groaned. "I'll go back to bed! I promise!"

"Okay, little man," I offered, "then *you* get the first hug!" I stood and scooped-up Dave into my arms, and proclaimed: "Happy Christmas Eve, Dave!"

"Happy Christmas Eve, Ferran!" he gleefully replied.

"Okay, *not fair,*" Clary grumbled. She reached out her arms towards me, and I leaned down and gave her a big hug. "Now, could you take your brother Dave back up to his room," I asked, "and go back to yours and go to sleep, so Santa will actually get to show up?"

"Okay," Clary said, turning to her big brother. "Kisses, Matt," she demanded. Matt gave her a kiss on the cheek, and only then did she get up and move to the door.

Dave ran over to Matt and issued the same demand, except his sounded more like a request: "Kisses, Matt!" and Matt kissed him on the cheek. Taking Dave's hand, Clary led him out the door, telling him: "Come on Dave, let's go hit the hay."

I ushered them both out the door, and they scampered up the stairs. I closed the door and looked over at Matt, with my heart full. He smiled at me and said, "Well done."

"I am so in love with you right now I might explode," I gushed.

"Don't do that. I need Ferran Hugs and Kisses."

I got onto the bed on my knees, took Matt in my arms, and kissed him again. My body vibrated like the floor at a rave. This is where I belonged. In the same space as him. Loved by him.

"I'm pretty nuts about you," he quietly announced.

"I'm glad," I said, "because I'm kinda head-over-heels for you."

Matt kissed me again, and we savored the taste of each other. We both laid down and turned onto our backs, looking upward at the fairy lights around the room. I felt like I was the happiest I'd ever been, but I knew I had to broach a subject that might be a tender one with Matt.

I didn't know how else to do it, so I just blurted it out: "I think maybe I need to see April."

"I *know* you do," he answered.

"Please don't think … you know … that anything sexual will happen with her. *It won't.*"

"Ferr, I really wasn't afraid of that. Did you want to convince me about that, or convince yourself?"

I felt out of my depth talking about it. I suppose I defaulted to behaving like a high school boy making a vain attempt at mansplaining something to a girl who knew better. I promised him I'd talk about my fears with him, so I did: "I was worried that you'd be as crazy as me," I told him. "I was worried that you might think I was cheating on you."

"Oh," Matt said, rolling his eyes and grinning.

"I would never, baby. And I'm sorry. I guess I have a scarcity mentality, but I'm working hard to overcome it."

"That's good, and I trust you. But don't let that make you think I don't sometimes get jealous," Matt confessed. "Everybody has to contend with that green monster. We get it foisted on us, Ferr. Think about it: the people who care for us as toddlers teach us to associate that kind of fearful grasping with our natural drive to get enough food to keep ourselves alive."

"I read about it in high school social studies class. And I remember hearing my parents give me the proprietary 'mine and thine' message pretty strongly. All my cousins would be around the table eating, and my parents would say stuff to them like, 'You have enough food of your own to finish. Don't put your hands near your cousin's plate. That's his, not yours; eat your own food.'"

"Right. I remember hearing, 'If you don't keep your crayons together, Sofie will break them and then you'll be left with nothing that's any good.'"

"Or, 'Play nice. You don't get to run away with Ricky's toys and he doesn't get to run away with yours.'"

"Jesus," Matt said with an eye roll. "I can remember so much of that. You see? That's an artificial mental link, but it's hard to break without having to process it to death. I actually do get jealous sometimes, Ferr. It's just that I have faith in you — that we would work it out between us before either of us would ever actually engage in any *extracurricular activity.* Keeping that in mind helps me override 'the stupid'."

"I'm sorry that *I* was so stupid, Matty."

Matt groaned. "Will you stop with the 'sorry'?" We learned the right lessons from our mistakes. We're moving forward from that, okay?"

I relented. "Okay, baby."

"I'm gonna do some one-upmanship on the Classics major right now. You ready?"

"Oh, this should be good."

"Have you ever heard that quote from St. John Chrysostom about 'mine and thine'?"

"Why are your questions always so erudite and profound?" I teased.

"Look who's talking, nerd. But have you heard it?"

"No, what?"

"He said: *'Mine* and *thine,* those chilling words which introduce innumerable conflicts into the world, should be eradicated from the community.'"

I mulled that over. "I feel like that ought to be my mantra."

"Mine, too."

"But even if we're both working to overcome our envy and our jealousy and our coveting," I asked him, "do you think you could you still be mine?"

Matt's emerald eyes glistened and he smiled at me. "Ferr, I'm always yours. Always."

"And I'm always yours, Matty."

"You'd better be," Matt said, chuckling.

Matteo

"Do you know what *chrysostomos* means in Greek?" Ferran asked me.

I supposed that this was my allotment for having a boyfriend who studied and spoke ancient languages. "I don't," I answered. "What is it?"

"It means 'golden-mouthed.'"

"I guess that fits, doesn't it," I chuckled.

"Now I'm going to kiss *your* golden mouth, puppy."

That was an idea I could support: "Yes, please." And there we were again, wrapped in each other and sharing soft, passionate kisses. "I could never get too many of these," I said. Ferran reminded me that after our first kiss, we both agreed we were going to need many more of each other's kisses.

But eventually, Ferran broke our kisses and looked down into my eyes. "I wanna circle back to the conversation about April, okay?"

"Okay."

"I haven't really spoken with April since back in September, Matty. Back then, we compared notes on getting settled at our dorms, and I guess we both got really busy. She texted me out of the blue yesterday. She wanted to set up something for us to catch-up while she's back here for the holidays. She and I have six years of growing up together as best friends, so I need to find out what's happening in her life and I need to tell her about mine. And I need to tell her about you."

"I get it."

"I'm glad you understand," Ferran sighed.

I offered him some options: "Do you want to take some time and drive down to Santa Nella? Do you want me to go with you? Or, do you want me to stay put?"

"I told her that Mama and Papa went to Spain for the holidays, and that I was staying in San Francisco. She said a couple of our friends from Los Banos High went to UC Berkeley, and they're going to be having a party. She's going there on the 29th and staying with them in Rockridge through New Year's Day or so."

"Okay," I answered, "that makes it less complicated."

Ferran turned to me and kissed me on the head. "Not if you and I *both* go to the party," he said.

"Was that an option?"

"April told me that our friends invited me, and I'm not spending New Year's Eve without you."

"Mmmmmm," I purred. "Well, good. Now, kiss me."

He did, and then he gave me a small peck on the tip of my nose. "I haven't given them an answer yet. When she's up here, April wants to come into The City and go to high tea at Lovejoy's Tea Room."

"Fancy."

"She loves that stuff," he chuckled. "I was thinking I could go to Rockridge and meet her at Crepevine for lunch. I can give her all the news and get caught up on hers. And if she survives all that, then maybe the three of us could go to Lovejoy's together?"

"That sounds like a good plan to me."

Ferran got a very serious look on his face. "Puppy, I just feel like I have to tell you again, because I need you to really know it. I'm not going to leave you behind *ever* again. It was the worst ninety-one hours of my life. April and I are not going to fall back into the old groove, I promise you."

I decided this trope would never end if I didn't try to subdue it. "Baby, I trust you," I repeated. "It was the worst ninety-one hours of my life, too. I know you're aching to tell her everything that's happened. You two grew up together in your relationship, and that's not going away."

"I'm really glad you get it."

I thought about what April looked like, and I couldn't help but be understanding about Ferran feeling a need to reassure me. I tried to ease his worries with some humor: "I do have to give you *major* props for not wanting to jump back into the sack with her. Don't forget, I've seen photos."

Ferran grinned at me. "She's hot, right?"

"Um, *yes!* Yes, she is. So, thank you for your restraint."

"Aha!" Ferran said, wrestling me around on the bed and giving me a big kiss. "You and I haven't really talked about restraints yet. But we can!"

"Beast."

"Thank you."

"I'm so lucky you're my boyfriend."

"I feel so incredibly lucky to have *you,* puppy. And not only do I get to be with you, but I've got this new place in your family's hearts, too."

I really adored this man. I stroked his cheek softly. "I'm glad I've been so welcomed by your family, too. And I definitely hope this is the first of many Winter Holidays together for you and me. You can see that Dave and Clary pretty much worship you; they wish we could both be here with them all the time."

"Maybe they could come visit us down in Santa Cruz sometime?" Ferran asked.

"That would be really cool, as long as it doesn't give your mother any ideas about how soon she can get us married and adopting grandchildren for her."

"Not that I hate that idea," he replied, "but I'm pretty sure she'll allow us to graduate and get gainful employment first."

"Well, how very gracious."

"I also think, the more they get to know them, the more both sets of our parents are going to like the chosen family we've gathered around us, and the kind of work for change that all of us are doing."

"I believe you're right about that."

"Do you really think what our friends tell us is true? That our bond with each other gives them strength to send out ripples of good trouble?"

"I think the love between us and the love we share with all of them is probably the desperately necessary stuff that can make things better in the world. I hope so, anyway. When I think about all of that, I'm just amazed at how lucky we are."

"Me too, *Beautiful Man I Someday Want To Raise Kids With.*"

It warmed my heart that he said it, but I wondered: "Is that scary for you? When we find ourselves talking about that kind of stuff so soon?"

Ferran laughed gently. "If someone had asked me last July if I'd be lying in bed in San Francisco during the

Winter Holiday listening to cheesy Christmas music with the man I love, I'd have told them they were delusional. But here I am with you, and I *am* totally in love with you, and I want us to be together no matter what. So, I honestly don't think I'm all that scared of it, Matty."

Finally — right then and there — I felt so happily and outrageously romantic that I couldn't imagine ever going back to trying to keep myself from feeling. "You're it for me, Ferran Bosch. Did you know that? You know how to keep me nice and warm in your love. When we go to sleep tonight, will you just keep holding me? Because, I live for that."

"Me, too, to all of it," Ferran answered, leaning in for a kiss "I love you, Matty. Happy Yule.

Close again to Ferran's lips, I whispered: "Happy Yule, Ferr. I love you, too."

A BETTER WORLD IS POSSIBLE

CONJUGATE

"Love is not primarily
a relationship to a specific person;
it is an attitude, and ordination of character
which determines the relatedness of the person
to the whole world as a whole,
not toward one object of love."
— *Erich Fromm*

*[Playlist reference: Colby Caillat,
featuring Jason Mraz — Lucky]*

Ekkheya

Chatting away at April's favorite San Francisco tea restaurant on a cold and sunny day, Matt and April discovered that they were both huge fans of Kathy Griffin.

Ferran, Matt, and April had met together at Lovejoy's Tea Room and were luxuriating in a high tea service for three. "Jam first, or clotted cream first?" Ferran asked as he sliced into a warm scone. "Cream first, jam on top," Matt and April said simultaneously.

"Jinx!" April called out.

"Monsoon!" Matt called back.

"O gods," Ferran groaned. "If I have to watch this game, you both owe *me* a zero-sugar Coke."

"Spoilsport," April teased. She offered a suggestion: "If all three of us go together to see Kathy Giffin's upcoming show, it would be a great way to hang-out and get to know each other better." As soon as the guys showed interest, she reached for her smartphone and started searching for VIP ticket deals.

Ever since she was a tween, April wanted to get the kind of tickets that would include a backstage pass for a meet-and-greet with Kathy after the show. Her parents would never agree to the higher fees. But April had been dreaming of it for years, and she visited all the key web sites to find the passes.

She managed to score three VIP tickets for January 2nd, to see Kathy Griffin do her one-woman show in San Francisco. It would be just before April had to leave to go back to New Haven for school. Matt and April were giddy with anticipation, and Ferran was ecstatic to see the two of them getting along so well.

After the show, as they waited in the VIP line to meet and talk with Kathy Griffin, April and Matt were reliving the funniest moment from the show. Ferran was even more amused by them than by the revisiting of the jokes. He told April, "I love that you like Matty so much."

"Look, Ferran," she said, "I keep you with me in my heart, and now Matt's in yours. It only stands to reason."

"Thank you," he said, getting a little teared up.

When it was their turn, the three approached Kathy, who was seated in front of a small desk. When she looked at the three of them, she dropped her jaw with an exaggerated gape.

"Who are you guys?" she asked. "You all look like supermodels. Are you gonna be the new version of the Mod Squad?"

April grinned happily, while Matt and Ferran were busy blushing. "No," April responded. "Just ordinary university students who *live* for your humor. I've always been a fan, and I started at fourteen to nag my mom to try to get VIP tickets so I could meet you."

Kathy wrinkled her lips. "Mom wasn't sold, huh?"

"She said it was too expensive. But this time I was determined to splurge with my friends."

"What's your name?" Kathy queried.

"April Challoner."

Kathy held out her hand and April shook it. "It is an honor to meet you, April Challoner."

"The pleasure is all mine," April replied with a little tip of her forehead.

Kathy again looked at all three of them, "You three have anything you want me to sign?" she asked.

"No, we literally just wanted to bask in your presence," April told her with a sheepish grin.

That gave Kathy a giggle. Turning towards the guys, she pointedly asked, "And who are these fine young men you have on your leash, April Challoner?" But before anyone could answer, Kathy very obviously gave Matt the once-over. "And you, young man. You are *gorgeous,*" she fawned. *"Like, really* gorgeous. *Please* tell me you're one of my gays."

Matt laughed nervously and corrected her: "I'm bi, actually."

"Good enough," Kathy said, with a perfunctory hand wave. "I probably sound like a cradle robber, because you're like — what — seventeen?"

"Nineteen."

"Nineteen," she repeated. "And stunning. And a queerling. *Please* tell me you're not a Republican."

"Oh, very much the opposite." Matt said, emphatically. "Politics student at UCSC, grassroots organizer, eco-socialist, surf pup." Kathy did her dropped jaw bit again, and Matt chuckled. "And my name is Matteo Poulsen," he added.

"Matteo," she repeated, seeming to savor the name. "Every bit of that information is good to know."

"And you, Sir," she said, turning her attention to Ferran.

"Ferran Bosch," he told her, smiling.

"You are also a strapping lad, aren't you." Kathy gushed. "This young lady has taste."

"She used to be my girlfriend."

"Used to be?," Kathy repeated, with emphasis. "Okay, spill the tea."

April was the one who took that challenge: "We agreed to break up because I was going to leave for school in New Haven. Really, we were just best-friends-with-benefits, and we wanted to grab hold of our new lives."

"That," Kathy commented with conviction, "is absurdly reasonable," Then she looked back at Ferran and, with a double hair-flip, she said: "So, are you still single, handsome?"

Ferran grinned, keeping his focus on Kathy to deliver the news. "No, I'm not," he answered. "Matt's my boyfriend."

Kathy mock-recoiled, acting as though the information had been shocking. "Oh, *this* story just gets *juicier!*"

Ferran laughed. "I hope you don't think less of us," he joked.

"Are you kidding?," Kathy asked, with apparent glee. "This could get you into my Hall of Fame!"

Kathy's eyes suddenly darted over the heads of the three, and she offered the slightest nod.

Now look, *kiddles,* unfortunately I have to move you along, because my assistant is giving me the side-eye. But you see where he's standing over there? I just gave him the special nod because someday, Mod-Squadders, I'm gonna pump you for more information about this exciting little drama you're starring in. So, if you guys go over there and give him your contact info, he'll make sure you get some *free* VIP tickets to my shows."

Matt answered excitedly: "That's amazingly generous."

"I assure you, *Matteo,* it's all self-interest,*"* she told him, adding a big smile. "Now scoot, you three. Thank you for coming to say hi."

All three of them thanked her again.

They left her, and walked over to her personal assistant, who already had his business smartphone ready, opened to the contact list. They gave him all their pertinent info and thanked him profusely. "She's in charge," he said, smiling. "I just show up."

As they walked into the hallway of the theatre, Matt told April, "I have to hug you right now. Can I hug you?"

"You'd better, boy," she said, pulling him in. She gave him a huge kiss on his forehead. Both of them looked at Ferran and, almost in tandem, they said, "Thank you, Ferran."

APPENDIX

"The only thing they have to look forward to is hope.

And you have to give them hope.

Hope for a better world, hope for a better tomorrow,

hope for a better place to come to

if the pressures at home are too great.

Hope that all will be all right.

Without hope, …the us-es, *the us-es* will give up.

And you, and you, and you:

You have to give people hope."

— Harvey Milk

[Playlist reference: The Police —

When the World is Running Down

(You Make The Best of What's Still Around)]

AT THE U.N. CLIMATE ACTION SUMMIT

PUBLIC DOMAIN TRANSCRIPT

Climate activist Greta Thunberg, who was 16 at the time, addressed the U.N.'s Climate Action Summit in New York City on 23 September 2019. In her remarks, she clearly stated the truth of what we face, but she has — and the greater scientific community have — been largely ignored by policy makers, for the sake of profit. Our only solution is putting love for people and the planet into action, and that may take some radical measures. Here is the full transcript of Thunberg's speech, beginning with her response to a question about the message she had for world leaders.

My message is that we'll be watching you.

This is all wrong. I shouldn't be up here. I should be back in school on the other side of the ocean. Yet you all come to us young people for hope. How dare you!

You have stolen my dreams and my childhood with your empty words. And yet I'm one of the lucky ones. People are suffering. People are dying. Entire ecosystems are collapsing. We are in the beginning of a mass extinction, and all you can talk about is money and fairy tales of eternal economic growth. How dare you!

For more than 30 years, the science has been crystal clear. How dare you continue to look away and come here saying that you're doing enough, when the politics and solutions needed are still nowhere in sight.

You say you hear us and that you understand the urgency. But no matter how sad and angry I am, I do not want to believe that. Because if you really understood the situation and still kept on failing to act, then you would be evil. And that I refuse to believe.

The popular idea of cutting our emissions in half in 10 years only gives us a 50% chance of staying below 1.5 degrees [Celsius], and the risk of setting off irreversible chain reactions beyond human control. Fifty percent may be acceptable to you. But those numbers do not include tipping points, most feedback loops, additional warming hidden by toxic air pollution or the aspects of equity and climate justice. They also rely on my generation sucking hundreds of billions of tons of your carbon dioxide out of the air with technologies that barely exist.

So, a 50% risk is simply not acceptable to us — we who have to live with the consequences.

To have a 67% chance of staying below a 1.5 degrees global temperature rise – the best odds given by the [Intergovernmental Panel on Climate Change] – the world had 420 giga-tons of carbon dioxide left to emit back on Jan. 1st, 2018. Today that figure is already down to less than 350 giga-tons.

How dare you pretend that this can be solved with just 'business as usual' and some technical solutions? With today's emissions levels, that remaining carbon dioxide budget will be entirely gone within less than 8 1/2 years.

There will not be any solutions or plans presented in line with these figures here today, because these numbers are too uncomfortable. And you are still not mature enough to tell it like it is.

You are failing us. But the young people are starting to understand your betrayal. The eyes of all future generations are upon you. And if you choose to fail us, I say: We will never forgive you.

We will not let you get away with this. Right here, right now is where we draw the line. The world is waking up. And change is coming, whether you like it or not.

Thank you.

— Greta Thunberg

GLOSSARY

There are some terms used in the writing that are technical, or are from languages other than the main language of the book. This glossary should help readers who don't know the terms to understand them better.

Åh mine guder! Danish phrase which translates to English as "O my God."

Amor meu. A Catalan term of endearment, which literally means, "my love."

Association Football. In most countries around the world, the word "football" refers to the team sport played between two teams of eleven players each, who primarily use their feet to propel a spherical ball around a rectangular field (also called a "pitch"). The objective of the game is to score more goals than the opposing team by moving the ball beyond the goal line into a rectangular-framed goal defended by the opposing team. In the United States, the term "soccer" is generally used to refer to *association football,* so as to distinguish it from the game of *American football,* which is a more chess-like, rarified variation of the more universal international game of rugby.

Brujas y brujos. Catalan and Spanish term(s) for practitioners of magick.

DL. An acronym for "down low." It is a term referring to hiding queer identity or sex acts in the secrecy of the closet.

Dulce de leche. The Spanish and Catalan term for caramel or soft toffee. The literal English translation is "sweet from milk."

El meu fill. The Catalan term for "my son," and the word, **fill** in this context means "son."

Gods. This is a distinction in usage. The term usually is used here as juxtaposed with the term "God." In the book, "God" most often refers to the concept of a deity, or of a "God" as understood in religious terms — as one or more anthropomorphic, supernaturally supreme beings that control people and events. The "witchy" concept of "gods," however, refers to the idea of a trajectory, or principle, or divinity that pervades the cosmos but is also beyond the whole cosmos, and can be vaguely conceived as aspects of the ultimately whole, essential, perfect, spiritual reality out of which the cosmos — in all its fractures and polarities and imperfections — is projected. Apart from that, however, the use in this book of the phrase, "God only knows," refers to the "witchy" concept of gods.

Hygge. A Danish word meaning a quality of coziness and comfortable conviviality that engenders a feeling of contentment or well-being (considered as a defining characteristic of Danish culture).

Jersei. The Catalan term used to refer to: a sweater, jumper, jersey.

Jove canalla. The Catalan term for a seductive young rascal.

Lares. (Singlular: **Lar.**) The Latin word in classical Rome that referred to archetypal spirits who, when they received appropriate offerings, would guard over the place and people of a community, and would help to guide them for the better. This concept was pervasive in the ancient world.

Les yeux sans visage. A French phrase that literally translates to English as "Eyes Without a Face." It is the title of a 1960 French-language horror film directed by Georges Franjou, based on the novel by Jean Redon. It revolves around the story of a plastic surgeon who is determined to perform a face transplant on his daughter, who was horribly disfigured in a car accident. He has long been conducting macabre experiments on using various parts taken from other living creatures to graft onto humans. Now he is willing to cannibalize parts and tissues from other living human beings, in his attempts to make his daughter look "perfect" again. As his daughter discovers what he is doing, it fractures her sense of herself, and she turns on him, leaving him to be mauled to death by the animals he'd abused. The title was used as a lyrical echo in the Billy Idol song, *Eyes Without a Face,* written by Billy Idol and Steve Stevens and released in 1983 (video released 29 June 1984). Ironically, after shooting the video, Idol nearly lost his eyesight when he had to be taken to the hospital to have his corneas repaired after his contact lenses had fused to them during the video shoot and subsequent airplane flight to his next performance venue. The song builds on the themes of the film and applies them to personal life and intimacy, exploring how certain kinds of overcompensating with rebellion can lead to inhumane harshness, dogmatism, acting-out, and a near disintegration into madness — a mess that undermines the very beauty of life that the rebel was supposedly seeking. "Les yeux sans visage" is, therefore, a phrase that succinctly summarizes such hypocrisy.

Ley lines. Invisible, mystical energy conduits that run through the ground of the Earth, much like the meridians that connect key circuits of life-force in the human body. They form a significant energetic network of straight, intersecting lengths not unlike a cobweb. Notable landscape features and settlements, along with ancient monuments, often mark their links and alignment.

LGBTIA2Q+. There are other variations on this arrangement of letters that stand for various orbits within queer communities: Lesbian, Gay, Bi, Trans/Non-binary, Intersex, Asexual/Aromantic, Two-spirit, Queer, etc.

Magick, Magickal. This spelling, with a "k," of these words is in reference to the ritualization and ceremonialism applied to one's intentions, in a spiritual or metaphysical sense. It separates the spiritual practice — of setting intention and directing energy to follow it — from the stage performances, sleight-of-hand, and fictional magic of fantasy films and other media. Magic is performative; magick is about aligning oneself with cosmic energies and natural forces, so as to manifest an intention — the "witchy" equivalent of prayer and contemplation. In mystic or gnostic thought — that is, in neopaganism, spiritualism (as distinct from materialism), and various forms of witchcraft, animism, and shamanism — spells and rites and ceremonies are used as techniques to evoke, elicit, and change a person's or group's consciousness so that they may better participate in the flow of a more ultimate reality.

Maricón. Spanish term that, when employed by a straight person, is a derogatory, misogynistic epithet, used to refer to someone as a "sissy," or an "effeminate homosexual."

Merda. The Catalan term for "crap."

Nonnina. An Italian diminutive term of endearment for a grandmother.

Pitch. Soccer (association football) field.

Pronaos. The vestibule at the front of a temple in civilizations of the classical period, enclosed by a portico and projecting sidewalls.

PrEP. An acronym for "pre-exposure prevention," or "pre-exposure prophylaxis." This is any combination of the approved antiretroviral medications that are used, in conjunction with a testing regimen, to prevent infection with HIV-1. At the present writing in 2024, these medications are approved in many countries (in a just world, they'd be universally approved and free-at-point-of-service). They include a generic combination of tenofovir disoproxil fumarate (TDF) and emtricitabine (a brand name of the combination is "Truvada") taken daily (safer) or in a 2-1-1 pulsed dosage for specific incidents; a combination of the gentler tenofovir alafenamide fumarate (TAF) with emtricitabine (a brand name of this combination is "Descovy") taken according to the same regimens as Truvada; and the cabotegravir extended-release injection regimen (or, brand name, "Apretude"). Any prospective user of such methods should consult with properly licensed medical professionals to ensure that they follow the protocols correctly. Studies report that, when used correctly, PrEP is 90-99% effective in preventing infection with HIV-1. (All information available from the US Centers for Disease Control and Prevention.)

Rei meu. A Catalan term of endearment used by lovers, which literally means, "my king."

Saludadores. Catalan term for naturally-based healers who may add the utilization of magick to their other methods.

Skipper. The captain of a soccer (association football) team.

Tankies. Also known as **Red Guards.** Both of these terms have historical contexts. Historical Tankies were anti-democratic authoritarians on the Left who held to the doctrinaire party line of the Communist Party of the USSR, and supported the authoritarian Soviet military crackdowns to crush the Hungarian democratic socialist revolution in 1956, and the Prague Spring democratic socialist revolution in Czechoslovakia in 1968. Historical Red Guards were a paramilitary social movement mobilized by Chinese Communist Party Chairman Mao Zedong, primarily composed of Chinese university students and other Chinese youth, to usher-in his Cultural Revolution to impose a doctrinaire, authoritarian party line on the populace. The Leninist-Stalinist Left and the Maoist Left had employed the same techniques as the Fascist right. As Hitler had mobilized the brownshirt Stormtroopers to usher in Nazism, and other authoritarian dictators had used similar paramilitary groups in other countries to usher-in other forms of fascism in their respective countries, the Soviets, and Mao and his Gang of Four, used these means to usher in their own control over people. As soon as each dictatorial regime, Right or Left, had gained control, they also quickly eradicated and banned their paramilitary shock troops, replacing them with terrorizing secret police. In contemporary use, referring to someone as a Tankie or a Red Guard is to equate them with the doctrinaire, antidemocratic, authoritarian, anti-socialist ethos of such shock troops.

Traife. A Yiddish word that means the opposite of kosher. It broadly refers to any foods that do not conform to Kashrut, the Jewish dietary laws held by strictly observant Jews.

Vita meva. A Catalan term of endearment used by lovers, which literally means, "my life."

Witchy. In this book, the term refers to any person who employs the use of magick. Such people do not consider themselves to be, of necessity, in opposition either to science or to particular religious ideologies, insofar as the dogmatism found in either does not infringe on or harm human rights and the sustainability of the ecosystem. There are, in fact, respected theoretical physicists who refer to both the study of quantum physics and of astrophysics as forms of magick. There are practitioners of all the world's major religions who directly refer to some of their own rites and ceremonies as "high magick," including (among many others) certain Buddhists from Sri Lanka or Tibet who utilize Raksha mantras, and certain Christians who mindfully celebrate the Eucharist. Witchy people are neither traditional theists (monotheists or polytheists), nor are they atheists. Rather, they accept four basic realities: Infinite Intelligence, qualified monism (also known as "vishistadvaita vedanta'), panentheism, and fourth order cybernetics.

A LETTER FROM
THE AUTHOR

Dear Reader,

Thank you for reading Chance Harvest. I hope you love Matteo, Ferran, and their cauldron of friends as much as I do.

Santa Cruz isn't just different on paper; it's different in real life. This humble novel is also different, and I suspect the readers of it will be different. This book is meant to give a platform to difference and to people on the margins.

I've been mindful during this journey of the example of the story of Dr. Who — that it always has been for remarkable participants in extraordinary times, and it is even more so as I write this, thanks to their returning show-runner, Russel T. Davies. Davies and I were both born in April of 1963; we are contemporaries who have both pushed the envelope for progress. He recently stated that there is now "a more open door," and rightly said, "We're still opening it further and further as much as we can. It's a heavy door that keeps slamming shut." Like Davies, I am one of those who intends to keep prying it open.

My pet project, *New Pacific Academy,* was born after my own time as an undergraduate at UCSC. I developed the idea further when I spent a year in 1988-89 as a Visiting Scholar at the Institute for Policy Studies, a progressive think-tank in Washington, DC. If you want you can look it up in Wikipedia or in various Queer Studies research materials. It was and remains a reflection of my life's work, both as an agent of political change and as a health worker.

My objective has been to re-deploy queer youth — from lives which, as a result of facing an awful world, had too much despair, self-harm, and suicide — into lives of community service and activism, liberation, and queer joy. I hope that *Chance Harvest* also will advance that objective.

It is not a widespread practice to write an essay about gratitude in place of the standard short acknowledgements for a book, but I feel it is right for this book and for me. Professional editors have a reputation for being jaded, but mine had the wisdom to see this essay not as an act of mere self-indulgence but as a manifesto. The world is in a period of collective grieving. Perhaps this letter can help to deepen your understanding of this story of hope.

Asked about hope, optimism, possibility, and beauty in a recent interview, Kit Connor said, "You do have a natural level of empathy, but that empathy is then fed by the people you meet, and the things that you learn, and the places that you go to." I agree on a very deep level, because I think and feel that the revolutionary reality of love is our only way out of our mess.

We human beings tend to grip the myths of our lives as if they were rails, even if we destroy ourselves in the process. But we too rarely seem to learn why we cling to ways of doing things that backfire on us. We all now live in an unusual and exceptional human existential crisis — personal and political, local and global, of people and the planet. So, I have shaped this sweet love story by our greater human context.

I have spent my life as an organizer and activist, and I have worked in the mental health field for a long time as well. I trust that this book and these grateful words will reflect how it all fits together. I hope that this story will be not only personally relatable, but also evocative of positive change for those who need it, and supportive of the ways in which each of us can do our part in this increasingly vulnerable world.

My life's work comes from my great love affair with people and the planet, and we should always acknowledge those we love. I myself continue to be grateful for and to believe in love in large part because of its embodiment for me in my longtime life partner, Dr. Leonardo Kusdra. I was able to set my heart on him because I also have a relationship with a far greater reservoir of humanism and of spirituality.

I also wish to acknowledge here those who helped make this project a reality. There are many people, especially some great talents in both the arts and crafts, without whom this book would have been impossible. There are also many who've already passed from this life, to whom I owe thanks for anything good I've done — and I'll see them soon enough to thank them.

If there had not been a writer named James Baldwin, however, I doubt I ever really could have known who I am. That also may be what helped make me a more voracious reader. But there are four relatively recent authors, all of whom were assigned female at birth but two of whom have come to express gender in other ways that help them thrive. They provided the riveting, swift, virtual kick-in-the-ass that led me to actually sit down and write this story — a story which had been lingering in my head for decades.

The first was Leah Thomas, an extraordinary woman whose book — and work through — The Intersectional Environmentalist is a blueprint for saving our future.

Next was Amy Lane, a master of the form, whose magical-realist and romance novels plunged me into the gripping world of her interesting characters and the fictional, ex-urban, liberated world they are building based in the east off the coast of North Carolina in Spinners Drift, and in the west in the hills north of Sacramento, California. I'd like to think that Lane's writing had something to do with manifesting a more progressive social climate in those areas over the past 15 years or so.

The third was nonbinary author Casey McQuiston. At a time when there has been growing authoritarian backlash and fascist bigotry, they have humanized queerdom to a global audience. Taylor Zachar Perez, Nicholas Galantzine, and the amazing cast and crew of *Red, White, And Royal Blue* have helped bring it to life on the screen. Their work is a gift to us all.

The fourth was an author and artist, Alice Oseman, who openly identifies as nonbinary and asexual-aromantic. I have frequently referred to them as a lovely, subversive genius. Frankly, I do not have enough thanks and praise for Alice Oseman. Alice's exceptional writing and art (which may be found in a full universe of books) led to the creation of *Heartstopper,* the enormously impactful streaming series from See Saw Films and Netflix.

For all the awards and kudos that the show, the books, and the actors have received, it remains underrated indeed. *Heartstopper* is accomplishing on a massive scale some of the same objectives I had with *New Pacific Academy.* We made history at our Academy and the model now pervades the movement, but we had nowhere near the immediacy, reach, and leverage that *Heartstopper* has at this writing.

It follows, then, that I am also grateful for the stunningly talented ensemble cast of *Heartstopper* — Joe Locke, Kit Connor, Yasmin Finney, William Gao, Tobie Donovan, Jenny Walser, Sebastian Croft, Fisayo Akinade, Cormac Hyde-Corrin, Corinna Brown, Kizzy Edgell, Rhea Norwood, Olivia Colman, Chetna Pandya, Momo Yeung, Leila Khan, Bradley Riches, Nima Taleghani, Haley Atwell, Darragh Hand, Eddie Marsan, Jonathan Bailey, Lara Decaro, Araloyin Oshunremi, Evan Ovenell, Joseph Balderrama, Georgiana Rich, Jack Barton, Alan Turkington, Bel Priestly, Ash Self, Thibault De Montalembert, Ashwin Vishwanath, Laura Hanna, Habib Nasib Nader, Vanessa Cruickshank, and all the rest — and to their directors, Euros Lyn and Andy Newbery, to their key executive producer Patrick Walters, to their additional musical geniuses (such as Adiescar Chase, Bella "Baby Queen" Latham, Olivia Hardy, and others), and to their crew and production team. They have created a truly moving, life-changing, global force for good.

Individually, jointly, and collectively, their efforts continue the impact of the show (and books) through their public lives — a phenomenon which is making genuine progressive change — and I do not mean that in a light or perfunctory way. Joe Locke helped force change at Tynwald that has had worldwide reverberations. Yasmin Finney (with thanks to Russel T. Davies) was able to help use *Dr. Who* to break the binary code. Bradley Riches, who is neurodivergent, has co-authored an accessible, groundbreaking book on autism as a superpower.

But, there's more. As a broadly consulted therapist, I literally know of lives saved, relationships salvaged and grown, disorders treated, healthier love and expression undertaken, boundaries and healthy communication improved, loving partnerships that had endured since high school finally represented, and queer joy that had been out of reach finally experienced, because of *Heartstopper* and the public lives of the cast. One need only look at the thank-you messages that Alice and the cast receive on social media to see people declaring all of that outright.

I'm also thankful that Connor Jessup and Sebastian Croft, along with several artists, teamed up with *Choose Love* and launched *QueerWasAlwaysHere.com* to secure futures for LGBTIA2Q+ refugees and displaced people around the world — telling the story of orange cartoon dinosaurs Dylan & Derek, who were in love in a time before humans invented homophobia. The folks at *Choose Love* are a powerful antidote to the evils of the plutocrats and oligarchs — and of their mouthpieces such as the Suella Bravermans and Rishi Sunaks, Nigel Farages and Alice Weidels, and Donald Trumps and Matt Gaetzes of the world.

I must also thank Sarah McCaffrey (Solas Support) for helping many show folk keep their sanity, especially members of the broad *Heartstopper* team, who've done work that has placed them under ridiculous public scrutiny, at the same time as it has demanded they turn-in their very best — which they have so far accomplished in ways that have lovingly pushed the bounds of the craft.

All of the *Heartstopper* family and their efforts, and Casey McQuiston's successes, and the inspiration of Leah Thomas and Amy Lane, made it an imperative for me that I finally write this book and seek to get it out to the world. The vision I see them making into a global reality is the vision that has always informed my work and informs the theme of this book.

Special thanks to my editors for believing in my work and making this story stronger. Many thanks to Lynette Greenfield and the wonderful Limelight Publishing team for bringing this novel to life, from all of the various departments.

In the writing process, indispensable help comes from the time and talent of those who agree to read early drafts of a book and provide their critical feedback. I very much appreciate the circle of critical readers who helped me: Nicole Alef, Robert Boone, Brian Bramlett, Shane Duran, Ken Gilberg, Kirri Grogan, Jane Metcalf, Douglas Rich, Carly Sharbaugh, Ann-Marie Swarbrick, and several of the other people I've acknowledged below.

My gratitude also goes to these global movers-and-shakers: Lisa Sterman, Leya Tanit (Pineapple Support), Rodney Karr, Frank Strona, and Steven Tierney — all longstanding friends — as well as to Jinkx Monsoon, Dylan Mulvaney, and Stephen Samuel Wrabel. Their impact on the people about whom I care, as well as on me, is beautiful and deserves great appreciation.

Thanks to Jane Fonda and Ted Danson for being among those who helped teach me to be a political organizer, to John Palmadessa for his rallying call that we are all in this together, and to Kathy Griffin for her grace under fire. Thank you also for my health care team and for all the Friends of Bill — the not-wrong-with-it village it takes to keep me lively in mind and body.

Thanks to Douglas Moran who, like me, was born in Connecticut, and who has been a "brother from another mother," an unstoppable ally, and my friend since we were both nine years old and stumping for Shirley Chisholm and George McGovern. Thank you to my brother AJ Brown, his wife Liza, and my inspiring niece (their magickal child) Giuseppina Louise, as well as to Tony Falcone and the other people who have kept connected with me over the years from Thomas Jefferson High School in Annandale, Virginia.

I am thankful for Anne Gabbard-Alley, my inspirational professor at James Madison University in the early 1980s, who pushed me to get out of Virginia to go make a greater impact on the world. I also want to thank every teacher, administrator, and student with whom I worked at UCSC in the 1980s — even the ones with whom I fought (and still would) — who indelibly marked my life for the better, as well as the founders of UCSC whose vision has thwarted many of the most relentless attempts to kill Ekkheya, the spirit of the place.

I also owe enduring thanks to eight of my own fellow *Cruzista* comrades who cheered me on in writing this book, and who remain good friends to this day: Kathleen Bryson, Jason Kendy, Haley Mack, Austin McInerny, Matthew Roberts, Sabin Speiser, Shamus Thornton, and Jeffrey Zurschmeide. I wish to thank Tom Lehrer for everything, both the personal and the artistic. A special thank you to the late David Mixner for the moral support, ever since Wilson vetoed AB 101. Last but not least, I am grateful that my tribe continue to inspire me: Chad Tynan, Brady Lee Sharbaugh, Eric Pytryga, Michael

Moody, Adam Heusinkveld, David Varela, Stephan Ferris, and the inimitable Miss Billie Bertan.

There are many others, too numerous to thank, but I have gratitude for all of them. They strive every day with love to make the global and local world better. I hope you will, as well.

—*Luke Adams*

United Nations World AIDS Day, 1 December 2024

[Playlist reference: Vanessa Carlton — A Thousand Miles]

ABOUT THE AUTHOR

A soft-hearted bisexual curmudgeon who believes that a better world is possible, Luke Adams can be found carrying out reconnaissance missions in the San Francisco Bay Area, Chicago, London, New York City, and elsewhere. He seems to be convinced that his objective is to help liberate queer spirit and to transform everyday lives. His late mother once asked him when he would stop collecting advanced degrees, certificates, and titles, and he simply shrugged. Additionally, he is a coffee and tea snob, as well as a hereditary psychic medium. From his dual childhood loves: the arts and social justice advocacy; to his second career in social and mental health and education; Luke has utilized and combined many disciplines to make ripples in the ponds of life — especially to empower marginalized young people. He can be found binge-watching videos with his longtime life partner Len (a reluctant scientist), as well as exploring beaches, forests, leather play-spaces, Elton John playlists, book nights, theaters, go-go bars, cafés, and — particularly if Sister Roma, Juanita More, Honey Mahogany, Mr. David Glamamore, or Chi Chi LaRue have anything to do with them — certain choice soirées and performances. Fiction writing is his latest fixation.

Never forget: Queer was always here.